I0572996

Between Heaven *and* Earth

REACHING

PEAKS TRILOGY

Between Heaven and Earth

Between Heaven *and* Earth

REACHING

PEAKS TRILOGY

BOOK 1

ASHLYN McKAYLA OHM

Words from the Wilderness
© 2025 Ashlyn McKayla Ohm

BETWEEN HEAVEN AND EARTH

Copyright © 2025 by Ashlyn McKayla Ohm

All rights reserved. Printed in the United States of America. No part of this book may be used or reproduced in any form or by any electronic or mechanical means, including information storage and retrieval systems, without permission in writing from the publisher. The only exception is brief quotations in reviews. No part of this book may be used or reproduced in any manner for the purpose of training artificial intelligence technologies or systems. The publisher expressly reserves this work from the text and data mining exception.

This book is a work of fiction. Names, characters, businesses, organizations, places, events, and incidents either are the product of the author's imagination or are used fictitiously. Any resemblance to actual persons, living or dead, is entirely coincidental.

For information, contact www.wordsfromthewilderness.com.

Cover design by Hannah Linder Designs

ISBN (paperback): 979-8-9992060-0-8

ISBN (ebook): 979-8-9992060-1-5

Library of Congress Control Number: 2025912233

Scriptures on page 5 (Epigraph), pages 186-187 (Chapter 10), and page 369 (Chapter 21) are reproduced from *First Nations Version: An Indigenous Translation of the New Testament*, copyright © 2021 by Rain Ministries, Inc. Used by permission of InterVarsity Press. All rights reserved worldwide. www.ivpress.com

Scripture on page 223 (Chapter 13) is taken from GOD'S WORD®, © 1995 God's Word to the Nations. Used by permission of Baker Publishing Group.

First Edition: October 2025

Hot Springs, Arkansas

10 9 8 7 6 5 4 3 2 1

30 29 28 27 26 25

❀ Formatted with Vellum

For Mama—

Your love has shaped not only the story on these pages, but also the story of my life. Thank you for leaving the flatland for the High Country, for choosing forgiveness with each new day, and for tirelessly teaching me how to fly. You are relentless in reflecting Heaven, and I love you more than you will ever know!

— A

O Great Spirit, our Father from above, we honor your name as sacred and holy. Bring your good road to us, where the beauty of your ways in the spirit-world above is reflected in the earth below.

— MATTHEW 6:9-10, FIRST NATIONS VERSION

CHAPTER 1

The morning sky over the mountains was breath-stealing blue. Bluer than the crystal-cut glacial lakes that glittered in the heart of the peaks. Bluer than the wings of the Steller's Jays that swooped among the alpine evergreen forests.

Avery inhaled the frosty air, tucking her chin into the collar of her anorak. Even in late April, mornings were still chilly in the Colorado Rockies. But she loved the mountains in all their moods. And soon, the sun would make good on the promise of spring.

She tugged on the door of her cabin, maneuvering the intricate dance of locking the old doorknob, and then jogged to her dented green truck. She'd bought the trusty little pickup long before she'd come to the mountains, and it had been saddled with high mileage even then. Yet despite its occasional crankiness, it was solid and reliable.

Much more so than most of the people in her life.

She slid into the truck and patted the passenger seat. "Come on up, Mercy."

Her black Lab gave an excited yip and scrambled into the cab beside Avery. As Avery started the ignition—it only took two tries— Mercy circled on the cracked leather seat, flopping down with a contented sigh.

"You're having a good day, aren't you, girl?" Avery smiled. Morning in the Rockies was its own kind of miracle, and as she drove along Devils Gulch Road, the gentle flutter of the first aspen leaves and the rich gleam of slanting sunlight and the clouds curling over Longs Peak twined together into a moment of peace.

Yes, she was blessed to live in this wonderful place—and to work for its protection at the Estes Valley Nature Center. When she'd begun working there, three years ago, it had been called the Estes Valley Raptor Rehabilitation Center, named after the primary function of the organization. But after years of pressing toward a wider vision for the center they'd founded, Skyla and Chayton had recently rebranded it, reflecting the hopes for expansion: continuing the rehab work but adding a native-plant garden, instituting a family nature discovery center, and offering conservation programs.

Which meant that once the new expansion was complete, Avery would be the director of said discovery center, the generator of such programs, and the general organizer of all things. Even now, in the planning stages, the work was the ideal blend of challenging and fulfilling. And best of all, it enabled her to pour her heart back into the mountains that had encircled her at her darkest, and later been the setting for her journey back to hope and life.

Her phone rang, shattering the stillness. Avery glanced at the screen. Tyler. She put the call on speaker. "What's up?"

"Avery." Her typically buttoned-up coworker sounded unusually frazzled right now. "Are you in Allenspark yet?"

"Nope." She'd just made the turn onto Marys Lake Road. "Why?"

"Someone's calling in for a bird on Tunnel Road. Injuries possible. Nest fall, I think."

Avery's heart clenched. Incidents like this were why spring—nesting season—was the busiest time of year for raptor rehab. "Okay. I'll go get it."

"You sure you can manage by yourself?"

She didn't normally make pickups alone, but—"Yes. Of course."

"I can come help, if you want to wait."

"It's fine. I've got it." She'd manage by herself. The way she always had.

"Okay." Tyler still sounded unsure. "Well, the address is 1965

Horn Drive. It's one of those side streets off Tunnel. It's supposed to be—uh—across from the hunting lodge."

"Got it." Avery's mental map of the area was clicking into place. She turned around in a driveway, then sped back the way she'd come. "Be there as soon as I can. Tell Liv to prep an enclosure."

The house at 1965 Horn wasn't hard to find—especially not with a woman standing helplessly in the front yard. She hurried over as soon as Avery pulled in. "Are you from the bird place?"

"I am." Avery put a firm hand on Mercy's collar, suppressing the dog's curiosity. She hadn't considered how Mercy would complicate this mission. "Are you the one who made the report?"

"Yes." The woman brushed back a strand of graying blonde hair and offered a lukewarm smile, worry crinkling her brown eyes. "I'm Martha Shaw."

"Martha, nice to meet you. I'm Avery." She summoned her dealing-with-people smile. Talking to strangers had gotten a little easier over the years, but it would never be her favorite thing. "Um, so tell me what happened."

"There've been hawks nesting right outside my window for a month now. Well, at some point, I quit seeing the parents coming and going. I didn't know what happened, but I kept watching. And now this morning I looked out while I was drinking my coffee and saw this little guy on the ground." Martha's eyes rounded with anxiety. "I think he's hurt."

This was a good woman, to care this much for the birds in her yard. "Let's have a look." Avery grabbed the pair of leather gloves and empty pet carrier in the back of her truck, shut the door on Mercy's eager panting, and fell into step beside Martha. Young birds tumbled rather frequently, and usually it was a simple matter of returning them to the nest. But if the bird was hurt, or if the parents were gone, that was a different matter entirely.

"Right there." Martha led the way around the side of the house and pointed. "That little one."

"Oh—I see." Avery crept closer, keeping her movements slow and gentle. An eyas—the technical term for a young raptor. This little guy was definitely a hawk—Swainson's, probably, given the time of year. He was a limp ball of white fluff, far too young to be on the ground. He'd hatched within the last three weeks at most. Probably more like two. And sure enough, his wing was folded awkwardly at his side.

She took another step, and the eyas turned his head at her approach. Well, good. At least he was still responsive.

"Hey, little one." Skyla would have begun crooning Lakota phrases at him, but all Avery could do was hope he felt her concern and care. "What happened to you, hmm?"

"Is he okay?" Martha hovered anxiously behind her.

"I'm not sure yet." She hated to take the young bird to the center if he could make it in the wild. It was always better to interfere as little as possible. But that wing just didn't look right. And if he was alone—

She tilted her head, scanning the treetop. "That's the nest there? When was the last time you saw the parents?"

Martha worried her bottom lip with her teeth. "Thursday morning, I think. Although—no, it may have been the morning before that. I didn't really pay attention, you know." She squeezed her hands together. "Do you—do you think he's been abandoned?"

Abandoned.

The sharp edges of the word cut into Avery with a force she hadn't expected. She kept her eyes on the eyas. "I'm afraid it's possible."

"Why?"

"Well, the female is primarily responsible for caring for the young, so—something may have happened to her. Or—" Avery took a deep breath. "She may have simply left the nest."

Martha's mouth tightened. "Not a very good mother."

Not a very good mother. Yeah, she knew about that. Bird mothers weren't the only ones who left their young.

"Do you think she'll come back?"

Avery swallowed, fighting to distance the question from taillights on the road and her sister's crying. "No. I don't think she'll be back."

She stared at the eyas. He was waiting. Lost, alone, unsure. He was panting now, his useless wings quivering as he stared at her.

Her own breath was coming faster, and then the trembling started—her fingers shaking with the force of the past. *No!* She couldn't give in to this. *Not now. Not here.*

"So? What are you going to do?"

Avery snapped herself loose from the memories. What was wrong with her? She hadn't felt that way since—

She stuffed her hands in her pockets. "I—I'm going to take him to the center."

She pulled on her gloves and retrieved the towel she kept inside the crate, deliberately slowing her breathing as she moved toward the bird. Fortunately her hands had stopped shaking, so he wouldn't feel her angst. "You're okay." Was she talking to him or herself? "I've got you now. You're safe."

He shifted himself sideways, but now that she was closer, she could clearly see the unnatural position of his wing. Chayton would need to look at that immediately. She scooped him in the towel, cradling him in her hands. He was underweight too. She settled him into the pet carrier and shut the door.

"Will he be okay?"

Goodness, she'd forgotten about Martha.

"Yes. He'll be fine." Just as she had been.

She slipped one of the center's business cards from her pocket. "If you want to check on his progress in a few days, you're welcome to call this number. Ask for me."

"Thank you." The woman clutched the card and nodded.

As soon as Avery opened the car door, she was met with Mercy's overzealous interest in the pet carrier. "No, no, girl." Avery nudged her back and settled the carrier in the space between the seats. "It's just a baby bird. You're used to them."

She tossed her leather gloves into the back seat, then cranked up the truck and headed out again. Another successful rescue.

Except that she'd almost blown it.

She let out a breath and flexed her fingers on the wheel. What in the High Country had brought those memories bubbling up? She'd dealt with dozens of abandoned eyases, and she hadn't thought about her mom in—who knew how long?

After all, she was past all of that. Fully and completely. She'd long ago left it back east. And the girl she'd been then was even more of a misty unreality than the folklore Skyla shared around the campfire.

So it didn't matter anymore, what had happened before the mountains. What did matter was that she was finally away from the darkness. Finally spreading the healing she'd found. Finally perfecting the one skill that had saved her over and over and over again as she'd run from the pain of her past.

Never looking back.

⧖

THE DAY DIDN'T SLOW down after the rescue. Avery had no sooner made it to the center and delivered the eyas to Chayton's care than Skyla had handed her a list of birds to exercise in the flight enclosures. That had kept her busy until she'd eaten a quick lunch and driven with Tyler to do a school visit in Fort Collins.

By four o'clock, her energy was all but gone.

"Almost back to the center, Elijah." Avery glanced over her shoulder at the oversized animal carrier in Tyler's backseat. She could barely see the majestic Swainson's Hawk as he huddled in the crate, but a soft squawk let her know he was listening. "We'll get you inside your own home soon."

"He's probably tired." Tyler scrubbed a hand over his hair as he turned in the driveway of the center. "I know I am."

"Yeah." Avery stifled a yawn.

"I gotta say, I don't love the school visits." Tyler nudged his glasses up his nose and shook his head. "Such a waste of time. And so little return on investment."

Avery bit back a reply. The definition of *value* was one of the many ways she and Tyler didn't see eye to eye. Sure, the school visit stipends weren't generous. But still, how could it ever be a *waste of time* to ignite wonder in the kids? To give them, even for a moment, a glimpse of the world outside their phone screens?

But she kept her voice light. "We got to talk to people. That's worth something."

"It is." The words were more question than statement. "But if we want to be able to keep talking to people—" Tyler glanced at the unfinished nature center building. "We have to get the money somewhere."

Avery frowned as she followed his gaze. Tyler's argument made more sense than she'd like to admit. "Skyla's still talking to the foundation."

"Yes, but—you know how that goes."

Unease rippled through her. The Harvey Foundation's grant had been a key piece of the funding needed for the new programs, but the directors had seemed hesitant about renewing for this year. "I'm sure they'll still come through."

"Maybe. We can hope." Tyler's tone sounded anything but hopeful. But then again, he was the business brain of the center. Being pessimistic about money was basically his job.

"Well—" Avery opened the car door and reached for Elijah's crate. She couldn't think about all the things that might go wrong. "I've got to get Elijah back in his mew." And then she would send thank-you emails to the school coordinators from today. A nice followup touch.

"Um, Avery?" Tyler's voice sounded more uncertain.

"Yes?" She hefted the crate and glanced at him.

He rubbed the back of his neck sheepishly. "You, uh—well, I just wanted to say you did a good job today."

"Thanks."

"I mean—" He cleared his throat. "You always do."

Good thing Addisyn wasn't here now. Her little sister had been commenting on Tyler's supposed interest for a while, and at first Avery had dismissed the whole thing, but now...Tyler's hints were starting to become alarmingly pronounced. She gave him a smile. Sincere, but cautious. "I think it went well today. Thanks for your help."

She turned away before he could respond. Tyler was a nice guy, even if he was a bit stuffy at times. But she wasn't interested in a relationship right now. Or ever. Not after...

She shrugged off the uncomfortable memories and headed toward the back of the center, smiling at the soft acoustic music coming from that direction. Liv must be out with the birds.

She followed the music to where small wooden pedestals poked from the ground like mushrooms. Liv was sitting cross-legged among them, coaxing beauty from her guitar. The sunlight slid along the strings on the battered instrument that was almost as much a part of Liv as the tattoos that marched up and down her arms. The song—something slow and delicately thoughtful—blended into the background orchestra of the mountain wind.

Avery stepped around the corner and applauded. "Entertaining our birds again?"

"Hey, Avery!" Liv smiled and swept a bow as if she were onstage at Red Rocks. "I'm entertaining myself. I don't know if the birds care for it."

"Oh, I think they do." Avery nodded to the pedestal next to Liv, where a tiny American Kestrel was soaking up the sun, the leather straps on his legs ensuring he didn't escape. "Adam seems happy."

"I think that's more because of the mice I just fed him than my musical performance." Liv fiddled with the tuning pegs on the guitar. "How'd it go today?"

"Good." Avery slipped on her thick mitt and drew Elijah out of the crate. He leaped willingly onto a vacant pedestal, ruffling his feathers slightly as she attached his leather straps—jesses, Chayton called them—to the attached hooks.

"Mercy's in the office, by the way." Liv raised an eyebrow. "Sleeping in the sun, last I saw."

Avery laughed. "Great. Hey, will you be out here a little longer to watch Elijah? I'm going to take care of his mew."

"No problem." Liv flipped her blonde beach waves over her shoulder with a smug grin. "I picked up his leftover food and hosed the mew down while you were gone. You owe me."

"Big time. Thanks." Avery chuckled to herself as she headed

toward the cinder-block structure behind the center. As much as she loved the birds, they were some of the messiest creatures she'd ever been around.

The enclosure building was much like a barn, with individual rooms—mews—like separate stalls. Elijah's mew was the second on the left, a snug room with tan cement walls and a couple of screened windows. True to Liv's word, the gravel underfoot was still damp. Grabbing the rake in the corner, Avery smoothed the gravel and pushed it over the rough cement edges, then emptied and refilled the water bowls. She stepped back and studied the space. All done until feeding time tonight.

She leaned for just a moment on the side of the mew and pictured the hawk, the slope of his strong shoulders, the fierce wisdom in his hooded eyes. This was the true joy—getting to connect kids like the ones today with the awe and wonder of the world they inhabited. How could Tyler not see the value in that? She understood the business mindset, but she'd never understand how he could reduce what they did to dollars and cents.

Although those dollars and cents were still necessary.

Well, maybe Skyla would get good news from the foundation. Speaking of, where was Skyla? She should have been around somewhere.

Avery headed down to Adam's mew—she could do Liv a favor by helping clean that area while the kestrel was outside. But by the time she'd refilled his water dish, hosed down the gravel, and picked up the pellets—a task which more than repaid any obligation she'd had to Liv—she still hadn't seen Skyla. She was writing down some stats on Adam's log sheet when she finally heard the woman's gentle voice behind her. "Avery, you have returned."

"Yes, I'm back. It went well." Avery blinked at the shadow on Skyla's face. "Is something wrong?"

Skyla glanced out the window, to where the mountains scraped against the sky. "We are having a gathering. I was waiting until you and Tyler were finished with the visit so that you could join us."

A gathering. Avery's pulse quickened as she followed Skyla toward the office area. Skyla's term for a meeting might have been informal, but it still meant business. Only rarely did Skyla assemble all the disparate staff of the center.

In the office, the other members were already waiting. Tom, another rehabber, was sitting next to Tyler. Chayton, Skyla's husband, paced at the front of the room. This must be serious indeed. Avery found an empty seat just as Liv scurried in, a little out of breath, and slid into the chair next to her. Her whisper was only loud enough for Avery. "You got the pellets! Now I'm the one who owes you."

Before Avery could respond, Skyla stepped to the head of the group, crinkled skirt swishing, and nodded at them. "Thank you for taking time away from your jobs to hear this announcement. We are indeed blessed by your presence." She glanced at her husband and ran a hand through her long black hair. "We received word today that the Harvey Foundation has decided not to renew their grant offer for this year."

A murmur of collective disappointment rippled through the room. Avery's stomach dropped.

"Hold on." Tyler leaned forward, looking just as upset as she felt. "They promised us that—"

Skyla held up a hand. "The clause in our agreement stated that the money was distributed per year and could be canceled at any time." She hesitated for a moment. "Due to—various factors, they decided not to renew this year."

Avery narrowed her eyes. *Various factors?* What did that mean?

"But the building's already in progress!" Liv crossed her tattooed arms, defiance squared from every inch of her being. "Where does that leave us?"

Chayton cleared his throat. "We'll have to reevaluate our plans until we can figure out alternative funding sources."

"I never thought it was a good idea to split our focus like this in the first place." Tom's tone was even more sour than normal. "Now we've got a half-completed building, and we've wasted time and money and personnel."

No surprise there—the gruff older guy had been suspicious of the expansion since the day Skyla first announced it. Still, Avery flinched. After all, her job duties were supposed to include overseeing the new programs and offerings. So now—

"Will there be any layoffs?" Tyler glanced at Avery. He must have had the same thought.

"No." Skyla's voice was still calm but held the undeniable ring of authority. She glanced around the gathering. "You are each precious to this place. And there are already choices before us. To start, Laz Jobe has kindly agreed to help with construction on the building. As you know, the building is in the dry, and the electricity is installed. Laz has graciously agreed to push this forward."

"Right." Chay nodded. "He'll do the sheetrock and flooring and interior. It will take a little longer, but it's the best option."

Trust Laz to step in. Avery smiled in spite of herself. The larger-than-life mountain man had become almost a father to her when she'd first arrived in Estes, and his friendship with Skyla and Chayton had spanned decades.

Tyler, however, looked skeptical. "Laz can actually handle the building?"

"He is well qualified to do so." Skyla hesitated. "He has—a background in construction."

Huh. Avery had never known that. But then, Laz possessed a wealth of mysterious talents.

"This will prevent us from being completely stalled while we discover an alternative source of funding. In fact—" she glanced at her husband—"Chay and I already have some ideas financially."

Tyler was scribbling on his notepad, his executive face in place. "So do I. What about the Gunther Foundation? They've been known to invest in centers of education. I also think that the Colorado Conservancy might be interested."

"Good thoughts, Tyler." Skyla nodded. "However, for the duration of this project, I have decided to focus on grassroots fundraising instead of foundations."

"Grassroots?" Tyler's pen froze. He frowned. "You've always used foundations before."

"Times have changed." Skyla shrugged. "No longer is that the only option. I believe that now, heart-projects hold greater power."

Chay nodded. "We've been talking about how the expansion is designed to reach people, to open their minds to nature. So what better way to begin that process now than by allowing them buy-in?"

Tyler's expression was still a locked gate. "Having the name of a foundation attached gives legitimacy to our endeavors."

Liv snorted and readjusted her backwards ball cap. "Until said fancy-shmancy foundation struts off with our money."

Tyler slid her an exasperated look and refocused on Skyla. "Raising money through donations is inherently unpredictable." Avery could almost see his mental calculator clicking.

"It is a new approach, yes." Skyla still didn't seem fazed. "But it is one that opens many pathways."

"Like what?" Tom's tone had dropped another ten degrees. Clearly he was in Tyler's camp.

Chay ticked off the items on his fingers. "Hiring a marketer, possibly. Finding partnerships with other nonprofits. Even paid advertising, if we were able to scale up to that."

"Great." Tom's sigh was more of a huff. "Throw more money away."

Skyla pressed her palms together. "The cycle holds true. When people care, they give, and when they give, they care." She clapped her hands lightly. "Thank you all for your time and attention. You may be dismissed now. Except—" Her gaze lingered on Avery. "Avery, could you speak with me for a moment?"

"Um, yes." Avery's heart stuttered into a faster rhythm as the others left the room. Skyla had said there would be no layoffs, but still, with the expansion on pause, maybe—

"Avery, I simply wanted to reassure you." Skyla's copper bracelets jingled as she crossed the room to Avery, carrying a file. "You are our program director, and your job will not change."

Relief softened Avery's shoulders. "Oh. Thank you. I—I wasn't sure."

"Even if the building is not done, we can still offer your programs for the summer. We will continue to host the school groups in the usual outdoor area. And if we are indeed able to make these partnerships, then you can also join hands with those."

So Skyla still needed her. Avery stood straighter. "Yes. I can do that."

"In fact, it is my hope that you will assist me with something special for the upcoming summer." Skyla tapped a finger on the file. "We have been approached by many schools over the last couple of years to prepare a path of lessons relating to the natural world and the work we do here. A curriculum, almost. Something that teachers can use, even in their own classrooms."

Avery nodded. The idea sounded marvelous—a way to connect the miracle of the mountains back into the everyday world.

"I have done some work on this, but the days are too full for me to give this the true vision. And I was wondering if, especially at this time, you would take this on."

Avery blinked. "You mean—develop the curriculum?"

"This is my hope, yes. You have already done the teaching in the schools. You are familiar with the students and the teachers. And you love this land." Skyla's face softened into one of her rare smiles. "I feel it is a calling for you. Especially now, until other paths open again."

"Oh—" Avery's throat pinched unexpectedly. Skyla was sharing with her the seeds of a magnificent project. "Thank you."

"Of course. In here are my notes, the bones of the plan. But please, Avery, make it your own. You have the heart and the hands for this work."

The weight of Skyla's trust draped like a mantle over her shoulders. Avery gripped the file. "Thank you. I'll start working on it right away."

"Good." Skyla smiled and glanced out the window. "Now, your birds are calling."

Avery laughed and headed back to the flight enclosures, her mind whirling with the new developments. Skyla's words echoed again.

You have the heart and the hands for this work.

The same words Skyla had given her years ago. She'd been lost then on the path of her life, and Skyla had invited her to work for the center full-time. And throughout Avery's three years there, Skyla had continued to repeat the encouragement. According to her, Avery had all the skills needed for any aspect of her work. Even developing a school curriculum.

If only she could share Skyla's confidence in herself.

Avery had no illusions regarding her qualifications. With no college degree, she'd been initially hesitant to step into the role, but Skyla had arranged for her to achieve her wildlife rehabilitation and outdoor education certification via two years of in-the-field experience. She'd believed in Avery enough to take a chance on her.

Avery would not let her down.

The uncertainty flowed out, replaced by determination, and Avery lifted her chin. It didn't matter what happened. She loved this center, and she loved these mountains. And funding or no funding, she wouldn't let all that they were doing here fall apart. She'd start now, with the curriculum, and she'd make sure everything was okay.

No matter what.

⎯⎯⟠⎯⎯

STUCK BETWEEN HEAVEN AND EARTH. The story of his life.

Creed Running Wolf shifted his weight, pressing his hands more tightly into the rough, sun-warmed cliff. Over halfway up the climbing route, but the next bolt was just out of reach.

Erica's voice floated up to him, but the wind had whipped the words away. He frowned. "Huh?"

"I said, how you doing up there?"

"Perfect. Never been better." He bent his knee and caught the rock edge with his heel, straining himself higher, savoring the satisfaction of his muscles' response.

A fresh gust of wind slapped at him, his balance wavering for a moment. He gritted his teeth and tucked himself against the cliff until the gust passed.

"Creed, you sure this a good idea?"

"Nope." The metal gleam of the next bolt poked from the rock.

He flexed his aching fingers as he clipped his rope into the carabiner. "But I'm doing it anyway." It had been a year since he'd had the chance to climb at Sinks Canyon. And the rock in these Wyoming cliffs was legendary.

The wind was rising again, whistling around the corner of the rock face and ripping at his thin T-shirt. Once more he flattened himself against the dolomite wall. This gust took longer to pass.

"Okay, that had to be forty, forty-five miles an hour." Erica's annoyed sigh was even louder than the wind. "I feel guilty encouraging this madness by belaying you. This is not safe, you know."

"Life's not safe. We live it anyway." Another tucking of his fingers into a crimp. Another demand on his burning arms and legs. Another fluid swing of his body, moving up the cliff. The rhythm was second nature, a dance learned years ago, back when he'd first discovered that challenging the mountains could mute the voices that haunted him. Even if only for a few minutes.

"Uh-huh." Erica's voice was farther away now. "And since I want you to *keep* living it, I think you should come down."

If he could complete this problem, it'd be the only time he'd managed a Sinks Canyon route *"onsight"*—a perfect climb on the first try. "Look, I'm almost—" His fingers slipped off the rock. *Shoot!* He grabbed air for a dizzying second, then snagged his elbow on a jut of the rock. *Careful, Running Wolf.*

"Creed, I saw that."

Creed rolled his eyes. "Of course you did. So why would I worry with an expert belayer like you on the ground?" Erica had years' worth of practice at maintaining the proper rope tension. Even if he fell—God forbid—she'd use her weight to lock the line down, holding him in place. As long as he clipped in as he went, he'd be fine.

"Yes, well, your expert belayer is telling you to come down. And Austin's gonna be mad. He specifically told the team to wait till tomorrow. This wind is not safe."

"Austin will get over it once he sees the footage I'm going to get this way." Sure, his boss could play it safe. But Austin was a YouTube channel manager, not a videographer. He didn't understand the way the world shifted on windy days, the way inclement conditions—dangerous though they were—led to heart-pounding moments on film. Moments of tension and beauty and man against nature. The focus of the adventure channel in the first place.

Which was why his GoPro was running, and if he survived this, he'd get the kind of footage that would thrill their three hundred thousand subscribers, serve folks a few vicarious moments of adventure that would keep them clicking for more.

And if the footage impressed Austin...if it reminded him of Creed's prowess...if it led him to finally promote Creed as a reward for his four years of hard work at the channel...well, that wouldn't hurt either.

On a ledge wide enough for both feet, he shifted his weight against the rock. "Tension."

"Tension on."

He took a moment to rest on the line Erica had tightened, letting the burning subside in his arms and legs. He brushed fresh chalk on his palms and tugged on the spider holster he wore, testing its security. It was sometimes awkward while he climbed, but he never made an ascent without his DSLR camera. Four years of shooting film for the channel had taught him that the most epic shots usually happened in the middle of unforeseen stories. And unforeseen stories typically tended to occur in moments like this.

So the camera climbed with him, and the other guys always joked about it. *Hey, Running Wolf, you can't fall off the rock, you know! Might put a dent in that sweetheart camera of yours! Be sure to give her a nice massage after all the action today.*

Well, in his experience, the camera was more loyal than any friend and less stressful than any girl. Even Erica.

He risked a quick glance down the cliff face, where his rope unspooled to her. Guilt needled at him. She hadn't come with him today because of the filming opportunities. And sooner or later, he needed to decide where they stood.

He glanced up. About twelve yards to go. Not too bad. He tucked his fingers into the narrow crimp, engaging his muscles again. "Climbing."

"Climb on." A pause. "Creed?"

"Yeah?"

"You lived close to here, in the Rockies, right?"

He nearly missed the next bolt. What made her ask that question? "Uh...yeah. Colorado. A lifetime ago. Before my parents divorced." He tried to put a period on the statement.

"Do you still have family there?"

"No." That answer was quick. "My mom is in Idaho."

"What about your dad?"

Creed shook his head. Easier than admitting he hadn't talked to the man in years. "South Dakota." A change of subject was in order. "How am I looking?"

"I don't know. The wind's picking up. You should head down."

Yeah, the gusts of wind were coming more frequently now. That was in keeping with the forecast. Another reason Austin had told everyone last night to wait to climb. But the bigger the risk, the bigger the payoff, right?

"I'm still good." He clipped in his next carabiner. "Just need to stay focused." A not-so-subtle hint to quit talking. "I'm only—"

Wind screamed along the rock, blistering a cloud of dust and sand in his face. Creed closed his eyes against the stinging and grabbed for the wall, pressing himself into a crack as the gust thundered by. It was at least sixty seconds before the wind's howling died to a mutter.

"That's it." Erica's tone was as unmovable as the rock face itself. "You're coming down."

"Look, I'm almost there!" He squinted up, blinking the grit from his eyes. Only two more bolts on the route. Maybe three. He could almost taste that onsight climb achievement.

Plus, that might justify his disobedience, should Austin somehow find out.

"Creed?"

Who made her his babysitter? He clenched his jaw, fumbling with the next bolt. "It'll just take—"

Suddenly the wind roared again, and this time, a shower of debris pummeled his helmet and shoulders. He ducked in the sheer blink of instinct, and then the cliff flew away from his hands as the carabiner he hadn't clipped released.

"Creed!" Erica's wail cut over the wind. The useless rope burned against his hands. He was plummeting downward, toward the last bolt where he'd clipped in, unless—

And then the rope jerked against him again. His vision cleared just as he was flung toward the cliff face, and he grabbed at a jut in the rock. His feet were dangling, but the dolomite was reassuringly solid beneath his hands.

"Oh my gosh, Creed!" Erica's voice was shaking. "Are you okay?"

"Yep!" The adrenaline rush was still throbbing through him. He shook his head to clear the whooshing in his ears. "You caught me. Thanks."

"Well—yeah. The bolt helped too."

"I'm coming on down." His breathing was steady again, but his arms were screaming. "Ready to lower."

"Lowering." Her voice was still breathless.

He swung toward the cliff again, pushing against it with his feet and following the rope down. "Whoo!" He let out a whoop as his feet bounced against the ground, laughing from the sheer intoxication of adrenaline. "That was amazing!"

"Amazing?" Erica's face was paler than his climbing chalk. "Creed, you could have been really hurt this time. Or killed."

"I know. That's what makes it so fun." He smirked at her expression and tapped the GoPro. "This film is worth dying for, but I'd rather be alive to make sure it gets edited properly." If only he'd gotten the onsight. Dang it.

"But you still—"

"Believer" by Imagine Dragons throbbed its rhythm across Erica's words. Creed dug for his cell phone, glancing at the name on the screen. *Uh oh.* He swiped to answer. "Hey, Austin."

"Yo, Creed." His boss's typical SoCal swagger didn't fool him. "Dave mentioned he saw you driving out earlier."

"Um, yeah. I'm not on base at the moment. Do you need something? I can be back in—"

"Well, I was just thinking—you wouldn't happen to be out climbing, would you?"

Explanation time. "Uh—well, I actually am. But—"

"That's what I thought." Austin's voice hardened to a tone scarier than anything he'd just encountered. "Mind heading on back to base? I'd like to talk with you."

CHAPTER 2

Creed's carabiners jangled from his climbing belt as he hurried through the campground. He needed to get back to his trailer and start editing the footage so he had something good to show Austin this afternoon at the team huddle. The last huddle before they left for Arizona tomorrow.

But instead, he had to pay for his morning's excitement.

"Hey, man." Rusty glanced up from where he was hooking his own trailer to his pickup. "Austin's been looking for you."

"Yeah, I know. On my way."

Rusty stared at the carabiners, his eyes widening. "You've been climbing? In this weather?"

"Yep. Me and Erica."

"You dragged Austin's sis into this?" Rusty chuckled and shook his head. "Dude, you are brave. Or dumb."

"How 'bout both?" Creed grinned. "Don't worry about me. Austin will eat this footage up."

"If you say so." Rusty raised an eyebrow and bent over his tow hitch again. "But first, get your rear into his office and eat a big slice of humble pie."

Pinecones crunched underfoot as Creed made his way to campsite 50. His dusty orange Jeep was already attached to the little teardrop trailer, ready to pull it five hundred miles tomorrow. When he'd first traded his F-150 for the Jeep—seeking better off-road capability—the salesman had pulled a skeptical face at the idea of the Jeep towing the camper. *"Just because it can don't mean it will."* And then, of course, he'd tried to interest Creed in the bigger—and far more expensive—Rubicon Jeep model.

What he hadn't counted on was that Creed could spot a sham from a mountain mile away. And he'd made a career out of doing what others said couldn't be done. It was a trait Austin had always appreciated in him. Hopefully his boss would remember that now.

He tossed his gear inside the trailer door, then headed three campsites over to Austin's camper—a roomy Class A—and knocked.

"Creed, my man!" Austin met him with a fist bump. "Good to see you today."

"You too." Creed held himself warily. Beneath Austin's groovy-surfer-guy manner was the sharp business mind that had built one of the most lucrative YouTube channels in the genre.

"So, have a seat." Austin gestured at a chair, then flopped onto the couch and ran a hand through his shaggy blond hair. "First of all—bro, you can't be climbing on a morning like this. You know the rules."

Explanation time. "Yes, but—" Creed summoned the charming smile that usually released him from tight spots. "You know how it is. The best footage comes in the most difficult places."

"Yeah, yeah, I get it. But—" Austin sat forward, the businessman overtaking the surfer dude. "We've been over this, man. Remember the time in Yellowstone when you almost got frostbite because you were waiting to film the geyser?"

Creed winced. "Well, but that was—"

"And when you went out in a thunderstorm on Wind River for lightning shots?"

"Uh—"

"And the rappelling in the dust storm in Utah?" Austin didn't wait for an answer. "You've got a track record, man. And I've been understanding."

Understanding? Sure, because that *track record* had bagged some of the best footage the channel had ever received. "You've always told me that you appreciated my efforts to—"

"Right, right. I know you've got that itch for adventure. Heck, that's what makes you good at what you do. You've got a wild heart, and you keep it lit. But I gotta make sure this channel's safe. No liabilities. You understand."

No, he didn't understand, and Austin could just—

Get your rear into his office and eat a big slice of humble pie.

Rusty's advice clanged a warning bell in his brain, and Creed choked down everything he could have said. "Okay. I got it. I'll be more careful."

"Great, great." Austin grabbed a can of Red Bull from the table and pulled the tab. "So, that brings us to something else I wanted to mention."

Great, what now? "Okay…"

"I've decided—" Austin took a long pull of the Red Bull—"I'm actually not gonna have you go with us on the Arizona trip."

The air sucked out of the room. "Wait—*what?*"

"Yeah." Austin shrugged and wiped the back of his hand across his mouth. "Dave's going to sub in for you. I talked with him about it just a minute ago."

Dave? That guy hadn't been here six weeks. Didn't know aperture from shutter speed yet. "Austin, I don't understand." He forced himself to pull back on his tone. Letting his bratty younger self resurface now would only get him in deeper trouble. "I was expecting to go. I already planned for—"

"Yeah, I know." Austin slid him a look. "But things change, man."

Things change. So Austin was punishing him, no doubt. Proving his point. Being the big man. Anger swelled, pressing against the inside of his chest.

Watch your temper, son. Wildfires start with sparks.

His dad's voice in his head, but he'd grown accustomed to ignoring it. "Look, this isn't right." He didn't bother to lower his volume. "I get cut out, just like that, even after—"

Austin held up his hands, palms out. "Hey, hey, bro. Calm down. You're a good dude. I have a different project in mind."

A different project?

"See, Creed, I know you're a stuntman. You've proven that."

Austin took another drink of the Red Bull and leaned forward again. "But are you a storyteller?"

A storyteller.

For just a moment, Creed was back on the Rez, and Charlie Manyhorse was standing in front of him again, his hands fluttering like bird wings against the sacred fire as he spun tales of spirits and men.

Creed blinked the image away. "I don't know what you mean."

"You've got a good eye. You're one of my best filmmakers. But to go farther, you need to go deeper. Not going to Arizona gives you a chance."

"A chance?"

"I want you to take a solo project."

A solo project? Creed's expectations slid sideways as confusion and elation warred within him. Only the senior videographers were trusted with solo projects. "Really?" *Play it cool, man.* "I mean, sure. A climbing project, right?" Chase had taken the last solo project—in Denali.

"Well, not exactly. I'm wanting to do some projects that are more —more thoughtful, I guess." Austin gestured with the Red Bull can. "You know, like, more heartfelt. Nature from a different perspective. Ways people interact with the wild. You get it."

That was pretty vague, but Creed nodded anyway.

"So, I'd like you to take on a project in the mountains. It's a great town. On the edge of a national park, lots of nature stuff. You'll partner with one of these conservation centers and—you know, tell a story about the work they're doing. You've got about six weeks to get the story together. And you'll keep me updated, of course. How does that sound?"

A solo project about *conservation*? The excitement drained away. He was supposed to be up on the rock face, finding the sweet intersection between risk and survival. So what was this, really? Just a way to sweep him aside?

He had to say something. He cleared his throat. "Wow. That's— that's great. Thank you, Austin." He couldn't help it if the words were a little stiff.

"No problem, dude. I'm excited to see what comes of this."

The whole offer was still disorientingly different. "What's the town?"

"Estes Park, Colorado."

Estes Park. Ice water drenched his spirit.

Austin must have noticed, because his brow wrinkled. "You know the town?"

Oh, he knew that town. He knew that land. He'd hated it years ago, and he hated it still. Sun that burned you in minutes. Cold that froze your bones. Mountains that didn't care if you lived or died.

And his dad's angry voice echoing through all of it.

But what choice did he have?

"Yeah. Some." He fisted his hands. "No problem. When do I leave?"

"Tomorrow, if you'd like." Austin drained the last of his Red Bull and crumpled the can. Conversation over. "Looking forward to seeing the story you tell, Running Wolf."

⟶ ⧗ ⟵

Avery's commute home was a long one. At least, her former city neighbors might have thought so.

First was the drive through the open expanses near Allenspark, the hills scalloped against the sky and Longs Peak gleaming larger than life to the west. Then came the deep downhill, where Avery rode her brakes between rock-cut cliffs back down into the Estes Valley. She passed the property where Laz had both his house and store, and Marys Lake, and the little pond where western chorus frogs were beginning to thrum their spring song. From there, it was stop-and-go through downtown Estes—maybe with a pause at Kind Coffee, on the evenings she had time—and then out of the town, into the higher lands again, winding with the road through Devils Gulch and up the staggered stones of Lumpy Ridge to the land and cabin that had opened their arms to her.

Normally the drive was relaxing—time to watch the sun change over the mountain peaks, to reflect on the day's events, to murmur the thoughts of her heart to the God of the mountains. But today, an odd sense of unease prickled around her. The peaceful view outside her windshield seemed strangely out of reach.

It couldn't be the incident with the eyas. That had just been a fleeting trick of her mind, a weird fragmentary phantom of old memories. Anyway, what had happened with her own mother simply didn't matter anymore.

What did matter, though, was the problem with the center. Avery tapped her thumb on the steering wheel as she pulled onto the lonely sweeps of Devils Gulch Road. Would grassroots funding really work? What kind of plan did Skyla have in mind? Maybe she should do some of her own research. See if she could find something to help.

Of course, she really needed to be focusing on the curriculum. Avery glanced at the file on the truck dashboard. She hadn't had a chance to go through it at work. She would tonight, when she got back to her cabin.

But when she came around the final turn of her driveway, a familiar blue Hyundai Elantra was parked crookedly by her back deck. Addisyn! And sure enough, there was her sister, waving from the porch.

Avery could hardly wait to shove the truck into park. "Ads!" She scrambled up the porch steps and tackled her little sister in a bear hug.

"Hey, A." Addisyn laughed and squeezed Avery back, then bent to rub Mercy's ears. "Well, hello, pretty pup."

"You didn't tell me you were coming." Alarm replaced some of Avery's elation. "Are you okay?"

"Yes, yes, I'm fine." Addisyn raised an eyebrow. "I called you. And texted you. About four times each."

"Oh..." Avery cringed. Come to think of it, where was her phone? In the truck?

"You have got to be better about checking your phone, A." Ads propped her hands on her hips and leveled a warning gaze at Avery. "Living out here by yourself—"

"Oh, Addisyn, we are *not* starting that again." They'd replayed this conversation so many times they'd worn ruts in it. To hear Addisyn talk, one would think Avery was a helpless recluse who lived off the grid and would have to resort to smoke signals in an emergency. "What are you doing here?"

"Moving in with you again." Addisyn made a silly face and gestured to the duffel bag slung at her feet. "You know the routine."

Avery laughed, remembering all their years as roommates. "For you, I'll waive the rent. But really, what's going on?"

"Oh, Darius had to fly back to Vancouver this weekend to deal with some clients." Addisyn shrugged. "Thought I'd come crash with you rather than rattle around the empty house."

This was one of the greatest things about Addisyn and Darius dividing their time between Colorado and Canada—the way Addisyn could often swing up to the mountains for a few days. But —"I thought you normally went with Darius for client auditions."

The briefest shadow fell over her sister's face. "Oh, well, not this time." She brushed the front of her shorts. "I, um, have work in Denver next week. Couldn't get away."

Hmm. Avery studied her sister. Something was different, wasn't it? Something about Addisyn's face—her soul. That was it. Something deeper.

"Well—" Time enough later to figure out what was going on. "You know this door is always open to you."

Addisyn grimaced. "Metaphorically, perhaps. But—" She ducked sheepishly, looking more like the scattered teenager she once had been. "I lost my key somehow."

Avery bit back a smile. Never mind that Addisyn was now a successful figure skating coach who worked for two different agencies and trained some of the brightest new skaters in the country—she'd always trail some amount of chaos in her wake. A few years ago, the clash between their personalities had almost separated them, but Avery had learned to accept her sister's quirks. She smiled and draped an arm over Addisyn's shoulders. "Fortunately, I still have my key."

Addisyn winced. "I think I know what happened to mine. I accidentally left my jacket in a taxi a couple weeks ago, and I'm pretty sure it was in my pocket."

Avery tried not to think about a total stranger stumbling upon her house key in the back of a taxi. Or about what other irreplaceable things had been in Addisyn's pockets. "Well. No problem. I'll get a new one made for you while you're here."

WITH ADDISYN THERE, Avery's normally lonely evening sparkled. They worked together to get dinner started, and while they ate, Addisyn filled Avery in on the details of her and Darius's new coaching jobs in Denver.

"So anyway, the center in Denver is happy with us." Addisyn shrugged and speared some zucchini. "I have nine clients with them now, which is quite a load, but it's working out."

"That's amazing." Avery had never fully understood her sister's world of skating and competitions, but she could still rejoice in her accomplishments. "And the competitions went well?"

"Yes, very well. But thankfully the season's winding down now. I can work more on technique throughout the summer and get ready for the fall." Addisyn swirled some spaghetti around her fork. "That's why Darius is back in Canada this week. Trent had some potential recruits he wanted Darius to audition."

Avery nodded. Darius's uncle, also a coach, respected his opinion any time skating was involved. But typically, Addisyn jumped at any chance to return with her husband to his Canadian hometown. "And so—you couldn't go this time—"

"Well—" Addisyn sighed and rolled her eyes. "Actually, Darius thought I shouldn't. He thinks I'm pushing myself too hard. He worries too much."

A stab of concern struck. Addisyn's husband was adoring and protective, but far from overreactive. If he thought something was wrong—"What does he mean, *pushing yourself?*"

Addisyn flicked the statement away. "Nothing. I've been really tired lately, that's all."

Avery tilted her head. "Tired like sleepy, or tired like—"

"Now, A." Addisyn held up her hand in mock sternness. "Don't you start in on me too. I've been training fourteen high-maintenance kids, working at two centers in two different countries, and digging out of a pile of preseason paperwork." She pulled a funny face. "Can't imagine why I'd be a little tired."

Avery's worry remained, but she laughed along with Addisyn. She wouldn't push her sister any more right now. Probably Ads was right anyway. No matter how much she enjoyed her job, the stress had to be intense.

Well, a weekend in the mountains would help her rest. Avery would make sure of that.

"Enough about me, anyway." Addisyn pushed back her plate and watched Avery expectantly. "How 'bout you? Anything new with Skyla and the gang?"

"Well, actually—" The shadow of the earlier news settled over Avery again. "Our funding has fallen through."

"What?" Addisyn's brow creased. "How can that happen?"

"The foundation decided not to continue their support. There was something in the contract, I guess."

"Why?"

"I don't know." What had Skyla said? *Various factors.*

"So now what happens?"

"We have to find another funding source." Avery slid her fork around her plate. "If we don't get more funding soon, we'll have to cancel the expansion."

Addisyn winced. "You can't let that happen."

"I know." She'd do everything she could to fight for what she loved. The way she always had. "Oh, and Skyla wants me to write a curriculum."

"Cool!" Addisyn nodded with interest. "What about?"

"About the mountains and the land. For science and ecology classes, I think."

"You'll be great at that!"

The doubt from earlier wriggled back in. "I don't know."

"Hey, you're the best at everything you do, A. And you make

stuff happen." Addisyn's expression turned serious. "I mean, you always did for me."

Well, she'd tried, anyway. When their mom had left them with their abusive father, Avery had stood in the gap for Addisyn, trying to shield her from the realities of their home life. Ultimately, she'd left home as a high school graduate, taking the teenaged Addisyn with her to finish raising her in a place of stability and love.

"I did my best." Although she'd never felt as if it had been enough.

"You did everything."

Avery shrugged, attempting to shake off the faint guilt that always pricked her when she thought about those years. What would Addisyn say if she knew exactly how much *everything* Avery had done? What would she say if she knew about that day on the sidewalk, when—

Enough. She'd decided long ago to never tell Addisyn that angle of the story. She'd done what she'd had to, but Ads would never understand.

After supper, Addisyn curled up on the rug with a novel, and Avery stretched out on the couch to study Skyla's notes. The structure of the curriculum was straightforward enough. Ten to twelve nature-themed lessons, each dealing with science and including a hands-on demonstration or activity. Simple and basic. But then Skyla had written something else, a brief note at the bottom of the page.

Not just science but also soul—Include reflection questions on each to promote healing.

Healing? That was something she understood. Something about the mountains, the space around them, seemed to bring peace, to help people through darkness.

She rubbed her eyes and glanced at Addisyn. In the soft light of the living room, she saw it again—that new depth. What was that about?

But her little sister also looked younger in this light. More like the preteen who'd clung to Avery on that horrible day and wailed with the brokenness of their story. *"Where is she, Avery? Where's Mom? When is she coming back?"*

The memory cinched an iron band around Avery's soul. But that horrible day had not been the end. Instead, it had been the beginning of her fight.

For Addisyn.

For herself.

Addisyn's head was drooping. Was she really that tired? Avery reached from the couch and gently shook her sister's shoulder. "Ads, you need to go to bed."

"Not yet." But Addisyn's protest was swallowed by a yawn. She tossed her book aside and flopped onto her back with a groan. "Ugh. I'm just worn out from the drive here."

The drive had never seemed to bother Addisyn before. Avery frowned and set Skyla's papers aside. "Ads, I'm worried about you. Have you been to the doctor?"

"Go to the doctor for feeling tired?" Addisyn opened her eyes just enough to toss Avery an exasperated glance. "I've skated with a torn meniscus, remember? I'll be fine."

"But maybe just a checkup—"

"Yeah, and when was the last time you had a checkup, A?" Addisyn pushed herself onto her elbows with a smug expression. "Seems like I should be the one worrying about you."

Avery grimaced. Caught. "I'm fine."

"Okay, but I really do worry about you." Addisyn's expression turned uncharacteristically serious. "I don't like you living up here all by yourself."

Again? "Oh, Addisyn, I have Mercy." As if on cue, the dog licked her hand. "And Laz and Skyla would come if I needed anything."

Addisyn flashed her an innocent look. "And Tyler."

Avery groaned. "Addisyn, do not start with me. We're friends."

"Uh-huh." Addisyn tilted her head. "I've seen the way that guy looks at you when you're not watching. And remember that day I was at the center, and he saved your life when you fell off the ladder?"

"Oh, Addisyn, please. Grabbing my arm when I lost my balance on a stepladder does not count as saving my life."

"It wasn't the grabbing your arm." Addisyn certainly seemed

fully awake now. She shook her finger, her eyes glinting. "It was the way he held onto it afterwards."

Avery huffed and rolled onto her back. "I'm not hearing any more of this."

"Yeah, but—" Addisyn hesitated. "Okay, Tyler aside, don't you want to get married one day?"

Avery stared up at the ceiling. There was no way Addisyn would understand—she who'd married a man who was a true knight in shining armor. "I don't think so, Ads."

"But why not?"

A single image flashed to her mind. Mom, trapped by her abusive husband in a hell of her own making—and letting her daughters inhabit it with her. She shuddered. "I—I'm independent, Ads." She waved her hand around the cabin with a weak laugh. "I do fine by myself."

"Okay. I know you say that." Addisyn shrugged. "But—you sometimes just feel sort of—unrooted to me."

"Unrooted?" What kind of crazy talk was that? "What does that mean?"

"Like—" Addisyn hesitated, obviously searching for words. "Like there's some part of your story still missing."

Oh, since when was Addisyn the prophet? Avery sighed. "Ads. I'm fine."

The concern didn't leave Addisyn's eyes, but she nodded reluctantly. "Okay."

"Now we need to go to bed, silly girl." Avery tossed one of the throw pillows gently in her direction. "I've got to be at work early."

But long after they were both in bed, she thought about her sister's words.

Some part of your story still missing.

Ridiculous. Her life was just as she wanted it to be. Especially now that there were no ghosts left to haunt her.

They were all on the other side of the Continental Divide.

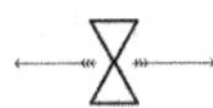

Estes Park. The last place Creed had ever wanted to see again.

He clenched his jaw as he pulled out of yet another campground. Was this the third or fourth place he'd checked? They were starting to run together.

He should have remembered the dates of the tourist season here. Should have checked online to see that most campgrounds weren't open this early, at the end of April. Should have anticipated the fact that finding a place to park his camper—especially for six weeks— would be harder than free climbing solo.

A jet plane streaked across the sky, nosing into the gathering clouds. Helping its lucky passengers escape godforsaken Colorado and the angry mountains that already peered at Creed with hostile eyes.

At the next red light, he squeezed his forehead, rubbing away the beginnings of a headache. Okay. He'd head to the national park. Maybe the campgrounds there were already open. Plus, the national park was the obvious destination for nature filming. Maybe he could even shadow a ranger, capture a story about the difference federal conservation made. Or something. He'd make it work.

The streets were different enough that he almost passed by the turn for the national park. He glanced around as he drove, comparing the present to the past. All the traffic patterns had been changed. A lot more new construction, too.

But the mountains were the same. Looming over the horizon like ghosts that still remembered all the mistakes, the avalanche of choices that had sent him tumbling a thousand miles away from the boy who'd once watched this world with innocent eyes.

They'd moved away when he was—what? Eight? Nine? This land should have released him long ago. Yet after nearly two decades, he had the irrational sense that the mountains were judging all his shortcomings. Disappointed in what he'd grown up to be.

Just like Dad.

His dad, the *missionary*. Huh. Creed locked his jaw. If God really existed, hopefully He was more like the gentle and faithful Creator his Native friends worshipped and less like the stiff-starched, fire- and-brimstone tyrant that his father boxed into church buildings.

Regardless, Dad was a sorry representative of any version of God. But why was he even thinking about it? Back in Colorado for only half a day, and already the man was on his mind. Just as he'd feared.

Focus. He rubbed a hand over the tattoo on his arm and tried to shift gears. Logical, orderly steps. He'd do what he had to here, and then he'd be off again. The mountains would shrink in the rearview mirror, and he'd be back to a world that moved too fast for these kinds of memories.

He looked away from the mountains, keeping his focus on the road ahead until he pulled into Beaver Meadows Visitor Center. The parking lot was crowded. Well, why didn't they go ahead and open the campgrounds, then?

He had to wait in a line of at least ten people before it was his turn to speak with the harassed-looking ranger. "Hello." It took more effort than usual to summon his charming smile. "Are the campgrounds open yet?"

"We normally open most campgrounds near the end of May. However, our winter camping season is still in effect." The woman's voice was flat, as though already the questions of the day had emptied her energy. She scanned a clipboard. "So, Timber Creek is inaccessible. It's across the Continental Divide, and the road is still closed for the season."

"Trail Ridge Road, right?" Weird, how the geography of this region was still mapped on his mind. "Highway 34?"

"That's correct." A hint of personality thawed the woman's voice. "You must have been here before."

"Yeah...when I was younger." Creed's headache was intensifying. "Um—any options closer?"

"Moraine Park is closed all season for construction. However, Aspenglen and Glacier Basin still allow winter camping." The woman raised an eyebrow. "No water or dump station. The restrooms are not operational, but there are portable toilets on site. And each campsite does have a fire grate."

A fire grate was a pretty poor trade for a flush toilet. Creed fought the urge to groan. He'd done his share of wilderness camping, but he didn't relish the prospect of roughing it for this long. Of course, it was only till the regular season opened. Three weeks. He could do anything for three weeks, right?

"Uh—okay. Which campground is closest?"

"Aspenglen." The woman tapped the laminated map on the counter. "Near the Fall River entrance."

"I guess I'll head that way."

"Go soon." The woman tucked her clipboard away. "Spots are limited for winter camping."

Yeah, well, he probably wouldn't have much competition for a fire grate and a portable toilet. "Okay." The line behind him was lengthening. He needed to be fast. "Next question. I'm actually here on business. I work for a YouTube channel. Guys in the Wild."

The woman's patiently blank expression didn't change. Okay, then.

"Anyway, I'm wanting to do some nature filming. I wondered if there's a process for—"

"All commercial filming or photography requires a permit."

Creed blinked. "Okay—so how do I—"

"Here." The woman rummaged under the counter and plopped a slab of paperwork in front of him. "You'll need to complete these forms and return them to any visitor center. Applications are reviewed and approved within ninety days."

Ninety days? "So—if I'm wanting to start filming this weekend—"

"I'm afraid that won't be possible. The application review process requires a waiting period as well and evaluation by our resource use team. New guidelines this year, as a matter of fact. That's why we now encourage content creators to fill out their paperwork ahead of time."

Creed clenched his jaw. "This was—unexpected."

"Well, this is the process." The woman's voice held the note of finality. She glanced over his shoulder at the next visitor.

"Um, last question." The pressure of the crowd behind him was almost unbearable. "Is there any way I could shadow a ranger or—"

"Sir, the National Park Service is a federal agency. We're not available for a project like this without prior approval. However, there's a place on the form to note any special requests."

Could *nothing* go right? He'd like to unload on all of it—the rule-rigid woman and Austin with his big ideas and the mountains that wouldn't stop staring at him.

Instead, he nodded. "Thanks."

Out in the sunshine again, he took a deep breath. What could he do? The only logical option was to drive on over to Aspenglen and stake his claim to what barren amenities he could.

He folded the paperwork and crammed it in the first trashcan he passed. Ninety days just to get filming permission? At that rate, he'd still be in Colorado at Christmas.

No, he'd come up with another plan. Just like climbing. He was good at that—getting stuck, getting mad, but ultimately stepping back and finding another route to the top.

And that's just what he'd do this time.

He swung into the Jeep with new resolve. First things first. He'd find the campsite and snag it for six weeks—although with any luck he could be out of Colorado sooner.

Just as he was pulling onto the road, an idea poked at him. If his memory was correct, there was another national park campground, wasn't there? In the Longs Peak area. Out by—what was that little town? Adamspark? No, Allenspark. That was it.

He hesitated. The ranger hadn't mentioned the campground. Most likely it was still closed too. But hadn't she said *most* campgrounds were closed? If it was an exception, he'd have running water and working restrooms—and a new lease on his sanity.

He waited for a break in the traffic and then made a clumsy U-turn, ignoring the honk of the white SUV behind him. Now, if only he could find the road to Allenspark.

It took a couple of wrong turns, but he was finally out of Estes, driving south on Marys Lake Road. Not much to see out here—the lake with water arcing from a penstock, some houses that looked like Lincoln Log replicas, a llama farm. Just past the farm was a little A-frame building with letters sprawled across a wooden sign: LIVE

BIGGER OUTDOOR SUPPLY. Interesting. Who'd put an outdoors store so far from the downtown district?

The double profile of Longs Peak and Mount Meeker was looming closer and sharper as the road wound higher. The campground had been somewhere out here, right? Maybe that was it—the collection of buildings to his left. He slowed, squinting at the sign. ESTES PARK MOUNTAIN CENTER.

Mountain center? Possibility sparked to life. Maybe it was a climbing center. Or an adventure hub. Or best of all—a place where he could film. If he talked to the people there, they might—

And then the symbol on the sign jolted through him, scattering his thoughts like leaves on a windy day. He hit his brake a little too hard. Surely it wasn't—but—it was.

The *kapemni.*

The symbol of his mother's Lakota people, familiar as his own last name. Two triangles, joined tip to tip in an hourglass shape. The same X-shaped icon drawn on the wall of his camper and even on his Jeep dashboard. The image he'd clung to when every other shred of his heritage had been stolen from him.

Well, X marked the spot, right?

He flipped on his blinker and pulled into the parking lot. He didn't normally believe in signs. Not anymore. Certainly not for him.

But this one was too obvious to miss.

CHAPTER 3

Avery leaned hard on the gearshift, shoving her battered old truck into park, and hopped out of the driver's seat. She peered apprehensively into the bed at the two elk antlers sprawled there. "Well, they survived the trip."

From the passenger side, Laz snorted. "Told you that you was worryin' for nothin'."

"I guess so." Laz had wrapped bungee cords around both antlers in what appeared to Avery to be a haphazard fashion. He'd laughed off her concerns, but she'd still taken every turn on eggshells, obsessively watching the rearview mirror. Even worse than losing the new teaching aids for the center would be sending them through the windshield of the car behind her.

"An ole mountain goat knows how to tie somethin' down." Laz winked at her and jerked his head toward the office. "I'll go find Miz Skyla and tell her I'm here to work on the buildin'."

"All right." As Laz's footsteps faded, Avery tugged on one of the cords and blinked. Well, if she'd known his seemingly careless system was this secure, she wouldn't have worried so much. Opening the tailgate for a better angle, she snapped the first cord free and dragged the bulky antler toward her.

She always forgot how heavy these things really were. And how unwieldy. She hefted the antler only to see a cord she'd overlooked still clinging to one of the points. Ugh.

"Skyla? Laz?"

Nothing except the distant croak of a raven. She was on her own.

Shifting the weight to her left arm, she braced her shoulder under the bulky antler and stretched her free arm until her fingers found the hook. There. Almost—just a little—

"Need some help there?"

The cord gave way, and the antler flopped down suddenly, pulling her sideways. "Whoa!" She stumbled, grabbing the tailgate just in time to regain her balance, and spun toward the voice.

"Sorry to startle you." A dark-haired guy about her age gave a half-wave. When he lowered his arm, the light caught a tattoo partially visible beneath his shirt sleeve.

"Oh—it's fine." Who was this guy? She'd never seen him before. "Can I help you with something?"

The corner of his mouth tipped up, amusement hiding in his eyes. "Well, I think you're the one with your hands full."

Ha, ha. Avery pressed her lips together and adjusted her grip on the antler. "I can manage." The words came out more abruptly than she'd intended. If only there were some way to hold these that wasn't so awkward.

"Here, let me." The guy brushed his hands against his canvas shorts and reached out. "I know how bulky those things are."

She didn't need help, but there was no dignified way to refuse it. Avery clenched her jaw and handed over the antler. "Be careful with it."

The guy's tanned face unexpectedly creased into a grin. "If some bull elk crashed around with this thing, I don't think I can hurt it too badly just carrying it for a moment."

Something about his tone made everything he said sound like a dare. Avery frowned. "Okay. Thank you." The words were flat, but she couldn't help it. She nodded toward the exhibit table set up just outside the office doors. "I'll show you where it goes."

"All right." The guy slung it over his shoulder in a way that looked irritatingly effortless. As he fell into step beside her, Avery studied him out of the corner of her eye. Deep brown hair, brush of stubble, lean build—he could have been any guy in downtown Estes. Yet there was an unfamiliarity about him, as if he were disconnected from his setting. So where had he come from? And why was he at the center?

"Right here." She pointed to the exhibit table.

"Like that?" He set the antler down, slid it a fraction of an inch with exaggerated precision, then grinned at her. "Looks like it survived me carrying it."

Avery glanced at her watch. Already past nine o'clock. The last thing she had time for was more of this man's swagger. "Can I help you, sir?"

He propped one hip against the exhibit table, apparently ignoring the way the whole thing tilted precariously. "Yes. I saw the sign for the mountain center and was wondering—what does that mean? Do you offer climbing or adventure tours or—"

"This is a *conservation* center." Probably not what this guy had in mind. "Our team performs raptor rehabilitation for injured birds. In addition, we offer conservation programs and education. For school groups, visitors, that sort of thing."

"Okay." The guy hesitated. "Uh—also—there's a *kapemni* symbol on your sign."

"A what?" Avery glanced around, but the parking lot was still empty. Where was Laz when she needed him? Even Tyler would have been welcome.

"The Lakota symbol. It sort of looks like an hourglass."

Avery blinked. And here she'd thought that was just a design element. "Oh. Well, our director is Lakota, so—"

"Really?" Interest flashed in his eyes. "Can I speak with him?"

"*Her.*" And she wasn't about to bother Skyla with this weird guy. "She's very busy today. Is there something I can help you with?"

"Well—possibly." He adjusted his stance as if settling in for a long story. Just great. "I'm Creed Running Wolf." His smile held a tinge of expectation. "I work for the Guys in the Wild channel on YouTube."

YouTube? The last time she'd been on the video website was to watch something Addisyn had sent her about funny dog antics. If he was waiting for recognition from her, he'd be leaning against that table for days. "I'm not familiar with that."

"Oh." Faint disappointment creased between his eyes. "We're an outdoors channel specializing in adrenaline-driven content for today's adventure culture."

She could smell a sales pitch. "Okay..."

"And we're at over three hundred thousand subscribers."

Addisyn would have been able to tell her if that was a good number or not. But why did it matter? "I'm sorry. I don't understand what this has to do with our center."

"Well—" His smile looked more hopeful now. "I'm here to do some filming in and around Estes Park. Do you ever allow filming on the center property?"

"No." The word was out of her mouth before she could attempt to soften her tone. With everything else on her mind, the last thing she could handle was this posturing showoff who wanted to disrupt everything at the center. For a YouTube video? *Really?*

He blinked. "Just like that?"

"I'm sorry, but this is private property." Her patience was melting like snow in the High Country sun. "We don't allow any sort of access for that purpose. Our property abuts the national forest in the back, and it is a managed conservation area." Raptors nested there in the winter, and elk calved in the spring, and endangered cutthroat trout frolicked in the creek. No way would this fame-hunting hound have the chance to wound her wilderness.

Mr. Three-Hundred-Thousand-Subscribers seemed definitely knocked off his stride now. He opened his mouth and closed it again, then sighed and softened his stance. "Okay. Maybe I didn't explain myself well enough. The land wouldn't be disturbed. I'm wanting to create some content regarding conservation work. And our channel would reimburse you. We always pay for filming rights."

Pay? Avery paused. Well, she still didn't like the idea. But with the foundation grant gone, what if—

And then suddenly the scene blurred so abruptly that the ground seemed to drop away beneath her. *A knowing.* Her soul shifted, the way it always did when the pictures came, and the darkness in her mind burst into—flames. Rushing rivers of fire, blazing in reckless abandon around the shadow of the man. Flames wild and untamed, flames relentless and raging, flames with words swirling through and around the roar of the blaze.

Let the fire fall upon the altar...

And then the vision snapped away, and Avery blinked back into the normal day. What on earth?

"—happy to put you in contact with my boss, if you'd like." The guy was still talking, oblivious. He slipped a business card from his pocket. "Here's my card. If you want, you could—"

"Avery? Who is this?"

Skyla was hurrying out of the main office, Laz on her heels. Oh, thank goodness. Avery stepped aside, her heart still thrumming from the knowing. "Skyla, this is—uh—" What had he said his name was?

"Creed Running Wolf." The guy turned and offered his hand to Skyla. "I'm here to—" He glanced over Skyla's shoulder—and froze.

Just behind Skyla, Laz had shrunk, his blustery mountain-man confidence leaked away, his face the color of ashes.

"Don't tell me." Acid curled around the edges of the strange guy's words. He took a step past Skyla, a thunderstorm kindling in his eyes. "Laz Jobe. Right here, hiding in the shadow of these mountains."

"Not hiding." Laz's voice was low. His hands were fisting and releasing at his sides. Over and over and over. "Jes' waitin'."

"Waiting for what?" The man's voice was climbing a staircase. "To crawl into some hole and—"

Okay, whatever was going on, this guy couldn't talk to Laz this way. Avery stepped forward. "What's—"

"Avery, girl." Laz held out a hand with a single shake of his head. "Let this feller talk."

"Talk?" The man huffed out a laugh. "After all these years, you think I want to *talk*?"

"After all these years—" Laz scuffed the toe of his boot into the dry soil—"I figure you got something to say to me."

"I have nothing to say to you." His voice cracked on the last syllable. For a moment there was something raw and broken in his face. "Nothing—except I wish I'd never seen you again." He wheeled for the parking lot, breaking into a jog.

"Wait!" Avery took a step forward, but the man jumped into a dusty Jeep attached to a camper. The next moment, he was back on the road toward Estes.

The car noise died away. A Steller's Jay flitted to the top of a pine, squawked, and glided on behind the office. Only then did Skyla sigh, her gaze still on Laz. "When I saw him—I knew. There was much the same about his face."

"Yep." Laz's shoulders were stooped under some invisible weight. A soft sound broke from him, more moan than cry, and then tears found the furrows in his cheeks, soaking into his beard.

Seeing Laz cry was like watching the mountains themselves crumble. Avery crossed to him and squeezed his arm, his pain stabbing at her own heart. "Laz—who—who was that?"

"That—" Laz straightened and sniffed, eyes gazing unseeingly westward. A cloud shadow hung heavy across his face. He swiped at his eyes and then finally met her gaze.

"That, Miz Avery, was my son."

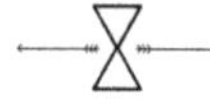

MY SON.

The words were no sooner out, hanging in the air between them all, than Laz spun on his heel and headed for his pickup. Skyla breathed something that sounded like a prayer and hurried after him, her expression pulled taut. "Laz, wait!"

The shock rooted Avery's feet to the dirt and her eyes to the scene. She watched as Skyla caught up with Laz near the pickup and said something to him. Laz adamantly shook his head and swiped a rough hand over his eyes. He reached for the door handle, but Skyla placed a gentle hand on his wrist. She was talking, her words no doubt flowing with the healing they always carried.

Avery shifted, caught in the crosshairs of indecision. Should she follow Skyla? But what good could she do? It was Skyla who apparently knew the secret chapters in Laz Jobe's story, Skyla who'd recognized the young man.

Laz's *son*.

Avery shook her head, the disbelief turning her inside out again. How was it possible for a single revelation to so completely topple everything you thought you knew about a person?

Since she'd come to the mountains, Laz had been almost a father to her—an infinitely better one than hers had ever hoped to be. She'd known there were blanks in his biography, tender places in the past he guarded with a wall of silence.

But this was a whole new level of unexpected. He'd never mentioned a family of any kind. No talk of a former wife or even a girlfriend. Certainly none of this storm-eyed guy.

And what had this guy said his last name was? *Wolf* something, right? Not Jobe. Maybe he was adopted? A stepson? Born out of marriage?

Whatever the answers were, they were only the beginning of the story. The slicing pain in Laz's face cut through Avery again. She'd never seen or imagined the blustery mountain man breaking down. But then, she knew better than most how much hurt could be held between parents and children.

The roar of Laz's pickup cut through her thoughts. He was pulling out of the center, turning the opposite direction from the man Avery couldn't yet think of as his son. Skyla was heading toward Avery, her steps deliberate, measured. She halted and sighed. "He is —hurting." Her own face was creased, as if she'd absorbed Laz's pain through osmosis.

"I—I didn't know he had a son." The words sounded weak.

Skyla glanced down the road, as if keeping watch. "Do you know why he came? Was he seeking Laz?"

"Uh—no. He was talking about filming—I guess he's a YouTuber, or something—"

Skyla's eyebrows rose a fraction. "Can you tell me what he said? All of it, please."

Avery fumbled through the description, the events now blurry from the shock that had chased them away. "So basically, he said he wanted to film at the center. With us, I think. I—I told him we don't do that. But when he talked about us getting payment for it, I wondered if it might be an option. I was going to ask him more, but then—"

"Then Laz came." Skyla shaded her eyes and glanced behind them, to the horizon and the faraway swoop of the Continental Divide. She stood for several suspended heartbeats, then nodded once, a firm decision. "Very well, Avery. Come with me. We shall find this young man."

"Wait, what? I—I don't know if it's a good idea for—"

Skyla was already heading toward her slate-blue Bronco. Avery bit her lip and followed.

Skyla's expression remained a meditative mask as they drove down Marys Lake Road. They passed Live Bigger, where Laz's pickup was nowhere to be seen. Where had he disappeared to?

At Marys Lake Campground, Skyla slowed and peered over the crowd of campers on the hillside below. "Not here." She nodded and resumed her pace.

"Where will you look next?" Avery peered at her. What internal compass Skyla was following, she had no idea.

"The national park campgrounds. Perhaps he is winter camping there."

That sounded about as easy as finding a spruce tree in a whole mountainside of firs. "How do you know he hasn't just left town?"

"Because." Skyla slowed to take a sharp turn. "There is a reason he is here. The mountains will not release him that easily."

Who knew what that meant, but she wasn't going to ask. "Uh—I —I had a knowing."

"Indeed?" Skyla slid her a questioning look. Only she and Addisyn knew about the words and images that sometimes hit Avery's heart. "What was this one?"

"Fire." She could still picture the shadow outline of the flames. "Around him, when he was talking."

"Fire." The word was colored with meaning. Skyla nodded slowly. "This rings true."

But the fire had had a wild feeling. Too close. Too strong. Avery picked at a loose thread on her hiking pants. "I'm not sure about it. If it was good, I mean."

"Well, then we shall have something else about which to ask the Spirit, yes?" Skyla squinted ahead as they slowed near The Mad Moose. "Starting now, it would seem."

Avery blinked. The dusty orange Jeep, trailer included, was crookedly cross-parked at the back of the lot.

THE WHOLE DRIVE OUT of the mountains had been the blurred sequence of a bad dream. Creed had kept the acceleration high, not caring when his trailer skidded on the curves. All his energies were concentrated on escaping. Breaking free from the judgmental mountains and the man they'd conspired to make him face.

The first decent-sized parking lot was for some kitschy store called The Mad Moose, at the corner of Marys Lake and Elkhorn. He pulled in and maneuvered to the side, then dropped his forehead on the steering wheel and tried to forget his father's face.

The last few minutes had hurt him worse than any injury he'd ever sustained on a climbing route. And the injustice of it made him want to throw up. All these years, while he'd been fighting to stagger out from under the shadow of his upbringing, the man who'd continually cut him down had been hiding out right here where everything had started. Coward, as always.

But of course. *He* hadn't had to live down rejection or watch his dreams be misunderstood or try to find a path when the right one had been yanked from under his feet. He'd breathed a sigh of relief when Creed was gone. Been happy to forget he ever had a son.

Anger and pain burned through his veins like a white-hot drug, and he slammed his palm on the wheel. "No!" The word was rough against his throat. "No!"

His eyes stung. Not with tears, surely. He'd cried his last years ago, when he'd watched the Rez disappear in his rearview mirror. He blinked hard and glanced at the hourglass symbol traced onto his dashboard. The *kapemni,* the one he'd drawn on that disastrous night when—well, when everything happened. It had been an act of defiance, he'd thought then. Now it seemed more like pure desperation.

Heaven and Earth. That's what Charlie Manyhorse had said. He could still see the old tribal elder, the fire dancing shadows and light on his face. *"The* kapemni *shows the intersection. What is done on Earth shall be done in Heaven. And in the mirroring of the obedience, the two realms shall become one."*

It had been a long time since he'd heard stories like that. Even longer since he believed them. And if there ever was a place where Heaven met Earth, it wasn't in these mountains.

He swiped a hand hard over his face, trying to think around the shock waves still submerging his soul. He needed to just get back on I-25. Head as fast and far from this place as he could run. He could call Austin and convince him that whatever vague *"nature footage"* he was hoping to showcase on the channel wouldn't be found in these hills. Maybe he could—

He was only faintly aware that a slate-blue Bronco had pulled up next to him. Even less aware that someone was getting out. Not until there was a gentle tap on his window.

He looked up. Well, no leaving town that easily.

Skyla Bluefeather had found him.

THE GUY HADN'T EVEN NOTICED when they pulled next to him. His head had been bent, as if in thought. Or sorrow. Avery had hung by the Bronco, but Skyla simply marched to his window and rapped on it.

The man jerked his head up, and his startled expression instantly locked into something much less approachable. He slowly opened the door and climbed out of the Jeep. "What are you doing?" His eyes flicked behind them in an unspoken question.

"Laz is not here, if this is your concern." Skyla's voice was calm, but her eyes held the probing gaze that could bring peace to the raptors and draw truth from the hurting. "We have come to discuss another matter with you, Creed."

The guy blinked, as if Skyla's use of his name had changed the air around them. Avery rolled the word in her head. *Creed.* The name suited him. Strong and bold and unapologetically different.

"Okay." He leaned against the Jeep door and folded his arms, his expression that of an injured mountain lion at bay.

Skyla glanced around. "You are not yet staying in a campground?"

"Couldn't find any open for the season. Didn't feel like winter camping. It wouldn't be the first time I've spent the night in a parking lot."

There was an odd defiance in his words, a shoving back of sympathy. Hard to believe this closed-door guy bore any relation to Laz's open heart.

Although apparently Laz hadn't been as open as she'd thought.

"But I'm busy." Creed glanced back at his Jeep and shifted. "So, what do you need?"

He'd win no personality points. Avery frowned and stepped forward. "You were telling me that you wanted to film on our land."

He squinted in her direction. "Yeah, and you said that you weren't interested." His tone could have given frostbite. "*Unavailable* is I think how you described it."

Avery narrowed her eyes at him. "That was before—"

"Before what? Before you realized you knew my dad?"

She liked this man less every second. "Before I gave you the chance to tell us what you were planning."

"That's for sure." His eyes snapped sparks. "You didn't even let me finish my sentence when you—"

"This is enough." Skyla's voice was still calm, but the weight of it flattened the argument. "Creed, as you have rightly seen, the past cannot be changed. However, the future is still open to us. Avery says that you are a videographer?"

"Well—yeah." Creed's shoulders stayed tight. "I work for Guys in the Wild, which has three hundred—"

Thousand subscribers. Yep. She'd heard this.

"Very well." Skyla didn't wait for the rest of his spiel. "And you are seeking to undertake what sort of project here?"

"My boss sent me here." His tone didn't sound too happy about it. "This is my first solo project. I'll be doing a lot of filming for a YouTube feature about nature in this area." He shrugged. "I was going to film in the national park, but I'm having a, uh, hard time getting a permit. I was driving around looking for alternatives, and I saw—" For the first time, something more vulnerable crept into his expression. "The *kapemni.*"

"Ah. Yes." Skyla nodded slowly. "Heaven and Earth, and the door that is always open between them."

Creed cleared his throat. "Yeah. Anyway. That's why I stopped there."

"I see." Skyla took a deep breath and gave a firm nod. "Well, Creed. This is my proposition to you. You may film at the center, on our land. We have extensive property. And we have a few campsites, for some of our summer staff." She gestured at the camper trailer. "You are more than welcome to park your camper there for the duration of your time here."

What? Avery spun to face Skyla. Surely she was joking.

"Are you serious?" Creed's tone sounded only slightly less horrified.

Well, for once they agreed.

"Yes." Skyla sounded as calm as if she were discussing details of an injured hawk's exercise schedule. "You need a place to film and a place to stay. We are in need of funding for the center." She spread her hands. "Let us help each other."

An odd hope struggled against something harder in Creed's face. "Look, don't do this just because—I mean, is this because of my— my—"

"I have known your father for many years. But the invitation I offer to you now is not tangled in his story. And if you wish, you will not need to speak with him at all." Skyla's voice turned more serious. "This is business, Creed. Not pity. We will thankfully accept the payment you mentioned. And we will rejoice in the increased exposure for the center. We will tell the stories so that the hearts of others are stirred." Skyla leveled a piercing gaze at Creed. "Something I know you have seen."

A muscle tightened in his jaw. "I know what you're thinking." He muttered the words. "But I don't do those kinds of videos anymore."

"You have the eyes for them."

"No." Creed bit off the word and sighed. He shoved a hand through his hair. "All right. I'll prepare the filming agreement."

"Thank you." Skyla pressed her palms together and bowed slightly. "It is an honor, Creed. Now, perhaps you would like to follow us back to the center."

ADDISYN SAGGED over the bathroom sink and turned the faucet on full blast. No wonder she'd been feeling so worn out the last couple of weeks. Apparently, she'd been coming down with a virus.

She rinsed her mouth out, then pushed her hair back and straightened. How many times was this now that she'd lost her lunch? Three? Four? Ugh. She *hated* stomach bugs.

She glanced at her reflection in the mirror. The girl staring back at her looked even more tired than she felt—chalk-pale with eyes rimmed in shadow. She sighed and shuffled out of the bathroom on wobbly legs. Back to the couch, where she'd spent most of the day— minus the time in the bathroom. Well, at least she hadn't gone to Canada with Darius. His time there would be hectic enough without adding a sick wife to everything.

She pulled out her phone and tapped out a text to him.

I think I'm getting sick.

Her finger paused over the *send* button. Did he really need to know that? It would only worry him.

She backspaced the text and slipped the phone back in her pocket. There was no need to whine to him. She could deal with this herself. The way she'd tried to do more and more since their marriage.

A twinge that had nothing to do with the nausea poked at her. Darius was a wonderful man, kind and compassionate and thoughtful. But sometimes she still found herself—well, holding back. Every need felt like a withdrawal from the overflowing account of his love for her.

And she couldn't bear to wake up one morning and find it overdrawn.

A key clicked in the lock, and then her sister's voice. "Ads?"

"In here." She cleared her throat and sat straighter on the couch. "And I'm—"

"You are never going to believe this." Avery rushed into the room like an alpine blizzard, her words tumbling out almost before she could peel her jacket off. "So, this guy showed up today and started telling me about his YouTube channel, and now Skyla—"

"Wait, what?" When was the last time she had seen Avery this chaotic? "Start over."

Avery gripped the jacket in front of her and took a deep breath. "Okay. This strange guy came to the center. Said he worked for a YouTube channel."

Addisyn was trying to concentrate, but the nausea was swelling again. "Uh-huh?"

"Yeah. And you'll never guess who—"

Nope. Couldn't wait. Addisyn scrambled off the couch and bolted for the bathroom, Avery on her heels. "Addisyn, what's wrong?"

By the time they left the bathroom, Avery's focus had completely shifted. "Addisyn, why didn't you tell me you were sick?"

Addisyn groaned and flopped onto the couch. "I didn't know until today. I've had some nausea for the last week or so. Ever since I started being tired. But today was the first day I was sick like this." She sighed. "I think this is five times."

"Five times?" Avery's eyebrows shot up. She pressed a palm to Addisyn's forehead. "You don't feel hot."

Addisyn shrugged. "I feel okay, except for being tired and sick to my stomach. I don't have any aches or chills or anything." This was a weird stomach bug. With her luck, probably some rare and fatal type. Six hours of vomiting followed by sudden death.

Avery's brow creased. "Any other symptoms? Does anything else feel different?"

Addisyn mentally scanned the past few weeks. When had things started feeling weird? "Uh—no. I don't think so. Except—" She hadn't thought of this before. "It must be messing with my hormones. The timing of my cycle is off." But that could have also been her hectic schedule at work. Really, the whole thing could be stress-related.

"*Off* like how?"

"Uh—long, I think." She knew some women who kept detailed female health apps and knew the day of their cycle to precision. She had never been one of them.

Avery's expression suddenly shifted. "Ads..."

"Yeah?" Sickness curdled in her gut again. She squeezed her eyes shut and ran a hand over the back of her neck. Maybe she really should tell Darius.

"Do you think you're pregnant?"

Pregnant? Addisyn's head snapped up. "What?" Her heart ratcheted into overdrive. "No way."

Avery hesitated. "Are you sure?"

"Yes." She said the word firmly enough to tamp down the doubts that were now stirring uncomfortably in her midsection. She and Darius weren't planning for kids yet. They'd been careful. There was no way she could be pregnant.

No way at all.

"Okay..." Avery dragged the word out long enough to show she wasn't convinced. "But—"

"But *what*?" Irritation prickled over her shoulders. *Pregnant.* What a ridiculous idea.

Avery hesitated. "There was something deeper in your soul this time. When I saw you yesterday. Like something had shifted. And at the time, it didn't make sense, but now—"

She'd never argued with Avery's ability to sense the patterns of hearts, but this time, her intuitive sister had to be wrong. "I—I really don't think—" What cycle day was it, anyway? She tried to picture the calendar in her head, mentally juggle the days into weeks. Wait. Had it really been over five weeks? Or—was it actually six? No, it was six.

The knot in her stomach pulled tighter. Oh gosh. She'd been so busy that she hadn't been paying attention, but—

"Ads, I really think this might be it." Avery's voice colored with rising excitement. "You're going to have a—"

"Avery, that is *not* what is going on here." Addisyn jerked to her feet, her eyes stinging. Tears, really? She was going to cry over her sister's far-flung theory?

Of course she was. Because she was moody with PMS, right? And any day now, her hormones would kick in, and her body would assure her that everything was normal.

She couldn't bear to think of the alternative.

"Wait, are you crying?" Avery wrapped a soothing arm around Addisyn's shoulders. "Hey. That would be a good thing, Ads. Can't you imagine how excited Darius would be?"

She could, which did not help. At all. "I'm—we're not ready for kids." It was the truth. The truth she'd anchored in her own soul. The truth she'd pushed against Darius every time he tentatively brought the subject up.

"Okay." But judging from Avery's tone, her mind was quite obviously made up. "Tell you what. Why don't you take a pregnancy test? And then we'll know. And if you really aren't pregnant—" her voice turned serious—"then you probably need to go to the doctor with all these symptoms."

All *what* symptoms? The exhaustion of working two jobs? Nausea that was probably from that stupid street-taco place where she'd stopped on her way to Estes Park? Cardiac arrest caused by even considering the idea that she was inadvertently bringing another human into the world?

"Well—" She shrank away from the idea. The test would be negative—of course it would be—but she just—well, she just didn't want to deal with it. But then again, how else would she get Avery off the idea? "Fine. Uh—where do you get one?"

"At Safeway."

She already couldn't bear the idea of having to walk up to the checkout counter with a pregnancy test. She'd be using self-check for sure. "Okay. How—do you know how to use one of those things?" So help her, she was *not* Googling that.

Avery didn't look certain, but she nodded anyway. "I think I know how they work. Hey, if you'll get the test, I'll help you figure that part out."

The tiniest sliver of relief cut through the chaos inside her. "Do you mind?"

"Not at all." Avery smoothed a hand over her hair and squeezed her close. "Don't worry, Ads. I got you."

And that was why she was so thankful for her big sister. Why every time her life slipped south, she found herself on the winding road to Estes Park. Because Avery stood solidly in her corner. And she always told the truth. And she could read Addisyn's heart without a single word.

But surely—surely this time Avery was wrong.

She just had to be.

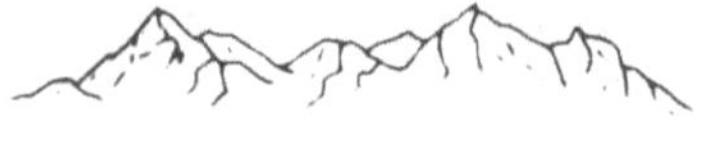

CHAPTER 4

Avery had held one purpose in her mind when she'd left work last night: to share the shock of Creed with Addisyn. But that had been interrupted by Addisyn's sickness.

Or pregnancy. Far more likely, even though her stubborn sister wouldn't admit it.

But once things had settled down, she'd finally told the tale. Addisyn's jaw had dropped. "Laz has a son? He never really seemed like the family type."

That was putting it far too mildly. "I know. And Laz was—" Describing the raw pain on his face almost felt like breaching his privacy. "Very upset."

"So Laz has a *son*." Clearly the disbelief was nearly too big for Addisyn to hold. "Wow. I always knew that guy had some secrets."

"Oh, and here's the other thing." Avery had gauged Addisyn's reaction. "This guy is some kind of YouTube hotshot. Works for some channel with three hundred thousand subscribers."

"Three hundred thousand?" Addisyn's eyebrows had lifted. So apparently that was a good number, after all. She'd snatched up her phone. "I want to see what Laz's son looks like. What's his channel called?"

The name had dangled just out of reach in Avery's memory. But when she'd left the house this morning, she'd promised Addisyn to find out today. After all, she'd be seeing the hotshot himself at work.

Rubbing her thumbs on the steering wheel, she groaned at the very idea. Mercy lifted her head from the passenger seat, the space between her ears scrunched in concern.

"It's okay, Mercy." Avery sighed. "Just gonna be a long day."

Why had Skyla offered Creed this chance, anyway? Clearly they'd known each other before, somehow. So was this her way of trying to help him? Or did she really think he was as important as he said he was?

Well, it was only for six weeks, anyway. And Mr. Movie Star was paying them, at least—payment that would help fund the expansion. That made it worthwhile.

As long as she could survive working with him in the meantime.

She'd left early this morning, giving herself plenty of time to stop by Laz's place on her way to the raptor center. If nothing else, the conversation with Addisyn had convinced her of one thing: it simply wasn't fair for her to conjecture about Laz's story. She needed to hear the facts from him. Before she saw his son again.

The sun splashed rosy warmth against the sides of the mountains, the tune of the new day singing stronger with the increasing light. Avery rolled down the window an inch, and the chilly morning air rushed into the truck, tingling with a sudden wide-awake energy. She breathed it in, pulled hard on the reins of her racing thoughts. The way she did every morning, or tried to.

God of the mountains...El Shaddai... She waited, rolling His Name around in her mind until the other voices in her heart settled. There were a million questions she could ask, a million requests she could make.

But her mind kept returning to the knowing, the fire she'd seen around Creed yesterday. Why had a vision come about *him*? Usually the words and images pertained to her own spirit, or Addisyn, or occasionally Skyla. But they'd always seemed reserved for people near to her heart. Never random strangers.

She sent her thoughts upward again. *Show me why. When it's time. And until then—* The little A-frame building of Live Bigger appeared around the curve. *Help Laz.*

The door at the shop still squawked on its hinges when she opened it. Mercy trotted in confidently, immediately busying herself with the all-important task of sniffing at display racks. Avery breathed in the familiar scent of the place where she'd worked for her first two years in Estes—wood and leather and the rubber soles of new hiking boots. "Laz?"

"Miz Avery?" Floorboards creaked, and then he appeared from the back room. "Waaalll, good mornin', gal. Shouldn't you be on yer way to work?"

The normal boom of his voice was diminished, but at least he was talking to her. "I am. I stopped for a minute." Avery worried the hem of her jacket in her hands. "Laz—I—yesterday." The questions didn't package neatly into sentences. "I'm sorry about—about whatever happened. With your son."

"Eh—" Laz broke her gaze and bent to rub Mercy's ears. "It jes' brought it all back."

So many times, she'd seen him take an injured bird or a stray puppy in those calloused hands, watched him soothe it back to peace. Now he was the one in pain, and the reversal hurt her own heart. "Is there—anything I can do?"

"Naw. Nothin' now." He sighed and finally looked up, scrubbing a hand hard over his beard. "Figger we was jes' too much alike, me and him."

Her fingertips were growing sweaty on the jacket hem. "Skyla offered him the chance to film. At the center."

His bushy eyebrows twitched. "She said somethin' 'bout that."

"I'll be working with him." She was marking time, waiting for the tightness in his face to release.

"That so?" Laz's mouth quirked. "Good Lord help you, then."

"He seems—stubborn."

"Stubborn?" His tone was rough, but the creases on his face looked more like sadness than anger. "That's for sure. That boy runs hot an' heavy like a lone wolf. Ever since he was a kid."

"So—you two don't talk."

"Nope." The word was heavy as granite. "Haven't seen him in— five years, I guess. No, almost six."

"Why?"

Laz scratched his forehead. "Cause we both as ornery as a pair of

Missouri mules. An' neither one of us ever' done nothin' but stick our clumsy hands where they don't belong. Only one ever had any sense was his mother."

His mother. Another question mark. "I didn't know you'd ever been married."

"Yep. A lifetime ago." A small smile softened Laz's face. "Beautiful gal. Natasha Running Wolf."

Running Wolf. Creed's last name made sense now. "She was Native American?"

"Lakota tribe." Laz's expression locked down again. "But she's gone now. Same as ever'thin' else."

Mercy pressed herself against Avery's leg. Avery automatically rubbed the dog's head, keeping her focus on Laz. "What happened?"

"Ain't no use talkin' 'bout it." He let out a breath and crossed his arms. "Yer lookin' at a man who done purty near ever' wrong a feller can do. An' I thought the Good Lord had done let me move on, but —" He glanced out the window, squinting as if the morning sun hurt his eyes. "Sure does seem like He's still got some lightnin' bolts to hurl my way."

The pain in his voice sliced her own soul. "Laz—that's not—"

"Git on with you, Avery gal." The gruffness in his voice didn't hide the tremble. He turned around and stalked toward the back of the store. "You gotta git up there to work 'fore Miz Skyla sends out a search party. Never mind me. I'm fine."

I'm fine. The same words she'd snapped at him, on her first day of work at Live Bigger, as a closed-off island of a girl. And he'd stopped right where she was standing now, cocked an eyebrow at her in a way that she learned not to disobey. *"Fine's what people say when they don't want help, Avery gal. When they ain't gonna take nobody's hand. So tell me yer mad or scared or stressed or fit to bust with fear, but don't tell me yer fine. Whatever's up, we're wrasslin' through it together."*

Together. Avery took a deep breath and willed her words to reach her truest friend. "You wouldn't let me say I was fine. Not ever."

Laz froze for a heartbeat. When he turned around, his face was softer than before. "Quit worryin' 'bout me, Miz Avery. An old mountain goat like me done knows how to hunker down in a storm." His smile didn't reach the pain in his eyes. "Now git. I done tole you all I plan to say 'bout this here situation. An' we both got places to be."

The stock room door banged behind him. Avery swallowed the ache in her throat and clenched her fists. A flare of anger at Creed struck a sudden match in her soul. Did he have to come back here and ruin Laz's peace? Why had he left Laz anyway?

Selfish, probably. Just like her mom. For a half second, those taillights glowed again in her memory. No brake lights. No second thoughts, no—

Mercy gave a soft whine and pressed closer to Avery's leg. Avery blinked away the memory and sighed. "I know, girl. Come on. Let's see Skyla."

The bell over the door jingled farewell as she headed back into the chilly air. She'd done what she could for the stubborn father.

Now, time to deal with the stubborn son.

—✕—

A DEAL WAS A DEAL, like it or not. Which was why Creed was at the office door five minutes before eight o'clock in the morning.

That, and the fact that his trailer was parked twenty yards from said door. Escape wasn't exactly an option.

"Creed." Skyla greeted him with the graciousness that seemed to be her rhythm now. "Thank you for coming."

Against his will. "Yeah, of course." He eyed Skyla warily. He'd last seen her when he was a teenager and she was a new college graduate making visits home to the Rez. But back then, she'd had a temper as swift as a snakebite. "You, uh, you said you're married now?"

"I am." She leaned against the doorframe, seemingly at peace in a way she'd never been on the Rez. "Chayton is a wonderful man. You will meet him soon."

Was that it? Her marriage had calmed her down? Yet the change in her seemed deeper than that. Somehow in the last decade, the storm within her had settled into stillness. "Great. You, uh—" How could he ask everything he wanted to know? "You've found a good place here."

"Yes." She turned her face to the morning sun and smiled as if she shared a secret with the sky. "It is a great blessing." Her keen glance flicked to him. "I am glad you were led here."

Led. He wasn't ready to think about what that word meant. Or about the staggering odds of turning up at his father's address, six years and three states removed from the past. "Well—uh—actually, I was driving by and saw the *kapemni* on your sign. That's why I stopped."

"Ah, yes." Skyla nodded. "It is there because the center exists for this reason. We are told to act in Creator's will in the earth below as in the spirit-world above. Is it not so?"

"Uh. Yes." He'd long ago stopped believing that, but he wasn't ready to test Skyla's apparent transformation by arguing.

"That is our reason for being. To reflect His greatness, and to stand with love in the open door between the worlds. And when we do that, He gives power. Heart-healing power."

When had Skyla, of all people, taken on his dad's faith? On the Rez, he'd once seen her spit on the church steps. "I, uh, I didn't know you were a—a—"

"A walker of the good road?" She smiled. "It was a journey for me. But it has been—wonderful."

"Well. That's good." He wanted to resent her for selling out to his father's faith. But on the other hand—well, *something* had changed her. And somehow, the way she talked about God felt much more welcoming than the strait-laced sermons at the cheap Rez chapel.

"And you are on a journey as well, I believe. There is a reason you came here, He Who Believes."

The name pricked part of his heart that hadn't stirred in far too long. "I—" He swallowed. "No one has called me that since your grandfather."

"*Kaká* was a farseeing man." Skyla swept her hair over her shoulder. "I am glad for his sake that he has entered the sky-world, but I miss his eyes."

"So do I." Charlie's hands, Charlie's voice in his mind again. "*To the truth you will cling, He Who Believes. And what you see, you will pull from Heaven to Earth.*"

"And he most certainly believed in you. As do I."

The undeserved trust stretched over his shoulders like a burden he'd never been strong enough to carry. "I—thanks." Creed shifted uncomfortably. What would his mentor say about him now?

The morning stretched silently between them until the awkwardness itched at him. But before he could come up with something to say, Skyla spoke again.

"As you can see, there is opportunity here for the stories you will tell." She waved her hand at the half-finished building across the parking lot. "We are in the process of expanding this center to accommodate more learning areas. Exhibits, classes." Again her measuring gaze turned to him. "This is yet again why I am glad of your being here. I have seen some of your work, Creed."

"Oh, really?" For some reason, he cringed to imagine what Skyla had thought of adrenaline-laced jocks bragging their way up mountainsides. "My Guys in the Wild work?"

"That, and—" Skyla paused and waved her hand vaguely. "Some of your older content. Your filming, your editing—it is clear that the gift to see is yours." She gestured to the sun-drenched land. "What artistry this place holds. And so you will tell that story, and others will listen. And as they listen, they will help. It is ever the way of things."

Gift of seeing? What the heck? Creed just nodded vaguely. Whatever Skyla meant wasn't important. This was a matter of filming, and filming he could do.

"And one more thing." Skyla glanced at a beat-up truck announcing its arrival with a clatter. "I have requested Avery to work closely with you in order to direct you and guide your time at the center."

"Avery?" He couldn't fully focus on Skyla's words for watching the old beater clamber over the potholes in the driveway. Heck, the rickety thing must be older than him. "Who's he?"

Skyla cleared her throat. "*She* is my righthand assistant."

Oh. Embarrassment squirmed through him before he blinked at the implication. There was a woman in that old truck?

"She is the one who came with me last night."

The one who—*oh no.* "You mean—"

The statement died as the woman he couldn't seem to escape swung out of the truck. And then a black dog the size of a small bear bounded after her. She brought her dog to work? Who did that?

"Hi, Skyla." The temperature of her voice fell several degrees. "Creed."

"Greetings, Avery." Skyla smiled and patted the bear/dog, who was slobbering and panting as if coming to the center were more exciting than finding a bone. "And to you, Mercy."

So the woman who'd judged him up and down had named her dog *Mercy*? Ha.

Skyla was still talking. "I've already explained to Creed that you'll be working with him today. I thought you could begin by showing him the center."

"Yes. Right." The woman—Avery—didn't look any happier than Creed felt with the arrangement. Having lost Skyla's attention, the big black dog slobbered over to Creed. He stepped back. *Not a chance, dog.*

"Mercy! Come here." Avery yanked the dog back as if Creed had smallpox, then studied him through narrowed eyes. "Are you ready to get going?" She glanced at her watch. "I have my first school group at—"

"I have already instructed Liv to take the first group today." Skyla slipped back through the office door. "You two take as much time as is needed."

The door closed, a period on Skyla's statement. Avery's mouth tightened slightly. Then she sighed and faced Creed. "I guess Skyla has explained the basics to you."

Well, sort of. "Yeah." He studied Avery, taking note of her appearance for the first time. Tall and thin like an aspen, with brown hair chopped off at her shoulders and clothes that looked as if she might leave on a hike at any minute. "I'm, uh, Creed. I mean, I know you know that, but—"

"Right." Her chin tilted slightly up. "I also know your father. Very well."

His father again. And her tone made it clear which side of the feud she'd claimed. Creed clenched his jaw. "So you know the story of what happened between us?"

"He hasn't told me much about that."

Right. Of course he didn't want to admit his part in it. "Then maybe you should consider the possibility that you don't know him as well as you thought you did."

Avery flinched. "Laz is my friend." Her voice was softer, but still determined. "I won't hear talk about him."

An old memory tugged on his sleeve. He'd been eight years old when he'd shoved a kid on the playground for calling his dad a *redneck.*" He hadn't really known the meaning of the term, but he'd still pummeled Tommy Jacobs into the ground until a teacher had dragged him to the principal's office—where he'd spouted off almost the same words. *"I don't let anybody talk mean about my dad."*

A strange ache filled his chest as he looked back at Avery. Well, good for her that the old man hadn't disillusioned her yet. "Fine." He bit off the word. "I have no desire to talk about him anyway." He shouldered his camera bag. "So, tell me about the center."

"It's easier to show you." She started walking. Apparently he was supposed to follow. "We'll go through the buildings first, then to the back of the property. It's a good piece of walking to there, though."

A good piece? Who said that? He'd bet his boots she wasn't originally from the West. Some of her words still harbored a trace of a New England accent. Boston, maybe. Or Philadelphia. Probably some posh big city where her wealthy parents sent her to stuck-up prep schools.

"The walking doesn't bother me." If she wanted to scare him off, she'd have to try harder than that. "I've been backcountry camping in the Tetons for a filming project. You'll be hard pressed to tire me out."

"About that." She cleared her throat as she opened the office door, Mercy trotting ahead of her. "What did you say the name of your channel was?"

Did she care? "Guys in the Wild. But it's not really my channel. I'm a videographer for it, and I do a lot of climbing too."

"Climbing?"

"Rock climbing." He glanced at the cliffs behind the tree line. He could really use a climb right now.

Avery nodded. "My sister asked me the name."

She had a sister? He peered at her as they stepped into the building, wondering what else waited behind that locked-off facade. "Oh. Have you, uh, ever seen any of our videos?"

"I'm not a YouTube person."

Well, then.

"Here are the offices." Avery gestured vaguely down a hallway. "And the business center is there, where Tyler is."

The guy—Tyler—peered from behind a computer that almost eclipsed him. "You must be Creed."

"That's me." Creed endured the guy's limp handshake.

"So, you're doing some kind of film project, right?" Tyler's round glasses gave him the look of an owl. An unfriendly owl.

"Yes. I work for an outdoors YouTube channel. We create adventure content." His spiel was starting to bore even him.

"Huh. Interesting." His flat tone buoyed when he looked at Avery. "Hey, Avery, I got the group schedule ready for next week."

"Thanks, Tyler." Amazingly, she actually smiled. "I'll pick it up when I'm done with this."

When she was done with *him*, she meant.

"Meanwhile, do you mind if Mercy stays with you?"

"Of course not." Tyler grinned at the dog as she pranced up to him. "Hey there, cute girl. Ready to help me with a budget?"

The way Tyler had gazed at Avery made it obvious why he was so sweet with the dog. Creed stopped just short of rolling his eyes. Well, he wouldn't be surprised if the two of them had some kind of thing going. They seemed made for each other.

Avery pointed to a desk in the corner of the area. "Creed, Skyla moved that desk in last night. She said you could work here and use the center Wi-Fi."

"Oh. Great." Being stuck next to Tyler didn't sound appealing, especially since the guy seemed no friendlier than Avery was. Why did everybody dislike him so much? Was it really because of his dad? Hard to believe the man could have won so many hearts. "So, uh, where does the actual work happen?" Nothing he'd seen so far was fit for a Guys in the Wild video.

"Well, the mews are out here." Avery led the way through the back door of the center and toward a barn-like structure not far away.

"The mews?"

"The enclosures for the non-releasable birds." She stepped inside the barn and opened the first door to the left. "Like Elijah here."

Creed blinked, his eyes adjusting from the sun—and sucked in a breath. On a tree limb swinging from the ceiling perched a brilliantly beautiful hawk, feathers like rich brushstrokes of auburn and charcoal. The bird's head pivoted, a raptor's sharp eye trained on them.

"Wow. Awesome."

"He's a Swainson's Hawk." Here with the hawk, Avery seemed more relaxed. "He came for rehab at the center eight years ago."

"He's very impressive."

"You could easily use the birds in your video." Avery's voice sounded hopeful. "Their journeys are often remarkable."

"Yeah. That's a thought." Although he was used to filming guys breaking their necks on rock walls. Not birds shut up in stalls. He frowned. "So, now he just has to stay in this room?"

The minute he heard his own words, he knew they were wrong. Especially when Avery's expression closed off again. *Think before you speak.* Dad's words, a hundred times over, yet they'd never taken root.

"He lost one eye in an accident, which does not allow him to have binocular vision. As a result, he can't hunt on his own anymore. He'd die in the wild." Avery crossed her arms. "The enclosure is designed to mimic his natural habitat as closely as possible. In addition, we take him outside several times a day."

Even the hawk seemed to be staring judgmentally at him with his one good eye. Creed sighed. "Okay."

After what was in fact *a good piece* of walking, Avery had shown him the flight cages, the rehab room—which looked like a vet's office —and the trailhead for the walking paths that wound through the back part of the property. "These aren't maintained well, though. I haven't had a chance to get out here yet this spring."

"You?"

"Yes." Her jaw tightened slightly. "I do all the trail maintenance."

Whoa. He wouldn't have guessed that, but he wouldn't let her see his surprise. He looked instead at the rough-hewn trail sign, carved arrows pointing out names like *Moose Way* and *Pika Point.* "Cool sign."

Her lips tightened. "Your father carved it for us."

Good grief, was there *anything* at this place that his father didn't have his hands on?

Fortunately Avery was already heading back the way they'd come, apparently not waiting for a response. "This is our new building. Or at least, it will be."

Even surrounded by the clutter of construction, the rustic structure was still pretty, with golden-new cedar siding and the skeleton of a wraparound porch. When Avery opened the door, the thick smell of sawdust and sheetrock billowed out. "Exhibits will be in there. Classrooms around the outer edge. We haven't been able to finish the interior yet." She hesitated. "We applied for a grant, but that fell through."

Hmm. This must be why they'd agreed to work with him. "Is that the plan for the Guys in the Wild payment?"

"Yes. That's going to be a blessing. This is the most important part of the whole center, after all. The way that people—" She broke off abruptly and stepped back, a flush rising to her face. "Sorry. I—I just love working here, is all."

Huh. Well, if she loved it that much, then maybe there was something about this place he could capitalize on for filming. Something more impressive than what he'd seen thus far. "Why is that?"

"Well—" She studied the unfinished boards beneath her feet for a moment. "Because of the healing. The birds come here and are mended. And people come here tired and worn out and hurting, and —and they see the wonder." The clouds reflected in her eyes as she looked back at him. "They see El Shaddai."

He blinked. "Who?"

"It's Hebrew." She gestured toward the peaks, sharp-cut against the horizon. "The God of the mountains."

God. So she was in league with not only his father, but also his father's God. Another Person who'd brutally let him down.

"This isn't a church." The words were rougher-edged than he'd intended.

Avery blinked. "No. But—don't you think God is here? More than anywhere?" Her gesture encompassed the sky above and the mountains beyond. "I think anywhere hearts change, He is there."

Well, hearts didn't change. That was the problem. "I don't know." The conversation itched him with irritation. "Any God up there probably brushed me under the rug a long time ago."

"That's not what God does."

"Oh, really?" She was seriously rubbing under his skin now. "And you are the expert on what God does, Saint Avery?"

The moment the words left his mouth, he knew he'd stepped over a line. Especially when Avery's eyes widened.

"I'm no saint." Her voice was softer now. "I just—"

"Never mind." He held up a hand. "I don't talk about faith." He'd let this conversation trigger him way too much. Probably because Avery was bringing Charlie's voice back. *And the Creator Who dwells in the high places beyond all time—*

No. *No* to Charlie and *no* to Saint Avery and *no* to whatever Power had dragged him back to these menacing mountains. He stepped back from the building. "I've seen enough to get started. Thanks for the tour."

And with that, he turned and headed away without looking back.

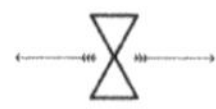

THE TASTE of her interaction with Creed was still sour in Avery's soul as she all but ran to the outdoor classroom area. As she stumbled into the little grouping of picnic tables, Liv threw her an uncertain look. "First group just finished. The ten-thirty one should be here any minute." She straddled a stool between two perches, occupied by an American Kestrel and a Great Horned Owl—both of them strapped securely with jesses and studying Avery condescendingly.

Avery sighed. "Great. I'll help you."

"Awesome. If you could take Solomon—"

"For sure." Avery slipped on the thick leather glove and unhooked the owl's jesses, allowing the bird to clamber onto her forearm while she wound the jesses around her other hand.

"You're good with him." Liv nodded approvingly. "He's a little big for me to handle."

"I think he's used to me by now." Solomon was one of the less predictable species ambassadors. Having been shot by a farmer, he'd seemingly retained a suspicion of humans even after his injuries healed. Now he tossed Avery a cynical look out of his impressive eyes. Great. Just what she needed, another arrogant guy in her life.

Liv shifted position on her stool. "How's Wolf Guy doing?"

"He's—well—"

"A pain in the part of your body where you sit?" Liv grinned.

Avery couldn't hold back a laugh. "Something like that, yes."

"He's cute, though."

Of course Liv would notice. Avery raised her eyebrows. "Matt would like to hear you talk like that."

Liv laughed. "That boy's got nothing to worry about. If he ever gets around to asking me, I'll follow him all the way to the altar. But I'm just saying..." She glanced back toward the path. "That hair and those eyes are a pretty electric combo."

The next group of students was filing in. "Enough about him." Avery waved her free hand. If only she could flick Creed away that easily. "We've got a group to lead." She glanced at the schedule. "Which school again?"

"Bear Point High." Liv's mouth quirked. "Probably a tougher group."

Avery swallowed a groan. As much as she loved leading these raptor education workshops, the high schoolers were just...difficult. Old enough to have lost the wonder. Not old enough to have found it again.

The kids clumped themselves at the picnic tables, most already yawning or fidgeting or just staring dully into the middle distance. Not even the birds seemed to get their attention. Although to be fair, Solomon was peering at them in a way that was less than welcoming. And he was tugging on the jesses more than normal.

Avery still assumed her brightest smile and waved to get their attention. "Hello, everyone! We're so glad you're here today at the Estes Valley Outdoor Center."

A few kids mumbled hello. Several had cellphones out. In the back, two girls whispered to each other, stifling giggles behind screening palms.

"I'm Avery, and this is Liv."

Liv waved and flashed her *onstage-at-Red Rocks* smile.

"Today we're going to be introducing you to our birds and talking about conservation work here in the mountains. Does anyone have any questions before we begin?" A kid in a black hoodie dragged his hand up. "Yes, you there."

"How long does this workshop last?"

Whether it was a prayer or a swear that Liv muttered under her breath, Avery couldn't tell. She fought to keep her smile in place. "An hour."

"K." The kid slumped lower on the picnic bench, the glow of his phone screen obvious beneath the edge of the table.

Avery gritted her teeth. An uphill battle. "Okay, well, we're starting off today by introducing our species ambassadors. This is Solomon."

As if on cue, Solomon somehow found a way to infuse yet more hostility into his glare.

"He's a Great Horned Owl, which is the most common owl in Colorado. You've probably heard these owls at night." Or maybe not, if the kids paid as much attention to their surroundings as they were to the class. "Now, these feathers here—the 'horns'—are called ear tufts, but they aren't truly ears. An owl's ears are flat on the sides of its head. But that doesn't mean its hearing is lessened. In fact, did you know a Great Horned Owl can hear a mouse moving under a foot of snow from up to seventy-five feet away?"

Younger—or older—groups usually received this fact with a proper ripple of astonishment. These teens didn't lift an eyebrow. Avery sighed. "And now Liv will introduce you to Miriam, our resident American Kestrel."

But despite Liv's most impassioned introduction, the students' faces remained locked doors. Avery's chest clenched as she watched them. This was the heartbreaking part—seeing kids who were numb to the wonder of the world around them simply because it wasn't as dopamine-driving as their screens.

On her arm, Solomon squirmed, as if he too were ready to be done with the workshop. His beak parted in panting—a sure sign of restlessness. Avery tightened her grip on the jesses. *No. Not right now.*

"—and so Miriam ended up at the center due to contact with West Nile virus. She suffered some neurological damage, so her balance isn't good enough for flight, but she still enjoys spending time outside." Liv glanced back at Avery.

Her turn again. Ignoring the squirming owl on her arm, she pointed at the laminated chart propped on the easel behind her. "One of the main questions we're asked is how birds fly. There are four different kinds of flight—flapping, gliding, soaring, and hovering. Flapping is what we most often picture when we think of bird flight, where wing movements drive the bird forward through the air. Soaring, however, is more common for many raptors." She pointed up. "Above our heads, right now, are invisible rising columns of warm air, called thermals. And raptors know how to ride those columns all the way into the clouds."

A couple of kids glanced up briefly.

"This enables our big raptors, like hawks and eagles, to cover a lot of territory looking for food while saving energy."

There were more than a few lit phone screens. Why wasn't their teacher doing anything about it? Avery glanced toward the back of the group to see the teacher—swiping on her own screen. Well, that explained a few things.

"Now, flight depends on feathers as well." She pointed to the shallow tray of feathers that she and Liv utilized for the workshops. "Miss Liv here is going to talk to you about how that process works."

"All right, guys." Even Liv's infinite enthusiasm looked to be wearing thin. "So first of all, who can tell me what feathers are made of?"

The kids looked nervously at each other before one girl sheepishly raised her hand. "Uh, leather."

Liv ignored the snickers from some of the other students. "Good guess, but not quite. Anyone else?"

Silence hung like a bubble that couldn't be burst.

"Well, they're actually made of keratin. The same material as our hair and fingernails, or the claws of your dog or cat at home. So the way this works is—"

While Liv delivered her presentation, displaying examples of different feathers, Avery watched the students with a heart-aching frustration. How could they all be sucked into screens when this was going on? There was so much out in the world to be seen and experienced. Her whole goal with these classes was to reach kids, to wake them up, to rattle them free from the confines of the familiar and send them into the world with wide-open eyes. And when she couldn't—well, it all felt like such a waste.

This was why she needed to get started on that new curriculum. And it needed to be bold. Interesting. Able to grab these kids by the throats and startle them into looking the world squarely in the eye.

Movement near the back row caught her eye. Creed? What was he doing here? He ducked between the trees and slipped onto one of the back benches, his camera panning until it rested on her like an all-seeing eye.

Wait a minute. She'd never given him permission to film one of the workshops. She froze, her nerves suddenly attuned to her every movement, every breath. All of this was going into his camera, her whole self paraded on display.

It's on you, Avery.

The words resurfaced from some basement in her memory, and she blinked. Her mom's often-repeated refrain. The explanation for why Avery had to take care of Addisyn, defuse their father's wrath, cover up the pill bottles she found in the medicine cabinet.

Because everyone was counting on her.

"Avery?"

She blinked back to reality. Liv was staring at her. And so were all the kids--of course, *now* she had their interest.

"Uh—" Her stomach was flipping, sweat prickling along her shoulders. "I'm sorry, what?"

In the back row, the science teacher frowned. Liv's forehead creased, but her tone didn't change. "I said you would talk more about what we did at the center."

"Oh! Yes. Of course." Avery fought for a deep breath, ignoring the trembling in her fingers. "Okay. So." She fumbled desperately for her train of thought. "Um—"

"When birds are injured, they come here for help." Liv's forehead crease was deeper, but her voice was still gentle. She was obviously trying to help Avery find her footing.

"Right. Exactly. So, uh—" All those faces. All those expectations. And the camera's omniscient eye. "Uh—the—the center exists to create a safe space for raptors—and—"

Solomon ruffled his wings. He was bound to feel her trembling through the glove. *Please, no.* She clenched a fist, trying to squeeze her muscles into stillness. "Uh—"

Her thoughts were gone, her mind as blank as a cloudless sky. The shaking tightened its grip, vibrating deep inside her chest in a way it hadn't for years. What was wrong with her? She'd led a thousand of these workshops and never had trouble before—

A wing suddenly smacked her across the face. She jerked back just as Solomon flapped again. And then, like a living lesson on flight, he sprang from her glove, ripping the jesses from her shaking grasp.

"Solomon!" Avery flung herself forward, accidentally colliding with the display table, which overturned, feathers and papers tumbling in the breeze. Solomon glided low over the heads of the kids—some of whom shrieked and ducked with more emotion than they'd displayed all day—then made for the trees at the back of the ring.

Apparently inspired by the escape of her teammate, Miriam was squawking, requiring all Liv's efforts to control her. Avery's heart throbbed in her throat as she ran after the bird. Solomon couldn't survive in the wild. If they weren't able to recover him—

But he fluttered to a halt on the lower branch of the biggest ponderosa—right next to Creed, who was still filming—and cast a disgruntled eye at them all.

"Solomon, hold still. It's okay, boy." Avery had milliseconds to recapture him. If that long. She shoved past Creed and stretched upward, straining for the jesses that dangled just out of reach.

"Here." Creed finally set the stupid camera down. He jumped, his grip closing on the jesses. "Now what?"

Okay. It was okay. They had him. Avery let out a breath, the panic melting into a relief that threatened to dissolve her, and held out her gloved arm. "Solomon." She swallowed and somehow forced a whistle past her dry lips.

Solomon eyed her for a moment longer, then with a flurry of feathers, settled grudgingly back on her arm.

Avery blinked free from the moment of crisis, delayed embarrassment finally crashing over her like a tidal wave. She turned back to the students. Every wide eye was trained on her—including the disapproving glare of the teacher.

"Glad we got him." Creed folded his arms with a grin.

Irritation snagged on the edges of her emotions. The inattentive students, the pressure of the camera eye—all of this was the fault of him and people like him. People who used YouTube and television and social media to suck more souls into a screen for simulated adventures.

She yanked the jesses from his hand. "Yes."

"Anyway, guys." Liv was obviously trying to lighten the moment. "That's the risk of flight!"

A couple of students gave a halfhearted laugh.

"Let's move forward with the next part while Avery takes

Solomon back to his enclosure." She nodded at Avery with a reassuring wink.

Avery all but ran back to the barn. By the time she'd returned Solomon to his mew and lectured him about appropriate behavior, her hands had stopped shaking.

It was okay. She would be more careful. She would make no more mistakes.

But she would keep Creed far away from her talks from now on.

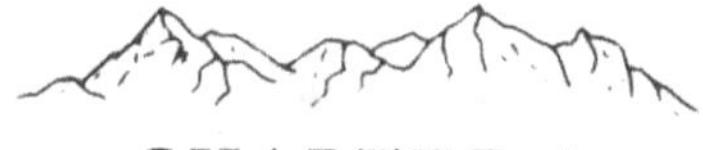

CHAPTER 5

Creed kicked a chunk of mud off his shoe and opened the camper door, letting it swing to catch what little breeze there was on this still evening. He squeezed past the narrow bench couch and settled himself at the strip of table space. The camper wasn't much, but it was home. Far more so than any other place in his turbulent life.

The Wi-Fi was too spotty to upload his content wirelessly, so he hooked the Canon to his laptop with the interface cable. *Back in the old days.* He opened the software and clicked through the prompts, then studied the stacking squares of uploading videos. Not much to work with yet. So far, all he'd really managed to capture were a few shots of the raptors in the enclosures and some B-roll footage of the land behind.

And shots of today's class, but he wouldn't be getting any more of those.

Escaping birds aside, there just didn't seem to be much *action* at this center. Sure, the long-term, big-picture goals were fine. Commendable, really. But—well, he needed something more tangible. More immediate.

Maybe he should throw in the towel on the whole place, try to scare up a story elsewhere. But what other organization would be willing to let him run all over with a camera, not to mention stay on the property?

Plus...there was the matter of the *kapemni.*

He stared at the hourglass marking traced onto the wall of his camper, Charlie's voice reverberating through his memories. *"Always, always, the worlds are reaching out for each other. When the earth-realm and the sky-realm are in agreement, the doorway opens. And our job is to live in the doorway."*

Live in the doorway. It had been one of Charlie's favorite expressions. In his view, believers had a foot in both worlds—bringing heavenly power to the things of Earth, and leading people to the things of Heaven. And regardless of whether that philosophy was true, there was no doubt that Charlie had made it real. He could pray like a thunderclap as joyfully as he could pound nails for a roof on a widow's house.

What would Charlie say if he could see him now?

Creed frowned and refocused on his videos. What other footage could he possibly get? Not Saint Avery's classes, for sure. When he'd had the idea to sit in on her group, he'd had the same feeling that came when he was trying to start a backcountry campfire and finally saw the first spark.

But she'd thrown a wet blanket over that spark that afternoon. *"Don't film during the classes. It's distracting to the students and violates our policies."*

Violating policies. Huh. More likely it had something to do with what had happened during Avery's class today.

What was weirder than the escaping bird had been Avery herself. One moment, she had seemed confident and relaxed. The next, she had a deer-in-the-headlights look and couldn't seem to get the words out. Whatever had happened to her was probably how the bird had escaped. Good thing he'd been there to grab it—not that she'd thanked him.

He sighed. He didn't need a mystery. He just needed footage. His buddies at the channel would never stop laughing if they knew he was sitting around with broken-winged birds waiting for a story to appear. But then, he hadn't heard from a single one of them since he'd come to Colorado. Nobody had checked in or texted or asked if he made it there okay or wondered how the filming was going.

Which was fine, really. They all maintained an unspoken buffer of distance between them. The way Creed preferred. Anyway, Austin was surely keeping them busy in Arizona right now.

Arizona. Man, what he wouldn't give to be there right now. He could almost feel the red-rough sandstone under his fingers, imagine swinging his body up the perfect cliffs of Sedona. Instead, he was stuck here on a foggy day in the mountains where, only a month before Memorial Day, it was downright chilly. Seriously, how could people stand to live here? Let alone love it, the way Avery seemed to.

Although—he had too. Once.

"Believer" jangled from his cell phone. He glanced at the screen, and the uncertainty already gnawing in his gut tightened. *Erica.* He forced his tone to lighten as he answered. "Hey, Erica."

"Hey there, Creed." Voices mingled behind her words. "How's it going in Colorado?"

"Uh—well—" He grimaced. "Not great."

"Aw. I'm sorry to hear that." A door closed, and the background noise vanished. "Having trouble?"

"You could say that." Creed hesitated. Spilling his heart could only muddy the waters more between them—but who else cared enough to absorb his frustration?

He leaned back in his chair and let the whole story tumble out. How he'd struggled to get a permit for the national park and instead found the raptor center. How he was having a hard time creating content out of that. How he was stuck living on the property. "And, uh—" He wasn't ready to share his backstory with her. "I ran into some—some people I used to know."

"Really?" She paused. "Wow. I'm sorry, Creed. I know that's got to be driving you crazy. But—" Her tone softened, an undercurrent of something more than friendship beneath her words. "If anybody can handle all that, it's you. You're the best there is."

Half of him wanted to surrender to that current. The other half knew he could drown there. "Well. Thank you."

"Of course." Her tone was still searching for something he wasn't ready to give. "You're missed in Arizona."

Creed sighed. "I doubt that. Austin basically exiled me."

"Austin thinks—" She checked herself. "Never mind."

"Wait." Creed pressed the phone closer to his ear. "Austin thinks *what?*"

"No." She sounded sheepish. "I shouldn't have said anything. You're not supposed to know."

"Aww, c'mon, Erica." He dialed up the charm in his voice, ignoring the twinge of guilt. "You can't just leave me hanging."

"Well—you can't tell anybody."

"Who am I gonna tell? I'm stranded in Colorado."

"You'll be the death of me, Running Wolf." But the smile behind her words told him he'd won. "All right. Austin was saying the other day how he thinks you have incredible talent. He said he's been watching your work the last few months, and you have a better eye with the camera than anybody else."

The words shimmered in his mind. After all his years of effort, he'd struck gold. "Austin said that?"

"Yeah." She hesitated. "Creed, don't tell anyone, but he's considering you for the international crew."

The international crew? Really? The possibility was almost too bright to look at. Since he'd started at Guys in the Wild, traveling with the international crew had been in his focus lens. The A-team crew explored all over the world. Adventures and salaries and creative freedom he could only dream of.

Erica was still talking. "So, the point is, I think he's watching to see how you handle this."

All this time he'd thought Austin was shuffling him aside—the guy was actually auditioning him? "I—wow." The word was weak. He let out a breath. "Man, I had no idea..."

"I don't know that last part for sure. It's just—he's said some things. I have a good guess. So, my point is, this isn't exile." She laughed. "I think it's a test."

"Wow." Again the word was too small. "I mean, thanks for telling me. I'd love to go with the international team."

"Yeah, pretty rad. And, you know, I'll be on the team next year."

Oh. A twinge of reality poked at his dream. "Uh, really?"

"Yeah, so—" Her tone turned velvety again. "We'd be doing it together."

Together. He scratched the back of his neck uncomfortably. "That—that'd be cool."

The conversation shifted to lighter things—Erica's annoyance with the desert heat, the different climbs they'd done, the funny story of how Rusty had found a scorpion in his sleeping bag. Creed laughed along, but when the call ended, he stayed at the table, watching the square of twilight out the window congeal into night.

Had Austin really said that? He closed his eyes, summoning the words again. *Talent. Better than anybody else.*

Words his dad had never been willing to give—but Austin was.

Although—an uncomfortable question buzzed around his brain like an irritating mosquito. Was all of this truly due to his talent? Or —had Erica pulled strings?

Creed frowned and swatted the idea away. No, she wouldn't do that. She was interested in him, sure, but not enough to stick her neck out. She and Austin had had their share of friction—the classic clash of competitive siblings. She wouldn't have asked her brother for favors.

At least, he hoped not. Because favors were usually traded for... other favors.

He sighed, his frustration turning inward. Erica was a great girl. Smart and funny, with a snappy wit and a mind in constant motion. And as for her looks—well, he would have had to be stone-blind to not notice that. Any other guy on the team would have pounced on even one of the hints she'd dangled Creed's way.

So why was he still—uneasy?

He rubbed his eyes. Whatever the answer to the Erica problem might be, it could wait, at least until he got to Arizona. But what couldn't wait was creating a video fantastic enough to banish any hesitation Austin might have.

He refocused on the glow of his laptop, a square of light in the darkness. Okay. He could do this. He'd dig out the most amazing story, and he'd present it in a dazzling way. Because the better his creation turned out, the more likely it was that he could achieve the one goal he'd been chasing ever since he drove away from the Rez.

Escape.

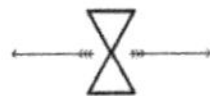

By Sunday afternoon, Avery had realized that despite Addisyn's repeated promises, she was never going to buy a pregnancy test. She'd had every opportunity. Good grief, on Saturday, she'd even gone to the stationery store right next door to Safeway. She'd come home with a package of ballpoint pens and a blank-eyed excuse. *"Oh…I forgot to stop by there."*

Uh huh, just as she'd always *forgotten* to show Avery any less-than-stellar report cards in high school. Avery rolled her eyes as she pulled into Safeway's parking lot. No need to play tug-of-war with this any longer. She'd take care of the situation the same way she'd handled most things in their lives—doing it herself.

The days were warmer now, but the wind still had a bite as it rushed off the dense snowpack of the High Peaks. Avery zipped her windbreaker and grabbed a shopping basket as she walked into the fluorescent frenzy that was Estes Park's only franchised grocery store. A maze of aisles swirling with smells and sounds tugged on the sleeves of her attention. And crowded tonight—too many people orbiting on collision courses, and a checkout line stretched all the way to the bakery.

"Excuse me." A woman swerved a cart around Avery just as the toddler inside wailed.

Avery jumped. "I'm sorry."

But the woman was already gone.

Avery clenched her jaw and tucked her chin into the collar of her windbreaker, plowing resolutely into the sterile wilderness of the supermarket. This chaos was why she never went to the store on the weekend. But this would be a short trip—just for the test. And maybe some more of those weird little pudding cups that Addisyn was crazy about lately. The few she'd brought with her from Denver were almost gone.

But the test came first.

The pharmacy was all the way at the other end of the store, wedged behind the bakery. Avery kept her eyes down, shutting the doors of her mind to the noise and hustle around her. She scanned the shelves—sunscreen, hand lotion, Band-Aids, tweezers. Where would pregnancy tests be?

She zigzagged down two more aisles. And then, in the last one, a skinny guy with AirPods was stocking vitamin bottles—right under a sign reading *Pregnancy.*

The sensible thing was to march up fearlessly, say *"Excuse me,"* and grab a test without caring who saw. Instead, Avery loitered by the end of the aisle, pretending to compare lip balm brands, until the guy pushed his cart to the next aisle, head bopping to the music she couldn't hear. Then she darted to the space he'd vacated. He'd been stocking prenatal vitamins, apparently. Come to think of it—was Addisyn supposed to be taking those? Maybe she should grab a bottle. But—hadn't she seen somewhere that some of them were toxic, or something? How did you know what the good kind was?

The noise of the store was getting more insistent. Avery rubbed a hand over her forehead. *One thing at a time.* They didn't even know that Addisyn was pregnant yet. Time enough to figure out everything else later.

The pregnancy tests were on the shelf just below the vitamins. How could there be so many different kinds? Weren't they all the same? Avery scanned the array of pink boxes. *Quickest...Most Accurate Results...Earliest Detection...*

The options stacked into a dizzying overwhelm, a sudden panic looming over her. What was she *doing*? She knew nothing about this, beyond the vague awkwardness of the puberty talk at school.

Once more, she could see her little sister, the way she'd looked the other night. Shocked and small, as if she'd stumbled into an experience too big for her. If Addisyn truly was pregnant, she'd need Avery to hold her hand and walk her through it. The way she always had.

But now—now Addisyn was entering a territory Avery had never explored and possessed no map for. So what if she steered her little sister wrong? What if she made a mistake?

The overwhelm was knotting itself into a more urgent feeling. The same soul-spinning that had first hit Avery when she'd moved away with Addisyn, when they'd stood inside the cramped apartment and the whole weight of adulthood had settled unforgivingly on her shoulders. Her heartbeat throbbed loud in her ears, her lungs squeezing until the terror pricked tears to her eyes. She couldn't do this again. Couldn't take a single step nearer to that vortex where anxiety waited to swallow her. She hadn't had a panic attack in years.

But the day with the eyas—and with her class—and now—

No. Stop. She gripped the display shelf and shook her head, blinking away her blurring vision. *For Addisyn. Do this for Addisyn.* She forced depth into her lungs, holding each precious breath until the store stopped spinning.

Okay. Good. She'd stopped the spiral. Talked back to her frantic shadow shelf. She rolled her shoulders back, shook out her trembling hands. She'd figure this out. She was the responsible one. The grown-up. After all, she hadn't known what she was doing when she raised Addisyn, but that had turned out okay. And this would be the same way. She'd make sure of it. For Addisyn's sake.

She studied the pregnancy test boxes with renewed determination, finally settling on one that touted itself as *#1 in ease of use.* What *ease of use* meant she wasn't truly sure, but certainly both she and Addisyn needed it.

She dropped the test in her basket and headed toward the snack aisle for Addisyn's treats. Weird, to think that the answer to such a big question was riding innocently along under her arm. Now, hopefully it came with instructions.

Something harder shoved itself into the cracks in her heart, and she paused, staring unseeingly at the store. Most girls had moms to lead them through moments like this. Not moms who'd driven away one afternoon without one look in the rearview mirror.

Once again, Addisyn's frightened face floated through Avery's mind. That look of fearful bewilderment was the same expression Addisyn had worn years ago beneath her anxious questions. *"When is Mom coming back? Will she be gone a long time? Can we go visit her?"*

A nine-year-old's brain wasn't meant to wrap around the big questions of why parents disappeared. A thirteen-year-old's brain wasn't either, but Avery had tried her best. And she'd never been sure which was sadder—the year and a half Addisyn spent asking the questions, or the day she'd finally stopped. Thankfully, in the years since then, Addisyn had rebounded. She hadn't brought up the subject since she was a teenager, and she'd come to accept the truth.

As she knew it, anyway.

The pinch of guilt was familiar now, like a blister rubbed by an ill-fitting hiking boot. Still...what would Addisyn say if she knew the whole truth? The story of everything that had happened behind the scenes?

Avery pressed her lips together. Addisyn wouldn't understand. That much was certain. And she'd be needlessly devastated all over again—the old wound ripped wide open.

Which was why Avery had long ago resolved to be strong enough to hold the secret for them both.

"Can I help you?"

She blinked out of the memories into the slightly concerned expression of the AirPods guy, who'd paused while pushing his stock cart. "Oh!" How long had she been standing there? "I'm fine. Thank you."

She ducked down the snack aisle. Enough high-fructose corn syrup and artificial coloring here to kill an elephant. When had her health-conscious, athletic sister started eating junk like this?

She couldn't remember the brand of the pudding cups, but she recognized the packaging. She grabbed a handful, pausing to check the best-by date—Addisyn would never remember to pay attention to that—and the flavor. *Double chocolate coffee?* Yuck. But Addisyn claimed they were the only food lately that didn't make her feel sick. Which might mean—oh, could it be a pregnancy craving? If so, did that mean something?

Yet another thing to research. Avery rubbed her forehead again as she headed down the aisle. Okay, when she got home, she needed to Google all of this. Prenatal vitamins, pregnancy cravings, and most of all, instructions for using the—

She turned the corner of the aisle and smacked against something solid. The basket flung from her hand, and she fought a losing battle for balance—and then a sudden tug around her upper arm jerked her back upright.

"You okay there?"

Creed, his hand still around her arm, uncomfortably close.

"Creed." She yanked her arm free and bounced back a couple of steps, ignoring the embarrassment blazing from her face. "Uh—I'm sorry."

The corner of his mouth quirked slightly. "I guess you're in as big a hurry everywhere else as you are at the raptor center, huh?"

Embarrassment shape-shifted into irritation. "And I guess you always make a habit of being where you're not expected?"

The words came out a bit sharper than she'd planned, but the amusement at the corners of his eyes only creased deeper. "I suppose that could be said." He bent toward the scattered pudding cups. "Here, I'll help you get these."

Great. Now he was going to think she was some junk food addict who lived only on pudding cups. "These aren't for me." Avery knelt and reached for the two nearest her. The sooner these were gathered, the sooner he would leave. "These are for—for my sister."

"Your sister?"

"She eats stuff like this. I mean, she shouldn't." She was chattering, trying to fill the space between them. "I've told her it's bad."

"What flavor are they?" Creed peered at the label with what was apparently his usual disregard for privacy.

"Double chocolate coffee." With his sleeves rolled up, the bottom of that tattoo was visible. Some—animal? Were those paws?

"Hmm, well, I always say—"

Creed's voice cut off abruptly. Avery followed his gaze—to the basket. Where the neon-pink pregnancy test box practically glowed.

The heat of humiliation made sweat prickle under her windbreaker. Oh, if only she could slide out of sight under the shelving. "That's for my sister too."

He cleared his throat. "Um, okay."

"She's staying with me now, and she thinks she might be—" *Stop.* She snapped her mouth shut. Addisyn would kill her. "Anyway, I just wanted—I'm not—I mean, it's not for—for me."

"Oh." The color of his face was higher now too. "Got it."

She grabbed the last pudding cup and scrambled to her feet. "Um—thank you. Sorry again for running into you."

"It's fine." He shrugged. "So, I guess I'll see you at the center tomorrow."

"Yes—I guess so." There was a basket on the ground next to him. A stack of frozen-meal boxes. Sort of sad, for some reason.

"I'll be there." He nodded in finality, then grabbed his basket and strode off with an undeniably eager stride. Probably grateful to escape from the single most embarrassing escapade of Avery's entire life.

Addisyn, you owe me big time.

Avery sighed and glanced down accusingly at the pregnancy test, still reposing innocently in the basket. She swiped the mound of pudding cups over it. There. Now to pay for all this—self-check, for sure—and leave. Before anything else could go wrong.

WAIT TWO MINUTES. That's what the directions had said. Addisyn gripped the edge of the bathroom counter and stared at the little stick dangling over the edge of the sink. Like a magic wand, able to rearrange her life in an instant. The whole process was taking too long for a Monday morning. Both she and Avery needed to get to work. She glanced toward the closed door. "Is it time yet?"

"Nope." Avery's voice was muffled through the door. "Fifty more seconds."

Of course her sister was the one supervising the whole process. Without Avery's help, Addisyn wouldn't have known where to begin using a pregnancy test. Why would she? She hadn't planned on being in this spot for a long, long, *long* time to come. If ever.

She still hadn't told Darius that she was feeling sick. Certainly not that she was taking the test. When he called, she kept the conversation light, sweet, casual. Letting him talk about what he was doing in Canada and how his family was and how much he missed her.

Would he be disappointed she'd taken the test without him? The thought wadded in her stomach for just a moment before she pushed it away. Too late now.

"Ten seconds." Avery's voice was somehow still calm.

"Okay." Addisyn squeezed her eyes shut. The heavy drumbeat of dread throbbed in her chest.

Her sister's phone timer beeped. "All right, Ads. You can look at it now."

Still she kept her eyes tightly shut. The test would be negative. Of course it would be. She had a stomach bug and PMS. That was all. And then she and Avery would laugh, and—

"Addisyn?"

"Um—" She opened her eyes. Drew in a shaky breath. Forced her gaze to the display screen.

Two lines stared back at her.

Unforgiving.

Unwavering.

"Ads?"

There was no air in the bathroom. She gripped the counter and stared at the test.

The door opened, and Avery slipped in. "Addisyn?" Her voice was gentle. "What's it say?"

"That—" Her voice was a croak. She swallowed and tried again. "It says—that—that I'm—" She couldn't bring herself to form the word.

Avery glanced at the display and gasped. A sudden joy glowed on her face like a mountain sunrise. "Oh, Ads! I knew it!" She grabbed Addisyn in a rib-crushing hug. "You're pregnant!"

Nausea unrelated to her physical symptoms rocked her stomach. "Uh—yeah." Over Avery's shoulder, her reflection in the bathroom mirror watched her with terrified eyes.

"This is so exciting." Avery pulled back just enough to smile at her. "You'll have a little girl, Ads. And you'll bring her on the weekends to see her Aunt Avery." Tears swam suddenly in Avery's eyes. "Ads!" She pulled Addisyn in close again, her breath catching over a sob. "I'm so happy for you."

This overpowering reaction from her normally even-keeled sister was only making it worse. Addisyn squeezed her eyes shut, but her own tears crept through. "Avery—"

"No, now, we can't both cry!" Avery laughed through a sob and grabbed a handful of Kleenex off the counter.

Addisyn choked out a nervous laugh and gripped the tissues. "I —you know, Avery, the test could be wrong. Maybe before we start—"

"I doubt it. Not with all your other symptoms."

"But—" So many questions. "How?"

"How?" Avery raised her eyebrows. "You really want me to answer that?"

Heat splashed over her face. "That's not what I meant." Only then did she realize her hand was resting on her stomach. She snatched it away. "It's just—you know—we've been careful." *Said everybody ever.* "I—we're not ready for kids. And Darius—and—my job—I—I have client auditions this week." Okay, that sounded stupid.

"Hey." Avery smiled gently and rubbed Addisyn's shoulder. "I know it's a lot to take in. But I'm here to help you, okay?"

"I—" How was this real? How was she standing in her sister's bathroom hearing that her entire world was turning upside down? "Okay."

"Of course it's an adjustment. I get that. But just think about it, Ads!" Avery's voice was turning giddy again. She squeezed Addisyn's hands. "You're having a baby! You've got to call Darius."

Call Darius and make this whole thing more real than it already was. Oh, she was definitely not ready for that. She edged toward the bathroom door. Away from Avery's unbridled joy and the accusing finger of the test. "I—I think I'll wait until he's home. Tell him in person."

"Well, all right." Avery pulled her into another hug, smoothing a hand over her hair. "Oh, Ads, this is such good news."

She rested her chin on Avery's shoulder and squeezed her eyes shut. If only she were sixteen again, when her sister could fix any problem. She took a deep breath and pulled away. "You've got to get to work."

Avery glanced at her watch. "You're right. But I hate to leave when—"

"A, it's okay. I've got to head out soon myself." She gripped the only fragment of normalcy left. "I have client meetings this afternoon."

But after they said their goodbyes and Avery left for work, she didn't get in the car right away. Instead, she went upstairs to her room, then closed the door and leaned against it. Finally, silence. Stillness where she could let the news catch up to her in its own way.

Her reflection in the mirror caught her eye. What had Avery said, that first night?

When I saw you, there was something deeper to your soul—

She moved closer to the mirror, squinting at her face. She didn't see any trace of that. Just deer-in-the-headlights daze. Exactly the way she felt.

She turned sideways, pulling her shirt tight against her and running a hand over her stomach. Nothing looked different. But— somewhere inside her, a *baby* was forming? An actual real human being?

The panic was turning her inside out again. She scrambled onto the bed and hugged one of the pillows. Everything was so mixed up she couldn't begin to sort through it all. She wanted to go home. Wanted to stay here. Wanted to run away.

Most of all, she wanted Darius. Wanted to be held safely in his strong arms and hear his soothing voice understanding, consoling, assuring.

But of course, if she called Darius with this news, she wouldn't get understanding or consolation or assurance. Instead she'd be blasted with an excitement even more enthusiastic than Avery's. And she couldn't face any more misdirected joy right now.

She flopped onto her back and stared at the knotholes on the pine ceiling. What Darius didn't understand was that she'd never been one of those girls that dreamed of babies and mothering. She hadn't even played with dolls growing up. And she'd always loved that Darius never expected her to do the whole housewife thing. Their life together was fast-paced and career-centered, sparkling with energy and vibrance and spontaneity. How would any of that survive a baby?

Shame trickled into her anxiety. This was her own fault. When she'd first married Darius, she'd been obsessively careful to avoid this outcome. But as the months had passed, she'd let herself release some of the caution. Relaxed a bit more unguardedly into his love. Ignored the nagging voice of fear and tried to simply enjoy what they had together.

Well, see where that had led her.

She blew out a breath and rolled off the bed. Time to head to Denver. What she'd said to Avery was true. She wasn't ready to be a mom.

But ready or not, here she was.

CHAPTER 6

By Wednesday morning, Creed still didn't know how he was going to make a video worth anything more than the pixels composing it.

This was ridiculous, really. What was Austin expecting? Without a clearer vision for this project, he had no idea what direction to take. Or where to even start.

He huffed an exasperated breath and rubbed the back of his neck. He'd try to figure it all out later. For now, he was shooting film of the exterior of the center. It was the perfect golden hour in the strengthening dawn, before the sunrise cast sharpened shadows—or the parking lot filled with cars. He panned across the office building, keeping the *kapemni* in the foreground. Stupid symbol. He was beginning to think it meant nothing at all.

He sighed and glanced wistfully at the granite peaks. The sheer cliffs almost glowed in the gentle light. He needed to be up on a rock face somewhere. Somewhere far, far away from Estes Park. And Avery, especially after the crazy Safeway thing. He'd been pondering the flavor difference between ranch and barbecue chips when Avery had hurtled into him. Although the awkward deal with the pregnancy test had seemed to knock her even more off balance. He'd actually felt sorry for her.

It seemed weird that her sister couldn't get her own pregnancy test. Oh well, though. Who knew how girls did things.

A pickup growled its way into the parking lot, kicking up dust like a smoke-breathing dragon. Great. So much for his unspoiled filming. Avery, already?

He shielded his eyes and studied the truck. No, this one was newer—and bigger. Dual back wheels. Pretty sweet ride.

The truck door swung open. His father stepped out stiffly.

The anger was instantaneous, like a fuse that smoldered in his chest just waiting for a spark. "What are you doing here?"

His father rubbed a hand over his beard uneasily. "I been workin' on the buildin'." He gestured at the construction site. "Been puttin' up drywall last couple of days. Helpin' where I can."

Nice. If only his father could have been that eager to *help* when his son was crying out for him. "Didn't realize you were over here that much."

Dad sighed and crossed his arms. "Don't worry. I ain't here to get in yer bidness."

Creed clenched his jaw and refocused his camera. He wouldn't waste any more time on the man.

"How—uh—how's yer mother been?"

Creed's hands tightened on the camera. "She's fine, Dad. Just fine." He spit the words between his teeth.

"She ever remarry?"

Really? Creed spun toward the man. "You divorced her twenty years ago, remember? I don't think her marital status, or anything else about her, is your problem anymore."

"All right. I get it." His father's voice was low. "Yer still mad at me."

Mad? He'd spent the last six years with an uncontained wildfire burning in his chest. And every time he saw the man's sorry face, the flames leaped ten feet higher. "Yeah. You could say that." The words scraped across his throat. "Why did you even leave the Rez? Thought that was your whole life."

"It was." Dad scuffed a boot across the gravel. "A man's life can change, I guess."

Well, Creed's certainly had. Because of the actions of the man standing across from him. "So you came crawling back here?"

"I came back here 'cause—" Dad stopped, sighed. "Never mind, boy."

Boy. He'd hated his father to call him that. As if he were some faceless cutout to order around and hover over. "I'm not a *boy* anymore, Dad."

"I know." His father cleared his throat. "Skyla says yer a, uh—" He waved his hand in the air. Searching for a word Creed wouldn't help him find. "Doin' the filmin' stuff."

Filming stuff. Still, that was how his dad saw his career? As some juvenile hobby he'd outgrow? "I get it. I know it's not what you wanted. You made that clear."

"Wait. That ain't what I meant." The creases in Dad's face tightened. "I had jes' always seen you as doin' somethin' in the ministry line."

Right. Preach, reach, or teach. Because his old-fashioned father couldn't imagine any career outside that narrow box having any value to the human race. "Dad—we've had this conversation."

"I know." Dad shook his head. "I'm jes' tryin' to explain where I was comin' from. When I was yer age, nobody ran around puttin' videos on the MeTube."

"YouTube, Dad!" His jaw was clenching. Deliberately he worked it, loosening it. He wasn't going to be dragged into a full-scale fight. Not today.

"YouTube, right." Dad shifted his feet. "I s'pose I made a few wrong turns along the way."

"A few wrong turns?" The laugh jerked from his throat. Seriously? That was how his father described his lifetime of horrible parenting? Creed took a step forward. "Dad, you hated my filming. Here was this thing that I loved, that I was good at, and you never—" His breath snagged. "You never even cared."

"That's not it. I jes' didn't—well, I never knew about nothin' more than—"

The lighting was changing fast. And this conversation was only wasting his filming time. Creed turned away. "Forget it. It doesn't matter."

"Creed?"

Creed. Not *boy* or *kid*. His name sounded foreign in Dad's mouth. He turned warily. "What?"

"Mebbe sometime we can—" Dad shrugged. "Talk?"

Talk. How often as a kid had he longed for a real conversation with his father? Tried to get the man's attention or concoct things to say that would grab his dad's interest?

Yet for his father, *talking* had only meant *scolding.*

Creed swallowed down the lump in his throat that ached for the kid he'd been. "There's nothing to talk about."

He walked off before Dad could say anything else, but his heart was still thumping hard and hurting as he crossed the fields toward the trails, the knee-high grass tugging against his stride. How did the man still have the power to trigger him so easily? How was it possible that just by being around his dad, he so effortlessly reprised the role of his bratty teenage self?

He took a deep breath, forcing himself to replace the anger from the encounter with a mental checklist of his work for the day. Whether Dad took his filming seriously or not, Austin did. So first, he'd shoot some landscape scenes out here. Then when Avery arrived, he'd probably have to shadow her. He rolled his eyes. He couldn't escape her. Or Dad.

He clicked through a few settings, trying to prepare the camera as much as possible for the images he wanted to take. Of course he could still make edits in postproduction, but doing the best job now saved time later. He checked the histogram reading on the camera and focused on the ridgeline. No, too dark. He dialed up the ISO sensitivity and lowered his shutter speed. There.

Working with his camera like this brought him the same focused calm that climbing did. As though he could channel the restless flicker of his energy into a laser, sending all of himself into something beautiful and powerful and bigger than his own life.

Which was why his camera had been the saving of him. After sixth grade, when his parents' divorce had finalized, his life had split into two raw-edged halves. The school year was spent with his mom in Idaho, but summers belonged to the Pine Ridge Reservation, where Dad's ministry was based. And it was in those years, as a confused kid shuffling between two homes, that he'd found the magic of film. He'd realized that he saw most clearly when he was looking through a camera. And he'd found a beautiful power to tell untold stories, to wrap often-ignored wonder around the world.

Too bad his dad had never understood that.

The ministry his father worked for, Hands and Homes, did so-called *evangelism* by building houses for some of the most easily forgotten people on the Rez. Dad had supervised multiple construction projects at a time, spending his days with two-by-four's and shingles and nail guns. To Dad, *work* involved calloused hands and aching muscles and sweat-soaked clothing. Mindlessly running a bandsaw? Work. Hunching over the computer for hours on end trying to render a video to precision? Laziness.

Useless. Worthless. Waste.

He'd tolerated his dad's criticism as long as he could. But it had all snapped like a dry stick that final summer.

Creed lowered his camera. The precious golden hour had slipped away, and now the sun was coming in harsh from the east, striping the land in shadow.

And maybe that was the saddest part. Not that he'd lived his life in the shadows.

But that he'd yet to see the light behind them.

—⧖—

It was the clenched fist of terror that jerked Avery out of sleep on Thursday night. She gasped and sprang upright, the shreds of her dream taking a moment to dissolve into reality. She'd been running. A dark tunnel, a howling wind, her mom standing at the edge of—

No. She was okay. She'd been—dreaming. *Dreaming?* She never dreamed. Not since—well, since then.

El Shaddai— There was no peace even in the prayer. Her heart was thudding in her throat, her body shaking like an aspen in a mountain storm. She swiped a palm over the slickness of sweat on her forehead. Even the T-shirt and shorts she slept in were soaked, her hair plastered to her neck.

She squinted at the little bedside clock. 4:22. She swallowed hard, trying to force down the rest of the panic. She needed to go back to sleep. She had work in the morning. Why was she doing—this—again?

Night terrors.

The term rolled around in her mind as she changed into dry clothing and slipped her pillow into a new case. The term used by the doctor she'd seen in New York, the one who'd recommended counseling sessions she'd never attended and a prescription she'd never filled. But the terrors had stopped when the dreams had. Years ago.

You're fine, Avery. She was, after all. This was just—an aberration. The stress at work and the emotional upheaval of Addisyn's pregnancy combined to send her nervous system over the edge. Good thing she hadn't done this while Addisyn was there. Her younger sister would be even less convinced Avery was okay if she'd witnessed that performance. Now she needed to settle down and go back to sleep.

But two hours later when the alarm went off, she'd spent the entire time retracing her steps through the nightmare. By the time she parked at the center, her gritty eyes were ready to close. Now that sleep was impossible, her body was ready for it. All thanks to her crazy mind.

"Hey, Miz Avery."

"Laz!" She spun toward the familiar voice. "I haven't seen you all week."

"Eh, well, I've been comin' to work in the evenin's and early mornin's so's I don't interrupt the action here." He focused on the drywall panels he was pulling out of his truck bed. "Jes' came by now to drop these off."

Disappointment sank. "So you're not staying?"

"Gotta get back to the store." His gaze lingered on the camper behind the office.

Avery's heart twisted. "Have you—uh—"

His expression told her he'd read her unasked question. "Saw him Wednesday mornin' when I brought some stuff by." He cleared his throat. "We didn't have much of a talk."

The pain in his eyes made her throat ache. "Is there—anything I can do?"

"Naw." He sighed and rubbed a hard hand over his beard. "I jes'—I hope one day he'll talk to me. I done made a heap o' mistakes, but he's—he's my son, Miz Avery."

Avery bit her lip. No way would she tell Laz the caustic words Creed had said about him. "I know. I hope he will."

"Eh, if prayin' can do it—" Laz shook his head. "Let's jes' say I been stormin' Heaven. Now git in there! Miz Skyla needs you."

As Avery stepped inside the office, Skyla was studying a paper with drawn brows. "Welcome, Avery." Her smile was tinged with hesitancy. "Before this news comes from another—there has been a complaint."

The morning light was hurting her bleary eyes. "A complaint?"

"From the high school teacher who brought the group on Friday." Skyla cocked her head. "Apparently—something happened during the demonstration? She felt we were not well-prepared."

"Oh...Skyla. I'm so sorry." Shame, hot and heavy, hunched across her shoulders. "I—I lost my train of thought. And I accidentally—well, Solomon got loose for a moment. We quickly recaptured him." The adrenaline that was just beginning to leave her system ratcheted up again. This was it. Skyla would fire her. Or at the very least, scold her for—

"It is of no worry to me, Avery. Mistakes are made by us all at times. Please be careful in the future, as I know you are."

That was it? No scolding? No job loss? Avery took a deep breath. Insomnia always brought the worst-case scenarios within arm's length. "Uh—thank you. Yes, I understand. It won't happen again." She would make sure of that.

"Very well, then." Skyla crumpled the paper and flicked it into the nearest trashcan. "The matter is ended. Now, I know your birds are waiting. I will not take your time."

Skyla could say the matter was ended, but Avery's brain raced circles around the news all the way down the hall. A *complaint*? The center had *never* received a complaint. This was all her fault. She'd caused problems for Liv and Skyla and everyone else, splattered her own mistake on the entire center. How could she have been so careless?

It's on you, Avery...

She fisted her hands and glanced into Tyler's corner. "Hey, Tyler."

"Hey." Tyler pushed away from his computer screen. Even this early in the day, his glasses were askew, and his ruffled hair looked as if he'd run his hands through it more than a few times.

Avery cocked her head. "How's the budget coming?"

"Not good." He sighed. "That grant would have been an absolute godsend."

"I know." Avery settled on one of the unforgiving metal chairs in front of his desk. "But maybe with the money from Creed's channel—"

Tyler rolled his eyes. "I don't like that guy. Mercy has better people skills than he does. You're an absolute saint to work with him."

Saint Avery. The name still rubbed raw against her. "I don't know about that. But—yeah, he's not easy to be around."

"I don't think he knows what he's doing. And anyway, raising all this hype around the center—it can't be valuable. Sure, he says this will bring us publicity and all, but his crowd isn't our typical donor base."

She could see his point, but—"Creed says his channel has successfully partnered with a lot of nonprofits."

Bitterness soured in Tyler's laugh. "And how is he defining *successfully*?" He scowled. "I don't know why he's here. I mean, I get that he's doing this story, and he knew Skyla way back or something, but seriously. We have enough problems without him hanging around."

The acid in his voice was surprising for a guy as easygoing as Tyler. Then again, Creed had just about pushed her to her limit too.

A throat cleared behind her. "Ready for another day?"

Avery spun in her chair. Creed. He gave a single nod that might pass for a greeting. "Skyla said I would find you in here."

"Uh, yeah." Had he heard any of their conversation? Hopefully not.

"I was planning to film in the flight cage this morning." He held up his camera. "Can I head that way, or—"

She wouldn't have him around her birds unsupervised. "I'm heading there now. Bye, Tyler."

Mercy trotted toward Creed, panting for attention as they headed out of the office. He sidestepped. "I still don't understand why he gets to come to work with you."

"Mercy is a good dog. And *she* is a girl." Did he think she would have named a boy dog *Mercy*?

"Oh." His head dipped slightly sheepishly. "Guess I should have realized that."

The flight cage had always been one of Avery's favorite places. The long lattice-walled enclosure was a sun-striped tunnel where the staff could exercise the birds recovering their strength. Today Avery was helping a Cooper's Hawk stretch his wings, jogging behind the bird as he swooped laps in the enclosure. There was a peace to the task, a harmony in the rhythm. Maybe she could work that into her curriculum somehow. Although with everything that had happened, she still hadn't moved past the first lesson.

As Avery ran, she watched Creed out of the corner of her eye. He was shooting film from a variety of angles, his hands steady on his camera, his brow furrowed in the concentration of creativity, his focus mirroring her own for the task at hand. No matter what Tyler said, Creed was good at what he did. Or at least, he looked that way.

He glanced up when Avery paused for breath between laps. "So why Mercy?"

Avery blinked. "I'm sorry?"

"Your dog." He squinted through the viewfinder again. "Why'd you name her Mercy?"

Was he always this abrupt? "Well—" Avery hesitated. He'd probably scoff at the story. "I got her when I first came to the mountains. She was a stray, and—" Laz had been the one to bring the whimpering puppy to her door, but she'd best leave that part out. "Anyway, it all felt like mercy. Mercy for her that I'd found her, and mercy for me that I was here in the mountains. Grace from El Shaddai."

"You mentioned that name before." He studied the camera screen, clicking through some settings. "That what you call God?"

"Usually, yes. It means God of the mountains."

"I know." He looked up, the morning sun splashing his face and highlighting the color of his eyes. The blue-gray of smoke or stormy skies. "I used to be religious like you."

Religious. The words felt like a straitjacket, pinching the breathing room from her faith. "I—I try to follow God. If that's what you mean."

"Right. Saint Avery."

She still couldn't tell if the name was a joke or a jab, but it scraped against her like sandpaper. "I'm no saint."

"More of one than I am. Or want to be." He shrugged. "God let me down just about as badly as Dad did."

The hardness was returning to his words, his eyes. Avery bit her lip. "What—happened? Between you and Laz?"

"Surely he's already told you the scoop." He frowned. "What a degenerate kid he has? All that?"

The sneer in his voice hurt. "No. He hasn't told me anything."

The anger on Creed's face rewrote itself into surprise. "Oh." He paused. "Well, he was a cruddy dad, that's what happened. Divorced my mom when I was a little kid. I spent every summer with him on the Rez."

"The Rez?"

"Pine Ridge Reservation. Lakota land." His eyes softened with something that looked like yearning. "South Dakota, on the prairie."

South Dakota. Laz had mentioned the state a few times, but she'd never guessed—"Laz lived there?"

"He worked for a ministry that built houses for the people." Creed sat back on his heels, staring at the lattice walls of the cage. "And he sure as heck thought I'd fall right into his footsteps. Grow up swinging hammers the way he did."

Avery crossed her arms, reading between the lines of the story. "And you didn't?"

"Not hardly. This—" Creed tapped his camera—"was my life. And Dad never cared a thing about it. Or me. All he ever cared about was his precious ministry. Houses and Jesus." He gave a humorless laugh. "Jesus loves everybody, I guess, but Dad sure doesn't."

Avery bit her lip. She was back in the memory, a terrified twenty-three-year-old alone in the unfamiliar mountains, standing in the snowy ditch into which her truck had slid. And then a black pickup had roared through the gathering snowstorm, and a burly man had swung out.

"Needin' some help there, gal?"

It wasn't just her truck Laz had pulled out of the ditch; it was her soul as well. He'd given her a chance by hiring her at his store. He'd shown up with a snow shovel after her first mountain blizzard. He'd given her the first pair of hiking boots she'd owned, covering the gift by asking her to *"try them out for the store."*

But looking at Creed's face now, she couldn't find the words to explain how Laz had again and again kept her on the road. "Your dad has been—a good friend to me." True and steady as the blade of one of his knives.

"A good friend." Disbelief flattened his tone.

"People change, Creed." His name slipped out in the urgency of her plea.

He rubbed the back of his neck and looked away, but not before she caught the pain on his face. "Not him."

She pressed her lips together. She and Addisyn had struggled through years of similar misunderstanding. But they'd eventually worked through that, so surely Creed and Laz could do the same. "Why don't you talk to him? Try to—"

His laugh was quiet but razor-edge ironic. "Try to what? Pretend everything between us didn't really happen?"

"No." The broken look on Laz's face swam in Avery's mind again. *I messed up...* She sighed. "I think he wants to talk to you."

The corners of Creed's mouth folded in. "All he did while I was growing up was talk to me. Or *at* me. Tell me everything I'd done wrong, all the ways I needed to change. I've got nothing else to say to him."

Nothing else to say to him. As though it were better to leave the raw gaping wound between the two men. Avery's frustration doubled. "But don't you see that—"

"Hey, I see your point, Saint Avery." Creed stood and turned toward the door of the flight cage. "But you didn't grow up with him, okay? You might know him now, but you don't know how he was then." He let himself out of the enclosure, tossing a parting shot over his shoulder. "Pretty soon I'll be gone, and then everything can go back to normal for him anyway."

His footsteps faded away. Avery groaned and leaned against the wall of the flight cage. Above her, the Cooper's squawked questioningly.

"Yes, boy. Let's try it again." Avery shook her head. If only she could convince Laz and Creed to do the same.

ADDISYN HAD SEEN ALL the reels on TikTok and Instagram: women revealing their pregnancies to their husbands in dizzyingly creative ways. Gift-wrapped pregnancy tests and witty wordplay cards and elaborate scavenger hunts that led to "World's Best Dad" T-shirts.

Instead, here she was, standing in their house with her heart beating out of her ears, waiting for Darius to get home from Canada. No flowers. No fanfare. No fun announcements. She'd be fortunate to make it through telling him without breaking down. There was no way she could plan some kind of detailed surprise to share joy she didn't feel.

She glanced at the mountain-themed clock by the front door. 6:24. Where was he? When he'd called almost an hour ago, he'd been leaving the airport. He should have been here by now. But then again, it was Friday night. The traffic on 76 was probably horrid.

Friday night. The fifth day of knowing that she was pregnant.

And for every second of those five days, she'd begged her body to cooperate. Begged her hormones to restart their clock and prove that the test was inaccurate and the nausea was from stress and Avery was overreacting.

But now, on the forty-eighth day—well, it was getting harder to cling to the idea that the test was wrong.

And telling Darius would be the hardest part. Not because he wouldn't be excited. But because he would.

And as a result, she had to be too. Somehow.

We've been so careful. Her words to Avery, but really, it was she who'd been the careful one. He'd been hinting about kids for a year now. Watching families on the street with softened eyes. Bringing up the subject in a dozen different ways. And she—well, she'd played noncommittal. So much for that.

She glanced around her at their Colorado home—the *Welcome to the Mountains* sign Avery had given them, the hook by the door where Darius's jacket hung, the braided rug she'd found at a trendy market in the RiNo neighborhood. It was because of her that they were here at all. Darius had been happy with his work in Canada, but when the skating center in Denver had offered them jobs, he'd jumped on the chance without blinking an eye. He'd known how much it would mean to Addisyn to be closer to Avery, to split their time between Vancouver and Denver.

The jobs here, the house here, the way he patiently arranged their travel back and forth, the tedious hours on airplanes—it was all for her. There was nothing he'd left undone when it came to her happiness.

Which meant she couldn't ruin this moment for him. Even though every part of her carefully constructed dream life was about to crumble.

Headlights blurred down their street, and then a car shuddered to a halt in front of their house. Addisyn's heart rate kicked higher. She brushed her hair behind her ears and readied herself. *Don't cry. Just don't cry.*

The door opened, and Darius stepped inside, the cool freshness of evening coming in with him. "Addisyn!" He dropped his travel bag and reached for her. "Gosh, that's the best part of coming home!"

Even after two years of marriage, the sight of him still stole her breath. She nestled into his arms, savoring his strength encircling her. His warmth relaxed the cold grip of anxiety. "How was your trip home?"

"All right. The traffic was intense." He kissed her forehead. "Kenzie says hi."

Addisyn smiled. Darius's cousin was one of her closest friends. "I need to call her. Did you see her skate? How's she doing?"

"She's doing fantastic, although she says her new coach isn't nearly as good as you." Darius chuckled. "And Tina was quite irritated that you didn't come. When I was leaving, she instructed me to tell you that she will officially not talk to you for a month now."

Addisyn laughed. She had reached a truce of friendship with Darius's other cousin long ago. "She doesn't mean it. I'll call her too."

"So all in all, a good trip. But—" his voice lowered, softened—"I missed you so much."

The warmth of his care glowed through her until what she had to tell him was a hazy cloud on the horizon. "Darius." She tucked her head on his shoulder and breathed in his own unique scent—the salt-tang of the ocean and the deep secret of the pines that crowded the Canadian coast. "I've missed you too."

He brought his lips to hers in the kind of kiss she'd been aching for all week. When he pulled back, he rubbed his hand along her shoulders. "How have you been feeling? I know you were tired."

And just like that, the news drenched her contentment like a face-splash of cold water. "Oh—" She stepped back, out of his arms. "About that. I—I need to talk to you."

"Okay..." Confusion crept into his expression.

The hallway seemed suddenly too small. "Can we go sit down?"

"Sure." He followed her to the living room, then sat on the couch and angled himself to face her. "What's wrong?"

"Well—" She tucked her knees under her. If only she could melt into the couch cushions and vanish. "While you were gone, I, um, I figured out why I'd been feeling tired and stuff."

"Okay..." He was watching her for clues. "What's wrong?"

"Um—" This moment was the first step off a cliff, and she couldn't bring herself to leap.

"Addisyn?" His face drew tight. "You're scaring me. Are you—is something—"

"No." He didn't deserve to be dragged through this suspense. She gripped his hand in both of hers and snatched a breath. "Darius —I'm pregnant."

Shock slackened his face. "Wait. What?"

"I'm pregnant." The words still felt surreal. "Avery—she realized it first. And then I took a test, and—"

"You're pregnant?" His voice cracked. He wrapped his other hand around hers. "We're going to have a baby?"

"Yes." She bit her lip. "We're going to have a baby."

His eyes were shimmering now. His laugh was more like a cry. "No way."

The same way she'd felt, but for entirely different reasons. "Yes."

"Addisyn!" He blinked, tears spilling onto his cheeks, joy shining fiercely with wonder in his eyes. "I'm going to be a dad!"

He was caught in the warm glow of delight. Just as she'd known he'd be. And she was standing out in the cold with her doubts— alone. Her eyes smarted. *Don't cry. Don't cry.*

"Oh, Addisyn..." He drew her against him, kissing her cheek, her forehead, her hair. "I can't believe it. We're going to have a baby..."

For some reason his kisses were making her uncomfortable. Wasn't this how she'd gotten herself into this mess in the first place? Punished for loving her husband. She gently pulled back, putting distance between them in a way he hopefully wouldn't notice. "Are you excited?" Dumb question, but she had to say *something*.

"Excited? My gosh." He was breathless, the emotion trembling through his voice. "I'm so excited. This is—this is everything."

"Yes."

A flicker of hesitation dampened his expression. "You—you're excited too, right? I mean—"

"Um—well, of course I'm still in shock." Putting it mildly. She summoned what Avery had always called her ice-rink smile. "It will be a big change, you know—I don't know about coaching, and—"

"Yeah, but it'll work out. This is what we always wanted."

We? She nodded in a way she hoped was convincing. "Yes. Of course. It's—" she nearly choked over the word—"wonderful." Ha.

His eyes welled with an almost reverent depth, and he pulled her into his arms again. "Addisyn, I love you so much."

"I love you too, Darius." And she did, with a love that took her breath away. A love that wouldn't allow her own fears to invade this moment for him.

"I've prayed for this very thing. That one day we'd have a family." His laugh still held awe. "And God answered."

She nodded, forcing her voice to stay steady. "For sure." He'd answered, all right. Answered Darius, not her.

"It was just yesterday that I was thinking about—"

Addisyn could no longer focus on Darius's words. Not without falling apart from the fear. She stared at the unlit fireplace across the room, her throat tightening. If only she could cry, or scream, or do anything to somehow exorcise the terror working its way through her. Did Darius not understand what this meant? That a baby—a *child*—would be totally their responsibility? Good grief, she couldn't even keep track of Avery's house key. How in the blazes would she take care of a baby?

Darius dropped a kiss on her cheek. "This is the best welcome-home news."

But she was more alone now than she had been before Darius had come home.

CHAPTER 7

The glowing numbers on the bedside clock said 4:38. Six minutes later than the last time she'd checked. The night was oozing toward dawn at the laborious pace of a snail.

Addisyn sighed and flopped onto her back again. Fatigue rubbed sand in her eyes, but her body was too taut to sleep, her mind a sheet of unbroken ice over which thoughts skidded and slipped but found no purchase.

Beside her, Darius still slept peacefully, undisturbed by her restlessness. Infuriating and endearing at the same time. She watched the rhythmic rise and fall of his chest. Tried to match her own breaths to his tempo.

No use. She sighed and sat up, hugging her knees. This was the third night in a row that her swirling mind had sucked her out of sleep just to drown in a midnight vortex of unrest. Not surprising, though. Having your life dramatically rearranged tended to produce that effect.

It didn't help that Darius was still floating on excitement. Every word and thought and memory seemed to lead him back to the baby. And the more she saw his excitement, the more guilt gnawed at her. Why couldn't she share his joy? Was something wrong?

Or maybe—did all women have these doubts? Maybe even her own mom had.

She closed her eyes and tried, the way she often had since her childhood, to picture her mom's face. After so many years, the image was fuzzy. A composite of daydreams and the faces of friends' moms and things Avery had said in unguarded moments. How old had she been when she'd last seen her mom? Nine, right?

She hadn't thought about that horrible day in years, but now the memories were coming back, surrounding her like the ghosts they were. She'd been walking home from school with Avery, but as they reached their driveway, they could hear Dad roaring curses at Mom all the way through the double-thick front door.

Avery's hand had tightened on hers. *"Ads, you know what? Didn't you need to go to the library and find a story for your book report? Let's do that now."*

But just then, the door opened and Mom stumbled out, her shoulders drooping beneath the weight of a bag in each hand.

Addisyn sighed now to remember how naive she'd been. She'd tugged on Avery's hand. *"A, look. Are we going somewhere? Mom's packing."*

She'd never forgotten how Avery's face had changed. How her sister's expression had hardened into equal parts realization and determination. She'd dropped Addisyn's hand and charged forward. *"Mom!"*

Mom turned toward the girls and froze. As usual after a fight with Dad, one of her eyes didn't look right, and red marks reached ugly fingers up her neck. But no injury could hide the shame behind her eyes. *"Didn't expect you girls back so soon."*

Still, Addisyn hadn't known what was happening, but the look on Avery's face wadded fear in her stomach. *"Mom?"* Her voice had sounded strange in her ears. *"Where are you going?"*

Avery caught her by the shoulders. *"Hold on, Ads."* She locked her jaw, steel in her eyes as she stared at Mom. *"Don't do this."*

"I don't have a choice." Mom mumbled the words, stuffing her bags into the backseat of her car. Even with her hands free, her shoulders drooped under some weight. *"Take care of your sister, Avery."*

"So you're not planning to take us with you?" Avery's voice soared, and she stepped forward. *"Are you going to be as selfish about this as you are about everything else?"*

"Oh, Avery, stop it. Just stop it." Mom groaned and pressed a palm

against her forehead. Her hands were shaking. *"You don't know what it's like, all right?"*

"Mom, it's not that—"

"Avery, your dad will take care of you. I can't stay here." She slid into the driver's seat and paused with her hand on the ignition. For just a moment, the worn-down weariness of her face had slipped into something more raw. *"I—I'm sorry—"*

Avery's hands fisted. And then she walked away.

Addisyn's fear was only sharpening. As if she were inches from falling into an abyss she couldn't yet see. *"Mom?"*

"Bye, Addisyn." Mom's face pinched with some inner war. *"You'll understand some day."*

"But where are you going?" Why would no one tell her what was going on?

Her mom turned the key. *"I have to—I have to go right now."*

"But, Mom—can't we go together? Right now?"

"Addisyn, stop it! Stop whining!" Mom's apathy had finally snapped, the words flicking like whips. She'd jabbed a trembling finger toward the backyard. *"Go find your sister. Stay close to her."*

The memories of what happened next all had the metallic taste of terror. The little sedan had careened out of their driveway and swerved onto the road, and Addisyn had started sobbing for reasons she still didn't understand. She'd chased the car uselessly—arms pumping, feet slapping the asphalt, sobs choking out the breath in her lungs.

And then she'd heard faster feet behind her, and she'd been caught in Avery's arms. She'd fought back, straining against Avery, frantic with anguish as the taillights blinked into nothing in the distance.

But Avery had hung onto her anyway. *"Ads—I'm sorry."* Avery's voice had been tight with tears she wouldn't let herself cry. *"I'm so, so sorry."*

"But—when is she coming back?" Addisyn had searched Avery's face for any hint of reassurance. Anything to say that there was still a way to wake up from the nightmare.

But Avery had pressed her lips together and hung her head. And that's when Addisyn had finally recognized the shape of the fear that chased her down that road.

Stop. Replaying this wouldn't help her sleep tonight. Addisyn rubbed her eyes, as if she could scrub the images from her mind. Sometimes, on nights like this, she wondered if the fear had ever truly faded—or if she'd just learned to live in its shadow.

How different would her life have been if Mom had kept them close to her? Surely Avery wondered about that too, didn't she? But Addisyn had learned years ago that nothing caused her older sister to clam up like questions about the past. Whatever Avery could recall, she never shared beyond broad strokes. The last time she'd broached the subject, Avery had shrugged it off. *"I don't think she was ready to be a mom, really."*

Not ready to be a mom. The thought fell into a familiar groove. Her own words to Avery.

A fresh wave of panic raced over her as the dots connected. She'd had a million reasons for not wanting to have kids. She'd been too busy with her job, and she wasn't the maternal type, and she wanted to preserve the independent lifestyle she and Darius enjoyed.

But under it all—what was it that kept her being so careful, that made her change the subject every time Darius brought up the possibility? Was it the fear that one day, she would do to her child what her mother had done to her?

A hollow ache throbbed behind her sternum. Other pregnant girls had their own mothers to turn to for advice. Others could remember their happy childhoods and raise their children with the wisdom they'd inherited from their own parents. But her only model was a mother who'd broken her. And with that kind of example, how could she possibly do any better?

The terror of the idea throbbed in her temples, and she gripped the quilt. If only she could put all these memories to rest for good. But the worst part of the whole thing had always been that it was so —so *unresolved.* The story had just—ended. Because their mother had never come back. Never spoken to them. Never even been heard of again. Somewhere in the crazy busy world, her mother's story had simply vanished.

Maybe that was part of the problem. Part of the reason her subconscious wouldn't let her rest.

But what if—what if she tried to get some closure? To fill in the details of what had happened before Mom had left? To piece together the rest of the story?

The idea slowly began to gain traction. Yes. This was the way. She needed to revisit the mental ground zero, sort through the rubble one more time. And she'd start by asking for Avery's help. Avery surely knew some of the details Addisyn had forgotten or never knew. At the very least, Avery would listen to her, help her talk out the situation in a kind and loving way.

Yes, Avery would understand. She'd help find answers about Mom. And then finally Addisyn could come to grips with her own motherhood. Relax into the expectancy without all of this turmoil.

The plan brought the first sliver of peace, enough to make her eyelids grow heavy again. She lay down, burrowing into the protection of the quilt.

Darius stirred. "Addisyn?" His voice was groggy. "Are you okay?"

Even half asleep, he was always looking out for her. Addisyn smiled and pressed closer to his warmth. "Yes. I'm okay."

Which wasn't true, yet—but soon would be.

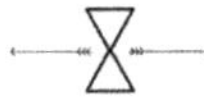

AVERY WAS HIKING through the desolate heart of Forest Canyon when her phone rang. She jumped at the sound and stared at the trees and cliffs. She had cell service *here*?

She fished her phone out of her backpack to see Addisyn's name on the screen. Quickly she swiped the call. "Ads?"

"Hey, Avery." Addisyn hesitated. "Are you busy?"

"In the middle of a hike, so I hope I don't lose service." Avery readjusted her backpack and kept walking, the phone on speaker. "What's up?"

"Um..." Addisyn cleared her throat. "How are things at work? With Laz's son and all."

"All right, I guess." Avery grimaced. If Creed called her *Saint Avery* once more, she might just shut him in Elijah's mew. But at least he was careful when he was filming around the birds. "He's difficult. But he won't be here forever. Just five more weeks."

"Yeah."

Silence pulled taut like a rubber band. Avery frowned. Addisyn hadn't called her up to ask about Creed. "So—is everything all right with you?"

"Yes." But the word was more than half question. "I—I actually have something I need to ask you about."

"Okay." Probably something to do with the pregnancy. Some symptom that Addisyn was embarrassed to discuss. She tried to infuse encouragement into her tone. "I'm here, Ads. You know you can ask me anything." Although she couldn't guarantee she'd know the answers.

"Well—I've been wondering about—about—Mom."

Mom.

Avery's ankle rolled over a rock. She stumbled to the side on the uneven ground, catching her balance at the last minute by grabbing a tree limb.

"A? You okay?"

No. Most definitely not. Still gripping the branch, she stared at the phone. "What did you say?"

"I asked if you were—"

"Not that." Her pulse was a drumbeat in her ears. "You said you wanted to ask me about—"

"About Mom. Yeah."

"Why?" Okay, that had been sharper than she intended.

"Uh—well—" Addisyn was quiet. Probably trying to manufacture a good reason, which didn't exist for a question like this. "I've been—I've been thinking about her a lot lately, for some reason, and —well, I never really had any closure. I just wanted to—you know, talk to you about her. Get details or stories or—"

"Addisyn, what do you mean, *stories*?" Her heart rate was too high for her to choose her words carefully. *Please, El Shaddai. Not like this.* "You were there too. You know what I do."

"Yeah, I know, but—I mean, I was a lot younger. I thought maybe you would be able to tell me more about what happened. Why she left, why she—" Addisyn's voice changed slightly—"why she never tried to come back."

And there it was. The reason she could not, under any circumstances, let Addisyn continue down this road. Avery squeezed the tree limb until the bark dug into her sweaty palm. Hadn't she always feared that someday, Addisyn would ask these questions? Questions whose answers would only destroy them both?

"A? Are you there?"

She'd never been so tempted to pretend to lose a call. Reluctantly she cleared her throat. "Yes. I'm here."

"So—can you help me?"

Of course she could help Addisyn—by diverting her interest before it was too late. "Ads, I don't think this is the best idea. I mean, you know everything I know." *For the most part.* She tried to keep her tone gently firm, choose words that would appease her prickling conscience. "I couldn't tell you anything else that would help you."

"But—" Addisyn sighed. "Don't you ever wonder about what happened to her?"

Waste mental energy woolgathering about the fate of the woman who'd thrown both of them away like garbage? "No." She released the tree limb and started walking faster, ignoring the burning in her chest. "I most certainly do not."

"You've never thought about what happened?"

Of course she'd thought about *that.* Relived her mother's taillights going down the driveway over and over and over. Heard Addisyn's screaming sobs in her darkest night terrors. Despised her mother's cowardice as their father turned his wrath on both of them instead in the coming years.

But Addisyn was still waiting. "Well—" Avery glanced down into the canyon, at the silver thread of the river far below. "I don't know. That was all so long ago."

"I know, but—I mean, don't you think it still affects us?"

A decade removed in time and a thousand miles in space? "I don't see how."

"Because we never talk about it." Addisyn's voice was gathering like a runaway train. The way it did when she was upset. "You say it doesn't bother you—"

"Because it doesn't." The volume was rising in her own words. Why was Addisyn so hung up on this? "We don't talk about it because there's no need."

"But we never got closure. We never got the chance to—I don't know, grieve what we should have had."

That sounded like some soundbite from a counseling guru on social media. Avery stopped just short of rolling her eyes. "We're past that, Addisyn. Water under the bridge."

"Water we could still drown in."

There was no reasoning with Addisyn when she got like this. Avery sighed. "Ads, look, this is a bad time for me to have this conversation, okay? I'm on the trail, and I'm about to lose reception." If only.

"Okay." Addisyn didn't sound convinced. "But—can we talk about this more later?"

She knew better than to hope Addisyn would forget. But maybe that would give her enough time to come up with a plan for rerouting her sister's curiosity. "Yes. Okay."

"All right." Addisyn sighed. "Bye."

Avery kept her voice easy. "Talk to you later. I love you, Ads."

But her sister had already hung up.

Avery slipped the phone into her pocket. Her hands were shaking, the trembling working its way through her body. What was Addisyn thinking?

A frustration years buried pressed its way upward again. When Mom left, Avery had watched her bright, confident little sister hollow into a frightened shell of herself, her entire foundation crumbling upon the fault lines of losing a parent. Poor Ads had been especially terrified of losing Avery too. She'd slept in Avery's bed for almost a year, and even then, she'd woken several times each night, frantic for reassurance that she wasn't alone.

And Avery had been there. Holding her close, keeping her safe, trying desperately to rebuild what Mom had razed. She'd fought tooth and nail to rise up from the rubble, to carry Addisyn out of the war zone into safety. And she'd done it. Finally, they were both in a place where they were safe at last.

And now Addisyn wanted to reverse all her efforts by ripping open a long-healed wound.

She clenched her fists. Maybe Addisyn didn't remember the trauma of their mom leaving. Maybe—hopefully—her young mind had blurred over the details. But Avery wasn't leading her back into that minefield. And she certainly would never tell Addisyn the rest of the story. The part her sister didn't know.

Why she never came back...

She closed her eyes and tried to imagine herself telling Addisyn the reason, finally unburdening the secret she'd carried all these years. She just couldn't do it. Addisyn would be torn wide open...and it would be Avery she blamed. She wouldn't understand how much Avery loved her, how hard Avery had worked to protect her from any more pain. And if she knew what Avery had kept from her...

Avery's lungs were shrinking, the familiar tightness squeezing her chest. The sound of the river blurred with a dull roar in her ears.

No! She couldn't have a panic attack. Not here, alone in an empty wilderness. She bent over her knees and forced herself to slowly breathe out until she could finally breathe in. *That's it.* Okay. Crisis averted.

She straightened, her legs still shaky. One way or another, she had to stop these recent bursts of panic. Yet another good reason to steer clear of the subject of their mom.

She kept drawing deep breaths until she felt her mind calming too. She glanced around at the mountains that had become her home —the blue sky, the whispering trees, the lingering patches of snow on the shady north slopes—and let the peace soak into her too. It would be okay. This wasn't a calamity. Just a small bump in the road that she could steer them around.

Because years ago, she'd given up everything to protect her sister.

And if need be, she'd do it all again.

THE DREAMS TWISTED like demented tornadoes in and out of Avery's darkness.

Her mom's face, that familiar resentful weariness in her eyes. *"Take care of your sister, Avery. As long as you two have each other, you don't need me. It's on you. You're the strong one..."*

Her dad's rage-rough voice, his hand broadsiding her mouth. She could taste the blood again. See her mom staring wordlessly for a moment before turning away.

The memories blurred into a confusing swirl of voices and faces and moments that no longer mattered. And then the confusion cleared again into Mom's face. Thinner. Older. More desperate.

"Avery, I need to see your sister..."

Avery snapped to a sitting position, bursting through the web of nightmares into waking life. She gasped, the room spinning around her for just a second before settling into the familiar shadowed shapes. Outside the window, the sky was the faint hopeful gray that came before dawn.

She groaned, her breathing finally slowing. This was becoming a torturous routine. Go to bed and fight the mind-whirl of insomnia. Finally get to sleep just in time to wake with her heart beating hawk-wings in her chest and sweat soaking through the blankets. How was she ever going to snap this cycle?

A warm tongue swiped her cold fingers, and Avery smiled in spite of herself. "Hey, Mercy." She stroked the dog's velvety ears. The warmth eased some tightness within her, even just a little. She'd done way too much googling over the last few days. The most common cause of night terrors, at least according to the disembodied opinions online, was stress. As though all the tension that accumulated during the day needed an outlet at night.

But she wasn't *that* stressed, was she? She just had a lot to juggle at the center, between Creed and the fundraiser and the looming deadline for designing her curriculum. It was nothing out of the ordinary. And as for the nightmares—well, that was Addisyn's fault for bringing up their mom. Which was why Avery needed to put a lid on that as soon as possible. So they could both return to peace. And so she could finally sleep again.

Sleep. Exhaustion strained behind her eyes, and the beginning of a headache was lurking in her temples. Her body was heavy, unwilling. It would be so easy to sink back into the bed, seek sleep that wasn't tortured by—

Mercy whined, pressing closer. The light was just strong enough to show the wrinkled worry between her ears. "It's all right, girl." Avery infused her voice with a peace she didn't feel. "I'm okay."

Because she was. She had to be. Too much was on her shoulders for her to be otherwise. And it was time to get up. Especially now that she had to take a shower before work.

By the time she was driving toward Allenspark, the dull headache had grown into a king-sized throb. Avery squinted into the rising sun and punched Addisyn's number on her phone. She couldn't go another day without resolving this.

"Hello?" Addisyn sounded groggy herself.

"Hey." Avery frowned. Usually Addisyn would have been getting ready for work by now. "Did I wake you up?"

"Uh—" Addisyn yawned. "No. Not really. I don't have clients till this afternoon, so I slept a little longer."

"Oh." Avery bit back her resentment. Sleeping in—or sleeping at all—wasn't a luxury she enjoyed anymore, thanks to Addisyn. "I'm on my way to work." She glanced at her dashboard clock. "I have an early meeting before my classes today."

"Didn't you go in early a lot last week too?" Addisyn's tone tinged with concern. "I think you're working too hard. You need a break."

Ha. As if. "Ads, I've been thinking about what you said about Mom."

"Yes?" Addisyn seemed to have magically rebounded to peak alertness.

"And I want to explain to you why I won't talk about this, because I know it's hard for you to understand." She forged ahead before Addisyn could interrupt. "We have a whole new life now. I have the mountains, and my work at the center." Although that wasn't going great. She forced the thought away. "And you have Darius and the baby."

"Yes." Addisyn's voice was hesitant. "The baby."

Avery narrowed her eyes. "Is something wrong?"

"No. Everything's okay."

Fine. Avery didn't have the strength to play Twenty Questions with Addisyn this morning. "Okay. Well, my point is that I just don't see how digging that far back into the past will help either one of us now."

"But—but it's hard."

The fight had drained from Addisyn's voice, and now she sounded like a scared little girl. Avery's heart squeezed. "Ads, I know it *was*. But we got through it, right? You and me?"

"Well—yeah." Addisyn didn't sound convinced. "But—"

"But what?"

"But don't you have some stuff? Stuff you brought from home?"

Home. Why in the world did Addisyn still call their abusive childhood abode *home* when Avery had labored for a decade to give her a healthy version of the concept? "Uh—I don't know where it is." Well, technically it was in some of the boxes of trash/not-trash she kept in the basement, but she didn't plan to dig through all that.

"Can I—could we look for it sometime?"

Avery took a hand off the steering wheel and rubbed at her temples. It didn't help the pounding. "Well, maybe. We'll see." Coded language for *no.*

"Okay. I—I just want to see if there are clues."

"Clues?" What was this, Nancy Drew?

"I want to know why she left."

Why she left.

Avery sucked in a reflexive breath. No. No, Addisyn didn't want to know that. The knowledge would crush her little sister like a cement block.

Which was why Avery had carried it for them both all these years.

"Ads, hey, I'm almost at work." She ignored the guilt that squirmed up her spine. "I've got to go."

"Okay." Addisyn still didn't sound satisfied. "Listen, I was thinking maybe I'd come up and see you this weekend."

"Uh—" Her sister's visits were always welcome, but right now Addisyn didn't need to be around the basement. Or the secrets. "I have classes on Saturday." It wasn't a lie.

"Okay. How 'bout Sunday?"

"I've got to do some writing on that curriculum."

"Oh, yeah. How's that going?"

The center loomed in front of her, Creed's Jeep already in the parking lot. *Great.* "Fine. It's going fine." The time on her dashboard clock was screaming at her. She couldn't be late. "Listen, I'll call you about this weekend, okay?"

She all but ran through the doors of the office, stumbling into the meeting room on the dot of the hour and dropping into the only empty seat—next to Creed. Perfect.

"Good morning, everyone." Skyla glanced around the room. "We're here today to—"

As Skyla continued her remarks, Avery focused on her breathing. Hopefully she didn't look as frantic as she felt.

"You okay?" Creed's question was low enough for only her.

Great. If he could see her distress, then everyone else could too. Avery tightened her jaw. "Yes." She found a fresh page in her notebook and—where was her pen? She always kept it in the spiral of the notebook—

Ill-prepared. The complaint email jabbed at her again.

She rummaged through her bag as quietly as she could. Had the stupid pen fallen out in her truck?

A pen that wasn't hers suddenly landed lightly on her notebook. She blinked and glanced at Creed. He tipped his head toward the pen with a half-smile.

"Thank you." He was watching her that closely? The thought flushed heat to her face. She forced herself to focus on Skyla.

"As we have discussed already, we are still seeking alternate funding sources for next year's expansion." Skyla glanced at Tyler. "Tyler has been considering some options for us."

"Yes." Tyler shuffled through his notes. "I'm looking into some more grants and foundations."

Liv cocked a skeptical eyebrow. "Grants and foundations are what stranded us in the first place. I thought we were going with a more grassroots approach."

Creed leaned forward. "Ever tried social media outreach?"

"No." Tyler's tone stopped just short of condescending. "We don't have money to throw away on online ads."

"I'm not talking about advertisements, although those can help." Creed shrugged. "At Guys in the Wild, we do a lot of cross-promos. Pairing up with similar creators so we can tap into each other's audiences. It's been a great form of networking for us. I mean, I realize this is different, but I bet there would be plenty of social media influencers willing to promote the center as part of their brand."

The idea was unfamiliar, but intriguing. Avery nodded.

But Tyler's frown didn't ease. "That kind of funding is inherently unreliable. Plus it requires us to work with content creator divas."

Creed's mouth twitched, but he didn't take Tyler's bait. "Well, here's another idea. Why don't you hold a fundraiser here? A banquet, or a festival. Or even a ribbon-cutting for the new building." His eyes were sparking with a rare unguarded enthusiasm. "You could sell tickets for a gala. Maybe put up some tents, hold it outside in the evening."

"Huh. Never thought of that." Tyler's tone was still stuffy, but there was no denying his face had thawed some. "That might actually be worthwhile."

"And during the day—" Liv rubbed her hands together—"people could tour the flight cages and the center."

"That's true." Tyler tapped his pen. "If we included a ribbon-cutting, we could involve the chamber of commerce, promote it to the downtown businesses."

"Creed, this is a thought of much value." Skyla smiled at him approvingly. "We could even invite philanthropy directors. Many of them may be looking for causes to join."

The idea gleamed with potential. Avery nodded. "That's a great idea."

"Or—" Creed's mind was obviously spinning with the swiftness she'd come to expect. "What if I show the video I'm creating there? To help donors engage with our mission."

"I think the focus should remain on the center for that event." Tyler's tone squashed disagreement.

Creed, however, seemed up for the challenge. "The video is *about* the center, so—"

"But it's still affiliated with your YouTube channel." The word *YouTube* sounded like an infectious disease. "I don't think we should mix our focus."

Creed's shoulders were stiffening. "It's no different than a sponsorship film, and I've done several of those at events."

Avery pressed her lips together. She wouldn't have envisioned herself siding with Creed, but in this case, his plan made perfect sense. Not that she would offer that opinion.

Skyla cleared her throat. "I understand your concerns, Tyler. However, Creed's idea holds weight. The video would allow prospective donors to see different parts of this work that they would not be able to experience that night."

"Plus, the branding for Guys in the Wild is minimal." Creed's eyes narrowed ever so slightly in Tyler's direction. "Don't worry. We're not staking territory."

Tyler's expression held grudging surrender. "How long is this video going to be?"

"Our full-length features are usually twenty minutes."

Tyler raised his eyebrows. "I'm not sure donors will want to sit through the length of that. They might lose interest."

"My job as a videographer is to make sure the audience doesn't lose interest." The spark in his eyes was igniting.

Apparently Tyler didn't notice. "Yes, well, these are serious professionals. Not your normal audience." Before Creed could respond, Tyler directed his focus to Avery. "At any rate, if we have to show the video, I at least want someone to speak afterwards. Recap things, present the mission of the center, call for donations. Avery, you'll do that."

"W-what?" Speak before an entire crowd of people? Especially now, when even her classes were triggering the panic? Avery's stomach dropped. "Oh no, I don't think—"

"Yes, you're the perfect one." Tyler scribbled something on his notepad. "You can talk about the expansion, and you can also share about the new curriculum."

The curriculum. A fresh wave of anxiety prickled over her. Avery took a deep breath, trying to keep the panic out of her voice. "Tyler, I think Liv or—"

"Avery, it's got to be you." A hint of annoyance was creeping into his tone. "You're the director of the expansion." He cocked his head, his voice softening. "Unless—is there some reason you don't want to?"

Creed, Skyla, Liv all staring at her. She clenched Creed's pen in her fist. "Um—no, that's okay. I'll do it."

"All right." Tyler gave her one more dubious look before he moved on down his paper. "So then, if we're going to do this, let's talk about logistics. I think—"

The rest of the meeting seemed to be happening to someone else, far away. Avery talked when she had to and kept her expression relaxed, but her mind relentlessly circled the looming threat of public speaking. In front of intimidating people on whose checkbooks the center was riding. The pressure would crush her like an avalanche. How would she do that without freezing up? Or worse...

Finally Skyla clapped her hands. "That's enough for right now. Thank you, everyone, for your contributions today."

With a final disgruntled look at Creed, Tyler gathered up his papers. "Avery, we'll talk later about your speaking part."

"Yes. All right." She pretended to study her notes as Tyler left.

"Hey. You okay?"

Avery blinked and glanced up. Creed was watching her with the same keen, unafraid gaze with which he shot film. She dropped her eyes, unable to meet his intensity. "Uh—yes."

"Public speaking isn't easy." He stood up, pushed his chair in.

So he could tell. Embarrassment burned through her.

But his voice didn't sound judgmental. "I had to learn that myself. When I started making videos."

"Avery?" Skyla was walking toward them. "May I speak with you for a minute?"

Creed glanced back at Avery. "We'll talk later."

He was gone before she could respond. Skyla moved into his vacant chair. "Avery—were you all right, in the meeting today?"

Heat swam to her cheeks. "Yes. I'm sorry. I just have a lot on my mind with—everything." She hesitated, but it was time for Skyla to know. "Addisyn is pregnant."

Skyla's eyes glowed with delight. "Oh, what great joy for all of you. Please tell her how excited I am. And I will pray many words of blessing over this child."

Great joy. Yes, it should have been, if Addisyn could have just focused on the baby and not tried to make this into some big catharsis from their past. Avery nodded. "Thank you. I'll tell her."

"How is the curriculum coming?"

The question wasn't an accusation, but Avery squirmed anyway. "Um, okay. It's coming—okay."

"Are you sure?" Skyla's gaze was probing. "Do you need help?"

"No." Skyla had entrusted her with this. She would figure it out herself. "I've got it. Well, I mean, I'm going to have it. It's—I'm still sort of organizing everything."

Skyla nodded. "When do you think you might have a sample lesson I could present to the board? Would the middle of next month be too soon? That is the time of our quarterly board meeting."

The middle of next month, and she hadn't even formulated her initial ideas. Panic pressed on her again. "Uh, no, that's fine. I'll have it to you before then."

"Good." Skyla's eyes searched her face. "Avery, forgive me for asking. But something weighs on you. Is it not so?"

For half a heartbeat, Avery considered telling Skyla the problems she was facing. Skyla was a woman of deep and rare wisdom. Maybe she could offer—

But what could Avery tell her? That she was revisited by the night terrors she thought she'd left behind years ago? That she was lost in her own internal wilderness? That she wasn't as competent or courageous as Skyla thought?

"No." She retreated behind the word. "I mean—not really. Everything has just been crazy, with me trying to help Addisyn, and all."

Skyla measured her for a few more moments, and then her shoulders drooped slightly. In—disappointment? "Very well. But, Avery—it has always seemed to me that you hold your pain tight to your chest. As do the birds with their broken wings."

The words struck close enough to the truth that Avery flinched. "But—"

Skyla held up a hand. "You need not say anything. It is indeed the nature of hurt things, yes? To tuck the pain tightly close to them. But the healing is found when the wing is opened. When the pain is released. When flight begins again." She glanced out the window, where clouds hovered over the mountains. "There is a place between the sky-world and the earth-world. It is in that place that we stand here. We bring Creator's vision to the earth, and we help others find Him in the sky. But to leave the ground, there must be flight." She stood and bowed her head. "Thank you, Avery. You may go back to your work now."

Avery gathered her things and left the room, Skyla's words echoing uncomfortably in her mind.

Healing is found when the wing is opened...

Wasn't that sort of what Addisyn had said?

Avery's headache throbbed harder. *No.* Addisyn didn't know what she was asking. Neither did Skyla. What she perceived as Avery hiding away the pain was actually Avery protecting her sister.

And that was worth any sleepless struggle.

Addisyn had given Avery three days. Three days to pick up the conversation that she'd so abruptly set aside. Three days to return to the topic and face the questions. Three days to talk about Mom.

She'd been patient. But she couldn't wait any longer. One way or another, she needed closure.

And the only person who could give it to her was the sister who was now practically MIA. Good grief, Avery hadn't even texted her for the last three days. When was the last time they'd had no communication for this long?

But maybe she shouldn't be surprised, considering how off-balance Avery had seemed when Addisyn had asked the question. Avery could say what she liked, but this was obviously a tender place for her too. Which was yet another reason for both of them to seek resolution.

Well, if Avery wouldn't initiate, Addisyn would have to prod her a little. She grabbed her cell phone and settled onto the couch. She'd taken the evening off, but Darius was still at work, so she had the house to herself. And Avery should be home from her job too. In other words, perfect timing.

The phone rang once. Twice. Maybe Avery wouldn't answer even now. At the beginning of the fourth ring, her sister's voice came over the phone. "Hello, Ads."

Already she sounded wary. Addisyn pressed her lips together. "Hey, A." She tried to keep her own voice upbeat. Not easy to do in light of a tense conversation, pregnancy hormones, and sleep deprivation. "Whatcha doing?"

"I'm fixing dinner."

Addisyn grinned. "In other words, your microwave is getting a workout?"

"Addisyn, that's not fair." Avery's words were even stiffer than before. "I cook a lot. When I use the microwave, it's to reheat leftovers."

She'd seen her sister nuke a frozen meal or two. But okay. "I was just kidding, A."

Avery sighed. "Look, Addisyn. I know why you called."

The undertone of her voice didn't sound promising. Addisyn bit her lip. "Well—I mean—you never called me back. After we—after the other day."

"I know." Every word had a wall around it. "I was going to. It was very busy at the center."

"But you had the weekend off."

"I had a lot to do at the house."

So either way, she'd conveniently found reasons to postpone an important conversation. Addisyn sighed. "All right." She couldn't press Avery too hard. Not if she wanted to walk away from this conversation with answers in her pocket. "So—did you—did you think anymore about what we talked about?"

"I did. I've thought about it—a lot, actually. And—" Avery's tone finally softened some. "That's why I didn't call you back right away. I was—I was thinking about how to approach this."

This was it. Avery was getting ready to give her answers. Memories. Closure. Addisyn pressed the phone closer to her ear. She wouldn't miss a single word.

"And first, I want to ask you this." Avery hesitated. "Why are you asking me now?"

So she had closure to stitch together the shredded pieces of the past. So she could breathe without pressure and sleep without worries and carry her and Darius's child without fear. But how could she put all that into words for Avery? "I've been thinking about Mom, I guess. And the more I think about it, the more it bothers me that I don't really know why she left or what happened to her or—or why she didn't take us with her."

"Okay." Avery was using the psychiatric tone that Addisyn had always resented. "But what brought this up now?"

Her hand was resting on her abdomen. This time she didn't move it away. "Being—being pregnant, I think."

"That's what I thought." Avery's voice gentled. "Listen, Ads. This is only normal, okay? It just makes sense that you're thinking about Mom at a time like this. Things are changing, and you're becoming a mom yourself, and so of course your mind would go there."

Addisyn wrinkled her brow. "Which means—"

"Which means that you don't need to worry about this. Thinking about Mom—it's not a sign that you have to figure anything out. Okay? It's just your body and mind trying to nail down loose ends for you."

Addisyn hesitated. Was Avery right? Were her emotions about her mother truly nothing more than an overactive subconscious superimposing the past on the present?

Avery was still talking. "And also, you know, your hormones are very—unbalanced right now. So any kind of anxiety or—"

Seriously? *Seriously?* She was having an existential crisis, and her sister was going to blame *hormones*? Addisyn jerked upright on the couch. "A, this is not a hormone thing. And it's not some fleeting fancy because I'm—pregnant." How many times had she wondered about her mom throughout the years? How deeply had the wound ached in the rocky soil of her heart? The pregnancy had unearthed it, yes. But the seed had been planted long ago.

"Wait. I'm sorry. That's not what I was getting at." Avery cleared her throat. "I'm just saying, you know, you don't have to rush into anything here. And you certainly don't have to add digging into the past to your list of things to do."

"I'm not doing this because I have to, A."

"No, I get it. You're trying to—get to the bottom of things, or whatever." Her sister's tone sounded as if that were a questionable pursuit at best. "But—I mean, you have a lot to handle right now. A lot to get ready and figure out and take care of."

As if she needed the reminder of how unprepared she was for all of this. And as if she could take on anything as long as she was strait-jacketed by uncertainty. "I know that." Was Avery ever going to quit stalling and give her answers?

"So—why don't we wait on this until you're in a calmer place. Okay?"

In a calmer place? What did that even mean? "A, it's not a big ask." She fought to keep the frustration out of her voice. "I just want you to tell me about Mom. One conversation. How time-consuming can that be?"

Avery sighed. "Addisyn, I get what you're asking. I truly do. But there's really not that much to tell." Her sister's voice closed off like a shutting door. "I don't know what happened to her."

What she'd expected, but the lack of closure still dropped in her stomach. "Okay." She grabbed for some other question. Some other chance at an answer. "Why did she leave?"

"Mom left because of Dad, of course. They were always fighting. You remember that even when she—"

"Yes." Instantly Addisyn regretted her interruption. She needed to let Avery talk, let the story unspool. "I mean, go ahead."

"Well, that's why she left. They couldn't get along."

But why would a mother fleeing abuse leave behind her children? "What about us?"

"What do you mean, what about us?"

"Why didn't she take us with her?"

Avery hesitated for a long time. Too long. "I don't know."

"And she never came back for us." At Avery's silence, Addisyn frowned. "Right?"

"What? Oh, right." Avery sighed. "She—she never came back."

Every question led down an infuriatingly open road, and she was no closer to arriving at a destination than she'd ever been. She sighed, switching tactics. "Okay. What else?"

"What else?" Avery let out a breath. "That's it, Addisyn. I've told you everything I know."

Her voice was getting more distant. She was already moving on from the conversation. Well then, if diplomacy hadn't worked, maybe directness would. "Look, Avery, you have to know more. Why won't you talk to me about this?"

"Addisyn, that's enough." Avery's tone sliced across the phone line and cut the question to shreds. "We're done talking about this. I've told you everything I can tell you."

Addisyn's eyes widened. Avery had always been the patient one, gentle and soft-spoken and long-suffering to a fault. Yet whatever territory Addisyn had stepped foot on was apparently protected by barbed wire.

"I'm sorry, Ads." Avery's tone was normal again. She sighed.

"That was abrupt. I just—this is just something I don't like to talk about, okay?"

"But—" She was being more cautious now. "Don't you think we need to talk about it?"

"I don't see why. I mean, it happened, but now it's over, and we're okay. So I don't see the point in dredging it back up."

We're okay. Yeah, sure, coming from the woman who had just flipped her lid at a simple question. Addisyn narrowed her eyes. "We're okay? Are *you* okay?"

"Of course." Avery's voice was taking on an edge again.

The conversation was making her temples throb. "Look. Do you think—sometime—you could tell me some stories about Mom?"

"I told you I don't know—"

"Not that. Just—stories. Things she told you. Things that happened before—" A sudden heat stung her eyes. She blinked it back. "Before she left."

Avery was quiet.

Addisyn swallowed hard and rushed ahead. "I—I want to know more about her, A. I want to know who she was and—" *And why she left us behind.* "And not just have this—this big blank in my mind where she should be."

Still, silence. Had the call dropped? "A? Are you there?"

"I'm here." Avery's sigh sounded weary. "I understand what you're asking, Addisyn. All I can tell you is—I'll think about it. Okay?"

Hope lifted its stubborn head within her. At least Avery hadn't said a flat-out *no.* "Okay. Thank you."

"Of course."

A faint beeping came from the background. Addisyn tilted her head. "What's that noise?"

Avery gave a soft chuckle, suddenly sounding much more like herself. "It's the microwave."

Addisyn joined her sister's laugh. "Told you."

"I know my limitations." Avery's smile wrapped around her words.

But even after they'd ended the conversation—Avery insisted she couldn't let her microwave dinner get cold—Addisyn wondered about Avery's words. Maybe her sister was right. Maybe the pregnancy hormones were distorting her logic more than she'd realized. The hormonal turbulence had been rougher than she'd expected. Just like everything else about the pregnancy. Already.

But still...

She closed her eyes and leaned against the couch cushions, her sister's assurance in her mind. *We're okay.*

Were they? When she was terrified about becoming a mother, and Avery was dodging a past that was still nipping at her heels? How much had they healed, and how much had they simply swept under the rug?

The longer she thought about it, the more convinced she was that they'd never be okay as long as the questions floated just out of reach. The only way back to solid ground was the one thing Avery refused to give her. The one thing she had to find at all costs.

Answers.

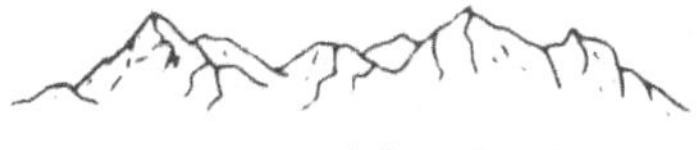

CHAPTER 8

"Back to the grind?"

The voice punctured the bubble of Avery's thoughts, and she jumped, almost dropping her bag in the dust of the parking lot. "Creed! You startled me."

"Sorry." He offered a sheepish smile as he straightened from the corner of the sign. "I was getting some more shots of the buildings." Mercy pranced toward him with a wagging tail, and he frowned. "Hello, Dog."

Avery rolled her eyes. "She has a name."

"I know. Mercy. See, I remember. And actually—" He patted Mercy's head. "She's not a bad dog."

Avery blinked. Had Creed actually said something *nice*? Was he sick?

Still petting Mercy, he darted his quick gaze at her. "What's up with you? It's Friday, but your face is saying Monday."

"I'm fine." Actually she'd spent another rough night, itching with insomnia while she replayed her interaction with Addisyn, then resurfacing between night terrors. But he didn't need to know any of that.

Creed's keen glance narrowed, but thankfully, he just shrugged. "Okay. Get yourself some coffee." He held up a travel cup. "Not much good coffee won't fix."

"Hmm. Maybe." Caffeine would solve exactly zero of her problems.

"But before you do—would you have a chance this morning to show me the walking trails? I want to get some shots in that area, and the lighting is good right now."

"Oh. Yes." Her first class wasn't for another hour. She'd planned to catch up on emails, but—"I can do it now."

"Thanks." He tossed her a grin as he fell into step beside her. "You gotta strike when the light is right, you know."

An answering smile tugged at her. "I guess so." Amazing, how much gentler he looked when he smiled, his rough edges softened.

"You have classes today?"

"Not this morning. I needed time to work." She hesitated, but what could it hurt to tell him? "I'm developing a new curriculum."

"Oh, really?" His interest seemed genuine. "For the center?"

"Well, possibly, but mainly for schools. It's supposed to help kids connect with nature to learn and explore. Seek wonder. Find healing." *Ha.* She was clearly the expert on that.

"Wow." He actually looked impressed. "That sounds cool."

"Well. Thanks." It would only be *cool* if she could climb over her mental block.

"So how's it going for you?"

"Uh—well, I'm still in the brainstorming stage." If staring at a blank page counted as brainstorming. "I might work outside today, find inspiration that way."

"Today's the day for it." He pushed up his sleeves and squinted at the sky. "It's warm. Feels almost like summer."

The tattoo was visible for the first time—a wolf. A running wolf, racing head-on out of evergreen-spiky mountains, with some kind of strange geometric symbols underneath it. It was intricate and surprisingly—beautiful.

"Wondering about this?" Creed tapped the tattoo.

Her cheeks grew warm. She wouldn't give him the satisfaction of knowing she was curious about it. "It's interesting."

"Got it on my twenty-first birthday." He underlined the symbols with his finger. "That's Lakota writing for *Running Wolf.*"

Lakota. She studied his high cheekbones, the reddish sparks in his espresso-colored hair. "Your mother's name."

His jaw twitched. "Dad told you."

She nodded.

He sighed. "Yeah." For a moment, he looked less like a rakishly irritating young man and more like a lost little boy. "I don't talk to her very often."

"Does she live near you?" Why was she asking? Creed's life was certainly none of her concern.

"Nah. She moved to Idaho. Did her own thing. Got remarried a few years back." He shrugged. "It's fine. I don't have a problem with her. That's over and done with."

The same thing she'd told Addisyn last night. Had she sounded as unconvincing as Creed did now?

"Seriously, though—" He stopped and squinted at her. "Is something wrong this morning? You really do seem down."

How had he read her emotions? Avery raised her eyebrows. "Why do you care?"

"I don't know." He gave that lopsided grin.

Huh. At least he was honest. Avery sighed. "It's fine. I had a difficult conversation this weekend with my sister and—" *Stop.* What was she doing, blabbing her private business to Creed?

"Hmm." He didn't seem ruffled. "This about the pregnancy?"

He'd remembered that this long? Embarrassment stung her again at the memory of the Safeway encounter. "Not really." How could she summarize it for him? "She wants to talk about—about something from our past. I don't think either of us needs to deal with it."

"Dealing with the past?" His eyebrows rose. "That's something we all do."

"Well, I suppose, but at some point, we get over it."

His laugh burned bitter. "Do we?"

"Of course." She started walking again, faster this time. "I did."

His mouth quirked cynically as he fell into step beside her. "And it never bothers you? You never think about it?"

Why would no one believe her? "No. It's over. It doesn't matter to me anymore."

"I don't believe you, Saint Avery. I think you just shove it down. Because you think you're supposed to."

If he didn't quit calling her that—Avery rounded on him, the tentative truce dashed. "I'm serious, Creed. This was years ago. It's done."

"Except it never is." His laugh was sad this time. "None of us get away from the past. Not really. Not ever."

His words jabbed at the tender places in her heart, but she ignored that. After all, he wasn't the best to be dispensing life advice. "I happen to disagree."

"But—" Creed's voice was softer now. Less acidic. "The past is what the future is built on."

"What do you mean?"

An undefinable sadness suddenly showed in his eyes. "Your life stacks on itself, you know? You can keep building layers on top, but underneath—" The wind tugged at his hair, wrapped around his words. "Underneath is everything you thought you left behind. You can't get rid of it because you can't undo it. Not without toppling everything you've built since then."

The words caught her off guard almost as much as the pain on his face. A burden she hadn't seen before.

Underneath his flippant facade, was *this* the weight he carried?

She shook her head. "Creed—" She was trying to look deeper. "What happened? With your dad?"

She knew the question was wrong the moment Creed's eyes hardened again. "He spent a lifetime assuring me that I never measured up to his lofty ideals. And then I made—I made a mistake."

She cocked her head. "A mistake?"

"Yeah." He blew out a breath. "I burned down part of the Rez."

Okay, not what she was expecting. "You *what?*"

"It's a long story. It was an accident. Partly, anyway. Not my finest moment, I guess." His face darkened. "And that's when I learned how my dad really felt about me." He turned away and strode off toward the trails. "I've got to get this footage before the light changes."

Avery stood still, the questions buzzing around her like a swarm of mosquitoes. She'd seen something different in Creed today. Something more broken than his usual bulldozer personality. Something that still ached along fault lines of the past.

Was that same ache inside Addisyn? Was that what was driving her sister's questions?

And Laz—he'd walked away from Creed? He whose heart was bulldog-loyal? Surely not. Surely he hadn't left his son the way her mom had left her.

The past is what the future is built on...

She watched Creed stalk off, his shadow following him into the morning light. Maybe he also knew something about the people who walked away.

And the pain they left behind.

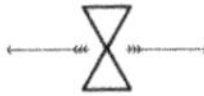

ADDISYN HAD EXPERIENCED her fair share of nerves in her life. As a professional figure skater, she'd undergone high-stakes performances and uncertain rankings and dicey media interviews. Now, as a coach, she dealt daily with the secondhand stress of watching her students take to the ice themselves.

But no case of nervous jitters had ever compared to the way adrenaline circulated through her body now.

She shifted on the exam table, the paper crackling beneath her. Why was clinical furniture always paper-covered? It was irritating. But then, so was everything else about the day.

"Are you okay?" Darius's forehead creased.

Another unintended side effect of the pregnancy—her husband had begun monitoring her like a science experiment. "I'm fine."

"Do you need anything, or—"

"Darius, I'm *fine*." She hated the edge to her voice. She should be grateful for his concern. And she was. Of course. She glanced at the door. "Shouldn't someone have been here by now to do the ultrasound?"

"They said it might be a few minutes."

Well, easy for him. All he had to do was sit there in the corner.

She, on the other hand, had already endured the gynecologist's examination, a gauntlet of embarrassingly specific questions, and a lab-rat litany of tests. She stared at the reproductive-cycle poster on the wall. Lovely.

"Are you excited for the ultrasound?" Darius beamed that Christmas-morning smile again. "We'll see the baby for the first time."

The baby. That pair of words still hit like a sucker punch. "Um— I don't think we'll be able to see much yet." Hadn't she read online that by six weeks the baby was the size of a grain of rice? Something like that?

"Yeah, but they said we might see a heartbeat, or at least the cardiac activity."

How did you *see* a heartbeat? And from a heart smaller than a grain of rice? The whole process didn't make much sense. Couldn't they just go home? She scratched absently at the inside of her elbow. The bandage they'd put on after the blood tests was itching.

"Are you sure you're okay?"

"Darius, I said *yes*!" The instant the words left her mouth, she sucked in a breath at how sharp her tone had been. "I'm sorry." Six weeks pregnant, and she was already yelling at her husband. By the time the baby was born, every ounce of joy would have been squeezed out of her marriage.

He shrugged, but the hurt in his eyes didn't leave. "Hey, it's okay." He stood and came beside her, curving an arm around her shoulders. "Are you nervous about the ultrasound?"

About the ultrasound. About the baby. About every wild way her life was about to change. About the answers she would never have regarding her own childhood. "I—yeah." Tears pooled in her eyes. What a mess she was.

"There's nothing to worry about." He rubbed her shoulder. "You've got this."

Sure. If that's what he wanted to believe. She nodded. Blinked the tears back. She couldn't put a damper on his exciting moment.

The door swung open, and a perky young nurse bopped in. "Hi there! I'm Jess, and I'll be doing your ultrasound today."

"Okay." The word was little better than a squeak.

Darius squeezed her shoulder again as they headed down the hall and directed his next words to Jess. "She's a little nervous."

Oh, so now he would speak for her too? Addisyn gritted her teeth but kept her smile in place.

"Aww, don't be nervous!" Jess was way happier than anybody should ever be. She led them into a tiny, dimly lit room. Like some villain's lair from an action movie. "If you'll just lie here for me now—"

As if she had a choice. Addisyn lay back on the slick vinyl bench. Someone had taped inspirational posters to the ceiling, but she couldn't read any of them in the dim light.

Jess was smearing some kind of cold goop on Addisyn's stomach and still chattering away with her excessive energy level. "And so we'll have a more precise due date after today, and we'll also be able to check for a gestational sac."

A *what*? Probably something Addisyn should have already known about, so she nodded.

Darius leaned forward. "Will we see the heartbeat?"

For crying out loud, why was he so hung up on that?

"Maybe." Jess retrieved some weird wand thing and tilted the screen toward them. "You can both watch along."

But as Jess began the ultrasound, Addisyn couldn't see much of anything besides black-and-white scribbles that looked like weird shadowy radio markings. Like a search for alien life. *Hello, out there...*

Had her mom lain in a dark room and watched for her on an ultrasound screen?

Maybe her mom hadn't wanted her any more than she wanted this baby.

The thought sliced through her, pain and guilt a double-edged sword. Why was this so hard for her? Wasn't pregnancy supposed to be about blissfully bonding with your unborn child, singing songs to your stomach and decorating a nursery?

"Good news, your pregnancy is in the uterus, not ectopic." Jess leaned forward to examine something more closely on the screen.

"And the gestational sac has developed properly. You don't have to worry about that."

"Oh. Okay." She hadn't even *known* to be worried about that. How did other moms know about this stuff?

"The embryo is about six millimeters long, meaning you're at six weeks exactly." Jess smiled at them. "Looks like you'll be having a December baby."

"December!" Darius matched Jess's level of enthusiasm.

For just a moment, Addisyn let herself imagine bringing a baby home at Christmas, when the house was full of greenery and presents and candles—

What was she thinking? All that stuff was dangerous for babies, right? Would they even get a Christmas tree this year? And why was she thinking about Christmas trees when she was getting her first ultrasound? Ugh.

"Also, it's a single embryo." Jess chuckled. "No twins."

Twins? Horrors, she hadn't even thought about the possibility of having more than one child to keep track of. Yikes.

"And—" Jess beamed at them both. "I can see the cardiac activity. There's a heartbeat."

Darius gasped. "No way! Did you hear that, Addisyn? Our baby has a heartbeat!"

"Yes." The word was all she could fit past the lump in her throat.

"Congratulations to both of you." Jess's smile wrapped around her words. "Everything looks perfect."

Perfect. A stone dropped to Addisyn's stomach. Even if the baby was perfect, she wouldn't be. Not when she didn't have a mom to follow.

And when Avery was apparently determined to give her no information at all.

A sudden surge of something harder than her earlier irritation slapped across her. These moments should be joyful. Exciting. Precious memories and firsts to treasure forever. Instead, they were slipping by while she was mired in uncertainty and isolation, all because Avery was determined to hold the entire situation with their mom at arm's length.

"This is wonderful." Darius's voice held the hush of reverence. Even in the dim light of the ultrasound screen, Addisyn could see the shimmer of tears in his eyes. And suddenly, her own eyes filled. Not because she felt his emotion.

But because she wished she could.

THE SEAT WAS HARD, but the Wi-Fi was good.

Creed shifted his position on the narrow picnic table bench and studied his laptop screen again. The Wi-Fi at the raptor center was, naturally, limited to the office. Which meant he could work offline at his camper and take the risk of not backing up his work—or work at the area Skyla had assigned him, uncomfortably close to Tyler and his apparent vendetta.

So he'd started driving to the Estes Park Visitor Center when he needed uninterrupted work time. Specifically, to the picnic table randomly stuck under a canopy near the parking lot. Not the best view, and plenty of traffic noise and distracting chatter from the tourists...but free Wi-Fi. That atoned for much.

Today he'd been reviewing film cuts, studying the hodgepodge of clips he'd captured over the last few days at the center. The best shots were the ones from the flight cage, when Avery had been exercising that bird.

Avery. He didn't know quite what to make of her. He'd been convinced she was one of those goody-two-shoes Christian girls, the kind whose biggest problem was deciding what Bible verse to aesthetically post on Instagram. Like the girls Dad had always wanted him to date.

But on the other hand, she wasn't all ditzy and giggly like those girls. She was quieter, deeper, with a seriousness for life that approached reverence. Plus, there was no questioning her competence, or the passion with which she poured her heart into her work.

A passion he'd once felt for his own.

Creed glanced up from the computer, settling his gaze on the clouds just blooming over the horizon. Guys in the Wild had started out so differently. Back then, they'd taken turns with the filming and the narrating and the editing. They'd all had moments in front of the camera to share their thoughts and their unique perspectives.

And Creed had been fired up about all of it. At the time, he'd been in a chaotic zigzag of bouncing between seasonal jobs in the backcountry—clearing trails, leading hiking trips, working in wild-fire management. When he'd had the invitation to join the rapidly rising channel, he'd believed that he'd found his life's work. And he'd been attracted as much by the brotherly companionship and the unified purpose as by the generous paycheck.

Plus, the job had offered something even more valuable, some-thing he'd craved ever since he'd driven Highway 18 south from the Rez: redemption.

But the job had shapeshifted since then. Austin had taken the lead as the channel expanded, slicing camera time for the others into smaller and smaller sections. And at the same time, he'd redefined *success*. Before, the views had naturally followed the content, but now their content was chasing the views—watching the metrics, counting the clicks, serving up the same story in a hundred weary ways.

Creed shrugged, shaking off the uncomfortable thoughts. Austin was a natural leader, after all. There was no denying the guy did great on camera. He was popular with their audience and had a charisma that could be felt even through the film. If the channel had narrowed its branding, or if the actual video legwork seemed to fall mainly on Creed—well, he could live with that.

And anyway, if he could just impress Austin with this project, he'd have a clear ticket to greater things. Things that would finally scratch that creative itch again.

The thought gave him fresh resolve, and he bent over the project with renewed determination, ignoring the chatting couples and giddy teenagers and panting dogs that streamed back and forth on the sidewalk. Just when he knew his eyes would cross if he studied another timestamp, "Believer" pounded out from his phone. He glanced at the screen. Erica?

Wariness tugged at him as he answered. "Hello?"

"Hey, Creed. Have you gotten lost in the mountains yet?"

He laughed in spite of himself. "No, not yet. What's up?"

"Nothing much." Her tone turned more velvety. "Just seeing how the handsome Mr. Running Wolf is doing."

Discomfort crawled over his shoulders. When he returned to Arizona, he wouldn't be able to put off this Erica dilemma any longer. "I'm all right."

"Oh, come on." Her teasing was like the tendrils of a vine, wrapping around him. "Aren't you going to ask what I'm doing?"

"You're having a great time in Arizona, I assume."

"Well, a *hot* time, for sure. The desert is no joke." Her voice turned quieter. "You haven't called."

"I—" Was he supposed to have? "Well, I've been busy here. I didn't know you were waiting to hear from me."

"I wasn't waiting." Her words were quick. "I just thought you would have."

What did that mean? Creed bit back a groan. Erica had always been bad about playing these games. At least that was something he never had to worry about with Avery. She was honest and direct. And refreshingly uninterested in him.

"How's the film project going?" Erica's voice was more normal now.

"Oh—" He sighed and stood, stretching his legs. "It's going. It's not the easiest thing."

"I bet." She laughed. "Trying to make a video out of a bunch of birds has to be hard."

Exactly his thoughts when he'd arrived, so why did her comment rankle him defensive? "The center is really cool. It does a lot of great things."

"Okay." Her tone still held a humor he resented. "If you say so. I just hate that there's no one to help you."

"There's Avery." The words slipped out before he could think.

"Who's Avery?"

He clenched his jaw. Why on earth had he said that? "Just—she works at the center. She's been sort of showing me around."

"Oh. Okay." Erica didn't sound too happy about that. "Is she—nice?"

Oh, no. The last thing he needed was another knot in the Erica situation. "No. She's irritating." He frowned. That wasn't fair. "I mean—she's got her own way of doing things."

Erica laughed softly. "Stubborn, huh?"

"Yeah. I guess." Why was this making him so uncomfortable? "She's just one of the workers."

"Okay." Thank goodness, Erica seemed to accept that. "So do you have the storyboard done?"

"Not yet."

"Not yet?"

He groaned. Fine. "Well, I can't get this video like I think Austin would want."

"Oh my goodness." A smile shaped her voice. "I think being in the desert is giving me hallucinations. I almost thought the world's most confident filmmaker just admitted he's not perfect."

Creed rolled his eyes. "Ha, ha."

She snickered. "Fortunately for you, the world's *second* greatest filmmaker might be willing to help you."

Hope lifted its head despite everything. Erica was frustrating sometimes, but she was a killer storyteller, always able to diagnose weaknesses and suggest improvements. Although—"In exchange for what?"

"Nothing. Just a friend helping a friend."

Her tone was a bit more than friendly. He hesitated. If Erica was doing this because of her interest in him, he needed to say no. But how could he pass up her expertise? He closed his eyes and ignored the blinking red light of his conscience. "Okay. Thanks."

"Sure. Anything for you." A door closed in the background. "All right. The doctor is in. Tell me what's wrong with your film."

"Um—" He squinted toward the mountains, struggling to fit his frustration into words. "Not enough—story, maybe? No through line?"

"Too episodic, you mean?"

"Yeah. That's it. It's like—I have good clips, but they're unrelated."

"Mmhm. I get that." Erica paused. "I think you need a central story. You can keep all the different pieces, but they should connect to some larger overarching idea. Like spokes from a wheel, you know?"

"Yeah..." The thought made sense. And it would definitely strengthen his film. "But where do I get that central story?"

"Good point. Uh—any big projects going on there right now?"

"A fundraiser coming up." He wouldn't mention that it had been his idea.

"No, not human enough." He could almost hear Erica's storyteller gears turning. "How about the people who work there? Does one of them have a cool or interesting story?"

"Well—there's Skyla. She started the center."

"Hmm, so why did she start the center?"

Good question. "You know, I'm not sure."

"Well, then maybe see if there's something there to spotlight."

Creed considered that idea. "Yeah..." No need to mention that Skyla wasn't much of a spotlight woman. Or that he was still wary of her.

"Check on that. And keep your eyes open. Maybe something will happen to point you in the right direction." Erica sighed. "I wish I were there with you."

"Uh, yeah." Somehow the thought of Erica at the center felt like an invasion.

"I feel for you, Creed. You're off the grid up there. I'm all for exploring, but I need to stay within an hour of the nearest TJ Maxx." She laughed. "I can't imagine how miserable it is, being stuck in that boring little mountain town."

Avery's face flashed to his mind. The way her eyes lit up with a rare kind of love when she looked at the land.

Avery would not call the mountains boring.

"Creed? You there?"

"Oh. Yes." Why was he thinking about Avery again? Especially when he was talking to Erica. He shrugged the thought away. "Thanks for your help, Erica."

"Of course."

He hung up and shook his head. His feelings about Erica were a confusing tangle. Almost as confusing as why Avery had come to mind for no reason. He sighed and closed his laptop. He'd work on Erica's suggestions later.

And then maybe at least one thing would make sense.

—— X ——

AVERY SOMETIMES SUSPECTED that there was more to Creed than she thought.

Yes, he was annoying. Yes, he was snarky. Yes, there were a dozen other people she would rather work with. And the day he left for Arizona couldn't possibly come too soon.

But at the same time, he sometimes had these rare flickers of—of *light*. For a moment, she'd see his soul. See something more real than his stubborn sarcasm. Something as fierce and fragile as the flames from her knowing.

And then the next moment he was right back to wearing down her every nerve.

She sighed and laid aside the book she'd been trying to read. Rubbing her eyes, she stared at the cabin walls, again replaying that rising fire. She still had no answers about the vision. Or about anything else regarding Creed. What had happened to bend and break him? And importantly, what was the full story of the fracture between him and Laz?

Mercy whined softly, snuggling her head in Avery's lap. Avery absently rubbed the dog's ears and compared the jagged, unmatched halves she'd been given of the story.

There was Laz's face, on one hand. The weight that pulled at his expression as he spoke of a family disintegrated and a boy gone astray. A voice rough with tears he'd never let fall. *Guess we were too much like each other.*

But then there was Creed's version. Where Laz had held him to a standard he couldn't meet. Punished him for chasing his creativity. Prioritized a career—even a Christian one—over his son. *All he ever cared about was his precious ministry.*

Neither version rang true. Avery couldn't imagine gruff, gold-hearted Laz walking away from *anyone* in distress, let alone his only son. Especially after the way he'd loyally protected her.

But on the other hand, the pain on Creed's face when he'd spoken of the past sliced deep. Hidden within him, some wound still throbbed.

Was it all related to his YouTube work? He'd said Laz didn't understand his videos. Which sort of made sense. Laz was tech-averse; he'd still been taking inventory with pencil and paper when Avery worked for him. But surely he could respect Creed's job, even if he couldn't understand it. From what she could tell, Creed's career was solid. The YouTube channel sounded very successful.

The channel. Hmm. Why had it never occurred to her to look at Creed's YouTube channel?

She didn't have the app on her phone, so she headed to her desk and powered on her computer. She clicked in the search bar and considered. What was the name of his channel? Guys in the Woods, right? No. Guys in the Wild.

She typed in the keywords, and immediately a channel sprang to the forefront of the search results. Guys in the Wild. Complete with a flashy logo and several video playlists, apparently arranged by location. *Arches National Park. Yosemite National Park. Yellowstone National Park.*

She tapped the Yellowstone playlist and picked a random video. The upload date was three months previous. Not that long ago, then.

Dramatic music pounded in over a swirling logo, and then some jock-type guy was standing in front of a rock cliff, his expression supercharged with intensity. "Wassup folks, this is Austin Snyder here, and you're watching Guys in the Wild!"

Was this Creed's boss? Avery studied him as he continued his intro spiel, something about *subscribing for more climbing culture.* Longish blond hair, contained with a fraying bandana, and a muscle shirt that said NO EXCUSES. He kept adjusting his sunglasses while he talked.

"Today we're gonna take an ascent right here at The Ovens." Austin's voice might burst from the hype. "We're gonna be heading straight up this limestone fin. There are five single-pitch routes here, and all of them are accessible for top rope, so to start, we'll review our basic knot protocol—"

The camera followed him as he retrieved some flimsy-looking rope from the ground and demonstrated a figure-eight knot. Then the background switched to a montage of climbing shots at creative angles. Clearly good filming. Was it Creed behind the camera?

"Anyway, it's gonna be pure awesomeness today." The camera cut back to Austin's million-dollar smile. "I'm so stoked for this climb. It's gonna be lit!"

Avery rolled her eyes. This guy was too much. Smoke and mirrors and bluster. Was Creed that way? Two weeks ago, she might have said yes. But now...she'd seen the flickers.

However, she couldn't take another second of this guy's blathering. How many problems must an ego that size create in a work environment? She swiped off the video and scrolled through the rest of the playlist. Austin, Austin, Austin. Creed had said there were a handful of guys who worked on the projects, hadn't he? So why didn't anyone else ever stand in front of the camera?

A thumbnail suddenly caught her eye. Was that Creed in the frame?

Quickly she clicked on the video—from last summer. The powerhouse intro rolled as before, but this time when the logo cleared, it was Creed on the screen. Leaning against a knotted pine tree, the sun playing patterns across his face.

"Hey everyone, I'm Creed Running Wolf, and you're watching Guys in the Wild." His voice was confident but calm, without the firehose feel of Austin's artificially amped delivery. "Today, we're filming from the majestic Yosemite National Park."

The camera shifted, panning around the landscape as Creed kept talking. "This is an amazing park, with eleven hundred square miles of wilderness and over seven hundred fifty climbing routes just in the

Valley. But today, we're going to do more than climb." The camera returned to him, and the kind of smile that Avery hadn't yet seen from him glowed across his face, softening his whole expression. "We're going to find the heartbeat of this incredible place."

Wow. Downright poetic. Avery leaned closer to the screen. The Creed she knew was terse, belligerent, and aloof. But the Creed on this screen looked at peace—at least for the video. Unlike Austin's power stance, he stood with his hands in his pockets, as if simply sharing with a friend. The wind tugged at his hair, its reddish highlights catching in the sun. And the light behind his eyes—well, she would have never guessed that was there.

Shame trickled through her. Just like Laz, hadn't she also criticized Creed's YouTube work? She'd pictured him as some posturing poser like Austin. But this—this looked like more than a job for him. It was a homecoming. Somehow, among the climbing and the cameras, he wasn't just helping others be lost in a video.

He was helping himself be found.

Which meant one very important thing: no matter how faint or fleeting, the flickers she'd seen must be real.

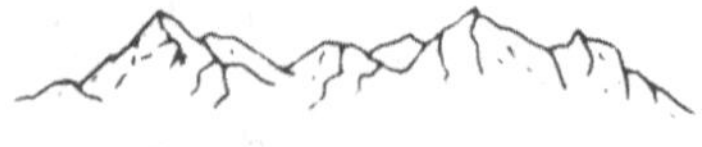

CHAPTER 9

Tuesday night, the terrors snatched away Avery's sleep yet again. She jerked from nightmare to nightmare, panic jolting like an electric shock. The third time, her own screams woke her up. She flew upright and was halfway out of the bed before reality could catch up with her runaway fear. She sank back against the pillow, her heart fluttering in her throat.

Something warm and soft nosed against her side. Mercy, frantically nudging her.

"I-it's ok-kay, girl." Her teeth were chattering with a cold that even Mercy's solid warmth couldn't melt. She flopped over and checked the clock. An hour until she was supposed to get up for work. Yet she was far too scared to go back to sleep.

How much more of this could she endure?

She hugged her knees to her chest and stared at the window. In the first reluctant wash of pre-dawn gray, a sullen mountain rain was pounding the trees. What she wouldn't give for a sleep without dreams. This was like it had been, back in—

No. She intentionally derailed the train of her thoughts. It wasn't like that. Not at all. At least this time, the anxiety left her alone during the day, or mostly. If it needed an outlet at night—well, then she would focus on managing that.

But how? Her thoughts leapfrogged among options and found nowhere to land. Maybe she really should tell Addisyn.

But by the time she was driving to the center—without ever

having been asleep again—she had talked herself out of the idea. Addisyn had enough going on. And really, what did she expect her sister to do? Touch her with a magic wand? No, she needed to try some other remedies first. Maybe magnesium. Another Google scouring had revealed that was sometimes helpful.

She'd no sooner dashed through the rain to the office than Creed waved to her. "Hey, Avery." He sidestepped Mercy's effusive greeting. "Liv said I could film a school group today."

Liv had told him that? They'd already had this conversation. "No." Avery shrugged out of her jacket, shaking off the rain.

"That's it?" His tone had an edge. "Just 'no'?"

"Creed—" Whatever softening she'd felt toward him after seeing him on YouTube was dissolving like summer snow. "I've made this clear. You can't film the class."

He cocked his head, his stance widening into defiance. "But Liv said—"

"Liv shouldn't have said anything." Her frustration was boiling over. "The class is mine, okay? Not hers."

"Okay, okay!" He flung out his hands in exasperation. "Testy this morning, huh?"

Testy. She'd spent endless nights being dragged through the gauntlet of her memories, she had Addisyn's questions breathing down her neck, and she was flailing in her responsibilities at the center. And now Creed wanted to talk about *testy*? She wheeled on him. "Creed, I'm really busy today. I don't have time for this."

He huffed. "Fine, Saint Avery."

The name was a matchstick on the brush pile. "Quit calling me that!"

He blinked. "Wait. What is *wrong* with you today?"

"What's wrong with me?" Her snarled emotions were running away with her faster than her common sense could catch up. "What's wrong with me is that you don't even have the respect to listen to what I tell you about filming my class!"

"Well, can't you see I'm in a bad spot here?" He flung his hands out. "You don't want me to film the birds. You don't want me to film your class. Good grief, what *can* I film?"

"That's not my problem. You're the one who showed up here—"

"Yeah, and you're the one who wanted to ship me off before you even heard what I had to say."

Oh, for crying out loud. "Will you forget about that?"

"Yeah, well, maybe it would have been better if you had run me off." The fire in Creed's eyes was flaming high. "I'm stuck here with no story because you're so hard to work with."

"Oh, *I'm* hard to work with?" Nobody had pushed her buttons this badly since Addisyn was a teenager. "You come in every day with a chip on your shoulder!"

"Well, not for much longer." He crossed his arms, elbows jutting defiantly. "I'm counting the days till I'm out of your hair." He hefted his camera. "I'll just—"

"Avery?"

Oh no, who had witnessed her tirade? Avery spun toward the voice. Liv peered at them apprehensively from the doorway. "There's a call for you in the phone room."

Avery blinked. "Uh—okay. Thanks. I'll get it." She hurried down the hallway, trying to disengage from the encounter with Creed enough to handle whatever this matter was. No doubt a school group trying to book or a rehabber at another facility asking a question. Whoever they were, they were a welcome and timely distraction. She picked up the phone. "Estes Valley Mountain Center, Avery speaking."

"Avery!" Addisyn's voice was almost a wail.

"Ads?" Avery gripped the phone, adrenaline surging. "What's going on?"

"I—I needed you." Addisyn's voice jerked over sobs. "I tried to call your cell phone—"

Her cell phone was still in her truck. "What's wrong? Aren't you at work?"

"I just got a call." Addisyn's sobs intensified. "Avery—Mom is dead."

The words bounced off her spirit like hailstones on the center roof. "What?"

"Mom is dead." Addisyn's words sounded as if they were being ripped from her. "S-somebody called me from New York and left me a voicemail."

A voicemail. Addisyn had found out this news from a *voicemail*. Avery closed her eyes. "Who?"

"I don't know." Addisyn was still sobbing. "The voicemail—I don't know, Avery, I couldn't listen—"

"Okay." A numbness was spreading through her, keeping the news from hitting her with its full force. Which was good, because right now, she had to help Addisyn. "Tell me the number, and I'll get in touch with whoever it was, find out what—"

"I—I—" Addisyn was drowning in sobs. "I can't handle this, Avery. I was already stressed, and this is—I don't know what to do, and—"

"Ads, listen, it's okay." She clenched her free hand until her fingernails dug into her palm. "Where are you right now?"

"I'm in my office. At work."

"Where's Darius?"

"He's doing auditions in Highlands Ranch today." Addisyn's breath caught on a sob. "I tried to call him. I can't get him. He won't look at his phone till he's done."

"Okay. I'm coming." The reply was the only thing that felt right. If only she could will herself across the distance to Denver. "Just hold on, okay?"

"You can't drive all the way down here." But there was an unmistakable hope behind Addisyn's feeble protest.

"I can, and I will." Avery glanced at the clock. If she left now, she could be there by lunchtime. "Take some deep breaths. I'm on my way."

She hung up and spun for the doorway—and nearly collided with Creed.

"Avery? Is everything okay?"

She stared at him, his question still belonging to the unreal world beyond her numbness. "I—"

"Hey." He stepped toward her, concern written across his face. "What's wrong?"

"My mom is dead. My sister called me." Addisyn was alone. Again, Mom had left Ads abandoned, crying and hurting and—

"I've got to get to Denver." She raced down the hallway, slapped open the center door, and sprinted into the rain. Her truck was parked next to Creed's Jeep.

"Wait! Avery! Wait!"

Creed's voice, and in a second, he was running next to her. "Your sister? She's in Denver?"

"Yes. At work." She skidded to a stop at her truck and fumbled in her pocket for her car keys. The shaking had set in, her fingers barely able to close on the metal.

"Hey." Creed grabbed her arm. "You can't drive all the way to Denver. Not in this weather, and not—" His expression softened in understanding. "Not like this."

He could tell, then. Could read how she was teetering on the very border of panic. "I have to—"

"Nope." He unlocked his Jeep, blinking at her in the dripping rain. "I'm driving you to Denver."

She could never let him do that. "I'll be f-fine." Okay, the stammering didn't help her case. "M-my truck—"

"I'll bring you back for it. After we make sure your sister's okay."

His words were a single flicker of hope. Yes. Addisyn would be okay, and the sun would come out, and when they came back for Avery's truck, it would be a distant memory that they'd stood here in the sullen rain.

"So come on, Avery." Creed opened the passenger door. "Let's go."

ONCE, on an emergency run to pick up a misdirected package of inventory for Laz's store, Avery had made the drive to Denver in just under an hour and fifteen minutes. Otherwise, she kept below the speed limit, respecting the difficult roads.

Creed's driving style was the reverse negative of hers. He flew down 36 as if blind to the alarming curves and had them zooming down the interstate within forty minutes. Avery glanced at his speedometer as they came past Mead High School. 83.

She was pretty sure that was almost ten miles over the speed limit, but with Addisyn waiting, she wouldn't point that out. She'd only heard from her sister once since they'd left—a brief text that she'd talked to Darius, and he was on his way.

"You're still shivering." Creed glanced at her, concern knit between his eyes.

"I'm okay." She'd angled the heat vents toward her, but the iceberg inside her refused to melt.

"Here." Keeping his eyes on the road, he stretched an arm into the backseat and yanked a red anorak over the console. "See if this helps."

The gentle comfort of the worn fabric eased a little of the tightness within her. "Oh. Thank you." A thought struck her. "Are you too hot in here? I know I turned the heat up—"

"Not a bit." He waved his hand as if ushering away the idea. The skyline of Denver was piecing itself together in front of them. "Can you help me find this skating center?"

"Yes." She took a deep breath, overriding the panic with her executive mode. *Find it. Fix it.*

Denver Ice Center was one of the city's biggest athletic facilities, with a complex ten times the size of the national park visitor center. Creed whipped into a parking space while Avery called Darius, but the phone went straight to voicemail.

"He's probably with your sister." Creed turned off the car and pointed at the front door. "Surely someone in there will be able to tell us where to go."

"Okay." Avery was three steps ahead of Creed as they burst through the front door, pausing only to tap a quick text to Darius.

The reception area was ensconced by dim statement lighting and a marble floor on which their wet boots squeaked. The receptionist studied Avery over her glasses. "Name?"

"Avery Miles."

The woman eyed her suspiciously. "Are you here as a client?"

The sudden consciousness of her rain-flattened hair and muddy work boots and Creed's oversized anorak flamed heat to her face. "No. I'm here to see my sister. She's a coach. Addisyn Payne."

"Payne…" The woman turned to her computer, scrolling a roster of names with maddening slowness. "Her office is in Room 317. In the meantime, you'll have to wait for someone to take you there."

"I can't—"

Creed stepped forward suddenly. "Ma'am, can Avery go on to the office by herself? Her sister needs her right now."

Avery flashed him a grateful glance, but the woman scowled. "That's not our procedure here. Someone will have to—"

"Avery! Avery, over here!"

Darius was waving from an adjoining hallway. "There's my brother-in-law." Avery spun but hesitated, glancing at Creed.

He waved her on. "You go. I'll wait in here."

She jogged toward Darius, refusing to look back to see how the stuffy woman was taking her rebellion. "Darius! I texted you and called—"

He grabbed her in the solid hug of a brother. "I know. I just now looked at my phone." He glanced toward Creed with a question in his eyes.

"That's my coworker." The easiest way to explain Creed at the moment. "Darius, is she okay?"

"She's not saying much. I think this just overwhelmed her." His face was taut as he led her toward a wood-paneled elevator. "She did tell me she was worried about you driving on the wet roads."

Well, that sounded like Addisyn. "Creed brought me in his Jeep."

Darius looked impressed. "Nice guy to drive you all this way."

Avery blinked as she followed Darius out of the elevator. She'd been so consumed with reaching Addisyn that she hadn't stopped to consider what a selfless thing Creed had done. She'd ditched him in the waiting room for goodness knew how long without even thanking him. And that was after nearly taking his head off.

Maybe he'd strand her and drive back to Estes Park. Except, somehow, she knew he wouldn't.

"Here we are." Darius stepped aside, ushering Avery into an office. Addisyn was slumped on a bench by the window, her head heavy in her hands.

"Ads!" Avery ran for the bench, pulling her little sister into her arms, holding her the way she always had. "Hey. I'm here."

"I—thank you for—" Addisyn's voice cracked, and she swiped at her face. Darius reached for the box of Kleenex on the desk. "I'm sorry."

"Don't be sorry." The pain in Addisyn's face made her own heart hurt. She rubbed soothing circles on Addisyn's back. "I'm your big sister, Ads. It's my job."

"Yeah, but you were at work, and—" Addisyn glanced at her and blinked. "What are you wearing? Whose coat is that?"

"Uh—Creed drove me here. He let me borrow his jacket."

"Creed brought you down here?"

"Yes." That wasn't important right now. "Okay, so—do you know who called you about Mom? Was it an attorney, or—"

Addisyn shook her head, her eyes roaming the opposite wall vacantly. "A friend of Mom's, I think." Her troubled gaze turned to Avery. "I've got to call her back."

She sounded scared and lost, once more like the little girl who still needed her big sister. Avery shook her head. "Give me your phone."

She stepped into the hallway to make the call. Addisyn didn't need to watch her process in real time whatever she found out.

"Addisyn?" A woman's soft voice on the phone. "Addisyn Payne?"

Avery cleared her throat. "This is Addisyn's sister, Avery."

"Avery, yes." The woman's voice tinged with recognition. "This is Lucy Stone. I—I was your mother's friend."

"Oh! Yes. Of course." She remembered the woman now—a vague shadow from her early childhood. But Mom and Lucy had drifted apart even before Mom left. "Addisyn told me—why you called."

"Yes." Lucy sighed. "I'm so very sorry."

Sorry. Such a weak word. Avery stared at an abstract-art painting across the hall. Something in shades of gray. "When did she die?"

"May fifth."

Around the time she'd started having the night terrors. She shoved the notion away. They couldn't be connected. "Why?"

"She had liver cancer. Toward the end, she—well, she didn't want treatment anymore."

So she'd died like she'd lived. Giving up.

Lucy was still talking. "We reconnected in recent years. I took her to and from appointments, that sort of thing. She'd asked me to make the arrangements, so there was a lot to take care of, and then I started trying to find you girls. I couldn't find any contact information for you, but I did locate your sister, through her skating career, of course. I hope it was all right to—"

The numbness from earlier was creeping back in, muffling Lucy's words. Avery shook her head, fighting off the fog. "Where is she?"

"I'm sorry?"

"Where is Mom—buried?"

"Greensdown Cemetery." She hesitated. "She asked for that."

The cemetery wasn't five blocks from their old house in Syracuse. "Okay."

"Now—" Uncertainty hedged Lucy's tone. "I have some of her things. I boxed up some of what I thought was sentimental. I wondered—well, I wondered if you and Addisyn wanted it."

Her mom's things? What value was there in the leftover remnants of her mother's unlived life? "I—well—"

"It's too much to ship, I'm afraid. You'd need to come and get it. And there are some legal arrangements in regards to her house, the estate."

Go to Syracuse. Walk back into the trap she'd escaped. Avery's hand trembled on the phone. "I—I'll need to see. I'll let you know."

"I'm really sorry to spring this on you."

"It's okay." The reply came automatically. Well-learned over a lifetime of having to handle what others left undone.

"I mean, I know things were—well—" Lucy sighed. "I'm just sorry. I wish things had been different."

Different. That her mom had never rotted her liver with pills. That she'd had a will to live. That she'd been surrounded at the end with her daughters instead of a friend who barely knew her.

Different. Yeah. A whole lot of things could have been different.

The conversation stalled to an uncomfortable end, with Lucy giving Avery her phone number and Avery promising to let her know about Syracuse. When the call ended, she blew out a breath and swiped her hands on her pants. Okay. Now she had to face Addisyn again.

El Shaddai, please, please, give me words. Avery clung to the prayer as she stepped back into the office. "All right." She pressed her hands together. "She passed away on May fifth."

Darius opened his mouth, then closed it again.

Addisyn's lip trembled. "How?"

"Cancer." Avery shoved her hands into her pockets and began pacing the office. Every answer felt as if she were stabbing her sister. Suddenly she was right back in the space she'd inhabited after their mom left. Forced to wrap harsh realities in words. Why did Mom always put her in this place?

"Will there—" Addisyn stopped. "I guess there's already been a funeral—"

Addisyn was worried about having missed their mom's funeral? Every day of the woman's life had been her funeral. "Yes. She's buried in Greensdown Cemetery."

"I remember it. The one with the big iron gates? By the library, right?"

"Mmhm."

Addisyn was quiet. Avery waited. She'd give her sister however much time she needed.

"What about—" Addisyn stopped. Breathed. Swallowed. "What about her things?"

None of these questions were easy, but this was the stickiest one. "Well, that's, um—" She couldn't lie. Not again. "Her friend asked us to come to Syracuse, pick up some things."

"Okay." Addisyn finally sounded the tiniest bit hopeful. "When will—I mean, we're going to do it, right?"

"Ads—" Pacing in the small room was making her dizzy. "We'll talk about it, okay? You have the baby—and I'm crazy busy right now, getting ready for the fundraiser. I couldn't possibly leave until after that's over." That at least was truth, not excuse. "After that—" She reached for the diplomatic answer she'd always used in Addisyn's teenage years—"we'll see."

Addisyn stared down at her feet, her expression a closed door. Behind that closed door, she was thinking something. And Avery didn't want to know what it was.

Darius cleared his throat. "Do you—need anything—"

Addisyn rubbed a hand over her forehead. "Something to drink."

"Oh, yeah. Of course." He stood so quickly he almost tripped over his feet. Probably desperate to escape the ominously quiet room. "Avery, are you going to stay here?"

Avery glanced at Addisyn again. "Well—I kind of need to say something to Creed—"

"Go on." Addisyn's voice was flat. "I'll be fine."

Avery bit her lip. "I can stay till Darius gets back and then—"

"Avery, *go*." The edge to her sister's voice sliced Avery's words off at the roots. "I want to be by myself."

Avery didn't argue. In the hall, Darius slid her an empathetic glance. "She doesn't mean it, Avery."

"I know." Even as a teen, Addisyn had used anger to avoid sorrow. "She's afraid and upset."

"I can tell." He kept his eyes on the tile floor. "She's, um, been that way for a while."

There was some cry for help in his voice. Avery tilted her head. "You mean—"

"She's just not herself." He groaned and turned to face Avery. "I mean, she's really emotional, and she always seems sad. Or stressed, maybe. And she gets mad at me, like, all the time."

Avery bit her lip. "Well, I mean, pregnancy—"

"No, I know, hormones and all that." He shrugged helplessly. "At first I thought that was the problem. Not that I told her that, you know."

"Right." Smart move there.

"But it's not getting any better, and she seems really—distant." He grimaced uneasily as they got in the elevator. "She talks about her mom a lot. I mean, your mom too, of course."

There it was. Avery closed her eyes and leaned against the elevator wall. The weight of all of this might crush her into the dirt. If only she could just—

"Avery?"

Grudgingly, she opened her eyes. "Yes?"

"Hey, I don't want to get in the middle of—" Darius waved his hand vaguely—"whatever's going on between the two of you, but— Addisyn says she's been asking you to tell her about your mom, or something like that."

The elevator pinged. Avery clenched her fists as they stepped off. "I've already told her everything I think would help." Diplomatic answer.

"I know, but—"

"Darius." Avery gentled her voice, facing the man who'd become her brother. She couldn't be angry with him, not when his heart was always for Addisyn. "I understand what you're saying. I really do. But when Mom left—Addisyn was younger, and so there are things she can't—" *Can't understand. Can't remember. Can't ever know.* "I just don't think it would actually help her."

"Okay." He still looked uncertain. "I respect what you're saying, Avery. But maybe not knowing is making her feel—"

"There's Creed." Avery hurried across the waiting room, dodging Darius's words.

Creed was sitting patiently on the slick leather couch, thumbing a magazine. He looked up as Avery approached. "How is she?"

"She's—" Avery bit her lip. "She's upset. But she'll be okay."

He nodded seriously, watching her with that same keen gaze he used to look at the world through the camera. Today, something about that unbalanced her. "Could you, um—" Shame burrowed through her. She was asking a lot of Creed, especially given the tension that tangled between them. "Can you please—wait just a few more minutes—it won't take much—"

"Hey, take all the time you need. I'm in no hurry." He waved the magazine. "I've got entertainment."

Avery studied the cover. "*Skating* magazine? That's your entertainment?"

"It's all they had. And I now know the difference between a Salchow and an lutz." His smile flashed suddenly. "That might save my life on a rock face one day."

Despite all the tension of the day, Avery's laugh escaped. "Well. I guess so."

Darius didn't bring up the subject of Mom again as they headed back up the elevator and entered Addisyn's office. "Here's your drink. Snapple."

Addisyn's face eased slightly. "Mango?"

"Now is there any other kind?" Avery waited for her sister to laugh, but instead Addisyn just gave a lukewarm side smile.

Thick silence descended, a physical force walling them in. Addisyn drank the Snapple, then stared out the window at the Denver skyline. "I really want to go."

Avery blinked. "Go—"

"To Syracuse. To get Mom's things."

So they were doing this again. "I know. I understand what you're feeling, but—"

"You don't get it, do you?" There was a new undercurrent in Addisyn's voice. A new tone stronger and sharper than her brokenness. "Our mom is dead, Avery! And you don't care."

Avery forced herself to wait for a deep breath. "Addisyn, that's not—"

"And maybe you don't care, because you can cut yourself loose from everything that happened and be just fine." Addisyn's voice warped under the weight of emotion. "You don't know what it's like to—to never be free from this!"

Never be free. A scarlet rush of anger swept through Avery like wildfire. "You're right. I don't understand." Sixteen years flashed before her eyes, and again she saw those taunting taillights disappearing down their road. "I don't understand why we're supposed to mourn for a woman who threw us away like garbage, who never cared what happened, who—" Her breath caught. She couldn't let the emotions make her say too much. "We'd lost her already, Ads." She relaxed her clenched hands, swiped her sweaty palms on her pants. "We had nothing left to lose now."

"Yes, we did!" Addisyn's voice was a cry. "I always hoped, you know? That Mom would—would come back." Her voice wobbled, balancing on the broken edge of pain. "And now—it will never be okay. She's never coming back."

Never coming back. Yet if Mom had reentered their lives, everything would have fractured in even more devastating ways. "What do you want me to do, Addisyn?" Her voice snapped razor-sharp. "I can't fix this, okay?"

"But you could at least try to listen to me! I've been telling you that we need closure, that we need—"

"I am listening to you. I've been listening to you ask about Mom for a month."

"Then what do I have to say to convince you of how important this is?"

Darius leaned forward tentatively. "Girls, let's—"

"Darius, no." Avery didn't like having this fight in front of her brother-in-law, but Addisyn had left her no choice. "Look, Addisyn, I get that you feel this is important. But it's a really, really bad idea." What could she say to drive the truth into Addisyn's stubborn head? "We're long past this. I don't see how revisiting someplace that—"

"Avery, will you stop saying that? That we're *past this*?" Addisyn pinched the words with air quotes. "We're not. Okay? We'll *never* be past this. This is part of our story. Until we face this, it's just going to keep wedging between us and hurting us, and we won't be able to get away from it." Addisyn's eyes snapped sparks. "So, fine. I don't have to have your help. I can go there on my own."

"No!" The word sprang out before Avery could realize how desperate it sounded. "Addisyn—you can't do that."

"I can." Addisyn jerked her chin up. "If you don't care that it's hurting me, then—"

"Really, Addisyn? You think I don't care? Do you have any idea how hard I've worked to make sure you were okay?" Anger and hurt and frustration tangled all around Avery's fear. "Don't you remember what it was like after Mom left? I was the one who held you together, Addisyn! When I took you away from home, when I made sure you were protected, when I—" Her anger was outrunning her words. "Good grief, why did I miss a day of work and come down to Denver if I *don't care*? I've answered all your questions and told you everything I think will help you. What more do you want from me?"

"I want Mom to be back!" The wail finally shattered Addisyn's fight. She caved over her knees, tears crawling broken tracks down her cheeks. "I hate this! I hate all of this!"

Something was ripping open in Avery. Something wild and raw, something that wanted to scream or kick or sprint out of the building and never stop running. Why was this happening? Why? All she'd given up, all she'd sacrificed, all she'd done and kept and fulfilled and lost to keep Addisyn safe.

And their mom was hurting her all over again.

She had to get away from the whole mess. From all the things she couldn't change and all the things she had tried to. Her legs were rubbery as she stumbled out of the office.

"Avery!" Darius hurried into the hall after her. "You're not—are you leaving?"

"I think it's best, Darius." She shouldered her bag. Her hands were already shaking. She had limited time before the emotions inside her split at the seams. "Go help Addisyn. Please."

He stared at her blankly. "But—"

"Darius, I can't do anything else for her." The tears were stinging, hot and hard. "I'll be back after—when she's ready. Tell her to call me if she needs me."

And with that, she began to run.

AVERY BURST down the corridor with no real destination except *away*. Tightness squeezed her lungs, cutting off her precious air. Her teeth clacked as the shivering began, the shaking that jerked its way through her whole body. The first sign that the poison of the panic was entering her bloodstream. *El Shaddai. Not now. Not here.*

Endless corridors swam around her. Walls tilting toward her. Doors like bared teeth. She stumbled to a pause at the end of a hallway. Wait. None of this was familiar. Which way was the elevator?

She was caught, caged, and the panic doubled.

"Excuse me, are you all right?"

She jerked at the sound of the voice. A worker, watching her through worried eyes. "Can I help you?"

"Th-the exit." She forced the words past her chattering teeth.

"The elevator is at the end of this hall."

No, not the elevator. She couldn't be trapped in that metal box right now. "What about the stairs?"

"Just around the corner." The lady pointed to the left. "Are you sure you—"

"Th-thank you." She turned and all but sprinted for the stairs. The panic chased her down three flights of cold metal, then propelled her into the reception room. Where was Creed?

"Avery!"

She gasped and spun. Creed was behind her, concern written on his face. "How's your sister?"

"I need to go back home." Nausea clenched her stomach. *No. No. Not again...*

"Back to Estes?" He blinked. "Is your sister okay?"

Her mind was blanking, anxiety beginning to throb inside her chest. "I don't know."

"You don't know?" He hurried closer, the concern carving deeper on his face. He was asking her something else, maybe something about Addisyn, but the sounds were bouncing off the surface of her brain.

"I don't know." She whispered the words this time. She was tired. Too tired of questions without answers, of faking her way through uncharted terrain. Addisyn was hurting, and Creed was waiting, and it was all on her, and it was all too much, and—

The world went fuzzy, swirling before her eyes as new scenes took shape. Addisyn, clinging to her in the middle of the chaos as their mom's taillights blinked down the road. A sudden pain knifed through her chest.

"Avery!"

Laz's voice. Her truck had slid off the road. Laz would help her. No, not Laz. Creed.

But the roaring in her ears swallowed his voice, and then the tunnel opened, sucking her inside, vanishing the light to a pinprick.

"Avery—"

The pressure in her chest swelled, forcing away all her air. She'd let everyone down. Despair clawed at her throat. Everything she'd tried to do had never been enough. She'd worked so hard, and here and now she'd failed again.

"Avery!" The voice was louder now, painfully close to her ear. "What's wrong?"

Air rushed in, a sudden merciful breath. She gasped, nearly choking as her lungs expanded. Warm hands gripped her shoulders, holding her to reality. And then her vision was coming back, fuzzy and dreamlike, and a face was peering into hers. Creed's face. And his hands on her shoulders.

Heat flooded her face. She jerked back, but his hands kept her steady. She was sitting on the marble floor, against the wall in the hallway. How had she ended up there?

"Avery?" The urgency in his eyes nearly matched what she'd felt.

She pressed a palm to her throbbing head. Slowly her mind was clearing, thoughts coalescing around the shadow of shame. Creed already thought she was stupid. Now he would know that she was weak. That in a moment of crisis, she'd folded completely. He'd taunt her or sneer at her or—

"Can you hear me? Deep breaths." His thumbs rubbed reassurance on her shoulders. "That's better."

This was still unreal, wasn't it? Just part of the daze of the panic itself? Because Creed's eyes could not be crinkled with compassion. Certainly not with understanding.

"Are you okay to sit here?" His voice was more gentle than she'd ever heard it.

She nodded. She was still shaking, her stomach still twisting with sickness, but the vortex had passed. "Y-yes. I—I need—" Her hands were trembling in her lap. She folded them together, rubbed her fingers.

"To go home? I know." Suddenly, surprisingly, Creed wrapped his hands around hers, rubbing away the freeze in her fingers and somehow bringing new strength. "Just breathe, okay? Take a few deep breaths, and we'll drive back to Estes."

She cautiously reached for a breath, her lungs expanding. Some of the tightness eased. She blew out the air in a long exhale.

"There. That's better." His voice was still soothing. He released her hands and stood. "Do you need anything?"

Her mouth was dry, her tongue like glue. "D-do you have water?"

"Not in the Jeep." He glanced toward the vending machine. "I'll get you a bottle. Wait right here."

He was gone before her fuzzy mind could protest. She slumped against the wall and focused on deep breathing until he came back with an ice-cold bottle of water. "Thank you." She tried to unscrew the cap, but her hands were still shaking. Drat it all.

"Here." Creed took the bottle from her and opened it, then handed it back.

When had he been this thoughtful? "Thanks."

"No problem." He shrugged one shoulder and held out his hand. "Ready to go?"

"Yes." She let him help her to her feet, then followed him outside on rubbery legs. The rain had stopped, the light washing through the dissolving clouds.

Silence cocooned them on the drive northward. Creed asked no questions, so Avery offered no answers. Instead, she closed her eyes, watching the reddish patterns of the slanting light play across the insides of her eyelids. Even the sun couldn't thaw the cold in her bones.

How long had it been since she'd had a full-blown panic attack, the way she had today?

The anxiety had hovered over her like a vulture's shadow for years. But once she'd come to the mountains, she'd outrun that darkness. She'd no longer awakened with the cold fear crawling down her back. No longer watched over her shoulder for the next attack. No longer found herself sometimes in the stranglehold of everything she'd run from.

So why now? The night terrors...the moments of freezing up at work...none of this had happened since—well, since that awful night. And now the panic attack...

Please, not again.

Was it because now everything she'd left on the other side of the Front Range was slinking back into her sanctuary? The secret. The memories. Addisyn's pain. Their mom...

A yawn stretched, and she sank more deeply into the seat. She'd figure it out later. But for now, the panic had wrung her out.

"Avery?"

She blinked back to alertness. All the shadows were slanted differently, and her neck hurt. Creed gestured at the road ahead. "We're almost back to Estes."

She'd fallen asleep? Could she embarrass herself any further? "I— oh. I'm sorry."

"Hey, nothing to apologize for." He glanced at her cautiously. "Are you—feeling better? Than earlier?"

Earlier. Heat squirmed up her shoulders. What must he think about her now? "Yes. I sometimes—" Her embarrassment slipped out as a breathy laugh. "I sometimes get nervous when things are really stacking up." *Nervous.* What an understatement. "Well, I mean, not nervous exactly, but—" Why was she telling him all this?

But his expression held the pure richness of understanding. "Yeah, I get it. I used to be anxious when I was climbing."

"Really?" She couldn't imagine his colorful cockiness washed out by panic.

"Yeah." He nodded. "Feels like the fear will grab you if you move."

He understood. Who would have thought? "Yeah." She rotated her stiff neck. "Actually I don't do it very often, not anymore. Not like I did when I was younger."

"No surprise it happened today." There was no judgment in his tone. "Getting news like that has to be rough."

"Yes, well—" She sucked in a breath. This required an explanation. "I was more upset over Addisyn. My—our mother left us when I was thirteen."

His face shadowed. "Gee. That's rough."

She smoothed the front of her pants, needing her hands to be busy. "Yeah."

"What about your dad?"

"He was very abusive." She shrugged, trying to create distance from the topic. "I left home when I graduated high school and took Addisyn with me. Got her out of that environment."

Creed stared at her. "That's a big responsibility."

"Yes." So big that her soul still felt the weight of it in ways she'd never heal from. "We got past it."

"Hard to get past something like that."

"Well...yes. That's part of—" How much should she say? "She's having trouble dealing with Mom's death. She—well, she wants to revisit a lot of that."

He nodded slowly. "I see."

"I don't know why she wants to bring it all back up. We got past it, and—it's done."

"I understand." His voice was slow, his words like careful movements up a cliff. "But remember what I said the other day? About the past always staying with you?"

"Yes." She still didn't really understand his words. "But—"

"I mean, well, it's sort of like these mountains." He waved a hand toward the horizon. "All these rock layers—they're built on each other, you know? All the growth and erosion, the good years and bad —they're undergirding everything today." He looked at Avery.

"Maybe that's what your sister is talking about. Maybe she needs to make peace with those layers underneath."

The idea sank into her. "Well...I never thought of it that way."

"Trust me." His laugh was sad. "The past never goes away. You just build on it and try to—I don't know, make peace with it somehow. But if you ignore the questions, they rattle around in your chest for years."

He was talking about more than her now. Avery cocked her head at him. "And you? You've made peace with it?"

"Touché." His grin was guilty. "I'll get there. One of these days."

The center was in front of them. Avery picked at a loose thread on her pants. Her hands were still cold, but they'd long since quit shaking.

Creed parked the Jeep next to her truck. Had it really been only that morning they'd stood there together? "I'm glad you feel better."

She nodded and climbed out of the Jeep. Three steps away, she paused. "Creed?"

"Yeah?"

"Thank you." Heat blazed in her face again, but she shoved forward. "For knowing what to do. At the skating center, and—" She was stumbling over her words, her thinking still tangled. She held up the water bottle. "Just—thank you."

A small smile tugged up one corner of his lip. "You're welcome. Glad I was there."

For the first time, she was too.

CHAPTER 10

As soon as Avery stepped back inside the office from the Denver drive, Skyla hurried to her, skirt swishing, compassion warm within her gaze. "Avery, I am so very sorry."

"Thank you." Now that the panic had ebbed away, she just felt... empty.

"How is your sister?"

"She's—" *Devastated. Hurt. In pain again.* Avery shrugged. "Working through it, I think."

"And you?" Skyla's gaze deepened.

"I'm okay." She had to be.

Skyla tilted her head. "You need not always be strong."

"Well—" She'd lost nothing except a woman who had already dwindled to a ghost in her mind. "There's no sorrow in it, really. Not anymore."

Skyla's mouth dipped. Her hand landed gently on Avery's shoulder. "There is sorrow in the lack of sorrow. And there is always more need of grief for what has never been. Please, go home and take some time."

Skyla's sympathy was inviting her back out of the emptiness, back into a world where she would have real feelings about this event. And that was something she couldn't afford. "I'm okay." She snapped out the words a little too quickly.

"Avery—" Skyla's penetrating gaze was the same one she used for assessing the injuries on a broken bird. "Much harm will come of running."

Avery ducked from beneath Skyla's hand and headed for the back hallway. "I need to take care of the birds." Feelings could come later. Or not at all.

"The place of healing is the intersection of pain and promise. You must learn to stand there."

A door banged outside. Liv probably, visiting the mews for the afternoon. "I know. But I need to do this right now. And really, I'm fine."

Fine was what she told herself as she hosed down the mews. *Fine* was how she answered Creed's question at the end of the day. *Fine* was what kept her cold company all the way home. But even inside her gate, her mountain stronghold felt strangely invaded. As though her safety had shattered.

She turned the truck off and leaned on the steering wheel, staring at her shadowed house. She really needed to leave some lights on when she was getting back this late. She glanced down and blinked. She was still wearing Creed's anorak. Oh, well. She could return it to him tomorrow.

Beside her, Mercy whined, a question mark.

"I know, girl. Don't worry. We're home now." She rubbed the strain from her eyes. Exhaustion gnawed inside her bones, hollowing her.

The evening air was chilly for the time of year. Avery shivered as she stepped inside the cabin, locking the door behind her with an urgency she didn't often feel. The silence was heavy, prickly. She flicked the light switch in the living room, the kitchen. Not enough. She moved through the house, Mercy at her side, flipping lights as she went. The bathroom. The laundry. Even the storage room on the second story.

She turned the light on in her bedroom last, then closed the door and huddled on the rug. Mercy pressed against her, and she stroked the dog's head.

What a day.

She hugged her knees and tucked her chin inside the anorak's collar. A strangely friendly aroma hovered around the worn fabric—pine trees, and coffee, and some subtle spicy scent that eased the tension in her chest. She fingered the softness of the fraying hem. Creed had been—well, he'd been amazing today. He'd driven almost four hours, given up his entire day, just to help her. All without pointed fingers or accusing questions or snarky defensiveness. Instead, his gentle strength had reminded her of the way he'd been in that video. The light that had been behind his eyes.

She needed to thank him, somehow, for what he'd done. And—she bit her lip—apologize.

She leaned into Mercy's reassuring warmth. Finally, her mind was slowing down. Her day so far had been an obstacle course of tasks to surmount. Get to Denver, help Addisyn, get back to Estes, finish at the center. But now—now she could finally open the drawer of her heart. Stare at the feelings folded inside. Wonder what it would take to sort through them.

And the one nearest the surface was...relief.

Hadn't she always worried, a little, that one day Mom would come back to haunt their lives? Show up on one of their doorsteps, upend the fragile peace they'd worked for? But now—she was dead. She'd never come back, as Addisyn had said. And the same truth that had flattened her sister's hopes brought Avery the release of a deep breath. Because now Mom could never hurt either of them again.

Guilt tunneled through her. She shouldn't feel that way. What kind of horrible daughter felt the death of her mom as a lifting of a weight?

There is sorrow in the lack of sorrow.

Skyla's words. She'd already known, hadn't she, what Avery would feel? Avery pressed her lips together. For a moment she considered telling the older woman everything. All the confusion of the event, all that she'd feared and wished and—

Ridiculous. What was the point of that? Wasting Skyla's time with burdens that didn't belong on her boss's shoulders? Mourning uselessly over what could never be changed? No, this was her load to bear. The way it always had been. Especially since that cold winter evening.

Not the day Mom left...but the day she came back.

Avery closed her eyes, and once more the memory lived around her. She was seventeen years old, about to graduate high school with honors. She'd just dropped Addisyn off for a sleepover at a friend's house. Their dad was away on one of his unfortunately infrequent business trips, leaving her mercifully alone at home.

She'd been walking up their sidewalk in the purple evening air when she'd seen an unfamiliar car parked by their mailbox, the headlights off. Fear had choked her, and she'd reached for her cell phone, quickly back-stepping down the sidewalk. There had been a string of break-ins not too long ago. Better safe than—

"Addisyn?"

The voice was a knife, stabbing right out of the past, and Avery froze. *"No."* Her voice sounded small, lost in the night. *"It's Avery."*

"Avery." There was more certainty now. And then Mom stepped from behind the car.

Rejection rose within Avery, and she took a step back. *"Mom."*

"It's me." Mom's smile was uneasy. She looked even worse than she had before she left. Hair faded and limp, face more deeply etched. Knobby collarbones stretched the skin above her tank top. *"Look at you. You've grown up."*

Yes, well, that happened when you left your teenager alone for four years.

"How old are you now? Sixteen, right?"

"Seventeen." Avery clenched her teeth so tightly her jaw throbbed. *"Mom, what are you doing?"*

Mom blinked. *"You're not happy to see me?"*

Did the woman think Avery would leap into her arms? Fury flashed hot within her. *"You left us, Mom. Forgive me if I'm not throwing a party now."*

Mom raised her chin, defiance seeping into her sunken eyes. *"Fine. I know how you feel about me. But I'm not here for you."*

Even through her anger, the words stung more than she would have expected. *"If you're here to see Dad, he's not—"*

"No." Mom glanced toward the house, scanning the second-floor windows. *"I'm here for your sister."*

With those words, the painful encounter morphed into a nightmare. *"What?"*

"I'm here for your sister." Mom stepped closer, just enough that Avery could catch the stale vinegary odor that clung to her clothes. *"Look, I know I did wrong leaving you girls the way I did. But I've come to make it right. I finally got a place. I'm taking your sister there."*

Mom couldn't do that. Could she? *"Mom, no. You're in no position to take care of Addisyn."*

"I am." Pleading underlined her words. *"I told you, I got my own place. I quit most of my meds too. I'm getting it all figured out. So, I thought she could stay with me. For a little while, at least."*

For a little while? The casualness of the words blazed a wildfire inside Avery. How could their mom upend Addisyn's whole life on a fleeting whim? And what would happen when her welcome wore out?

"No, Mom." She crossed her arms. A barred gate between her sister and the woman who'd never been a mom. *"Not unless I come too."*

Mom huffed out a laugh. *"Are you serious?"*

"Yes. I don't know. Maybe." The sudden sorrow pierced the callouses she'd formed over the pain. *"Why not, Mom? Why have you never wanted me? Why—"*

"Oh, Avery, shut up!" Mom clapped her hands to her head, her fragile façade slipping. *"Don't you ever give me any credit? Can't you see I'm doing the best I can? I'm trying. I'm trying."*

Her mom's slogan. Guilt trip and lame excuse and insincere apology all rolled into one sickening sentence.

"Don't you want her away from here?" Mom swept a hand at the house. *"I know what Ulys is like. I know how he treats you girls, how he—"*

If her mom knew things were so bad, why had she left them? *"I'm watching out for her here. Okay?"* A surge of protectiveness gave Avery the strength to step forward. *"I'm not letting you sweep in and take her back to wherever you came from."*

"You don't get to say!" Mom jabbed a bony finger at her chest.

"Your dad won't care. And you know your sister will want to go with me."

The truth struck like a spear, and suddenly, the whole idea solidified into a dire threat. *"Addisyn doesn't need any more turmoil, Mom."*

"She wants to be with her momma." Mom squinted, her face hard to see in the streetlight. *"I do care about you girls, you know."*

Care about. A slippery substitute for love. Avery stepped forward. *"If you cared anything about either of us, you would have taken us with you."* She was taller than her mom by a couple inches now. *"Do you have any idea how upset Addisyn was when you left? How devastated she was? How long she cried all night with nightmares and had to sleep in my bed, holding my hand, because she was terrified I would leave too? I'm not going to let you hurt her again when—"*

"Please!" The word broke open, raw. *"I never said I didn't make mistakes. You just don't know how hard it was. How tough it was to—"*

"Mom, spare me." Avery gritted the words out. She'd heard the woman's self-pity spiel all her life. *"You need to leave."*

"I've gotta see Addisyn."

"She's not here. She's spending the night away. And I don't think it would be a good idea for you to see her anyway." Avery took a step closer. *"Trust me. The most loving thing you can do for Addisyn is leave her alone."*

"You don't understand." Something like steel hardened in her mom's voice now. *"You don't know the truth."*

The words slithered like a cold snake up Avery's back. *"What do you mean?"*

Enough. Avery opened her eyes and drew in a deep breath, unwilling to follow the memory any further. Besides, there was no need. Because even now, a decade later, she could remember every second of what happened next. Every tone of every word that her mom had told her. Every way the woman had dismantled her entire world in five seconds flat.

And she could still remember her own reaction. She'd turned away, rejecting the razor edges of the new reality. She'd raced into the house, locked the door, and shut herself in the bathroom, panting like a hunted animal. And there, on the unforgiving coldness of the tile, she'd given in to her first panic attack.

She'd thought she was dying. Believed that the truth Mom had stuck like a dagger in her chest was killing her entirely. But when her hands had stopped shaking and her breath was no longer a fluttering bird in her lungs, she was still alive. Surprisingly so. And she'd resolved two things.

Keep Addisyn away from Mom.

And never tell her the poisonous truth.

She hadn't heard from Mom again, but that hadn't stopped her from worrying that the woman might infiltrate their lives. Catch Addisyn at school or show up at a friend's house or be waiting again under the porch lights to drag Addisyn into her own broken world. And so, in the days that followed, Avery had systematically built her plan to leave home, piece by determined piece. She had to get Addisyn away—not just from their father, but from their mother too.

The low-grade guilt the memory held simmered under the surface again. She'd done the right thing; she still believed that. She'd protected Addisyn from being lost in her mother's shadowy underworld. And from something even more deadly—the truth. But that hadn't kept the secret from weighing like a wound on her heart ever since that evening.

But now...

Now she'd never have to listen to the hiss of guilt. Never have to live looking over her shoulder. Never have to fear that someday, somehow, Addisyn would unwittingly step on the land mine of the truth.

Because the secret she'd held for a decade had now been buried with her mom.

Long after Creed had stretched himself on the narrow camper bed, he lay awake, Avery's face, Avery's voice, in his mind.

Thank you for knowing what to do.

A simple statement, really. Just a polite acknowledgement of help rendered. But coming from Avery, it was an outstretched hand, reaching across the sharp-edged tension he'd created between them.

And the strange thing was, it made him feel—different, somehow. Brave and capable and able to do the right thing. As though he were actually the kind of guy his dad had always wanted him to be.

And the thing was, really, he *hadn't* known what to do. But somehow, in the moment of urgency, he'd done it. When he'd seen the anxiety wracking her face, his chest had all but burst with the need to intervene, to help. It had been almost surreal—watching Avery the ever-capable crumble. Yet in the midst of her fear, he'd also seen her strength—her determination to reach her sister, her ability to push through her own inner turbulence, even her white-knuckle grip on his hands as she willed her way through the panic attack and out the other side.

He hadn't suspected she had that ironclad strength in her soul. But even from the brief snips of her past she'd shared, it was obvious that she was strong because she'd had to be. Why hadn't he known that she had such a scarred story?

Because you didn't care.

Remorse sliced through his soul. Had he ever really talked to her —let alone listened? No, he'd just slapped his own half-baked ideas onto her identity. And all the time he'd been busy judging her, she'd been fighting battles he'd known nothing about.

He'd been too quick. Too sure of himself. The way Dad had always said.

And as bitter as it was to admit—there might be a taste of the truth in a few of his dad's warnings. Today had slapped him in the face with everything he'd assumed he knew. Yet still, Avery had been gracious. Allowing him to help. To fumble his way into something a lot more like friendship.

Thank you for knowing what to do.

When had he last heard those words? Not from Dad, who'd undercut his confidence. And certainly not from Austin. He couldn't imagine his boss taking note of his efforts with anything besides an unspoken *of course*. But today—today he'd redeemed himself. The glow of gratitude in Avery's eyes told him that much.

So what if—what if that could continue? What if he could actually do better? Be something besides the guy who always goofed up? Maybe he could even help Avery some more. Especially right now, in all the stress she was facing.

But how to do it?

He rolled onto his back. Outside the little camper window, the stars were vivid pinpricks. He stared at them, waiting for inspiration. Firstly and obviously, he needed to make the film about the center great. But—well, his ideas for that were still chasing their tails. He needed something else. Something that specifically eased some of the weight Avery carried.

He scrolled through the litany of concerns he'd half-listened to her mention over the last three weeks. Her sister. The funding. Her curriculum...

Her curriculum. An idea sprang to 3D life. While he was still trying to organize his thoughts around the project, what if he helped her with her curriculum? Maybe—hey, maybe he could create short videos for her. Brief introductions to what she was teaching, videos that would bring her topics right into the classrooms.

Excitement sparked around the edges of his thoughts. That was it. Surely that would help Avery. Just having another set of hands on the project would probably boost her morale. And really, it might thaw the frozen gears of his own brain, help him think through new directions that he could then apply to his own project.

And it would enable him to hear those words again, the ones that continued to echo as he sank into sleep.

Thank you for knowing what to do.

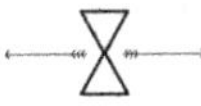

WHEN AVERY OPENED HER EYES, she swirled with a brief moment of disorientation before she blinked back to reality. She was in her bedroom. In bed. And there was—light. Sunlight, streaming through the window and splashing the floor.

She'd slept all the way through the night.

She sat up, a laugh that was half surprise and half joy slipping out. No night terrors? Had she really just been gifted a full eight hours of dreamlessness?

She stretched, basking in the renewal of it. A calm she hadn't experienced in far too long followed her as she walked with Mercy down to the mailbox and made breakfast and washed the dishes, even though the insistent finger of guilt jabbed at her. After all, her mom was *dead*. And she felt as if a cage door had been sprung. That had to be wrong.

But she couldn't talk herself into emotions she'd never felt. And really, wasn't it better to just enjoy the brief moment of peace, as long as it lasted? With the dark wings of the anxiety lifted, she could approach all of her problems differently. Especially the issue with Addisyn.

She hadn't handled that situation the best. She'd let her fears color her reaction. But this was about her sister, not her own feelings. And Addisyn still needed protection, guidance, help. Just as much as she had on the day she'd uselessly chased the taillights.

Maybe your sister needs to make peace with those layers underneath.

Creed's words rolled around in Avery's head again. If she didn't help Addisyn, would her little sister end up like him? Hounded by the past, staggering beneath its weight? No, Avery couldn't let that happen.

So now was the time for Avery to understand, to honor Addisyn's feelings. And her sister wanted to talk, to grieve, to remember. And to go to Syracuse. Avery grimaced. That part, they could talk about later. After the fundraiser, for sure.

But for now—now that the threat of the secret was removed— Avery could finally give her something. Some mementos, some memories to hold like smooth stones in her hand. She'd help Addisyn move on, and then things would be back to normal.

As if nothing had ever happened at all.

She took a deep breath and pulled out her phone. She almost hoped Addisyn wouldn't answer, but her sister's voice came across the line on the first ring. "Avery?"

"Hey. I wanted to check on you."

Silence, and then Addisyn sniffled. "I—" Her sister's voice wobbled. "I'm sorry, Avery. I shouldn't have snapped at you yesterday."

Avery closed her eyes and brushed aside the stings from her sister's words. "It's okay. I know you're upset."

"It's just—" Addisyn drew in a ragged breath. "I always hoped, you know? That Mom would—would come back." Her voice unbalanced again. "I always hoped everything would be okay. One day."

Avery swallowed. She couldn't fault her sister's hope. Addisyn didn't know all that lay behind their mom's departure. Or all that would have exploded if she had ever forced her way back into their lives.

"I understand, Ads. I'm so sorry. I know this isn't easy for you." She bit her lip, shoved ahead. "Ads, I've been thinking. If you still need to hear about Mom—I'll respect that."

"Really?"

"Really." She focused on a knothole on the opposite wall. "If you're free Saturday, you can come up here, and I'll show you the stuff I have. Photos and things."

"That—that would be great." Her sister was clearly trying not to let her enthusiasm fully explode, but excitement fizzled under her words. "I'd love that."

Why was this so thrilling for her? "Okay. See you then."

"Avery?" Addisyn cleared her throat. "Thank you."

Avery sighed. "You're welcome."

After she ended the call with Addisyn, she descended into the basement, where she'd stacked the mismatched odds and ends of her old life. She propped her fists on her hips and studied the assortment of shoeboxes and cardboard moving crates. At least she'd labeled each one. Finding their mom's stuff should be easy.

Too easy.

Mercy brushed past her legs and smelled suspiciously at the

corner of one of the boxes, then glanced at Avery with a quizzical whine. "I know, Mercy. It's not familiar, is it?" Avery scratched the dog's head and sighed. "Not to me either." Not anymore.

She pulled off the top box, waving a hand to banish the poof of dust. Dressed in her neat handwriting, a single word marched across the flap. *School.*

So that box was textbooks and school choir programs and probably her high school diploma. She'd been a straight-A student, excelling in the environment where right and wrong were as concrete as a true or false test. But once she was in the real world...

She sighed and reached for the next boxes in the stack.

Addisyn's School. Her sister's diploma was probably in there.

Files. Whatever that was.

House Documents. Must be the paperwork associated with her purchase of the cabin.

Why was everything in the basement of her life so—*boring*?

Syracuse.

The single Sharpie word on the box slammed into her soul like an iron fist. And in a blink, she was back in that life where a picture-perfect facade of a wealthy family propped itself against the rotting timbers of their private world.

Syracuse. The ghosts peered at her from the dusty corners of the basement. She could hear her father's curses, taste the blood after his fist found her face, see Addisyn cowering in the corner with a fear no child should ever have to—

El Shaddai. She gripped the cardboard, the sharp edges of Syracuse curling in her stomach. *Help me...*

For Addisyn. This was for Addisyn. She took a deep breath. If this was what it took to help Addisyn, she could do it. She could pick her careful way into the minefield of their past, and she could help her sister sidestep the dangers Addisyn didn't even know were there.

She had to do this. Because only she could.

CREED'S INSPIRATION stayed with him as he slept and tapped him on the shoulder as soon as he awoke in the morning. When he hurried down to the office, the parking lot held only the slate-colored Bronco that he'd learned was Skyla's. The main buildings were still dark, but the door to the exhibit building was open.

"Skyla?" He stepped through the unfinished doorway, blinking as his eyes adjusted to the shadowy interior.

"Creed?" Surprise marked Skyla's tone. She stepped from behind a new wall section. "You have come early this morning."

"Yeah—I had a new idea I wanted to talk to Avery about, but she's not here yet."

Skyla adjusted her copper necklace. "Avery told me you drove her to Denver yesterday."

The approval in her tone sent his eyes to the concrete floor. "Anyone would have done the same."

"Not anyone." Skyla smiled. "To help is to have courage, Creed. And I am thankful to you." She pressed her palms together in a slight bow.

Her praise itched awkwardly along his neck. "Well—thanks. I mean, it was no problem."

"Avery says that you acted with no thought for yourself."

Avery had said that? The thought warmed him. "I'm just glad I could help." He studied Skyla's face, but there was no hint that she knew about Avery's panic attack, so he didn't mention it. To change the subject, he nodded at the in-progress interior. The drywall was up, doorframes cut with clear precision. "This looks good."

"Thank you." Skyla folded her hands. "Laz has been working in the evenings."

The mention of his dad still twisted his gut, but the anger didn't pound as hot as normal. "Well. That's good."

"Bringing order from the chaos takes time, but it is always so."

Order from chaos. Like editing a video. "Avery said exhibits will go in here."

"Yes. Some we already have in storage." A brief shadow fell over Skyla's face. "The rest we will buy, if we are able to receive other funding."

Other funding, like the donors who might be inspired by his work. "That makes sense."

"This is where we believe that your work will help."

We believe. She trusted him totally. Why? Surely Dad had told her all his shortcomings by now. "Well—I hope so too."

"You are quite gifted." Skyla's voice was soft. "You have strength in your story, Creed. But now—you bend it for the vision of others."

Austin's brassy bravado burst into Creed's mind. "Yeah." He shrugged, lightening the frustration the image brought. "Gotta eat, you know."

"Yes." Skyla's voice was thoughtful. "But perhaps there are other ways."

He cocked his head. "What do you mean?"

"For one thing, I am well acquainted with someone who has been on the board of the Rocky Mountain Video Project for years. I am sure my friend would be willing to write you a recommendation based on my word."

Creed blinked. The Rocky Mountain Video Project was legendary. "Seriously?"

"Of course. That would open many doors for you, I hope. And you could take it wherever you would wish to work next."

A recommendation from one of the premier outdoor video companies—based on Skyla's unmerited trust in him. He swallowed. "Thank you, Skyla. I—that means a lot."

"Of course. We can talk more about it when your time here is done." She cocked her head, studying him. "Your eyes are good, Creed. But your heart is still bound, is it not so?"

Sometimes Skyla reminded him so much of Charlie that it was uncanny. "What do you mean?"

"What is bound in the earth-world is bound in the sky-world."

"I don't—"

"The Son of Creator taught us to pray. *'Bring Your good road to us, where the beauty of Your ways in the spirit-world above is reflected in the earth below. Release us from the things we have done wrong, in the same way we release others for the things done wrong to us.'"* Skyla's voice had slipped into storyteller mode. *"Remember, our Father from the spirit-world above will release you from your wrongdoings in the same manner you release others from theirs. But if you fail to release others, this keeps your Father, the Creator, from releasing you.'"*

The truth of her words was in sharp focus before his eyes. But he couldn't look at it. Not yet. "Skyla—"

"Think on my words. You need not respond now." There was still no judgment in her eyes. Only an overflow of compassion. "I am glad you came here, He Who Believes."

He glanced out the door, toward the sign. From here, he couldn't see the *kapemni,* but he could still trace its shape. "So am I."

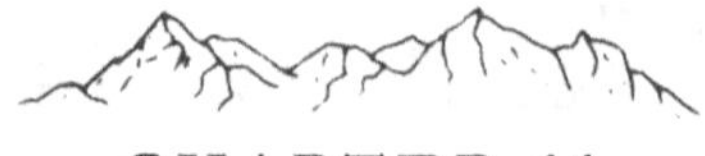

CHAPTER 11

"You want me to do *what*?" Avery eyed Creed suspiciously. She'd just walked through the door of the office for the first time after her morning class, and already Creed had ambushed her with some new idea that didn't sound particularly appealing. "An interview?"

"More like a lesson." Creed's enthusiasm seemed undampened by her wariness. "You're working on your curriculum, right? But you want to make it interactive. Real. Personal. So this is your chance." He spread his hands, glowing with the excitement of his idea. "Teach about things here—the birds, the mountains, the trees. And in this form, the whole natural world can fit right inside a classroom."

The idea sounded more plausible. And she'd never seen Creed this brim-full of passion about a possibility. But the very idea of standing in front of a camera churned in her stomach. "Liv would be better at that. Or Skyla, or Chay, or—"

"Or you." His grin widened. "C'mon, Avery. The camera doesn't bite."

She fought unsuccessfully to keep an answering smile off her face. "I never said it did."

"Then let's try this." His expression turned more serious. "I mean, you were just saying you wanted to make progress on your curriculum, right? This might be the breakthrough you were looking for."

He was right about that. "Yeah, but—I have work to do today. I have to check on some incubating eggs in the raptor building, and—"

"Perfect. That can be the first lesson. I'll film while you work."

Answering questions wouldn't be as bad if she had something else to occupy her hands and didn't have to return the stare of the camera. But still..."This isn't for your project, is it?"

"No." He waved his hand. "This isn't connected to that. I'm kind of—well, I'm a little bit at a dead end on it right now. I'm waiting for a fresh idea. So, tell you what." He flashed her his most charming smile. "Do one video, just one, and I'll buy you lunch anywhere you like."

Was that his idea of a bribe? Avery rolled her eyes. "You don't have to do that. I'm just...not a stand-in-the-spotlight kind of girl."

"No." His expression shifted, something more serious entering his eyes. "I know you're not. That's why you're perfect for this." He moved closer, his voice growing quieter. "This isn't about a spotlight, Avery. It's about you telling your story. You love these birds and this place so much. Tell us why."

Well, when he put it like that—Avery wavered. Surely she could do that, couldn't she? Talk not about herself but about the mountains she loved so much? And what if this was the key—the breakthrough that would enable her to move forward on this project? If it would help the center, there was nothing she wouldn't do.

"All right." She sighed. "I'll do it. As long as it's not for your YouTube channel."

"It's not." He shrugged. "I mean, I might use some of the B-roll, the birds or whatever. But I can ask you about that when the time comes."

"Okay." She would never be part of some video that would be consumed by thousands of people. But if this was just practice between her and Creed, a chance to try a new avenue for her teaching —well, what could it hurt, really?

Still, by the time Creed had finished setting up all his paraphernalia in the raptor building, she already regretted her agreement.

"All right." He adjusted his tripod and grinned at her. "Ready?"

"I guess."

"The camera is rolling, but I can edit any of this out, okay?" He peered through the viewfinder, then stepped back and crossed his arms. "All right. Just talk to me first. Get yourself warmed up. How do the eggs look?"

"Good today." Avery twisted the dials on the incubator. This felt weirdly performative, as though her every move was part of a choreographed routine.

"What are you checking?"

"The temperature." She needed to be giving him more than two-word answers, but her words seemed frozen.

"Okay, what temperature are they set on?"

"Thirty-eight degrees Celsius." Her hands were shaking. *No. Not already.* "Most studies find that to be the best temperature."

"Is that a constant setting?"

"No, actually." She focused on the sleeping roundness of the eggs inside the incubator, forced herself to block out the camera and relax into the details of the process. "The hatch rate is actually better if the temperature is cooled twice during the day. That's to mimic the action of the mother bird leaving the nest to find food."

"Oh, wow. That's neat." Creed adjusted something on his camera. "So what are you doing with them now?"

"I'm going to candle them."

Creed made a face. "Um, explain for the newbies at home."

Avery laughed. Surprisingly, the anxiety wasn't getting any worse. Without the mic wire twisting over her shoulder, this might have almost felt like a normal conversation. "Holding them up to a light helps me see the embryos inside. I can tell how close to development they are and what the hatch date will be."

"Sort of like an ultrasound for a baby?"

"Yes. Sort of." Which Addisyn had undergone earlier in the week. All her sister would say was that everything looked fine. No details.

She forced the strained situation with her sister from her mind and brought herself back to the task at hand. "So, I'm starting with Egg 1." She slipped on her gloves and opened the incubator, the oven-like heat blasting her face. "This is the largest egg and believed to be the one laid first, so its hatch date should be well ahead of its siblings."

"So when do you expect these eggs to hatch?"

"Well, these are Ferruginous Hawk eggs. Their typical incubation period is anywhere from twenty-eight to thirty-six days, and we're estimating these eggs at thirteen days. So, about two or three more weeks." She blinked as the realization hit her. Creed might be gone before the eggs hatched.

She brushed aside the odd pang the thought carried. "Creed, can you get the lights for me?"

"Oh, yes." He flipped the switch, and the room dropped into darkness except for the reddish glow of the incubator.

"Okay, so—" Avery reached for her candling light. It looked like an ordinary flashlight, but the rubber ring around the tip allowed the egg to rest securely next to the bulb. As she settled the egg in place, it immediately glowed with the fiery colors of a sunset.

"Whoa!" Creed's voice soared. "That's incredible."

"It definitely is." Avery smiled, appreciating his reaction. "Now, if you'll look closely, you'll see the top is a dark red, with lighter yellow on the bottom. And you can probably see the membranes inside."

"I do. Those dark spiderwebby things?" Creed was once again hunched behind the camera, the zoom lens extending. No doubt he was getting a close-up of the egg. "So what does that mean?"

Avery gently settled the egg back into the incubator. "It means this egg is fertile. And the embryo is developing." She never tired of seeing the miracle within each egg, where, in the depths of the invisible, El Shaddai was bringing forth the mystery of life.

"Does it all look right?"

"Yes. Everything is normal. The baby birds are healthy and growing as expected."

"Well, so this is something you do a lot here at the center, Avery. What are some other things that happen on a day-to-day basis?"

In spite of her hesitations, Avery had to admit that Creed was an expert interviewer. With disarmingly casual questions, he kept her talking as she candled the other two eggs and recorded her observations. She told him about the mission of the center, the plans for the expansion, and the training required for the work. Just as she was returning the last egg to the incubator, he swiveled the conversation to her. "So what about you, Avery? Work like this requires not just skill, but heart. So where did you find your passion for this?"

"Well, Skyla offered me a job here three years ago. At the time, I was working at—" *Don't mention Laz.* "I was working at an outdoors store in Estes Park and volunteering here on Friday afternoons. Skyla gave me a chance." She'd be forever grateful that the woman had believed in her. "And she helped me work through the classes and certifications I needed."

"That's really cool. Skyla is a pretty awesome woman." Creed flipped the light switch back on.

"Yes. She is." Avery blinked in the new brightness and peeled off her gloves. She was done with her tasks here, but Creed was still talking.

"What motivated you to want to do wildlife rehab?"

The question was a big one. She twisted the gloves together, her nerves stretching tight again. "Well—I think—"

"Just talk to me, Avery." Creed's voice was reassuringly warm. "You're doing great, by the way."

Her laugh trembled. "I am?"

"Yeah, totally. You're crushing it." He smiled at her, compassion in his smoke-gray eyes. "Talk to me like you'd talk to a friend, okay?"

She took a deep breath and pulled her eyes from the gun-barrel glare of the camera lens. Instead she looked at Creed. Drew a breath from the encouragement she saw in his face.

"I wanted to work in wildlife rehab because I wanted to bring healing." The rightness of the statement settled into her soul. "Many things in my life were—were broken before I came here. I wanted to be where I could help mend hurts, help wounded creatures fly free again." She was gathering strength now, losing herself in the burning of what she believed. "I'm passionate about the mission of this center. Skyla has a vision to bring wholeness. Not just to the birds, but to people. She wants to build a place where people can connect with nature and see the miracles and leave a little more healed themselves."

Creed was nodding. "Sounds like you really love this place."

"I do." Her love for it was too expansive for words, but she would try. "When I first came to the mountains—I knew it was God's country. I feel Him here. I see Him. This—this is my home. And I want to to be a part of His healing in this place."

"Good for you." A sad sort of smile hovered over Creed's face. "I think it's great that you know what you believe. That you've brought something good out of the bad."

The words hung between them for a moment, and then Creed abruptly punched something on the camera. "And that's a wrap."

Avery blinked. She'd been drawn so deeply into the telling of the story that she'd completely forgotten the filming. "I did okay?"

"Way better than okay." He grinned. "You were amazing."

The praise trickled warmth through her. She shrugged, refusing to let him see how deeply she felt his words. "Well, I'm glad."

"Yeah. Now I'll put together the first lesson for you. It will be ready to see tomorrow."

"Hmm. Okay." A hope she hadn't felt in too long rose within her. This might be doable. It was a way to move forward with the curriculum. And it might even help her practice speaking ahead of the fundraiser. If they really could make this work—then maybe everything would get better.

She raised her eyebrows at him, the hope glowing through her. "I like this idea, Creed. But you better edit out some of that."

He laughed. "We'll see. Now, where do you want to go for lunch?"

She stared at him blankly. "Lunch?"

"Yeah." He coiled his camera cord, shoved it back in his bag. "I told you I'd buy you lunch if you did the video."

He'd been serious? "That's not necessary."

"Hey, I promised." He grinned and held up his hand in a Boy Scout vow. "Can't go back on my word."

Avery hesitated, searching his eyes. There was no hint that he saw this as anything more than a simple lunch between coworkers. But still...

"Come on." He folded up his tripod, glancing over his shoulder. "Anywhere you'd like. And we can talk more about the videos too."

Yeah, but what would Liv say if she found out? Avery cringed. "I don't like to eat in restaurants very much. If anything, I get a to-go box downtown and bring it back here to eat." There. That would talk him out of it.

"That sounds awesome! Especially with the nice weather today." He slung the camera bag over his arm. "We could eat at the picnic table out by my camper."

Well, he was persistent, if nothing else. And a simple lunch between coworkers at the job site didn't mean anything, did it? "The Aspenglow has amazing chili."

"Chili, huh?" He grinned. "Haven't had decent chili since the winter I worked in Texas."

Was there anywhere he hadn't been? "Well, that might change today."

"Hmm." He nudged her shoulder as they headed back down the hall. "I warn you, I'm a snob about chili."

The bright sunlight warmed her as they stepped outside. "Just about chili?"

"Ouch!" He clutched his chest, feigning a wounded expression. "Are you calling me stuck-up?"

Avery raised her eyebrows. "If the shoe fits."

He grimaced. "Buying you purportedly the world's best chili won't redeem my mistakes?"

"Hmm." This was fun, the air easy between them. She let her laughter join his. "It might be a start."

Talk to me like you'd talk to a friend.

She would have never seen this coming, but Creed Running Wolf was truly becoming a friend.

It might be a start.

AVERY HAD LONG KNOWN that the best chili available at the Aspenglow was the Fire Eaters Bowl. But even she wasn't always in the mood to eat food that made her sweat. As a result, she'd tried to steer Creed toward an option with a little less drama, but he'd laughed her off. *"Remember, I lived in Texas. You can't get chili too hot for me."*

She didn't believe him. Not when he ordered the jalapeño-laced dish, and not when his first bite ended in a choking noise.

"Too hot for you?" She shifted position on the picnic table bench, unable to keep a smirk from her eyes.

Across the table, Creed downed half of his soft drink with frantic urgency, then pulled in a deep breath and flashed her a grin. "Nope. It just surprised me there for a second." He swiped the back of his arm over his forehead and took another bite—smaller this time. "It really is as good as you said."

"And as hot as I said?"

His grin turned sheepish, color rising behind his tan. "Maybe."

Avery laughed. "Glad to know it meets your standards." From here, the backbone of the Continental Divide was visible, the mountains still gleaming white under their snowpack. "The scenery probably helps the taste, you know."

"For sure." Creed followed her gaze. "This is a beautiful land."

"Mmhm." Avery rotated her neck, letting the warm sun soak into the places in her spirit that had been cold for so long. Birds chattered like cheerful sentinels in the watchtowers of the pines.

It must be a peaceful place to camp in. She glanced over her shoulder at Creed's teardrop camper. All the times she'd seen it behind the center, she somehow hadn't paid much attention to how tiny it was up close. The thing looked barely big enough to stand straight in.

"This is one of the prettier places I've seen." Creed seemed to be moving his spoon through the chili more than he was eating it. "And I've seen a lot. This would be a neat place to live."

Something in his voice sounded—wistful? Avery studied him. "Are you thinking about camping here longer?"

"Well—" He hesitated, finally setting his spoon down. "Skyla actually talked to me about a chance with the Rocky Mountain Video Project."

"She did?" Even without a film background, Avery had seen the brilliant artistry of the RMVP. They'd even been the ones to create one of the films shown at the national park center. "She's involved with that?"

"No, but she knows someone on the board, apparently." Creed shrugged. "She said she could write me a recommendation."

"That's amazing." Avery studied him, trying to read his feelings on his face. "Are you going to look into that?"

"I'm very grateful she trusts me. But—no, I don't think so." He shrugged and dug into his chili again. "My work with Guys in the Wild is good. I like getting to travel."

She'd started out counting the days until Creed left. So why did she shrink now from the thought of him leaving? "Well." She poked her spoon at one of the beans in her chili. "You travel a lot, don't you?"

"A good bit of the year, yeah." His eyes sparked with adventure. "I like that life. Seeing the whole country, meeting different people. Always something new ahead of you."

"And you travel in that thing?" She glanced again at the tiny camper.

"Of course." He grinned and scrambled up. "Wanna see the inside?"

Avery had expected a Spartan interior, complete with the mess that might be expected as a natural overflow of Creed's randomness. But as she ducked through the doorway, she blinked. The interior was—a home. A window spilled light over a wraparound couch with smoke-gray cushions, and a galley kitchen was tucked into the other end. A door in between most likely led to a bathroom. A dream-catcher spun from the side window, its beads glittering in the sun, and on the opposite wall, a row of odd designs marched across the white paneling.

"The couches fold into a bed." Creed shrugged uneasily, glancing around as if seeing it for the first time. "It's not much, I guess."

"I like it." Clearly he worked hard to make this his own, to take care of his cabin on wheels. The thought tugged at her heart for some reason. She turned toward the suite of stenciled designs. "Those are cool."

"Thanks." He ducked his head. "I drew them."

"You *drew* them?"

"Yeah. They're Lakota symbols."

This guy surprised her more all the time. She touched one gently with a fingertip—a circle sliced into four quadrants. "What's this one?"

"That's the medicine wheel." He crossed to stand beside her, the floor creaking beneath him. "It's the sacred circle of life. It shows the path of spiritual knowledge."

"Really?"

"Yeah. It's the four points of the compass, and each one stands for a different part of life. And the Great Spirit is supposedly at the center." He shrugged and touched another symbol, this one drawn from a continuous curve. "Then this is the bear sign. Bears represent healing."

"That's interesting. It's the same for the Squamish people in Canada, near where my sister lives." She'd learned that on her adventures with Addisyn and Kenzie in British Columbia.

"Hmm. That's neat." Creed tapped the next symbol. "And this is a *kapemni*."

The hourglass sketch jogged a memory. "Hey. That's the symbol on the center sign."

"I know. I saw it the first day, when I was driving by." He gave a quiet laugh. "That's why I stopped."

"That's right. You mentioned that." He'd said something about it at their first meeting, but she'd never followed up. "That's why you came?"

"Yeah." His brows bunched together. "I thought it might be a sign."

"What does it mean?"

"It symbolizes Heaven touching Earth. The center of it is supposed to be the doorway between the spirit-world and humans."

The words carried the faint aroma of a blessing. "Oh. I like that."

"Well—" He sighed. "I don't know if I believe it."

"But you drew it."

"Right. A lifetime ago. A prayer, maybe. Or just a wish." He blew out a breath and turned away, pointing toward the back of the pod. A clear exit from the conversation. "The dinette can be converted to an extra bunk."

"Wow." There was beauty in the way that every square inch was creatively utilized. "It's nice in here. Cozy."

"Uh-huh." He leaned against the doorframe, absently rubbing the wolf on his arm. "It's home."

Home. Avery tilted her head. "You don't have a house anywhere?"

"I rent an apartment back in South Dakota, just outside Ardmore."

"So, that's home base?"

"Not really." He rubbed a hand over his stubbled jaw. "I don't spend enough time there for it to really belong to me. It's mainly a place to store stuff, I guess."

So everything that mattered in Creed's life could fit between these tiny walls. For some reason, the thought made her want to cry. "How much of the year are you traveling?"

"At least two thirds, if not more." He shrugged. "I don't love South Dakota. Not anymore. I stay on the road whenever possible. I don't think I'm back there more than three or four months out of the year."

"And the rest of the time you live in this?"

"Yeah, just heading to different film locations. And staying in campgrounds. It's a good life. I get to film and travel and climb. My three favorite things." His laugh was more sad than bitter. "If you keep moving, you don't give yourself time to think."

The words sank harder than he'd probably intended. Avery glanced at the wolf on his arm. Where was the animal running to?

"It sounds—" She stopped. It wasn't her place to say.

"Sounds what?"

"Well—lonely." Ha. The same accusation Addisyn had leveled about her own life.

A heaviness settled over his face for a moment. "It can be. But most of the time it's fine." He shrugged. "Don't you ever just want to leave it all behind sometimes?"

"Back in New York, yes. And once I was able to, I moved here." Here, where she'd been set free from the panic and the pain. At least until lately. "But now I'm rooted here."

"Because you love the land." He nodded. "You said that in the video."

He'd paid that much attention? "Yes. I do." She rubbed at an invisible mark on the wall. "Where will you go next?"

"From here, I'll go to Arizona. The rest of my team is already there. And then when we're done filming in Arizona, I think Austin wants to shoot in Texas next. We usually go to El Paso and climb at Hueco Tanks at least once a year. Makes for great footage."

"And then you'll go back to South Dakota?"

He hesitated. "I'm hoping I'll have another option by then."

Avery raised her eyebrows. "You mean—"

"Well—" He rubbed the back of his neck, his tone casual in a way that couldn't hide the glint in his eyes. "Austin is considering me for his international team."

International. Why did it matter that Creed would be that far away? Avery blinked. "Oh—wow. Is that—is that what you want?"

"More than anything. Always has been." Enthusiasm brought a rare openness to his face. "I've never been out of the country. I'm itching to do some real traveling. See the rest of the world." He glanced out of the window—to the mountains and beyond. "But Austin hasn't made the decision yet."

"Well—congratulations on the possibility, anyway." The words sounded weak. What was wrong with her? Avery forced a smile, attempting to inject some levity. "Mercy will miss you."

Creed laughed. "She's the only one."

Not true.

"Anyway—" A hint of bitterness crept into his tone. "Dad will be happy when I'm gone. Life can go back to normal for him."

Avery bit her lip. A week ago she wouldn't have bothered, but— "Can I ask you something?"

He lifted a shoulder, his eyes intent on her. "Sure."

The flames of her knowing rose vivid in her mind again. "Did you really start a fire?"

His mouth twitched upward. "Yep."

"You don't seem like the arsonist type."

There was a sadness behind his laugh. "It was an accident." Again he rubbed the wolf on his arm. "I was—well, I was out of favor at the ministry, I guess. I worked there, you know."

He'd worked for Laz's ministry? Avery blinked. A whole new angle to the father-son conflict. "No. I didn't know."

"Yeah. It was Dad's dream. Him and me working together, changing the world." He sighed. "I wasn't cut out for that, you know? I was off making videos all the time. And—well, some people in the ministry might have described me as—different."

"Different?"

The smile lurking in the corner of his mouth deepened. "Heretical."

"Skyla says that's sometimes a label for people who are too close to the truth."

"See, that's why I like Skyla." Creed's laugh turned serious. "Anyway, it's a long story. I was sort of in a rough place, and—well, in Lakota tradition, to pray seriously, you build the *péta wakan*. The sacred fire. And your prayers rise on the smoke." He sighed. "I—I was trying to find something. Someone. God, I guess. And I built that fire and—it got away from me. Burned two adjoining fields and part of a shed nearby." He gave a bitter laugh. "The ministry leaders were already looking for an excuse to get rid of me. They gave Dad an ultimatum. Either I went or he did."

Avery could see the ending coming around the curve of the tale. "And he stayed."

"After letting me know his disappointment pretty loudly." He glanced out the window, squinting as if the past were painful to look at. "I hit the road."

The rift between them made sense now. Avery shook her head. "Creed—did he ever try to talk to you?"

"He wants to now." For just a second, his face hardened in the old way. "I don't care what he has to say. It doesn't really matter. There's no undoing what happened." He sighed and studied his dusty boots. "I made my own mistakes. I get that. But he just turned his back on me. The only thing important to him was his ministry." His smile twisted ironic. "Guess I got the answer to my prayer, though."

The raw pain under his words hurt her own heart. Avery kept her voice soft. "What were you praying for?"

"Well—" Creed's eyes settled on his *kapemni* for a moment before he shook his head. "It doesn't matter. Not now." He backed toward the door of the camper, the shutters in his eyes closing again. "Guess we better get back to work."

⋈

THE PROJECT still didn't fit in the shape he wanted, but at least it was moving again.

Creed turned the Jeep onto Marys Lake Road and checked the GoPro balanced on his dashboard. He'd driven into Estes for groceries this evening, and by the time he'd started back toward the center, the lighting was perfect—sun sinking behind some low-hanging clouds, a soft glow in the air. It was the ideal moment to catch film of the road there, maybe even some creative angles of the light through the flight cage bars. No one else would be there this time of day, so he could experiment.

The unspooling road into the mountains would make for a great intro scene. If only he were so confident about the rest of the project. In the spirit of Erica's advice, he'd shadowed Skyla some this week, letting her untangle the story of the center while she worked, sharing her heart in her quiet way. It had made for good footage, especially when she'd let him film the splinting of a wounded bird's wing.

Still, though, it seemed—off. Skyla had done an outstanding job, certainly. But how could he translate that into action? Into a film that had people reaching for their tissues right alongside their hefty checkbooks?

He shook his head. Maybe he just needed to spend more time working on the storyboard. Adding some voiceover, supplementing with shots like the one he was capturing now—it could all end up working. So far, he simply hadn't had a chance to really focus on it, what with filming the new lesson clips for Avery.

At least those were going well. Avery had a natural conviction, a passion for what she was doing that practically glowed around the edges of her words. Besides, every day she seemed more comfortable around the camera—and him. And the filming was more fun than he could have expected. Avery had a subtle wit he hadn't guessed at first. Now their banter made him laugh out loud.

He sighed. Too bad they hadn't reached a truce earlier. In a little over two weeks, he'd wrap this project and be on his way to Arizona, the story of their newfound friendship left unfinished.

Unless, of course, he accepted Skyla's offer.

The center came in sight, and he turned in under the now-familiar Estes Valley Mountain Center sign. He stepped out of the Jeep and unpacked his camera. He'd need a lens with a lower aperture tonight, in the dimming day.

He couldn't stay here, of course. Hadn't he sworn long ago he'd never get attached to a single place again? He needed the constant action. Needed to be waking up in new places, around new people. Didn't he?

Or did he just need to stay one step ahead of everything that lay behind?

He shook his head. He couldn't think about that now when the day was draining away, taking the light with it. He crouched in the tall grass near the sign and adjusted his ISO for the conditions, then did a slow panning shot of the facilities. Excellent. It'd be a good opening. Maybe underneath a voiceover.

Working on a project like this was nice, helping him stretch his creativity beyond the monotonously similar adrenaline-junkie videos he made for Austin. This was different. More artistic. Aesthetic. Slow enough to make him stop and remember all the reasons he'd loved filming in the first place.

I want to show people stories that change the world.

The words popped into his head unbidden, like a note from his past self. The sentence he'd written on his application to the film program his first summer out of college.

Dad hadn't wanted him to go, of course. His father had still been holding out hope that he'd trade a Nikon for a nail gun. Join the old man building houses. Roofing the Rez.

But he'd stood his ground. Paid the hefty entrance fee from his savings. And started work on a project that he'd thought his father would be proud of.

Instead—

A throat cleared nearby. "Miz Skyla's done gone for the day."

He jerked, nearly losing his grip on the camera, and looked up. His father was shadowed against the sky, as if his memories had brought the man to life. "I know."

Dad nodded at the camera. "Filmin' tonight?"

His hands tightened around it. "Yeah." Weird, how defensive he still felt. As if his father would scold him for filming the way he had when Creed was a teenager.

"All right." Dad squinted up at the sky. "Light is right nice tonight."

His father had noticed? "Yeah. It's the cloud cover. Cuts the glare and softens the shadows. Not as much contrast." He pressed his lips tighter. What was he doing? His father didn't care about his technique.

But Dad nodded. "Makes sense."

"Uh-huh."

The conversation lulled awkwardly between them. Skyla's words echoed in the stillness.

As we release others...

Creed studied his dad. The man ten years ago had been a no-nonsense giant with a gruff voice and little patience. But somehow now his dad seemed smaller. Or maybe just older. Lines in his face like cracks in a cliff. White softening his beard. And a gentleness in his eyes that hadn't been there before.

Was he right that he'd changed?

"Creed?"

It was still weird, hearing his name on his dad's lips. "Yeah."

"Can I jes' say somethin'?" Dad cleared his throat. "An' then I'll leave you be."

The light was already changing. If he wanted to keep this view, he had to act fast. "Sure."

"I was wrong in what I said. About the video for that workshop thing."

And like that, Creed was back in that summer workshop, and he'd just completed the project that had been his best and his worst. All at the same time.

Dad was still talking, scuffing his boot along the ground. "You worked hard on it." A faint, sad smile came. "I 'member I didn't even hardly see you that summer. You was always off filmin' somewhere."

He blinked. Was that one of the reasons his father had hated his filming? Because he'd spent the summer doing it, when summer was all the time he had with his dad?

He shoved against the idea. Of course not. Dad had never cared about him that much. "I wanted it to be good." He pressed his lips together. "I wanted you to like it."

"I know." Dad's voice was low. "I see that now."

He'd spent all summer working on the project—homage to the Rez. Laboring for hours to capture the perfect film. Interviewing dozens of the tribal elders. He'd endeavored to show both sides, the glory and the grit, of the place he'd viewed as his home. And he'd been sure his dad would be impressed.

Until everything had blown up in his face.

Dad sighed. "If not for the fire—"

The fire. Of course. Creed flinched and scrambled to his feet. He was through filming for the night. "Never mind."

"Creed." Dad's voice held a pleading, a brokenness. "For what it's worth—I shoulda not said—what I said."

Creed paused. His dad was asking him for something. Something he wasn't ready to offer. Not yet.

But he was closer than he'd ever been.

Dad didn't seem to mind that he hadn't responded. "I know you'll be leavin' soon. But if you could, when yer not too busy—"

He nodded at the camera in Creed's hands—"I'd be right thankful if you'd talk to me. Jes' once."

Avery's words whispered back in his ear. The way she'd wanted him to try to make amends. "I—I have to think about it."

"I understand." Dad shrugged. "Miz Skyla told me about some of the stuff you been doin' here. I don't know too much 'bout filmin', but sounds to me like yer doin' a good job."

A good job.

What else had he wanted to hear from his dad all his life?

Dad turned, boots crunching on the gravel. "Anyway. See you later."

As we release others...

As Dad's footsteps dimmed, Creed glanced at the wolf on his arm.

Maybe there was still hope for release.

CHAPTER 12

Addisyn had been counting down the hours all week, and finally, Saturday was here. The day Avery would at last blow dust off the boxed-up past, open the lid, and give her some kind of answers. Something she could hold onto.

And then she'd be able to settle down. She could face the pregnancy without fear and end the tension between her and Avery and finally feel the excitement she pretended around Darius. Everything would go back to normal. Well, as normal as it could be, given what would be happening in seven months. A terrifyingly brief period of time, if you thought about it.

But today wasn't a day for thinking about it. Today was a day for answers. And she announced as much to Darius once breakfast was over. "Remember, I'm going to drive up and see Avery today."

"Okay, babe."

His voice sounded uncertain, and Addisyn narrowed her eyes. "What's wrong? I told you I was going earlier in the week."

"No, I know." He studied his cup of coffee. "It's just—are you sure—"

Addisyn waited, but the rest of his sentence didn't come. "Am I sure *what*?"

"Are you sure you still feel up to driving all that way?"

Irritation scratched like sandpaper. She was pregnant, not porcelain. "I'm fine, Darius." She no longer tried to abate the frustration in her voice.

"Okay, but—maybe I should come with you."

As if she had to be chaperoned? "Darius, I'm just going to visit Avery. I won't get into trouble if I'm left unsupervised."

"Okay, okay. I get it." He held up his hands, a frustration on his face that matched her own. "I was just checking."

Checking. Addisyn dragged her spoon through the soggy cereal still left in her bowl. She didn't need more checking.

"What time do you think you'll be back?"

"Late afternoon probably." She fought to keep from screaming. Who made him the hall monitor? "I won't be driving back in the dark."

"That's not what I meant." His face turned hesitantly hopeful. "I —I was wondering if maybe you wanted to do something tonight. You know, just the two of us. Maybe go out, get dinner?"

It was the sort of way Addisyn would have normally loved to spend Saturday night. But now the prospect of having to dress up and do her makeup and navigate a crowded restaurant just sounded exhausting. Not to mention the fact that Darius would enthuse about the baby the whole time. She bit her lip. "Uh...I'll see how I feel when I get back."

His face drooped slightly, but he nodded. "Okay. Just thought it might be fun."

He stood and stretched. Gosh, he looked good this morning. Why hadn't she noticed earlier? She let her eyes drift along his familiar solid stance, the topography of his muscles under his T-shirt, the thick beard that had grown longer in the last few months. His hair, still damp from the shower, curled along his shoulders.

Something she hadn't felt for too long fluttered inside her. A longing that soothed her soul into a softer shape. She should go to him now, settle into the safety of his strong arms, brush her hand through his beard, and tell him—

A strange mix of shame and resentment soured in her chest. Well, wasn't that how she had gotten herself into this trouble in the first place?

"Everything okay?"

"Yes." She jerked her gaze away and stood, shoving her chair in and her feelings down at the same time. She brushed by him without looking at him again. "I'll be back this afternoon."

But the frustration of the morning still grated on her as she drove to Estes. What was happening to their relationship? When she'd first met Darius, one of the things she'd loved about him was the way he respected her independence. In contrast to Avery's big-sister hovering—albeit deserved, at that time in her life—Darius had given her the trusting space to make her own choices.

But now he seemed to think he had to be attached to her every second. Come with her to see Avery, indeed. Oh yeah, that would be just great. The last thing she needed was Avery and Darius whispering together about her welfare. Especially when Avery was already constantly and needlessly worried about her.

Frankly, if Avery needed to worry about someone, it was herself. After all, Avery was the one living alone way up in the mountains. Nobody to check on her, really. And she could claim she was fine, but Addisyn wasn't convinced. She was stressed, for sure. And definitely overworking.

Addisyn frowned as she turned onto Highway 36. Maybe neither of them was doing as well as they wanted the world to believe.

She shoved the thoughts away, turned up the radio, and tried to focus on the beautiful scenery as the road soared upward into the mountains that were only a filigree on the Denver horizon. By eleven o'clock, she was turning into Avery's driveway. Her sister's farm gate was open. She must be home.

But at the top of the driveway, there was no battered truck. Only an orange Jeep waiting there instead. Addisyn raised her eyebrows as she parked next to it. Had Avery gotten a new car? Maybe that ratty old beater had finally kicked the can.

She slipped out of her car and studied the Jeep. Beefy tires were splashed with mud, and a mountain stencil traced above the running boards. The back window was crowded with decals: a Bigfoot silhouette, a Yellowstone National Park sticker, a stylized camera with trees in the focus lens. No, this could not be Avery's car. And the house was dark too. What was going on?

A flicker of movement caught her eye, and she peered over the

Jeep. *There.* A figure was slipping through the trees between the house and the little stream.

Who was snooping around her sister's house? Addisyn's protective instincts propelled her toward the tree line. "Hello? What are you doing here?"

Branches snapped and bent, and then a guy in khaki cargo pants and a green T-shirt backed out of the brush, something cradled in his arm. He turned toward her and blinked. "Wait, who are you?"

Suddenly the full vulnerability of her position hit. What was she doing? This guy could be a serial killer. Addisyn shoved her hand in her pocket, wrapping her fingers around Avery's house key, and stepped backwards toward the cabin. "This is private property."

"I know." He shifted whatever it was he held—a camera. One of those big fancy ones. "I—I was just getting some pictures."

Okay, so far he wasn't giving serial killer vibes, but still—"Pictures for what? My sister owns this land."

"Your sister?" The confusion on his face suddenly cleared. "Ah! You must be Addisyn."

Her wariness only doubled. "And you are—"

"Creed Running Wolf." He tipped his head and gave a slight salute. "I work with Avery at the raptor center."

Creed! Addisyn's relief spilled into a laugh. "Oh! Yes, she's spoken of you." She wouldn't tell him what exactly Avery had said.

"I'm sorry." His smile turned sheepish. "I guess I did look awfully suspicious."

"Well, maybe just a little."

"Yeah, I get that." He leaned easily against the nearest tree. "Avery told me to stop by this morning. She's got the flyers for the fundraiser printed, and I'm going to take them back to the center for her. When I got here, her gate was open, but her truck was gone. I saw those pretty woods, and—" He hefted his camera. "I thought I'd just get some practice shots while I was waiting."

"That's neat." Curiosity was having a heyday with her. Not much resemblance to Laz in this good-looking guy. Chocolate-colored hair, heavy shadow of stubble, an athletic build. Addisyn hadn't known that Laz's son was Avery's age.

Or that he was this attractive.

Her mountain-loving sister...this outdoorsy guy...an idea was practically screaming in her ear. But she needed more information. "So, Creed, how are you enjoying being here?"

"It's a—nice area." He looked at the trees the same way Avery did. "Peaceful, I guess."

"Avery loves living here." Addisyn pointed toward the house. "She's been in the mountains for almost five years now."

"That long?" He nodded slowly. "She does a wonderful job at the center."

This was promising. "She truly does. She's just an amazing person." Was he hearing what she was saying? "I hope I'm like her one day."

He laughed. "I can see why. The way she's made a home here, her love for this place—it's inspiring. I've never been in an area long enough to find a groove, like she has."

Inspiring. Okay, this was promising. And he'd given her a clear route forward. "Yes, I guess you must travel quite a bit with your job?" She was leading him. One step at a time. "Avery mentioned you worked for a YouTube channel."

"Yeah. I like the traveling, though. I've been all over the western half of the country. Arizona, California, Nevada, Wyoming. Did a winter in the Southwest. Even went up to the North Cascades in Washington once."

"That's really neat." Addisyn silently congratulated herself on her ability to deftly maneuver this conversation. "But I guess your wife probably doesn't like you being gone that much."

"I'm not married." He shrugged. "Too much going on."

Aha! She fought to keep the jubilation off her face. "I can understand that." She gazed at the mountains, affecting nonchalance. "I mean, that's how it is with Avery. She's always been too busy with work to be married, she says."

"Uh-huh." He was studying something on his camera, pressing a button and squinting at the screen.

She was building to her climax. "Of course, I think there's more to it than that. I just think she hasn't found the right guy."

She paused expectantly, waiting for his reaction, but he was looking over her shoulder. "Hey, there she is."

Addisyn turned toward the crunch of tires on gravel just as Avery's truck lurched to a stop. Well, drat the interruption. Another thirty seconds, and she could have hinted that—

Avery climbed out, worry written across her expression. "Ads! Have you been waiting long? I'm sorry. My errands took a while."

"No problem. I've only been here a few minutes." Addisyn crossed to the truck and gave her sister a hug. "And I got to meet—"

Avery was already looking over her shoulder. "Creed, there you are."

"I'm here." Was it her imagination, or was there an extra spark in his eyes as he looked at Avery?

Avery brushed her hair absently behind her ears. Her cheeks were pink. From the hurry? "I'm sorry I wasn't here on time. The posters are in my truck."

"Oh, I was fine. And it was nice meeting your sister." Creed tipped his head toward Addisyn and smiled. "You two look a lot alike."

"Everyone always says that." Avery cleared her throat. "Ads, you can go in the house. I've just got to give these to Creed. It won't take long."

"Sure. I'll wait for you inside." Addisyn took her time strolling onto the porch and leisurely untying her shoes. Just before she ducked through the door, she glanced over her shoulder again. Creed and Avery were standing close together—very close. Avery was talking, pointing to something on the papers she held. Creed was nodding along, but from what Addisyn could tell, he was watching Avery more than the papers.

Hmm, interesting. Addisyn allowed herself a smirk as she reluctantly stepped into the cabin. She'd always worried that Avery would lose herself in her head-down work ethic and never find time for romance. Or that she'd settle for some boring guy. Somebody like Tyler, who had the stability—but also the personality—of a rock.

But Creed...well, Creed had potential.

And unless her instincts were totally off, he might have already had the same thought.

⧗

Earlier in the week, Avery had carried the box back upstairs and set it squarely on the dining room table. Where she couldn't overlook it or ignore it or convince herself to brush it aside again. Where it was still looming when she finished with Creed and hurried inside. "Addisyn? I'm here."

"Okay." Addisyn was perched sideways on a chair, staring at the box. Predictably. It was a miracle she hadn't ripped into it yet.

"Sorry I was late." Avery shrugged out of her jacket and snagged it on the wall hook.

"That's all right."

Why did Addisyn sound so—smug? Avery narrowed her eyes. "What's wrong?"

"What do you mean?"

"You know what I mean." She wasn't happy about this task anyway. She certainly wasn't going to begin it by playing mind games with her sister.

"Well—" Addisyn's eyes glinted with the secret-mischief look that had been terrifying when she was a teenager. "You didn't describe Creed accurately to me."

Had she described him at all? "Meaning—"

"Meaning I did not know he was your age." Addisyn smirked. "And single. And hot."

Oh, for crying out loud. Avery groaned. "Addisyn! Will you stop being ridiculous?"

"Ridiculous?" Addisyn raised her eyebrows. "That is one interesting man, Avery. I'd explore that possibility, if I were you."

Avery fought to keep from rolling her eyes. "We're coworkers, Addisyn. Friends." She busied herself straightening the wall photo of Mount Meeker. "Anyway, I'm sure he has a girlfriend, or something."

"He doesn't."

"You *asked* him?" She couldn't keep the words from coming out as a yelp.

Addisyn shrugged one shoulder. "Not really. Don't worry, I was slick about it."

Slick. Oh, what had she done?

"But he's definitely single." Addisyn paused long enough to give her next words weight. "And I think he likes you."

An annoying surge of heat rose to her cheeks without her consent. "I've told you, Ads. Stop with the matchmaking thing. I mean it."

"Okay." Addisyn was still using an *if-you-say-so* tone. "But if you signaled to him that you might be interested—just dropped a hint or two—"

"Addisyn, if you don't stop, I will drop a hint that you should go back to Denver." She pointed at the box. Her ultimate bargaining chip. "Do you want to see this stuff or not?"

Addisyn's expression immediately turned serious. "Yeah."

"Okay, then." If they had to do this, no sense wasting time. Avery pulled the scissors from her desk drawer and cut the tape. Like opening a bitter backwards gift. She pulled the flaps back and peered into the box—

Straight into her mother's eyes.

The framed photo stared back at her, and her hands froze on the cardboard. Where had she picked up this photo? Why didn't she remember it from their belongings in Syracuse?

Addisyn peered over Avery's shoulder and caught a breath. "That's her." It wasn't a question.

"Yes." Everything about the woman's face was sickeningly familiar. The pinched creases between her eyes. The slight droop to her mouth. The eyes that already held a flatlining fatigue.

Addisyn pulled the photo out, holding it gingerly with the concentration of a child peering into a mirror. Which, in a sense, she was. "This was before us." She glanced at Avery. "She looks like she's about your age."

"Yep." Avery pulled in a long, deep breath. Ridiculous, to be shoved so off-balance by a single photo. She couldn't react like that to every item in here. *Strong. For Addisyn.*

Addisyn scrutinized Avery. "Your eyes are a lot like hers."

Avery flinched involuntarily. "Her eyes were darker than mine."

"They look pretty light in this—"

"Addisyn, do you want to see the rest of the stuff in here?" If Addisyn was going to linger this long over every piece, the task might just outlast Avery's resolve to complete it.

"Yeah." Addisyn set the photo aside and rose on her knees in the chair. "What else is in there?"

"Well—" Avery shuffled through a few more framed photos. Mostly older relatives, some she didn't even know. Then her fingers found smooth plastic. "Oh, this." She pulled out the teal baby book. "Mom made you this."

"She did?" Addisyn stared with wide, reverent eyes. "When?"

"Right after you were born." Avery flipped to the first page. "Here's the photos of her with you at the hospital."

"Wow." A smile tugged the corner of Addisyn's mouth up. "I was pretty small."

"Yeah. You were." Avery glanced from the blanket-bundled baby to the expression of the woman holding her. She'd never quite figured out what was written across Mom's face in these photos. Resentment? Disappointment? Maybe simple exhaustion.

Addisyn turned the page and gasped. "A, look! There we are."

Avery chuckled in spite of herself. In the photo, she was between three and four years old, face incandescent with joy, arms wrapped protectively around her baby sister. Already trying to shelter her.

El Shaddai, help me protect her again. For her. Not for me.

She swallowed some aching emotion and slung an arm around Addisyn's shoulders. If only she could hold them both together through all that lay ahead. "Yeah. Best day of my life." She cleared her throat and tapped the page. "Mom wrote something."

"She did?"

The hunger in Addisyn's eyes nearly brought tears to Avery's own. What kind of mother would leave her daughter so ravenous to hear a single word from her?

Addisyn was focusing on the page, squinting at the untidily scribbled words. "'Baby Girl born April 13. Addisyn Grace Miles. Weight seven pounds, five ounces. Length eighteen inches. She is healthy and happy and already loves spending time with her big sister.'" Addisyn grew quiet, something darker filling her eyes.

"What's wrong?" Avery kept her voice gentle.

Addisyn hesitated. "Did she—did she write anything else?"

Avery bit her lip. "No." She sighed. "I've looked through it before. The rest of the book is blank."

Addisyn nodded slowly, flipping the empty remaining pages. "I —I just thought maybe she would have said something else."

"Like what?"

"Like—" Addisyn shrugged one shoulder. "Like maybe she was, you know, excited—or that I was special—or—" She lifted her chin and flashed her ice-rink smile. "You know, the mushy stuff that moms are supposed to say."

The hurt behind that artificially brave smile sliced right through Avery. She gripped the edge of the table. Even dead, their mom was reaching back through the past to hurt Addisyn. And she was powerless to do anything about it.

Frustration snarled with her sorrow. Why was Addisyn so desperate to scavenge crumbs of affection from a nonexistent mom? Especially when it was Avery who had always been there for her?

Addisyn was watching her. She had to say something. The first of many delicate evasions she'd have to make. "There could have been a lot of reasons she didn't get the chance to write more, Ads." *Because she wasn't excited. Because she didn't care.* "But—"

"It's okay." Addisyn folded the book shut and shoved it away. "I mean, I get it. She was probably really busy with a new baby and everything."

Busy? Busy feeling sorry for herself. Busy visiting those pill bottles that lived behind the bathroom mirror. Busy mixing them with the alcohol Avery had found in the laundry room that summer. "Ads—"

"It's fine." Addisyn shoved her hands in her pockets. "Can I— can I ask you something?"

Breathe in. Breathe out. Measure words in her palm. "Sure."

"Did Mom—" Addisyn rubbed at an invisible spot on the table. "Was she, you know, happy with me?"

"Happy with—"

"When I was born." Addisyn looked up, the question stark within her eyes. "Was she happy?"

A stone sank in Avery's stomach, and a thousand images swam through her mind. The way Dad had roared in tirades. The way their mother had early on laid Addisyn in Avery's arms and never seemed able to pick her up again. The way their parents' marriage, so long fractured, had crumbled into nothingness.

All after Addisyn was born.

And now, twenty-five years later, here was her little sister, looking mostly like the lost nine-year-old whose mother had just disappeared.

Waiting to hear if she had been wanted.

Avery dug her fingernails into her sweaty palms, her throat tightening. "Addisyn—" What she wouldn't give to make her voice the only one her sister heard. *You matter. You are special and wonderful and valued. Mom lost the greatest gift when she turned away from you.*

"Mom had—Mom found it hard to be a mother." The kindest way out. "I think she just wasn't cut out for that role."

Addisyn glanced down. Back into the apathetic eyes of the woman in the photo. "Okay." She spoke her next words without looking up. "Do you think—she ever tried to find us?"

Avery's heart hammered into overdrive. *No, El Shaddai. No.* "What do you mean?"

"Just—" Addisyn shrugged. "We were in New York after you graduated. So maybe—maybe she tried to find us and couldn't. Dad didn't know where we were."

"Okay, but Addisyn, you were skating. Remember?" Avery fought to keep the panic out of her voice. "If she had wanted to find us, all she would have had to do was Google your name."

"And you're sure—there were no signs she ever looked for—"

"Addisyn, what do you mean *signs*?" Avery couldn't control the frayed edge to her voice.

"I mean—" Addisyn studied her with searching eyes. "You never heard from her. Right?"

There it was. The black and white gate looming before her. Avery swallowed down the bitter taste of the lie. "Right." A single word that bound her to a truth she would die to conceal.

And to her relief, Addisyn seemed to accept it. "Well—okay. But maybe she tried." Addisyn turned pleading eyes on Avery. "Don't you think?"

"Well, she didn't try hard enough." True on so many levels. Avery snatched up the photo frame. "That's all that's in here."

"Can I take this stuff back home? To look at more later?"

Her heart was still pounding, the sick taste of the lie still curling in her gut. "Well—" She didn't love the idea, but she couldn't exactly say no. It was as much Addisyn's stuff as hers, anyway. "Sure. Let me make sure there's nothing else in here I wanted to show you." And more importantly, nothing she *didn't* want to show her.

For all her careful labeling system, some unrelated things had still managed to make their way in here. A messy set of files related to her job in New York, an old high school trophy with a now-chipping label, and—

Her fingers touched paper. A letter? An envelope? What was some stray envelope doing here at the bottom of the—

She shoved the files aside. Her name stared up at her from the front of the envelope.

In Mom's handwriting.

"So I was seven pounds, five ounces?" Addisyn was flipping through the baby book again. "Is that big?"

"What?" Her heart was throbbing out of her chest. She remembered the envelope, of course. But she hadn't remembered sticking it in here. She had to distract Addisyn somehow. Had to get this out of the box without her noticing.

"I was just wondering, because that sounds big to me, but the nurse at my appointment actually said that—"

The one thing that would blow the whole secret wide open, and she'd inadvertently placed it right under her sister's nose. She'd never wanted to see that envelope again herself. But she certainly, certainly, couldn't have Addisyn finding it.

Ever.

"Avery?" Addisyn sounded impatient. "Are you listening to me?"

"Yes. Of course. That's about average size. But your baby might be smaller, because it's your first one. They say that's the case." That was some old wives' tale, but at least it would temporarily occupy Addisyn. Avery casually lifted the slipping stack of files, tucking the envelope underneath. "These are from my job. I don't know how they got in the box. You can take the rest of this stuff home."

"Okay." Addisyn slid the baby book on top. Then she leaned against the table and looked earnestly at Avery. "Thanks so much, A. I really appreciate this. It's helped me, getting to hear everything from you."

Not everything. The bitterness burned in Avery's throat. The only lie she'd ever hidden from her sister, and it was tightening its tentacles around her soul. "Well, yes. Of course."

Addisyn pulled out her phone and checked the time. "I guess I need to be heading home. Darius will be wondering where I am." She hefted the box and headed for the door. "I'll bring this stuff back to you soon."

"That's fine." She'd be happy to never have the stuff again. But watching Addisyn carry the box away felt like sending a short-fused grenade home with her sister.

On the threshold, Addisyn paused and threw a smile more real than any she'd given all day back over her shoulder. "I love you, A."

Would she still if she knew the truth? Avery blinked back the stinging in her eyes. "I love you too, Ads." If only her sister could know how much. If only she could understand that what Avery had had to do, she'd done out of that love.

And then Addisyn was out the door, carrying all the boxed-up past. And Avery was left staring at the item that had reappeared with the persistence of an ominous curse.

The last words she had from her mother. The secret the woman had spilled on that day she'd come back.

The envelope flap was already broken. Years ago, Avery had

opened it after finding it in their mailbox when she came home from school. And inside was still the one item she remembered. She slipped out the dog-eared business card and stared at the name on the front.

Lance Potter.

—⧖—

IT WAS RAINING. Again. A depressing, dull drumming on the roof.

Lance frowned out the window as he pulled a breakfast burrito from his freezer. Here, in the earliest hours of the day, the light hadn't broken through. Streetlights still shimmered on the wet road. A car splashed by, spraying its headlights through an arc of water. His commute would be rotten today. Again.

He plunked the burrito in the microwave and hit the express button, watching the food spin slowly in the faint glow. The things tasted like cardboard, but they were easy to buy and fast to cook. Invaluable for a guy always running out of time.

The microwave beeped. He retrieved the soggy burrito and glanced at the clock. Ten minutes till he had to leave for the office. He opened his tablet while he ate, flicking through the pages of the electronic newspaper. Usual sorry stuff. Crimes, tragedies, world events. The same onslaught of disaster that dominated every morning's headlines—and kept at least half of his clients coming to his office. Every other psychiatrist in town probably felt the same way.

And that's why he was there. To absorb the weight of what his clients could no longer hold. And then to write them a prescription for short-lived peace.

Well, where was the sports section? Classifieds...local news...obituaries. He was swiping quickly through the born-lived-died pages when suddenly a picture leaped out.

Beth, true to life. Staring at him with those hazel eyes.

His heart jolted. What was this? Surely she wasn't—

His eyes raced for the text below the picture.

Elizabeth Scranton Miles passed away on May—

The gut punch of the news slugged all the way through him. His stomach twisted through a funnel, and he swiped a hand hard over his face. Dead. Beth was *dead*. Her tortured path through life had finally run into a wall. Or over a cliff. Or both.

He gulped in a gasp of air—had his lungs worked since he'd seen her picture?—and tried to focus on the rest of the article. It was terse, tight. The way she'd been. Who had been left to write it?

A lifelong resident of the Syracuse area, Elizabeth was living in Aston at the time of her death.

Another gut punch. Beth had been in Aston? Just fifteen miles away.

She passed away in her sleep after a long battle with liver cancer.

Liver cancer, huh? More likely she'd just given up.

"I hate life." He could still remember the night she'd whispered those words to him. There had been such raw pain in her eyes. The kind of pain that warped human souls into strange shapes and never let them expand to life again.

"Hey, now. It's not so bad." He'd tried for a moment of levity. *"Not with me in it, right?"*

"Lance, I'm serious. I've ruined my chance. And when I die—" She'd stared out the window, where the city lights drowned out the stars. *"It will be the best day of my life."*

Even then, the undercurrents of her voice had chilled him. The words would have waved a red flag for anyone, but especially for him, with his decades in clinical work. But that was one of the last times Beth had bared her heart so openly to him. Shortly after that, she'd cut him off entirely.

He looked back at the article.

She is survived by her daughters, Avery Miles and Addisyn Miles Payne, both residents of Colorado.

If possible, his heart rate kicked even further into overdrive. Her daughters. That was the crux of it all, wasn't it? The beginning and end of his dealings with her.

He scanned the sentence again, turning over words for clues. So both girls were living in Colorado. And Addisyn must be married. How long ago had that happened? She'd be—twenty-four? No, twenty-five. Gosh, how was that possible?

He leaned back, the weight of the last three decades settling across his shoulders. So many broken roads for him. Missed opportunities. Disastrous decisions. In his office, he was calm and wise and soothing, a repository of trust to wounded souls. Yet in reality—

In reality his story wasn't any different from theirs.

And now Beth was dead.

Dead.

Gone.

Mortality was a ghostly face pressing against the still-dark windows. Where was Beth now, anyway? What happened to her? Like, really?

He frowned. Ulys and he had argued this topic several times. Ulys always swore the afterlife was a fairytale. *"Once the biochemical processes of life cease, brain waves stop. The end of consciousness. Just like unplugging a computer."*

Which made sense, but—Lance had heard more stories from his clients than he could deny. Too many of them seemed to find something bigger than that. Unexplainable signs connected to departed loved ones. Or life transformations they credited to religion. And remarkably, he'd seen some of the most guilt-ridden or fear-dazed radically revive, claiming to have experienced some sort of *"forgiveness from God,"* whatever that meant. Something almost like—well, call it *grace* if you wanted, but it made a difference beyond what his medications and therapies could do.

As a result, he'd always been hesitant to subscribe to Ulys's confined worldview. But as he stared into Beth's newsprint eyes, for the first time he found himself hoping it were true.

Better by far to disappear into nothingness—than to give an account of his dealings with this broken woman.

And he needed no higher power to tell him what he already knew: he could never be forgiven.

CHAPTER 13

Red-tailed Hawks were always striking. No matter how many came to the center, Avery would never stop marveling at the shimmer of their rusty feathers, the proud fierceness in their sky-seeking eyes.

And this one was no exception. Even if he wasn't in top shape at the moment.

"Hey there, boy." Avery opened the enclosure door. Huddled on the ground, the hawk ruffled his feathers and clacked his beak half-heartedly at her approach. A bright-white bandage stood out against his wing.

No wonder he didn't feel the best. After being hit by a car, he'd come to the center only yesterday. Chayton had been forced to perform surgery to restructure the broken bones. Now it was just a matter of letting the hawk rest while his body recalibrated toward healing, the way it was designed to do.

So for now, he was in Avery's care.

Moving softly to avoid stressing him more, Avery bundled him in a towel, gently pinning his wings and talons so he couldn't escape. The very first bird she'd helped with had been a Red-tailed in much the same situation. Isaiah, his name had been.

"You know what, buddy? You need a name too." She crooned to the bird as she scooped him up and carried him to the exam room. Laz had begun the tradition of giving the birds Biblical names, and Avery thought through the available possibilities. They already had a

Gideon at the moment. Skyla was talking about using the name Samuel for the little Kestrel that had come in Monday. Avery needed something else. A prophet name. Not Isaiah, or Jeremiah. How about—

"Ezekiel?" She settled the bird on the exam room scale, peering at the readout. Good. His weight was on target. "What about that for a name?"

The bird seemed content to lie still, so she left him just long enough to flip quickly through the pages of the little Bible Skyla kept in the exam room. There it was, in the middle of the Old Testament. Ezekiel's story.

On the fifth day of the fourth month in the thirtieth year, while I was living among the exiles by the Chebar River, the sky opened, and I saw visions from Elohim.

The sky opened. Hmm. Like Creed's *kapemni*? Avery nodded. "That's a good name."

The hawk was beginning to squirm slightly, so she hurried to lay soothing hands on him again. "I'm back, Ezekiel. Is that better?"

She smiled, remembering how she'd held Isaiah so tightly, terrified of letting him go. Laz had gently rebuked her. *"Don't hold wild things too tight."*

That wisdom from her mentor had helped her in many areas of her life—including in her relationship with Addisyn, which had been rocky at the time. But now she wondered what else had hidden behind Laz's words. According to Creed's story, Laz had done a fair amount of straightjacketing him too.

But Laz was trying to repair things. Trying to let the brokenness heal. If only Creed would talk with his dad at least once before he left.

Avery pressed her lips together. Her own mother would have never dreamed of seeking healing. No apologies or repentance or steps toward reconciliation. Nothing except the sharp edges of excuses.

She shook her head and continued her examination of the hawk, moving methodically through the sequence and jotting her observations on the yellowing notepad. He looked good, so far. In no time, he'd be able to practice flying again.

"You'll like that, won't you, boy?" There was always something deeply right about seeing the birds back in the sky.

She carefully removed the bandage and inspected the incision. Chay had done a good job, as always. The mending was in progress.

She'd have to tell Skyla the name she'd chosen. The woman would approve, no doubt. Skyla held a deep respect for hawks and frequently referenced their place in her myths. According to Lakota belief, she'd said, they were messengers from the spirit realm. Creatures on the blurry edges of the spheres, inhabiting the space between the earth and the sky worlds.

Again it sounded like Creed's *kapemni* belief. Heaven and Earth, mirroring each other. Locked in an interrelated dance, where a move made in one affected both, and they met like a sacred kiss in the space between. The space Creed seemed achingly desperate to find.

Avery bundled the hawk again and carried him back to his mew, glancing out the window at the way the sun threw light against the mountains. For her, the crossroads of Heaven and Earth were here. She felt the breaking in of Heaven in every flush of alpenglow before a mountain morning, every gleam of the Milky Way across a dark velvet sky, every wheel of a healed hawk's wings against the sun-brushed clouds.

The God Who'd made these mountains was still breathing upon them. Of that she was sure. It was what had drawn her here in the first place.

Yet somehow—she still wondered. If this was where Heaven touched Earth—then why did God seem so far away?

Her faith was normally an easy cadence, a gentle rhythm that ebbed and flowed through her life like an alpine stream. But the last few days—weeks, really—her spirit had cracked in barren drought. She'd had no knowings—not since Creed's mysterious fire-shadow. She'd heard no gentle whispers, felt no breath of Spirit stirring the terrain of her soul. It had all been as empty as a cloudless sky.

But maybe it was her fault. She hadn't been praying as much.

Hadn't been reaching skyward. Which she needed to change, starting now.

El Shaddai— She stepped back from the hawk's mew and headed outside, blinking in the blazing midday sun. *Thank You that things are better.*

Because they were. She and Addisyn were finding more peace, Creed was easier to work with, and best of all, the night terrors hadn't returned. Whatever had made the anxiety resurface—she refused to credit a connection with her mom's death—had subsided. Her equilibrium was restored.

Right?

She took a deep breath, tried to refocus on her prayer. *May things go well for the fundraiser. Give Skyla wisdom. Help Creed with his video.*

She didn't pray for herself. That would require her to talk to Him about Mom. Which she wasn't ready to do. Not yet. After all, there was nothing to say.

But just being here, spending time with Him—well, this was what she had needed. To press in harder, pray more diligently. Be more faithful. What she felt was probably just the natural result of all she'd been through emotionally. Things would feel all right again in a few days. Most likely after the fundraiser.

Above the tops of the pines, a hawk soared in spiraling circles. Perhaps one of the ones who'd been ground-bound at the center, now flying free.

Avery smiled. So maybe she was still in her healing stages. But pretty soon, she'd be back in the sky again.

As if nothing had ever gone wrong.

✕

"LONG DAY, HUH?"

Avery looked up to see Liv leaning on the doorframe of her workspace. "You could say that." She shoved her computer away, pressing her fingertips into her scratchy eyes.

Liv slumped into one of the metal chairs in front of Avery's desk. "Good news is the weekend is only four days away."

"Haha. Very comforting."

"Hey, you know me. Always bearing glad tidings." Liv pointed at the wall clock. "It's almost six."

"I know. But I've got to get these schedules done tonight."

Liv cocked her head. "They'll wait. It's been a busy week getting ready for the fundraiser. Skyla will understand."

"Well, I'd rather get them finished now." In the past, leaving things undone at work had seemed to worsen her insomnia. And she couldn't risk triggering *that* again.

"Yeah, but why are you even here this late?"

Because as long as she was at work, her fragile peace would hold. But going back to a dark, hollow house, with nothing to occupy her hands, might send her mind into endlessly roaming the halls of her memories again. Avery narrowed her eyes at Liv. "Why are *you* still here?"

Liv laughed. "Touché."

"Seriously." Avery flipped her papers to the next stack. "Why aren't you with Matt?"

A shadow of uncertainty dimmed Liv's face. "Matt...well, he's out of town this week for work." She shrugged as if moving past the idea. "Sometimes I'd rather stay here and be useful than go home and —think. You know what I mean?"

"Yeah." Oh boy, did she. Avery hesitated. What if she told Liv what was happening to her? Opened up about—

"How are things with Creed?"

Avery blinked, the change of subject yanking her away from the moment. "He's—" What could she say?

"A cross between a mountain blizzard and a prickly pear?"

Avery laughed. "You could say that. But—he's not so bad."

"Uh-huh." Liv nodded. "He knows what he's doing. And he really is cute."

Avery rolled her eyes. "You've pointed that out."

"Yeah, but don't you think so?"

Unbidden, an image of Creed popped into Avery's mind. The

way those smoke-gray eyes could hold the entire sky, could see wonders through the camera lens, could read her like a story she didn't even know she was telling.

A strange feeling shivered inside her chest—a feeling that made her downright uncomfortable.

"He's all right." Irritation—at Liv for introducing such nonsense and herself for entertaining it—sharpened her words more than she'd intended. She winced. Liv didn't deserve her snappishness.

But Liv just slid her a maddeningly knowing glance, then reached for the stack of papers on Avery's desk. "If we're both still here, at least I can help you with this."

"You don't have to—"

"No arguing." Liv's grin made her look more like Addisyn. "Let's knock this out so we can both go back home to our super exciting lives."

Thirty minutes later, they were just finishing up the schedule when Tyler peered around the corner of the door. "I thought I heard voices in here."

"Liv is helping me with the schedule for next week." Avery clicked through the spreadsheet. "Guess we're all here late."

"Yeah, and Skyla's working in her office still." Tyler cleared his throat. "Uh, Avery, so I had a question for you."

"Uh-huh?" Maybe about the curriculum. Good thing she was finally prepared to answer.

"It's not work-related."

"Oh. Okay." Avery clicked one of the empty cells on the spreadsheet. Why wasn't the color coding showing up?

"Would—would you like to go downtown with me on Friday evening?"

Avery jerked her head from the spreadsheet and stared at Tyler. Oh wow. Oh no. "Um—"

"Are you—" Liv snapped her mouth shut, sank in her chair.

Color burned high in Tyler's face, a vulnerability in his eyes that was usually hidden beneath his business-minded defenses. "I mean—if you want to. I thought we could get some frozen yogurt."

"Tyler." Avery shook her head, still scrambling to align her suddenly shifted reality. "Are you—asking me out?"

"Well." He straightened his shoulders. His smile was sheepish, but not apologetic. "I guess I am."

"Like—a date."

"Yeah."

Liv stared between them as if she were following a tennis match.

Words had entirely abandoned her brain. A date? Dating wasn't remotely on her radar screen. And Tyler, of all people. He was just a friend. A coworker, for crying out loud.

But his face was so hopeful it hurt. She couldn't bear to let him down. Especially in front of Liv.

"Uh..." She could survive one date, couldn't she? "Yes, Tyler. That sounds good."

He released an audible breath, his face brightening. "Great. Text me your address. Can I pick you up at, say, seven?"

She got off work at five. That gave her plenty of time. "That works."

"Thanks." He nodded, backing out of the doorway. "Looking forward to it."

"Yes."

He'd already fled back down the hall. Avery collapsed against the back of her chair and stared at Liv. "Wow."

"So he finally got up the nerve." Liv shook her head and grinned. "Hey, look at you, girl! You got a date!"

Avery sighed. "Liv, I'm not looking for a relationship right now." That was putting it mildly. She hadn't been on a date since high school prom, when that guy with the braces had asked her. What was his name?

"Okay, sure." Liv shrugged. "But hey, keep an open mind. It might be fun."

Avery nodded vaguely, her thoughts already leapfrogging through the ramifications. She'd have to wear something nice. Find something to do with her hair. Miss her usual after-dinner reading time. Oh, already she was regretting this.

"I think this is super exciting." Liv's smile glinted mischievous.

"And to think, I was right here on the scene when it all went down. I demand full details after the fact."

"You sound like my little sister." Oh, Addisyn could never find out about this. Avery sighed and stood. "Come on. Help me print out these spreadsheets so we can go home. Before anything else crazy happens."

THE TRAIL FORGED UPWARD through a thick curtain of pines, and Creed savored a breath of the mountain-scented air. He'd be sore tomorrow from this hike, but the journey was exhilarating. Why had he waited until now—four weeks into his stay—to explore?

Yesterday, he had been watching Avery exercise one of the birds when she'd mentioned that she was going to hike at Lake Haiyaha this week. He'd furrowed his brow. "Lake *what*?"

"Lake Haiyaha." Avery had stared at him as if he'd asked what the Statue of Liberty was. "It's one of the prettiest lakes in the whole national park. Right on the ridge, near the glacier."

Glacier. His attention had been snagged. "A *real* glacier?"

She'd grinned. "Very real. I only work half a day tomorrow, so I'm going to Haiyaha afterwards, since the weather's so nice."

Which was why he was spending his Wednesday afternoon trudging up an arduously vertical trail—still snowy, at this elevation —with his camera strapped to his belt, letting Avery lead him into the beating heart of the park. He swiped the sweat from his forehead as they rounded yet another turn.

"You can see the whole valley down there." Avery swept a hand toward the panorama below without breaking stride. "We can stop on the way back and take pictures."

"Oh. Wow." The other glacial lakes were dotted across an expansive view that unrolled between the stern faces of the peaks all the way to the hazy horizon. The trail had certainly gained a lot of elevation, with no sign the climb would slack off soon. "And—how much farther is this, exactly?"

"Oh, it's just right around the bend."

He gave a mock groan. "That's what you've been saying for the last thirty minutes."

"Right." She tossed a smile over her shoulder. "I'm estimating."

"Great." He shook his head. "I see how it is."

She laughed, the sound mixing with the mountain wind, and he smiled. Regardless of his pretend complaints, this was the most fun he'd had since—well, a long time.

Avery was gaining ground on him. He jogged a few steps to catch up. "You hike fast."

"Just habit, I guess." She was barely out of breath. Infuriating and amazing. "The faster I can go, the farther I can go."

"That—makes sense." His breathing was getting away from him. But he'd lose a lung before he'd ask her to slow down.

"Anyway—" Avery pointed ahead, where the trail suddenly swooped into a downhill section. "We're going to go down for a bit here."

He blinked. "Really?"

"Really." She was gaining on him again, hopping across the rocky terrain and the remnants of the snow with practiced agility. "How else could we climb on the way back?"

The trail continued its descent, burrowing into a valley, and then changed its mind and swelled upward again. Creed had nearly given up on ever reaching a destination when Avery pointed ahead. "Here we are."

He scrambled up the last section and blinked. A jumbled boulder field in front of him encircled a sad, grassy puddle that might, at its greatest, be called a *pond*. "That's, uh, that's the lake?"

"That?" Avery's look was half exasperation and half pity. "The lake is behind the boulders."

"Oh." He cleared his throat as he followed her into the boulder field. "Makes more sense."

Sure enough, as he made his way through the tumbled stones— most of which were taller than him—snatches of blue-green water began to appear. Just as he ducked around the sprawling roots and branches of a particularly gnarly old tree, the full glory of the setting burst upon him. "Wow!"

The lake shimmered green like cut glass, dancing in the face of the alpine sun. Behind, a thick wooded ridge hemmed it in protective arms. And to the left, the sheer rock profiles of the High Peaks seemed close enough to touch, a white milky spill cradled in a dip in the ridgeline.

Avery pointed. "The glacier."

"This is—" His laugh was born of sheer wonder. "Amazing."

"I know. It's the best." There was a music to Avery's voice that hadn't been there in the valley. She gazed across the water with the loving familiarity of an old friend.

"I've got to get some shots of this." He reached for his camera bag, but a much larger boulder on the water's edge caught his eye. "Can we get up there?"

"Sure, if you want. It's a little steep, though."

"Hmm." He toed his shoe into a crack in the rock and braced his hands against the sun-warmed granite. A heave and a scramble, and he was up. The stone was massive, its crown large enough for three people. He looked down at Avery and held out his hand. "Care to come up?"

She hesitated for just a moment before slipping her hand into his. Her grip was gentle, but strong. Just like her.

Something trembled strangely in his chest. If he didn't know better, he would think—

"Thanks." She swung into place beside him and pulled her hand away.

"Uh, sure. No problem." He busied himself with his camera, dismissing the odd sensation. The lighting was perfect, the mountains seeming to gleam in the afternoon haze. Even his finest camera work couldn't capture the glory of the scene, but he would do his best. He panned some video, then switched to still shots.

Beside him, Avery was lost in another world, a peaceful daydream hovering over her face, the sun glowing on her hair, and the trees darkly protective behind her. On sudden impulse, he turned the camera on her and snapped the still shot. He'd send it to her later, after he downloaded everything to his laptop.

He lowered the camera and studied her. "What are you thinking?"

"Nothing really, I guess." Her voice was soft, almost reverent. "Just that there's more glory than we know. All around us, all the time. But people don't see it a lot."

He hadn't, when he'd first arrived in the Rockies. But his eyes were starting to come awake. "Yeah." He rubbed a thumb over the familiar shape of his camera. "Sometimes film can fix that. Help people see things in a different way."

"That makes sense." Avery crossed her legs, adjusting her position. "I looked at your channel, actually."

"Guys in the Wild?"

"Yeah."

He should have been proud, but as he thought of all the fake-hype videos he'd edited, an odd sense of shame squirmed inside him instead. "Oh—and—"

"Your filming's really good."

"Well—thanks." He cleared his throat. "It's not the kind of content I want to be making forever, but right now, it pays the bills. And Austin has connections. This could open a lot of doors."

"Like the international team?"

She'd remembered? "Yeah. Like that."

"So—" She turned and squinted at him, raising a hand to shield the sun. "What *do* you want to be making?"

He stared at the light dancing on the water. Usually such heavy questions tangled his tongue, but somehow, here with Avery, he could go deeper without drowning. "When I entered my first film workshop, it was a summer program. I put together this video about the Rez—Pine Ridge, you know. How beautiful the people were, how enduring the culture was, but how hard the conditions were. How people were living in poverty and struggling to get by, but they were still making something that was beautiful and lasting and part of—part of their heritage." The words were tumbling out, the story unspooling. "I wanted to honor the people of the Rez. And I wanted others to see what was happening, to be moved to want to help."

"That sounds like an incredible video." She was listening with her whole heart. That was obvious. "What happened with it?"

The rock was suddenly harder beneath him. "Well—the leaders of my dad's ministry weren't really—on board."

"Why not?"

A flare of the old anger flickered in him. "It didn't fit in their Christian box. A box that got smaller all the time, by the way."

"Oh." The syllable was heavy with empathy. "I'm really sorry, Creed. I hope you know that God is bigger than the people who speak for Him."

The simple statement sank into his soul. "Thanks, but—I don't really know where I stand with God." He'd spent years blaming everyone else for the distance between him and the Divine. But now he knew he'd taken a broken trail too. "I've done some stuff I'm not super proud of."

"We all make mistakes."

This coming from the woman he'd called Saint Avery. He'd wager her mistakes were a lot smaller than his. "I guess."

"That's where grace comes in." Avery glanced to the sky, squinting against the brightness of the day. "El Shaddai gives it and gives it like the sun gives light."

El Shaddai. He'd never asked, but—"That's what you call God. Why?"

"Well—" She smiled as if sharing a secret with the mountains. "The first Bible I had was a beat-up Names of God version. I bought it at Goodwill for under two dollars, and I was flipping through it, and I saw that name. El Shaddai. You know what it means?"

"I've heard it, but I don't remember." He'd forgotten a lot about God.

"God of the mountains."

Understanding washed over him. "So when you say you came to God's country—"

"I mean it." Avery shrugged. "He's God of everything. But to me —He's the God of the mountains."

A longing tugged inside him. At one time, he'd known God with the kind of simple trust Avery seemed to have. Then, when the tie with Dad had broken, so had the one with his Heavenly Father. But here, in the holy bowl of the glacial valley, he could almost imagine himself believing again.

That's where grace comes in…

He stretched out his legs, letting his thoughts drift slow as the sunlight. Before him, the waters of Lake Haiyaha held the face of the sky back up to itself. A reflection.

"Have you ever heard of earth-sky mirroring?"

The words were out before he realized how abrupt the question must seem. But Avery didn't look fazed. "Sort of. The *kapemni*, right?" She shrugged one shoulder. "The idea that the other world is close?"

"Yeah, that's part of it." The concept had defined his life since Charlie had introduced him to it, and here he couldn't find the words to explain it. He sat up, struggling to fit the symbol in a sentence. "It's more the idea that—well, that what we do matters. That the responsibility of Earth is to mirror the spirit world. And that what happens in the spirit world affects what happens on Earth. They're connected."

Avery nodded slowly. "I believe that. I've seen it." She tilted her head thoughtfully. "There's a Scripture about that. That what we bind on Earth is bound in Heaven, and what we release on Earth is set free in our spirits."

Normally he was wary of Bible verses, after watching the ministry leaders lob them like grenades. But these words sounded gentle, freeing. And like what Skyla had said. "Hmm. That fits, I guess."

"We live in a reflection of Heaven." Avery stared at the mountains. "I love that thought."

A reflection of Heaven. Really? The hurt he'd carried since the Rez hardened again. "But—" He caught the question before it slipped out. Avery was a Christian, after all.

"But what?"

"Well—" No need to cast the shadow of his disillusionment over her too.

"Come on, Creed." She turned toward him, the sun catching the lighter glints in her hair. "You can ask me."

"Well, how do Christians—" No, that wasn't right. He cleared his throat. "How do *you* feel about when the mirror is—broken?" He spread his hands, trying to explain. "When—well, when God doesn't seem like—what you thought. Or what you were told He was, maybe. And if God was—you know, Who He said—things would be—different."

The question had all but limped out, but Avery seemed to understand. She looked back at the water. "I've wondered that myself, lately." Her voice was gentle. "I think it's like—well, look at the lake. Right now, you can see the clouds so easily. True?"

The puffy summer clouds peered at him upside-down from the greenish glass. "Yeah."

"But I've been up here when the wind was racing down the peaks, and the water was all choppy, and there was no reflection at all." Avery shrugged. "The sky doesn't change. But the reflection depends on the water."

The truth settled into his soul. "On us."

Avery nodded. "We don't mirror Heaven all the time. Or in the right way. I know that more than most people. But—" She gazed at the mountain peaks. "I think we have to try."

He swallowed hard. *Saint Avery.* The nickname he'd given her in mockery was nothing but admiration now.

He allowed himself to sink into the silence alongside her, letting the spring day sing for them both. The mountain air filled his lungs like the release of a prayer, and the sun burned brighter than any sacred fire. He hadn't yet found the place where Heaven and Earth touched.

But here, high in the mountains, in the country of Avery's God —he was closer than he'd ever been.

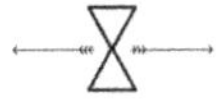

No matter how many times Addisyn stared at the page of the baby book, things still didn't add up.

She smoothed her hand across the paper, studying the single photo. Rereading the words she'd already read a hundred times since Saturday.

Baby Girl born April 13. Addisyn Grace Miles. Weight seven pounds, five ounces. Length eighteen inches. She is healthy and happy and already loves spending time with her big sister.

Nothing else. Just this fact-clipped statement.

Already loves spending time with her big sister.

For some reason, the words swelled an odd resentment. Of course she'd loved spending time with Avery. Avery was the anchor in her earliest memories, the one she ran to when she scraped her knee or needed help tying her shoes, when she struggled with a difficult math problem or flinched under middle-school taunts. And Avery was the one who'd always rescued her—then, in the midst of their chaos, and later, when she'd burst the padlocked prison of their old life.

But still, a hard edge ground inside her soul. Somehow those words in the baby book sounded like an excuse. Why hadn't her mom been the one to parent and protect her?

Because she hadn't been excited when Addisyn was born.

Oh, Avery hadn't come right out and said that, but Addisyn had seen the careful way she sidestepped the issue. It had been a dumb question to ask, anyway. Childish. Clearly her mother hadn't felt for her what most moms did. Otherwise, she would have never walked away.

And where did that leave Avery?

A guilt she hadn't fully expected settled in her chest. Was that why Avery was mad at Mom—because she felt as if Mom had foisted Addisyn on her? After all, she'd never had a choice about taking care of her younger sister. And she'd sacrificed much of her future to give Addisyn one.

But surely Avery didn't resent that.

Or did she?

Avery, I'm sorry.

Frustration tangled around her other emotions. See, this was the worst part. She wanted to work through this, wanted them both to talk through the story and finally accept the ending. Mostly, she wanted—well, she wanted Avery to be there for her. The way she always had been.

But every time Addisyn dared to bring up the topic to Avery, she might as well have argued with Longs Peak.

Addisyn forced the uncomfortable feelings away and studied Mom's picture again. Regardless of Avery's denials, she really did resemble their mom. Same high cheekbones, same hazel eyes, although Avery had always had more of a farseeing expression. In this photo, Mom's smile seemed frozen, her expression subtly desperate. Had she been strategizing her escape from their lives even then?

A mom who leaves her kids isn't a mom. That's what Avery had said.

But she'd been a mom at one time, hadn't she?

Addisyn's early memories were hazy, like blurry shots taken with a cheap Polaroid. Most were just disconnected snatches—the aroma of the walnut muffins her mom sometimes baked, or the Santa candy cane holder she put out at Christmas, or her silhouette standing in the doorway on summer evenings, shading her eyes and calling the girls back inside.

But one memory stood out, sharp against the confused cloud.

Before Addisyn had started kindergarten, she'd hated the beginning of the school year, when Avery rode away on the bus and left her for the entire dull-dragging day. One afternoon, she'd moped so much that Mom had taken her into the backyard for a tea party, complete with little cucumber sandwiches. And after their meal, Mom taught her to blow soap bubbles. She'd spent the rest of the afternoon racing after them, until she was finally, happily tired.

Then she ran back to the picnic blanket and flopped onto Mom, whose sudden silver laugh was as bright and airy as the bubbles. *"That's my little girl."* Addisyn squirmed with happiness at the affection in her mom's voice. *"My beautiful little girl."*

And then she saw Avery, apparently home from school. Watching them with an odd expression.

"Avery!" She'd sprung up and raced to her sister, tackling her in a hug. *"Come here and look at—"*

But Avery's eyes were still on Mom. And Mom was studying the grass. Then Mom quickly stood and gathered the picnic things. *"It's time to go back inside."*

She'd disappeared into the house with the finality of the screen door's slap. Avery must have seen the tremble in Addisyn's lip, because she'd quickly squeezed an arm around her shoulders. *"Hey, are you having a tea party? Can I play?"*

Addisyn blinked out of the memory. She'd replayed it so many times that it was stretched and sagging, like a worn-out vinyl recording. But she'd never understood why her mom had acted so weird toward Avery.

It wasn't even just that day. All their lives until Mom left, she and Avery had never really seemed to get along. Whatever the cause might have been, it had floated well above the level of Addisyn's juvenile awareness. But maybe—maybe it was the reason Avery was so mad at Mom now.

And maybe it was why, all those years ago, Avery had seemed to immediately accept that their mom was gone. She'd locked into executive mode as soon as the taillights disappeared, marshaling them to face the logistical changes, the schedule interruptions, the practical pieces of the event. By contrast, Addisyn would sit on her bed at night and will each set of headlights on the street to turn in their driveway. She'd pictured it all—how her mom would get out of the car and stand silhouetted in the headlights with open arms, how Addisyn would run downstairs and into the fresh coolness of the evening, how her mom would catch her in her arms and hold her so tightly she'd never let go again.

My beautiful little girl.

Steeping in the memories was making Addisyn's chest ache. And making her wish even more that Avery would just talk to her about this, would let her spill her feelings and then help her untangle them, the way she always had.

Honestly, every time she talked to Avery, something just seemed off. It was almost—well, if she hadn't known any better, she'd almost think Avery was hiding something. As if her sister knew more than she let on.

Nonsense. She really was losing her mind, to think that Avery would ever deceive her. Her sister had gold-standard character. And honesty was something she took very seriously. She'd never resorted even to a white lie.

She glanced at the clock and reached for her phone. Avery would be off work by now. Maybe she could try to talk with her one more time.

Her sister answered on the second ring. "Hey, Ads."

"Hey, Avery. How was work?"

"Oh—" Avery sounded exhausted. The way she had for months now. "Long." She yawned. "But it's getting better. Creed is helping me develop my curriculum."

"Oh?" This was a new twist. Addisyn smirked, grateful Avery couldn't see her. "That's nice of him."

"Yes, for sure. He's doing the filming for me. It was his idea."

I bet. Addisyn grinned. That was another reason she needed to come to Estes soon. Not to matchmake, of course. Just to—investigate. "Hey, I was wondering if I could come up Friday evening. Darius and I are going to Steamboat on Saturday, but I still want to see you this week."

"Uh—actually, I'm busy on Friday evening."

Busy? Her antisocial sister? Addisyn narrowed her eyes. "You started night hiking?"

Avery's laugh halted uneasily. "Well, um, no, I have a—a thing."

"A thing?"

"I'm going downtown."

"By yourself?"

There was defeat in Avery's sigh. "No. I—I guess you could call it a date."

A date? A *date?* A real-life, honest-to-goodness, roses-and-kisses date? "A!" Addisyn jumped up, her chair clattering to the floor behind her. She righted it with one hand and smashed the phone to her ear with the other. "Wait a minute. You never told me! Like a real date? What are you doing?"

"Yes, a real date. Frozen yogurt downtown, is what he said."

So Creed had finally mustered the nerve. Hallelujah! "Now do you think I was right about Creed?"

"What does Creed have to do with this?"

Addisyn blinked. "The date—is not with Creed?"

"No!" Indignation scorched the word. "Addisyn, Creed and I are just—coworkers. Well, friends now, I guess. The date is with Tyler."

Oh. Addisyn flopped back into the chair. Tyler was significantly less interesting than Creed. He was one of those straight-laced, stiff-collared guys that she'd always secretly worried Avery would end up with. But still, if her sister was happy—and at least she was dating. That was a start. "Well, hey! Tyler is a good guy."

"Addisyn—" A warning hung in Avery's voice. "Don't start."

"Start what?"

"You know what." Her sister's tone left no room for argument. "It's just a date between friends. It's not—not serious."

"Okay. Whatever you say." She grinned, then blinked as the most important thought struck her. "Wait, what are you wearing?"

"I haven't thought that far ahead yet."

Oh, no. No, she could not leave her fashion-blind sister to her own devices for this. "A, I'll help you. Okay? Pick out some possibilities"—could Avery be trusted with even that small measure of responsibility?—"and FaceTime me beforehand."

"It's really not that big of a deal. It's just casual."

Casual. Avery would use that word as an excuse to show up in a wrinkled graphic tee and hiking pants. "Look, casual or not, it's still a date. You need to look like a girl, at least."

"Addisyn—" There was a groan behind her name. "I'm twenty-eight, okay? I can dress myself." Avery's tone softened. "Listen, I'll send you a picture beforehand so you can approve. All right?"

Well, that was probably the best she could ask for. Addisyn sighed. "All right. Can you just promise me this? No hiking pants."

Avery actually laughed. "Okay, Ads. Deal."

CHAPTER 14

Although Monday had been a long day at the center, Tuesday, Wednesday, and Thursday were even longer. Between helping Liv with the school groups, prepping for the fundraiser, and filming her lessons with Creed, Avery was stretched to the breaking point. By the time Friday evening mercifully ended her work week, the last thing she felt like doing was dressing up and driving downtown to eat frozen yogurt with Tyler.

Why had she agreed to this, anyway? What she'd told Liv was true. She simply wasn't looking for a relationship. She had the mountains and the birds and the beating wings of her faith. Why couldn't that be enough?

She had stayed late at the center—one of the raptors accidentally re-injured his wing, and both Tom and Chay were off work, meaning that the care of the wound fell to her. By the time she was home and getting dressed, she had only twenty minutes until Tyler would pick her up. Great.

At least she didn't have a lot of preening to do. Last night, she'd already selected her outfit—not an easy process. She'd rolled her eyes at Addisyn's disparagement of her wardrobe, but an exploration of her closet had revealed that all her clothes truly did fall into two categories: hiking garb on one hand, and the artifacts of her *"business casual"* job in NYC on the other. Not much in the middle.

Regardless of her promise to Addisyn, she was strongly tempted to opt for her outdoor clothes. Tyler saw her in them every day at work, anyway. But instead, she found a stiff pair of jeans and an over-sized T-shirt with the words *On Mountain Time* stenciled above brightly colored peaks.

She snapped a quick mirror selfie and texted it to Addisyn. Her little sister would no doubt complain it wasn't glamorous enough—and probably scold her for the lack of makeup. But Addisyn wore lipstick to the grocery store. Her standards were significantly higher than where Avery was aiming.

She ran a brush through her hair just as a light *beep* sounded from outside. She glanced out the window to see Tyler's sensible Honda Acura nosed expectantly by the porch. Well, time to meet her fate.

Outside, Tyler reached across the passenger seat to open her door. "Hi, Avery. You ready?"

"Yes!" She manufactured a bright smile. Wow, Tyler was dressed up. He was probably the only guy she knew who would wear a polo and dress slacks to eat frozen yogurt.

He raised his eyebrows at her. "Nice shirt. You look comfortable."

Comfortable. Thank all that was holy that Addisyn hadn't heard that.

He turned the key, and the car started with a compliant purr. Not much like her truck. "Did your class go well today?"

"Yes." Why couldn't she think of anything to add to that?

Tyler maneuvered slowly down her driveway, but a cloud of midsummer dust still swirled around his spotlessly waxed car. "It looked like a big group."

"About twenty-five kids from Northrup High."

"That's good."

The conversation stalled awkwardly. Great. Thirty seconds in, and they were already out of things to say.

Avery's jeans were damp where she'd been squeezing her thighs. She folded her hands in her lap. "So, um, where are we going for yogurt?"

"I thought we could go to The Glacier. We'll get some yogurt and go to the River Walk." He waited a beat before adding, "As long as you want to, that is."

Did she really have a choice? "Yes. That sounds great."

Another protracted pause.

Avery's phone vibrated. She glanced down to see a text from Addisyn.

You should have worn makeup.

Of course.

A second text swooped in.

But otherwise, you look good. Have fun!

Tyler drummed a finger on the steering wheel. "Fundraiser should go well."

"For sure." She gripped the topic with relief. Work talk they could handle. They did this every day. "We need to start the setup next week."

"Agreed." Tyler nodded. "You still think we should take the tents outside?"

"I think so." They'd agreed earlier that tables set under canopies would bring a creative aesthetic to the event.

"I agree. And Laz should have the new building completed by then, so I'm thinking we can use that as a backup in case of rain."

Classic Tyler. His plans had baby plans of their own.

Talk of the fundraiser carried them along until they reached The Glacier. Avery expected more awkwardness about who was paying, but Tyler ordered his yogurt without asking her what she was having. Okay, then.

"What will it be?" The redheaded young man behind the counter looked at her expectantly.

Normally she kept her orders here light and simple—the orange dream, or the raspberry ice. But to get through the rest of the night, she needed something much more heavy-duty. "I'll take the double chocolate delight, please."

As they headed onto the River Walk, Tyler peered at her yogurt with a hint of disdain. "I learned long ago I can't handle that much sugar. It gives me indigestion."

As Addisyn would say, *TMI.* Something about Tyler's tone made Avery feel low-grade rebellious. She didn't mention that she normally avoided sugar too.

"Nowadays, I stick mainly to fruit." Tyler held up his sorbet, Exhibit A in his presentation. "Like this."

Well, no one was giving bonus points for healthy eating tonight. Avery swirled her spoon in her incriminating chocolate and shrugged. "Probably better."

"That's because the resistance starch in fruit is actually easier on your digestion." Tyler's eyes rounded with the conviction of his opinion. "The fructose breaks down more slowly in your bloodstream."

Avery stared at the flame of the sunset over the mountains. Pity that she had to hear the word *digestion* while looking at that view. If anything, this conversation was just making her need the chocolate more.

The daytime crowd had thinned, but there were still plenty of people on the path: a family with three exuberant kids lining up in front of the river for a picture, a man reading a book on one of the iron benches, a woman jogging with a Jack Russell Terrier on a lime-green leash. And for good reason. The River Walk was magical this time of evening, with the friendly glow of the restaurant windows, the sparkling fairy lights strung along the canopies, and the last pale shimmer of the Big Thompson to their left. Normally a dusky walk along the path could always soothe Avery's soul. But tonight her energies were absorbed by the strenuous task of enjoying herself.

Fortunately, Tyler had switched back to shop talk of the fundraiser. "At any rate, I think it could be big for us. And the response to our promotions so far has been very favorable."

"That's what Skyla was saying." The breeze rustled through the shimmering green leaves on the aspens. "Aren't those pretty?"

Tyler looked around. "What?"

"The aspen leaves."

"Oh." He stared blankly at the tree. "Yeah. Anyway, I think the posters were a good idea. We've received several hits on the link I added. The landing page that the QR code leads to."

"That's good." Avery glanced over her shoulder at the tree one last time. "Creed is going to put up some more posters for us this weekend."

Tyler scowled. "I still don't like that guy."

The acid in his tone made her flinch. "Well—he can be stubborn, I know. But—" She'd seen the flickers of light in his soul. "He's a good guy."

Tyler's mouth only tightened. "He's got an agenda. He's here because of his channel. That means whatever he produces is going to be what's good for *him*. Not us. And that, I don't trust."

I don't trust. Hadn't she worried about the same thing when Creed had begun helping her with the curriculum videos? She'd been suspicious that he might have an alternate agenda, that he was collecting footage for some other reason than helping her. But so far, he'd been trustworthy. Was it really fair to doubt him now?

"Assuming he's still working on that video, anyway." Tyler jabbed the button for the crosswalk a bit harder than necessary. "Seems to me he spends most of his time following you around."

Wait a minute. Was *that* the root of Tyler's dislike? Avery cleared her throat. She had to at least set this record straight. "He's helping me with my curriculum. We're doing some videos for it."

Tyler's eyes narrowed for just a second. Then he nodded. "Well. That's good."

A thick pause pressed around them that Tyler seemed to have no need to break. Too tired to forge any farther into the conversation, Avery instead took refuge in the silence. Why did Tyler—and Addisyn—keep assuming Creed had *that* kind of interest in her? True, he was a nice guy. Smart and creative and downright funny. And with a much bigger heart than he wanted others to see.

For just a minute, she imagined herself in a different reality, where Creed was the one walking next to her right now. He'd be wearing the cargo pants and T-shirts he always did. They'd be chattering about the mountains, or the clouds, or the way the light angled through the aspen leaves. Being with Creed was—to quote Tyler—*comfortable.* She could imagine it all—the way they'd walk, and talk, and when they crossed the street, he'd hold her hand—

Hold her hand? She jerked herself loose from her train of thought. Why was she imagining something so ridiculous?

"Avery?"

Heat rushed up her face. "Yes?"

Tyler's look seemed to question her sanity. "I asked if you were ready to head back to the car."

"Oh." She stared down at the empty yogurt cup in her hand. "Yes."

Avery did her best to concentrate as she and Tyler walked back to the car and drove home. Why had she been thinking about Creed at all when she was on a date? This had nothing to do with him. *She* had nothing to do with him, not really. He'd finish the job here and be on his way to Arizona within two weeks. Then after that, the world. Fulfilling his dreams. The end.

Her phone buzzed again. She glanced at the screen discreetly. Addisyn.

How are things going???

Avery slid her phone back in her pocket. She might not have a lot of dating experience, but even she knew that a successful date didn't involve counting the minutes until you were away from the guy.

"At any rate, I think this fundraiser could be the start of much bigger things. Even if Skyla is still resistant to foundations, there are more flexible options." Tyler turned onto Devils Gulch Road. Only five more minutes now. "I've been doing some research into strategies other nonprofits have used, and I think if we—"

Avery's attention had long since been exhausted. What Tyler was talking about was meaningful and important, of course. But they dwelt on these topics five days a week. For tonight, couldn't they talk about something besides work?

Then it hit her. They couldn't. They had nothing in common besides work. What else would they talk about?

The realization made her desperate to get out of the car. "Yes. I agree." To whatever his last statement had been. As soon as Tyler pulled into her yard, she scooped up her purse and pushed open her door. "Thank you, Tyler. I—I enjoyed tonight." A blurred fib, but what else could she say?

"Thank you for coming." Tyler cleared his throat. "Avery?"

She paused halfway out of the car. So close to freedom. "Yes?"

He opened his mouth. Closed it again. Maybe the disconnect had hit him too. "Uh—I'll see you Monday."

"See you then." She waved goodbye as personably as she could. Then she started for the house, breathing in relief like the cool evening air. Unwilling to peer too deeply at how she'd felt tonight.

Or why she'd rather have been with Creed.

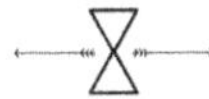

"Well?"

Avery dragged her eyes from the lesson plans she was preparing and blinked at Liv. "Well, what?"

"Well, what happened on Friday?" Liv's grin danced with mischief. "I've been waiting all weekend. Spill it."

"Oh—" Avery sat back and rubbed her eyes. Mid-morning on Monday, and she was already tired. She'd stayed up most of last night working through more plans for the fundraiser. She and Creed were set to film another of her lessons in less than an hour. And she still had to work on the itinerary for the fundraiser. "It went okay."

"Okay?" Liv rolled her eyes. "C'mon. Give a girl some details."

Avery had already endured this conversation with Addisyn and had no desire to rehash it. "It was nice. He picked me up, and we got frozen yogurt and went to the River Walk."

"What'd you do on the River Walk?"

"Walked and talked." Avery tilted her head. "See? Normal. Boring."

"Not necessarily. What did you talk about?"

"Oh—" *Digestion.* "Work, mainly."

"Huh." Liv didn't look satisfied with that answer. "Did he kiss you?"

"Liv!"

"Okay, okay." She held up her hands. "You're right. Not my business."

Avery made a shooing motion. "Don't you have a class to get ready for?"

Liv laughed and backed away. "No. But I can take a hint. See you later."

Avery sighed and shook her head as she printed the finished schedule. Liv and Addisyn never needed to join forces. The two of them would engineer Avery's love life at breakneck speed. Although at least the drama of the date had distracted her younger sister from the Syracuse issue. For now, anyway.

By eleven o'clock, Avery had finished her office work and was ready to film again. She found Creed at the picnic table by his camper. "Hey."

"Hey yourself." He closed his laptop and smiled. The broken sunlight through the pine branches brushed over his face. "Ready to film?"

"Yes." Over the last couple of weeks, speaking on camera had become much easier, even fun. Creed was skilled at making the whole thing feel more like a natural conversation than a performance.

"All right." He gathered his camera bag from the ground next to the table. "What are we filming today?"

"Rocks."

He wrinkled his nose. "Sounds exciting."

Avery laughed. "It will be." She pointed toward the back of the property. "Let's go where the granite field is."

They swished through the tangled hair of the meadow grass, heading for the treeline. Grasshoppers spiraled into the still air, their clicking chorus joining the background of the summer day. Creed cleared his throat. "So, I hear you went on a date this weekend."

"Seriously?" Avery groaned. "News travels fast."

"When Liv is involved, it does." He chuckled. "I assume she begged you for all the details this morning."

"Oh yeah. Where we went, what we did, if he kissed me."

"Wow." He shaded his eyes with his hand. "Sounds like a full report."

"There was no *report*." Receiving the third degree after this date wasn't making her want to go on another. "We walked downtown and got frozen yogurt, and then he drove me back home."

"Did you have a good time?"

Avery hesitated, wavering on the line between kindness and honesty. "It was all right."

Silence settled around them until they reached the granite field— the jumbled leftovers of a rockslide, a river of mica-sparkled rocks flowing down the hillside. Creed whistled. "Pretty impressive."

"I think so too." Avery took the clip-on mic from him and positioned the battery pack in her back pocket. Threading the wire through her shirt, she fumbled with the clip on her collar.

"Good backdrop, too." Creed was still studying the rockslide. "Afterwards I'll do some close-ups."

"Sounds good." What was wrong with the mic today?

"Here." Suddenly Creed's hands were on hers, taking the mic. "Hold still. I'll fix it."

"Oh. Okay." Gosh, he was close. Close enough she could smell that same earthy scent his anorak had held. She kept her eyes on the mountains over his shoulder.

"Just a second. The little clip thing is stuck." His breath was warm on the side of her face. "So—did you kiss him?"

"*What?*"

"Tyler. This weekend." The mic clip snapped shut. Creed stepped sideways, back into her field of vision. "Did you kiss him?"

His smoke-gray eyes held an unfamiliar look. Half teasing, half an almost fearful sincerity. The sun struck the reddish sparks in his hair and deepened the shadow of his stubble.

Something unfamiliar and heady swelled in her chest. Her stomach flipped unexpectedly.

"He didn't kiss me." She laced her fingers together. "He didn't even ask to."

"Would you have? If he had asked?"

A question she'd posed to herself last night, with no answer. But now, standing in front of Creed, she suddenly knew.

"No." The word was a breath. A whisper. Maybe a confession.

He started to say something, then stopped. He was still too close. She should look away, step back, close the door. But whatever had charged the space between them was pulling her closer to—

"Creeeeeed! There you are!!!"

Avery jerked away from Creed just in time to see a strange woman marching up the field, waving with a violent cheerfulness. "Who is that?"

Creed's expression suddenly froze. "Oh—"

"Creed!" The woman all but pranced across the remaining distance to attack him with an enthusiastic hug and smack a kiss near his cheek. This was—someone he knew. Very well, obviously.

Avery's stomach knotted. She stepped back and crossed her arms.

"Erica." Creed gave that artificial smile, the one he used as armor. "What are you doing here?"

"We're done filming in Arizona, and I had a few days free. So, I decided to run up here and help you finish your project before the shindig Friday night." Erica blinked as if noticing Avery for the first time. "Who's this?"

"This is Avery. She—"

"I work at the center." Avery's heart was slowly sucking through a dark funnel. But with the strength forged over years of hiding anxiety, she held out her hand, forced a smile. "Nice to meet you."

"Oh, yes!" Erica gripped her hand a little too tightly. "Creed has talked about you."

He had? Well, she couldn't say he'd told her anything about Erica. Including her existence.

Creed cleared his throat. "Erica and I, um, work together at Guys in the Wild."

"Yes. I'm his friend." Erica slid up to Creed's side and smiled confidentially at him. "He's amazingly talented. It's so much fun to work with him."

Creed edged a step away. "You're too kind."

"So?" Erica flicked a hot-pink fingernail in his direction. "Where's your camper? Let's look at your project."

"Well, actually." Creed gestured to his camera bag. "Um, Avery and I were just getting ready to film a—"

"That can wait." Avery took a step back. She needed to get away. Away from the gaping scar of the rockslide and the ground that had just slid from beneath her own version of reality.

"No, really, Avery." There was pleading in Creed's eyes. "Let me just—"

"It's totally fine." Avery yanked the mic free and thrust the battery pack in his direction. She couldn't even remember what she'd planned to talk about now. "We'll do it later."

Without waiting for his response, she turned and headed back to the center, cold fingers numbing her chest. *Friend.* It didn't take too much brainpower to figure out what kind of *friend* Erica was to Creed.

All this time, he never mentioned he had a—a girlfriend. Addisyn had even asked if he were single, right?

"Hey." Liv's eyes were alive with curiosity when Avery walked in the office. "Who's the girl? She showed up in here looking for Creed."

"She's his—" Ridiculous, to stumble over the word. "Girlfriend."

"Oooohhhh." Liv stretched the syllable into an entire statement. She glanced behind Avery. "Is he still—"

"They're at the rockslide site." Avery headed toward the back door. "I'm going out to the mews."

"But wait, wasn't he—"

She let the door swing shut on Liv's question and kept moving, forcing her feet toward the mews and ignoring the way her eyes wanted to stray toward Creed's camper.

It was fine that he had a girlfriend, of course. Totally fine. It was just—well, it was odd he hadn't mentioned that. Not that he owed her any personal information.

Regardless, it was none of her business anyway. Nor did it change anything as far as she was concerned. After all, he'd still be leaving next week as planned.

The sooner the better now.

YESTERDAY, Creed had watched Chay tending a bird who'd come to the center with a concussion. Chay had flicked a small light into the bird's eyes, nodding seriously. *"He needs a dark, quiet place. A concussion causes confusion and disorientation."*

Confusion and disorientation. Right now, Creed felt exactly like that bird. And he'd be only too thrilled to hide in a dark, quiet place. Somewhere far away from the woman who'd just ambushed him.

"So, Creed." Erica perched on his picnic table bench. "You haven't said much yet."

"Just never expected this." That was putting it mildly. He forced a grin as he opened his laptop. "You didn't say—"

"I know. That's part of the fun of it." Her eyes twinkled with her delight in the surprise. "Actually, I didn't even know myself till last week. We wrapped up in Arizona earlier than we thought. I asked Austin if I could have a few days off to come check on your progress and help you, and he said sure. So here we are."

"Well, that was—nice." And it was. But—Creed glanced toward the office again. He still didn't see Avery. Where was she? What was she thinking?

The guilt that hung heavy wings over him was unnecessary. It wasn't as if he and Avery had anything like—*that*. But still, they were friends. Avery had to be wondering why he'd never mentioned Erica.

Because he hadn't needed to. Because he hadn't *wanted* to. And because he'd certainly never expected this.

"—at least three days ago." Erica was still talking. "Anyway, Austin says hi."

"Oh. Yeah." Creed yanked his mind back to the present. After coming all this way, Erica deserved his focus, at the very least. He'd have to explain to Avery later. "How'd Arizona go?"

"Excellent. We got some awesome shots. And the last day, there was a derecho." Erica shivered dramatically. "Wild weather for sure and really scary, but still, the shooting was amazing. The light was streaming in rays under the dust. Looked like Heaven coming to Earth."

The *kapemni* flashed across his mind, but he pushed it away. "Wow! Hate I missed that." His soul was tingling again with that old itch to explore, to chase, to move.

"Hey, you'll be there next time." Erica raised an eyebrow and tapped his laptop. "Assuming this is good."

"Yeah..." His excitement cooled. "I still need some help."

"Well, you're asking the expert."

"I know." Erica's storyboard skills were legendary, whatever else could be said about her. He pressed his palms together in a mock bow. "I am grateful for your assistance."

"Of course." She shrugged out of her jacket, watching him out of the corner of her eye as she adjusted the straps of her white tank top. "Anything for you."

It would be good if she would quit saying that. And if she would put the jacket back on. Creed cleared his throat and pushed the laptop toward her. "Here. See what you think."

"Hmm." She rested her elbows on the picnic table and leaned forward, her suggestive smirk replaced by keen attention. "Wow. These are great clips. You've clearly done a lot of work on this."

Well, he had. Just not in the last few days, when he'd been distracted by Avery's project instead. "Thanks."

For the next fifteen minutes, Erica watched the screen, and Creed watched her face. As the music he'd chosen for the credits swelled, she nodded and leaned back, a cloud shadow of thought over her expression.

"Well?"

"Well—you have great videography. Of course." She sighed. "But —it's missing something."

She was right, and the confirmation settled like a rock in his gut. "Oh, man. I knew it." He smacked his palm lightly on the picnic table. He should have asked for help sooner. Dang his stubborn independence. "What is it missing?"

Erica tapped her chin with a finger, eyes still sharp on the screen as she scrubbed between the clips. "Um—continuity, I'd say. A through-line. You've got great shots here, and you've got cool micro-stories about everything that's going on at the center. What you can't seem to do is connect them all to each other."

Creed shook his head, trying to process the suggestion. "So, like —better transitions?"

"No." She shook her head. "Some overarching story. Some big reason to care." She held up her hands. "Your stories right now are separate train cars, right? You need a track for them all to be running on."

The fullness of the story brings healing.

The words flashed into his mind as if it had been yesterday. Charlie Manyhorse, looking at Creed's first clips for the Rez video. He'd nodded with approval. *This is good, He Who Believes. Keep going deeper.*

Go deeper. Ha. He'd put too much of his soul as it was into that project. All for nothing except to get burned.

Creed blinked the memory away. Ridiculous, to superimpose the past on the present. This was a whole new project. And what mattered now was completing it with flying colors.

"There's good stuff here." Erica sat back and tugged her tank top higher—thankfully. "You're just not mining it all the way."

That made sense, but it didn't help the panic wriggling under his skin. "Okay, but—what can I do now? The fundraiser is in only four days, and—"

"I know." Erica squeezed his arm sympathetically. "Don't worry. I'm going to help you. Deal?"

Wariness wrapped around Creed's soul. Why was Erica so invested in this project? If he accepted her help, what unspoken agreement was he underwriting?

But Austin was watching, Creed's efforts the door to his future.

And more importantly—others were watching too. Skyla. Dad. Avery.

Avery.

If for no other reason, this video had to be good for her. To help show others the center she loved with all her heart. He swallowed the last of his hesitation and looked back at Erica.

"Deal."

Everything was almost ready.

Avery stretched onto her toes, straining to tack down the corner of the poster on the pole. Ugh. If she just had a couple more inches...

"Here, I can get that for you."

Creed's voice, and the walls she'd had in place since she'd first seen him with Erica thickened. She didn't look at him as she stepped back in silent permission.

He tacked the corner with ease, then glanced around admiringly. "This setup looks great."

Avery couldn't resist a surge of pride as she followed his gaze. They'd brought in a portable stage on Tuesday. Yesterday, she and Liv had wrangled their way through unfurling the white-canopied tent in front of the stage. Today she'd designed bright infographics about the center and its role in conservation.

They weren't done yet, though. Laz was bringing the tables and chairs to set up this afternoon. Liv was making all the centerpieces. And Tyler was supposed to give them an updated RSVP list this evening.

Creed straightened the corner of the poster. "You've done a fantastic job."

"Thank you." She couldn't keep the words from sounding stiff.

Creed shifted his feet. "Um, so, is everything ready?"

"Just about."

"Good."

Silence stalled between them.

Creed cleared his throat. "Hey, you know, we never filmed any more of your videos."

Of course not, with Erica there. "It's fine. I probably have enough to get started."

"I—I'm still hoping I have time after the fundraiser to do more for you."

Empty promise. After the fundraiser, Creed would disappear back into his normal life.

"It's just—" He raked his hand down the side of his face. "I've been so busy trying to get my video done for Friday."

There was worry in his voice, and frustratingly, she couldn't suppress the urge to help him. "It's not done?"

"No." Tension tightened between his eyes. "It's—it's my fault. I didn't—" He spread his hands as if trying to catch hold of his vision. "I need a bigger story that connects. Erica is helping me with it."

Erica. Just her name was like freezing water poured down Avery's back. Which was absurd. "Well. Good thing she's here to help you."

"Yeah. She's an excellent videographer. Has a good eye, you know?"

Well, great. They were perfect for each other then.

"Uh, Avery?"

"Yes?" She glanced at her watch. Laz would be here any minute with the tables and chairs. If Creed had something to say, he needed to say it and be done.

He cleared his throat and rubbed the back of his neck. "Listen. Um, I've been trying to catch you the last couple days, but I just never found you at a good time."

Since she'd been actively avoiding him, that made sense.

"Uh, I—I don't know what you thought about Erica and me, but we're—"

"Creed." She stepped back, fighting the rush of heat in her face. "It's fine."

He blinked. "I—well, I thought you might wonder about, you know, her and—"

"No." The word slipped out with an ease that surprised her. "It doesn't matter."

"Oh." He looked down and scuffed the ground. "Look, Avery. I sort of—"

Gravel crunched on the driveway. Laz's beefy pickup, towing a trailer stacked with the tables for the event. Avery stepped backward, out of the conversation. "It's fine, Creed. I'll see you later."

Her chest hurt as she jogged toward Laz's truck. But pretty soon, she wouldn't have to worry about any of this. Creed would be gone. Back to his videos and his climbing.

And his girlfriend.

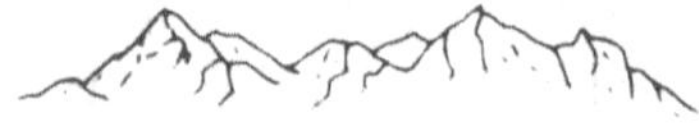

CHAPTER 15

The cranky old coffeemaker stowed in the camper had never worked so hard. Creed had lost count of how many cups he'd had so far. And not even the caffeine was helping him now.

He drained the lukewarm remnants of his most recent cup—was that five or six?—and made a face at Erica. "How will I ever get this to work?"

She shook her head, absently stacking a Styrofoam tower of her own empty cups. "Let's think again. What's something viewers can really connect to?"

Creed leaned back in the narrow chair and rubbed his eyes. He didn't glance at the clock, but it had to be past midnight by now. That meant it was early Thursday morning. He'd need every ounce of the time remaining before Friday evening to restructure the content and render everything, so this problem had to be solved tonight—no excuses.

"Um—the birds." He scraped his hand along his stubble. He needed to shave before the fundraiser. "Right? I could stitch it along the lines of the birds the center has helped..."

"But the focus now is more on the expansion, correct?"

"Well...true."

"It needs to be a more human element." Erica's fourth cup wobbled, and the tower tumbled down. She sighed. "Okay, what about this? Do you have film of the classes here?"

"Some." Creed tipped his chair onto the back legs and let his head rest against the wall. "It's too late to film any more."

"Yeah, and that would require waivers and such anyway, since it's including minors." Erica gave him a look. "It would have been helpful if you'd let me see this before now. Email and Dropbox are a thing, you know."

"I know." His eyelids were too heavy to fight gravity. "I thought I could get it on my own."

"Want my advice?"

He kept his eyes closed. "Ask the expert earlier next time?"

"That, yes." He could hear the half smile in her voice. "But actually—quit trying to do everything on your own."

Creed opened one eye and studied her. Instead of her typical flirty expression, she was watching him with what looked like real compassion. "Hmm." He closed his eye again. "I'll think about it."

"Okay. Think hard. In the meantime, mind if I look through your clips again? See if there's anything that sparks an idea?"

"Be my guest." If this wasn't successful, there'd be no international team for him. The thought jabbed with fresh anxiety, and Creed sat up, pulling himself back to alertness. "I have good footage, Erica. Surely there's some way I can use a voiceover and show how it ties together."

"Mm." She was distracted, peering at something on the computer screen. "What's all this?"

"What's all what?"

She rotated the laptop. "All these clips of that girl you work with."

A dozen thumbnails of Avery's videos stared at him. "Oh...that's a different project." He reached for the laptop.

Erica pulled it out of his reach and started scrolling through the clips. "A different project?"

"Yeah, so—" He busied himself by getting up and pouring another cup of coffee. He'd crash from the caffeine later, but he needed it now. "Avery was needing to record some instructional videos for a program she was directing. Nature in schools, that sort of thing. They're—well, they're sort of educational."

"Really?" Erica spun the computer toward him. "Okay. Show me one."

For some reason, showing Avery's videos to Erica felt like a breach of trust. But he shrugged. "Okay." He pulled up the one they'd recorded at Lake Haiyaha and hit *play*.

The camera panned over the landscape, and for a minute, he was back there again. The pine-spicy, high-altitude air tingling in his lungs. Wind-scrubbed sky like a billowing blue sail overhead. That had been a good day. A day when he'd felt something bigger than everything else. When life, not lukewarm caffeine, throbbed alertness in his veins.

"This land was born from ice." Avery's voice, soft but strong, as the camera panned upward toward the glacier patches on the mountainside. "And now all the rocks tell a story."

The transition blurred, and then there was Avery herself, standing on the shores of Lake Haiyaha, blue water diamond-tossed behind her. The sun was shaping the curves of her face, the wind tugging her hair. Her forest-colored jacket brought out the green of her eyes.

"Behind me you can see Tyndall Glacier." She pointed over her shoulder. "These glaciers are just a couple of the few left in the park today, but at one time, the ice spanned this area as far south as…"

The power of the footage pinned Creed to his seat. He hadn't yet edited this one, or even watched the raw cut. Now, the true beauty of it burst on him. Avery was a better storyteller than he'd ever be. Why had he never told her how powerful her words, her light, her love for the mountains was?

"As the ice moved through the valley, it created the unique geology of the mountains now." Avery paused and glanced to the jagged peaks behind her, then focused again on the viewer—on *him*. "The pain of the process gave rise to the beauty of the mountains."

The clip ended, and Erica let out a breath. "Wow." She stretched the syllable slowly, as if trying to find her footing again. "She's—very good."

"Yeah." Avery's picture was frozen perfectly in the final frame. He tore his gaze away and kept his tone casual. "She loves this place."

"I can tell." Erica dropped her chin into her hand and studied him.

He tilted his head, trying to break her gaze. "What?"

She shook her head. Her smile looked a little sad. "Nothing—I just didn't—" She cleared her throat. "Well, anyway." She tapped the screen. "This is it. This is your human element."

"What?"

"These videos, of course." Erica gave him an exasperated look. "Everything about this is perfect. Weave those in, and she'll take your viewers on a journey. It becomes the story of her, and her love for this land."

The idea expanded within him like a sunrise. Of course! How had he never thought of that before? Never realized that Avery's voice had the power to carry the whole project forward?

"This might really work." Hope overwrote the fatigue in Erica's eyes. "Listen, do you have any clips where she talks about her backstory, maybe? Her journey to the mountains?"

"Yeah, I do." He took the laptop back, scrolled through the library. "And I even have some still shots I've taken of these areas. And clips of her working at the center."

"That's perfect." Erica's voice held the excitement of a breakthrough. "So? What do you think?"

"It's awesome, but—" A sudden splash of reality doused his excitement. "I—I forgot. I don't know if Avery wants me to use that footage in my project."

Erica looked impatient. "Did you talk to her about it?"

He had, hadn't he? That first day? What had she said? That he could use some of it if he needed to, right?

"Uh—a little. She wasn't opposed to the idea, I don't think—"

"Meaning yes or no?"

Creed rubbed his chin. He needed an answer now, but he couldn't call Avery at one o'clock in the morning. Especially since he hadn't really talked with her since Erica's arrival.

But Avery wouldn't mind, would she? She'd probably be fine with whatever would help the center. She'd never said he couldn't use the clips. And it wasn't as if any of them were intensely personal.

Heck, she'd planned for them to be shown in schools. Obviously, they were intended for the public.

He nodded and forced down the twinge in his gut. "Go for it." He could always double-check with Avery before the fundraiser.

"Great. I'm going to go ahead and start splicing. Mind if I go through these?"

"Not at all." He yawned. "But I can—"

"Nope." She pointed a finger at him. "This is me helping you, okay? I'll try to do a rough storyboard tonight, and we can work on it in the morning. Right now, get some sleep before you split your face yawning."

He was too tired to argue. "All right." He rolled onto the little foldout bed and let his eyes close for good.

But even as he sank into sleep, he could still see one thing: the sun on Avery's face, and the dream behind her eyes.

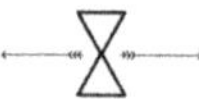

Thursday blurred into Friday as the fundraiser approached. By the time Avery was dressing in her room on Friday afternoon, she was already exhausted. And the event hadn't even started yet.

She turned on her indie folk playlist, but today, hearing about bare feet in mountain streams didn't bring her the peace it normally did. So much was riding on tonight. Tickets to the event had already surged their donation account. But if prospective donors were impressed with what they saw, even more could be accomplished.

And for that to happen, she had to be perfect. She couldn't stumble over her words or slip in her speech. Couldn't freeze when spoken to or let her hands start shaking. Otherwise, she'd embarrass Skyla. Reflect poorly on the center. And prove that she should have never been hired at all.

She took a deep breath, forcing the thoughts from her mind. There was no reason to think anything would go wrong. She was a little nervous, sure, but the anxiety had been so much better the last few weeks. Fortunately, Addisyn had also agreed to drive her there so that she could read over her speech on the way. She just needed to take this one step at a time.

And four hours from now, she'd be back home, and she could finally relax.

Avery finished getting ready five minutes before Addisyn was expected. She studied herself critically in the mirror. How long had it been since she'd dressed up for anything? The feeling was uncomfortably foreign. She adjusted the collar of her green dress and tugged at the ends of her hair. In times like these, she wondered if she should let it grow a little longer. Shoulder-length hair, especially as straight as hers, wasn't the easiest to coax into any kind of style for an event. She'd just left it alone.

She shrugged at herself in the mirror. Well, it would all have to do. She headed down to the living room, carrying her dress shoes. Where was Addisyn? Already she was two minutes late.

Addisyn answered on the first ring. "Hey, A! On my way. I'll be there in ten minutes."

"Ten minutes?" The clock on the wall was screaming at her. "Ads, I cannot be late."

"Aren't you getting there, like, an hour early anyway?"

Easy for Addisyn to say, when all she had to do was sit in the audience. Avery clenched her jaw. "Trust me, that will barely be enough time. Creed and Liv will be waiting, and I've still got to go over my speech and arrange the chairs and—"

"Okay, I got it." Addisyn still sounded maddeningly laidback. "Less than ten minutes, okay? I'm coming through downtown." She paused. "The traffic is awful. Any idea why?"

As if she could sense traffic patterns from her cabin? Avery rolled her eyes. "If you're not here by five till, I'm leaving without you." Although then she wouldn't be able to look over her notes on the way.

"No! I'll be there, okay? Promise."

When arrival times were concerned, Addisyn's promises had never been worth the breath she wasted making them. For the next twelve minutes, Avery paced and tried to keep Mercy from rubbing dog hair on her dress. She should have made Addisyn come earlier.

Although her younger sister had driven straight to Estes from work.

Speech or no, she was about to just get in her truck when Addisyn came driving—at entirely too leisurely a pace—up the driveway. Avery had the passenger door open almost before Addisyn stopped. "Addisyn, that was longer than ten minutes."

"I'm sorry!" Addisyn reached for her purse and began sifting through the contents. "I'm telling you, the traffic in town—"

"Never mind. Just *go!*" Avery's nerves were tangled around the last sparking ends of her sanity.

"Just a second." Addisyn was still rifling through the purse. "I know I had some gum in here somewhere—"

Gum. *Gum?* She was so nervous that her legs were already sweat-stuck to the leather seat, and Addisyn was looking for gum? Avery yanked the purse away from her younger sister. "That's not really a priority right now!" She jabbed her finger at the time on the car clock. "Is that accurate?"

"Okay! Good grief!" Addisyn shot her a sulky look and headed out the driveway—thankfully at a faster clip. "And no. It's a couple minutes behind."

Great. So she actually had *less* time than she'd thought. "When I tell you to be here at four forty-five, I mean four forty-five!" She gripped the sides of her seat as if she could somehow force them forward faster.

"We're getting there. Relax, A."

Relax! As if everything she'd worked for wasn't riding on this evening.

By the time they entered the outskirts of Estes, Avery's worry had only doubled. "Addisyn, at this rate, I'm not going to be there until five thirty. The event starts at six, so I'll only have half an hour to do everything that I have to take care of before—"

Taillights suddenly glowed red around the curve into downtown. Addisyn hit the brakes hard—unnecessarily so—and Avery jerked forward into the dashboard. "Addisyn, what are you doing?"

"Trying to keep us from having a wreck!" Addisyn flung her hand forward. "I told you about the traffic!"

Sure enough, Elkhorn Avenue was a caterpillar of brake lights all the way to the Marys Lake intersection, at least. "What on earth? What's going on?"

"I asked you that same question." Addisyn threw her an exasperated glance. "Maybe next time, instead of blaming me for being late, pay attention to—"

Avery didn't have time to play the apology game with Addisyn. "How far does this go?" She didn't see a disturbance anywhere. And this was way more than a few tourists enthralled with their first sight of a deer.

Addisyn shrugged in a *not-my-problem* way. "I don't know. Like I said, I told you that—"

"Oh, drop it! Just drop it!" Could Addisyn not give her a little grace right now? "Help me figure this out."

"Okay, okay." Addisyn seemed to thaw slightly. "Hey, it's not that far to the intersection. Maybe Marys Lake is clear."

"Maybe."

The cars inched forward, and Addisyn groaned. "Or maybe not."

Marys Lake Road was blocked from both directions by police cars, blue lights twirling. A truck was nosediving into the ditch, while a wrecker laboriously removed another car.

"Oh, you've got to be kidding me!" Avery deflated into the seat. All of this preparation...

"Okay, tell me what to do." Addisyn suddenly looked worried. Finally. "Uh, is there a side road? Some way to get around this?"

Avery scanned her mental map. There was Riverside, but they were past the intersection, and from the jammed opposite lane, there'd be no getting back. They certainly didn't have enough time to try to get back to 36 and come into Allenspark from the south.

The upended plans were enough to unbalance her precarious calm. And now her hands were shaking. *No! Please, El Shaddai. Not tonight.*

"A? What do you want to do?"

They hadn't moved more than six inches since they'd first seen the wreck. Avery glanced between the sneering numbers on the dashboard clock, the blue strobe of the police, and the mileage on the sign they were creeping past. ALLENSPARK 23 MILES.

She swallowed the dryness in her throat and reached for her phone. "I guess I better call Skyla."

By Friday afternoon, Creed had tried no fewer than four times to ask Avery about using her clips in the video. But every time he'd approached her, she'd cut him off. *"Just a minute. I've got to get these files input."* Or *"I'm sorry, Creed. There's a phone call waiting in the office."*

Even this morning, in all the last-minute prep, he'd hardly seen her. Probably it was nothing more than her nerves over the event and the stress of the preparation, but whatever the reason, she was keeping her distance. And when she wanted to, she could be as inaccessible as a sheer rock wall with no footholds.

It wasn't a matter of asking permission any more. The film was done, and—judging by Erica's excitement and his own videographer eye—it was awesome. Yet somehow, the uneasiness remained. True, Avery had never said he couldn't use the clips. Still, he would have liked the chance to just tell her ahead of time what was going on. Not that she'd mind, but it was the courteous thing to do. Well, maybe he could catch her when she arrived at the center, try one last time to explain.

He watched his video once more, then shaved and dressed in the one loosely professional outfit he'd brought—charcoal slacks and a button-up plaid shirt with the fringed leather jacket he'd brought from the Rez. The getup was no three-piece suit, but he was, after all, a Lakota story chaser who lived in a teardrop camper. Surely nobody could expect him to be entirely conventional.

He busied himself helping Liv arrange the centerpieces while he waited for Avery to arrive. But by five fifteen, he was growing concerned. It wasn't like Avery to show up less than an hour before showtime.

"Hey." He glanced at Liv. "What time was Avery supposed to get here?"

"Not sure. I've been wondering that myself." Liv frowned toward the road. "Maybe Skyla has heard—"

A small blue Hyundai veered into the center parking lot, announcing its arrival with a dramatic cloud of dust. A figure burst from the passenger side and jogged toward them. Avery. In a *dress*. Okay, now he'd seen everything.

Her breathless fragments of explanation preceded her. "I was waiting on Addisyn—the traffic—downtown, and—" She skidded to a halt in front of him and Liv, all but panting. "They were cleaning up a wreck. I—we got here as soon as—"

"Hey, it's okay." Liv squeezed her arm soothingly. "We've got the tables set up. Nobody's arrived yet."

"I—okay." Avery's shoulders softened slightly. "Then I probably have time to go over my speech. I planned to be here much—"

He needed to be focusing on her words, but he was still too busy processing the image of Avery in a dress. And—she looked—well, *beautiful*.

An odd warmth spread through him. The dress was the soft color of a springtime forest, and she had the gentle grace of an aspen tree, the shape of—

He jerked backward, nearly choking on his own shock. What was he doing? He had no business noticing her in that way. Let alone feeling the way he—

"Creed? Are you hearing me?" Avery was watching him with wide, clear eyes. Eyes that, in harmony with the dress, shone even more green than usual.

"Uh—" Heck, what was wrong with him? He cleared his throat, forced his eyes away. "I'm sorry?"

"I asked if your dad was here." Avery glanced around. "I need to make sure he has the building open."

"Yes." He'd seen the man earlier, in the kind of suit he'd once worn to preach at the Rez. "Uh, nice dress you got there." The words tripped over themselves clumsily. "You don't normally—look like that."

"I don't normally look nice?" Avery narrowed her eyes at him. "Gee, thanks. I can dress up when I need to, Creed."

"No, that's not what I meant." He was sweating beneath the leather jacket. Was it possible for him to give a simple compliment without tangling his tongue? "I mean—you look great. Very pretty."

"Oh." Avery's cheeks stained pink, but she didn't look upset. "Thank you." For just a moment, the wall in her eyes softened slightly. "Did you get the video done?"

The video. The words doused cold water over whatever the moment had just been. He had to tell her. "Yes. It is. And, also—"

"Great." Avery gave an abstracted nod in his direction and spun away. "If you don't need me, I'm going to go find Laz."

"Wait—Avery—"

But she was already gone, all but running toward the office. A car turned into the parking lot, another one following. Well, it was what it was. The first guests were arriving.

By six o'clock, Creed had shaken more hands than he could remember. There were the twelve board members of the center and their plus-ones, the leaders of different conservation organizations, and networks of volunteers and activists—all of whom seemed more interested in telling him about their own work than in hearing about what the center did.

Fortunately after the initial introductions, his part was pretty much over until the video. As people hobnobbed under the main tent, he hung back in the shadows and frowned. Even though this had been his idea, he sort of hated events like this. Heaven knew he'd had enough of them at the ministry.

How was Avery doing? He scanned the crowd until he saw Skyla leading her from group to group with an obvious air of introduction. Avery smiled at an older woman and extended her hand, then nodded at something the man beside her said. She certainly looked poised, regally confident. But then, Avery could hide feelings even better than Creed could.

Skyla touched Avery on the shoulder and said something, then ascended to the stage and tapped a microphone. Creed glanced at his watch. Five fifty-nine. Showtime.

"Greetings to all of you tonight." Skyla's clear voice carried over the grounds, and the hum of conversation and pleasantries dwindled into an expectant silence. "We are very thankful that you have come to meet us and to learn about the work we do. It is our prayer that this night is a blessing to you."

Creed glanced again at the folded itinerary in his hand, squinting at the type in the dimming light of evening. Once Skyla finished, Tyler would share the center's *strategic initiatives*—that should be riveting. After Tyler's talk was Creed's video. His redemption moment. And then Avery would follow him.

"—in this most beautiful place." Skyla gestured to the mountains behind her. "Tonight, you will learn how all of us may help others experience the healing of this place and the power of these mountains."

Erica slipped up beside him, heralded by a wave of perfume. "Going well so far." Her black pants were snakeskin-tight and bedazzled to boot. Could she not have been a little more understated tonight?

"Yeah." He could feel her gaze, but he wasn't going to return it. "So far, so good."

"It's a good turnout too. I wouldn't have expected this many people, here in the boonies."

Erica's voice was just a little too loud. The people at the back row of tables glanced toward them. "Uh—yeah."

"Still, I'm sure you'll be glad to be back in Arizona on Monday."

Creed's stomach lurched. "Monday?"

"Yeah." Erica inspected her fingernails—now a shocking lime green. "Austin texted me this afternoon. We're starting a new film Monday afternoon, and he needs you there for it."

Well, he'd known he was leaving next week, right? "Yeah. No problem. I'll be there Monday." Somehow the words felt like a betrayal.

"Good." She leaned a little closer to him, uncomfortably so. "In the meantime, enjoy tonight. This is your moment."

Your moment.

Creed took a deep breath. Erica was right. All the thoughts in his head would have to wait. Because right now, he was about to fulfill the objective he'd had since he was a kid.

Succeed so grandly that even his dad would have to agree.

AVERY WASN'T sure who she was right now.

Certainly she was not the woman cordially greeting people and saying the right things at the right moments and generally harmonizing with the social symphony. Even now, as she perched on an uncomfortable folding chair and tried to focus on Skyla's words, she was somewhere else. Floating above all the lights and noise and people, watching herself play this role.

If only the mental distance could last long enough for her to give her speech.

She'd gripped her papers tightly enough to wrinkle the edges. She deliberately released her hands and managed another shaky exhale. Okay. She was ready, wasn't she? She'd practiced with Creed, outrun her fears through the lens of his camera. When she stood on the stage tonight, she'd do so with the ghosts of her anxiety firmly behind her.

She shifted in her seat just enough to look out at the expectant faces. Board members, donors, activists, volunteers. The center's future rested on the shoulders of these people. Hard to impress. Easy to let down.

"Hey." In the seat next to her, Addisyn studied her with a probing expression. "Are you okay? You look like you're going to pass out."

Great. "I—"

"If you're nervous, don't be." Addisyn tapped the papers in Avery's hand. "You'll do great. And this is a huge success so far."

All the more reason why she couldn't be the one to drop the ball.

"Miss Miles?"

She turned toward the voice as a heavyset middle-aged man dropped into a nearby chair with a definite air of duty. He held out his hand. "Rodney Perkins. I'm the chairman of the board."

Her stomach flipped again. "Yes, Mr. Perkins. How nice to meet you." She gestured to Addisyn. "This is my sister, Addisyn Payne."

"Pleased to meet you both." Mr. Perkins shook Addisyn's hand with a distracted expression, then returned his attention to Avery. "Mrs. Wingo speaks highly of you."

Avery twisted her hands in her lap. "That's very kind. She is remarkable."

"Yes, yes, certainly. And the board trusts her judgment." He shifted, the chair squawking a bit beneath him. The overhead lights glinted off his bald head. "I will say, some members were—shall we say, skeptical regarding your qualifications. You had very little formal training, if I recall correctly."

Avery's hands were trembling. *No. Not now.* She folded them beneath her. "That's true, but I did take classes and receive a certification in—"

"Yes, that." Mr. Perkins dismissed Avery's experience with a wave of his hand. "As you no doubt remember, we prefer candidates with at least a four-year degree in environmental science." His glance measured her. "But Mrs. Wingo insisted you would do well. It appears she was right."

"Thank you, sir." *Was* that a compliment? Avery's stomach quivered. "I hope I can—"

"—would like to introduce Creed Running Wolf." Skyla stepped back from the microphone, and a wave of applause crossed the tables as Creed stood, pulling his jacket tighter.

Addisyn leaned close enough that her words were only for Avery. "He cleans up well."

Wow, Addisyn was right. Avery had been too flustered earlier to notice, but Creed really did look good tonight. His normally rumpled hair was tamed, and the shadow of stubble on his face was gone. His clothes were down-to-earth—somehow, it was a relief he wasn't posturing in a three-piece suit—but his leather jacket was its own bold statement. Like him. He looked—well, very striking. If Avery were more like Addisyn, she might have even said *handsome.*

And he had told her she was *very pretty.*

A flutter totally unrelated to her upcoming speech shivered through her. What had he meant by that?

"Good evening." Creed adjusted the microphone and flashed his smile like sunshine. "Thank you, Skyla, for the great words you've already spoken. I'm a little upset I have to try to follow that."

A ripple of amusement went through the crowd. Avery smiled. Creed was in his element, making magic the way he always did. She glanced for Laz but didn't see him. Surely he was watching his son.

"Tonight, I'm proud to present you with my latest film, a project of the Guys in the Wild outdoor YouTube channel. Tonight, you will experience the amazing mission and the incredible work that's done by this center. This film—" He paused slightly. "This film is a tribute to the healing found in wild places. And to the people who love those places."

His eyes seemed to land on Avery, but surely it was her imagination. She dropped her gaze.

"Please enjoy this brief film, 'Healing in the High Country.'"

A sustained note of music swelled up from the mountains and the trees and the deep dusk around them. And then slowly, slowly, colors began to wash across the screen. An early-morning sunrise over the peaks behind the center. Clouds swimming in a sea of glory.

"This is the High Country." Creed's voice behind the footage, resonant with conviction. *"The place where mountains rise and valleys dip and the sky is a handbreadth away."*

He'd written this voiceover? It was downright poetic.

The dawn blurred into the keen gaze of one of the hawks. The feathery needles on a pine tree. The splash and scatter of the Big Thompson River.

"But this land is not only a beautiful ecosystem. It's a haven of spiritual renewal."

The *kapemni* on the center's sign appeared center screen, the camera slowly panning out to reveal the rest of the sign and then the buildings beyond. *"This is the mission of the Estes Valley Mountain Center, and of one of its workers in particular."*

"I believe this is a place of healing."

Avery's breath caught. That was *her* voice. Her words from the day when—

And there she was, her face on the screen. Too close. Too big. Her words warping in the air around her. *"I came to these mountains when I was very broken, and they—they have a way of bringing all the broken parts back together. Of helping new things to spring up."*

Addisyn grinned at her. "Cool! You're in the video! You didn't tell me."

"I didn't know." An odd tingling was crawling over Avery's arms and legs. What was this? The face on the screen was her-but-not-her, her voice somehow foreign.

And then she was holding the candled egg as the voiceover came through again. *"Avery Miles has dedicated her life to furthering the mission of the Estes Valley Mountain Center through education, information, and transformation."*

What was going on? Her breathing was accelerating, her heart bounding in her chest like a runaway rabbit. What had Creed done? Why hadn't he said anything? She'd never dreamed—

A laugh. *Her* laugh. And then a clip from the day at The Loch. *"All places are holy. That's what I think."*

Her thoughts, her words, her self—all exposed and vulnerable on a screen the size of her anxiety. The video was still going, but she couldn't watch anymore. She sank into her seat, a hard realization heavy upon her. *This* was why Creed had gone to such trouble to befriend her, to help her, to record the videos for her curriculum. Not for the center. Not, as she'd so stupidly started to believe, for her.

But for his project.

"A, are you all right? It's a good video."

Oh, of course Addisyn would think so. She who was used to the spotlight, who wasn't learning that everything Creed had ever done had been a lie. He'd clearly come to wring a story from Avery and then be gone.

As the video continued, the humming in her ears rose to a dull roar, and the pinpricks of anxiety crawled over her skin. *No, no, no. Not here.* She cried out the words inside, a plea, a prayer—

Applause crashed, and she jerked in her seat. Addisyn was watching her with concern, saying something, but Skyla was on stage now, her words muffled…"—will now hear from Avery, our program coordinator, as she reveals what our hopes are for the center going forward."

No. She couldn't. She couldn't go up there and face these people. It was impossible. The black tunnel was opening, swallowing her, shrinking the evening into a single—

"Avery?"

Skyla's voice was light years away, all the way at the end of the tunnel. And Avery couldn't breathe. Couldn't speak. Couldn't stand.

Yet somehow she did.

Her feet were unreliable beneath her, her body as light and wavery as a fragile candle flame. She forced her quivering legs forward, and then she was standing in front of the crowd, gripping her paper. Bright lights slanting in her eyes.

Silence, heavy, thick. Sweat crawled down her back. All those people, thinking she was the confident face of the center. Looking at her with expectations she'd never be able to satisfy now.

It's on you, Avery.

She looked at her paper, but the words spun senselessly. She looked at the people, but she couldn't pick out a single encouraging face. She was frozen in this spotlight. Her voice, her words, herself—

The kick drum of her terrified heartbeat throbbed in her throat. Black spots twirled before her eyes. Pain stabbed lightning through her chest. The papers spun like snow from her hands.

And then she was moving, her shaking legs stumbling blindly to a safety she couldn't see. When the lights were behind her, she finally allowed the coiled spring in her chest to snap free.

And she ran. Over the fields, toward the dim outlines of the mountains, into the concealing comfort of the dark until she fell to her knees beneath a sky with no stars.

CHAPTER 16

Forcing the panic back took longer than it ever had, but Avery finally shoved the fear behind the flimsy gates in her soul. Once the sweat dried on her forehead, she stumbled back toward the lights. From a distance, she could see the faces within the tent, hear the melodic catch-and-croon of Liv's guitar. The event was still okay, even if she wasn't. How she'd face anyone later was a problem she didn't have to solve at the moment.

More from habit than intention, she crept to the office. It was locked, of course, which was fine with her. She couldn't be trapped within walls right now. Not when the whole night sky was hardly big enough to contain everything wounding her.

She sat on the porch, out of the warm circle of the little outdoor light. She hugged her knees, allowed the dreary emptiness of the truth to hollow her. She'd failed, utterly and completely. There couldn't have been a worse time for the panic to show up.

And it was Creed's fault.

Anger seeped in, fortifying her against the fear. How *dare* he use the videos he'd taken for her? She would have never given him permission for that. And here she'd thought he was her friend.

"A? A, where are you?"

Addisyn. Avery braced herself for the explanations. "I'm here."

"Where? Oh, I see you." Addisyn scrambled onto the porch, worry wrinkled across her face. "A, what on earth happened? Are you okay?"

All these weeks of carefully hiding her fear from her sister. "Uh—"

"It's the anxiety again, isn't it? Like you had in New York?" Addisyn dropped to her knees and studied Avery. "How long has this been going on? Why didn't you tell me?"

Because I'm the strong one. Avery shrugged.

"Skyla was worried about you."

Skyla. Another person she'd let down. Avery stared at the jagged edge of the trees. In the dusk, they looked like sharp teeth. "Go tell her I'm fine."

"But listen, we need to talk about—"

"Addisyn, there's nothing to talk about." Avery didn't try to make her voice less hard. The panic had sucked away all her strength for anything except breathing. The last thing she needed was for Addisyn to play therapist right now.

"Avery, I just don't understand why you didn't tell me you were—"

"Because I don't want to talk about it, okay?" Avery forced herself to her feet, ignoring her wobbly legs. "Just go tell Skyla I'm fine and—"

A throat cleared at the edge of the porch. "Avery?" Creed's face moved into the light.

Her stomach clenched.

"Are you okay?" He hopped onto the porch in a single smooth motion. "I came as soon as I—"

She stepped back, swallowing the metallic taste. "You lied."

His face crinkled in confusion. "What?"

Addisyn opened her mouth, then shut it as she glanced between the two of them. "Uh, I'll go tell Skyla." She scampered into the shadows without a backward glance. Traitor.

Creed ignored her, his gaze locked on Avery. "What are you talking about?"

"Your film. You—you took all those videos just for your project. I thought you were helping me, but—"

"No, no!" He groaned, scrubbed a hand over his face. "That's not true, Avery. I can explain. I *was* helping you. But then this week, I still didn't have a theme and I was running out of time." He hesitated. "Erica thought it would be great to use your clips. You did so well."

Erica. Avery's jaw hurt. "And you didn't think to ask me?"

His gaze dropped. "I—I wanted to. It was only on Thursday that we decided—and I kept trying to catch you and couldn't—"

Well, she had been avoiding him, but that didn't give him a pass. "So what about texting me? Calling me? Coming to my house?" Her runaway emotions were rebounding into anger. "Instead, you blindsided me. I'm sitting there, I'm already nervous, and—and then you —" The pain of it was too big to be packaged in words.

"I—I'm sorry." Creed stepped forward again, spreading his hands. "But the video wouldn't have been nearly as powerful without—"

There was a plea in his eyes, but she wouldn't let herself hear it. "Creed, is that what it's all about for you? You don't care that I was embarrassed in front of everyone as long as your video is *powerful*?"

"No. Of course I care." He raked a hand through his hair, a frustrated breath escaping. "But you've got to understand my perspective. My assignment was to make a great video that—"

"Yes. Of course." The anger was protection, a shield around her wounded soul. "A great video. And all along that's been your only purpose."

His eyes were starting to spark dangerously. "That was my assignment, Avery, but that doesn't mean—"

An *assignment.* The impersonal edge of the word was a blow. "And so nothing else matters? As long as your videos are successful?"

A muscle in his jaw twitched. "Avery, you're not being fair. My job has to matter to me. Because this weekend, I will drive out of here and be back in the real world. Okay?"

"The *real* world?" Her outrage jerked loose in a laugh. "This *is* the real world. Healing and helping and—and moving forward. And you won't do that. You're trapped in this imaginary world of videos, and—"

"Imaginary world?" His voice soared. "Oh, now you sound like my dad."

She'd gone too far, but she wasn't putting on the brakes now. "If you never face your own story, you end up trapped."

He huffed. "I live on the road. That's the opposite of trapped."

"Trapped inside yourself, Creed!" She couldn't see the wolf on his arm, but she could picture it. "You can't just keep running."

"Oh, really?" He had that locked-down look again, the way he had when he'd first come to the center. "You mean the way you have?
"

The words sliced, and she blinked. "I haven't been running."

"You talk a big talk about healing and moving forward and growing, Avery. About putting it behind you and how easy that's all supposed to be." Every word felt like a whip. "But you know what? You're so scared of your past that you won't even face things with your sister."

The fire inside her shocked into ice. "Stop it, Creed."

"Fine." He crossed his arms. "But your sister is right. Until you're brave enough to face everything with her, neither one of you will end up anywhere."

"This isn't your problem, Creed." The ice was numbing her face, her hands. "I'm over my past. I've worked hard for that. You have no right—"

"You worked hard to bury it." He spread his hands. "So where do you think your anxiety comes from? Why do you think you can't bring yourself to talk this out with your sister? Ask yourself those questions, Saint Avery. See what your answers are." His eyes flashed. "I think you'll be surprised to find we're not as different as you think."

"Fine, Creed." She'd been right about him from the beginning. The light she'd imagined in his eyes had never been real. She dug her fingernails into her sweaty palms. "Have it your way. Go back to Arizona. But there are things that can't be outrun. One day you'll realize that."

"That's not—" He paused, his shoulders softening. He took a step closer to the porch light. "Okay. Avery—what I meant was—"

"Go away." She was seconds from breaking down, but she wouldn't do it in front of him.

He worked his jaw, and for just a moment, all the words hung between them.

Then he shrugged and stepped back. Out of the light. Off the porch. His footsteps died away, leaving her just as she'd asked to be.

Alone.

CREED HAD KNOWN something was wrong the minute Avery stepped onto the stage. He'd recognized her deer-in-the-headlights panic from that day in Denver. So when she'd rushed off the stage, he'd known what had happened. But he hadn't known that he was why.

And he'd certainly never dreamed he'd bungle the whole situation into such a mess.

The hurt on Avery's face throbbed in his mind, and he groaned. He'd done it again. At his moment of redemption, he'd failed. And now he was standing in the ashes of a burned-out story while everyone around him felt the pain of the fallout.

Just like the Rez.

"Creed!" The overpowering perfume arrived at his side before Erica did. "That was so good!"

"Uh, thanks." No, he couldn't deal with Erica. Not right now.

"I knew it would work. Taking Avery's story was perfect."

Taking her story. The truth of the statement sickened him. That was what he'd done, wasn't it? He'd taken Avery's story. Stolen it without her permission. Made it into something from which he could benefit.

She was right to be angry.

"I thought it was good myself." Why had he said that? His hypocrisy disgusted him. He was just as bad as Avery said. "Hey, give me a minute, okay? I'll catch up with you afterwards."

He didn't wait for Erica's reply before he hurried back to the parking lot. The little Hyundai was turning onto the road. Avery's sister must be taking her home.

A throat cleared to the left. "Creed? That you?"

Dad. His jaw clenched. "Yes."

Dad stepped out from behind his pickup, the glare of the overhead lights harsh on his face. "What done happened? Miz Avery seemed mighty upset when she come through here."

So his dad was more worried about Avery than him. An odd resentment twisted in his soul. "I—I used those clips of her without asking her permission."

"I see."

The question hung between them before Dad asked it.

"Didn't you think that—"

"Stop it, Dad." He couldn't take any more condemnation. Not when he was already drowning himself in it. "I didn't have a chance to talk with her about it beforehand." His excuses sounded weaker every time he repeated them. "And I needed those clips to make the video good."

"To make the video good." Dad sighed. "You cain't git to filmin' an' forget what you're doin'."

Creed sucked in a breath, and anger surged to fill the wound. "Oh, yeah? So that's why you hated my filming? Why you never watched a single one of my videos? Why you told me to 'get a real job'?" The sting of that statement punched him as if it had been yesterday. "I was sixteen, Dad. Sixteen! What was I supposed to be doing, managing a bank?"

His words ran out. But still his father stood there. Unmoving. "I done tole you, I made my mistakes."

Why did his father always use that word? As if his parenting failures were no bigger than spilled milk.

"But you never gave me the chance to explain. Jes' up and left."

Oh, was that how his father remembered it? "You told me to go away. Remember, Dad?" He took a step forward, jabbed his finger toward the man.

"I know." Dad lifted his chin. "After the fire."

The fire. The pivot on which his whole life had shifted. He could still smell the acrid smoke, still see the technicolor twirl of the firetruck lights. Still remember the ambulance ride and the pain that zinged through his burns for weeks.

Still remember his father's words.

"So we're back there?" He crossed his arms. "Back at the fire?"

"Creed—" Dad rubbed a large hand over his face. "We been at that fire for six years now. You won't ever—"

"Yeah, the fire was my fault. I get that, okay? But you were the one who showed up at the hospital and yelled at me until the whole floor could hear you screaming!" He'd been burned and broken, and then his dad had finished the job. "What kind of father does that? Huh? Your son was at his lowest point, and your only interest was telling me how my filming had destroyed everything. Which I already knew."

"It wasn't the fire. I done tole you that." His dad held out his hands. "It was that you didn't tell me what was goin' on. Jes' ripped ahead with yer project even though I was beggin' you to quit."

"You were begging me to quit because the ministry didn't like what I was doing." Sarcasm strained his laugh. "I was a heretic, you know. Trying to celebrate my mother's culture made me a heathen." His breath caught on the sharp edges of the memories. "And you proved it when you came to rip me up at the hospital and ended by telling me I needed to leave the Rez. I know how it went down. You knew the board was already mad at me. And you wanted me gone so I didn't interfere with your precious church friends."

"That ain't true." Dad's voice was rising. "Sure, they'd talked to me 'bout you. 'Specially since you never went out o' yer way to make friends with any of 'em."

"They all hated my work. And me. And it doesn't look like they were any fonder of you." Outrage roughened his laugh. "I guess your plan to buy favor didn't work. Otherwise you'd still be at the Rez. So how long did it take for them to turn on you too? A month? Two weeks? Was it worth it?"

Dad shook his head. "If you'd listen for half a—"

"I'm done listening." A different fire was flaring. The one that had smoldered so long inside him. "I've been listening all my life, you understand that? Listening to you berate me and push me and demand more from me! But *you* never listen to *me*!"

"You never let me! You push an' push an' keep me at arm's length. An' didn't you ever stop to think that mebbe I was human too? That mebbe I was tryin' to do my dead-level best an' didn't always get it right? I know I screwed up. Good Lord knows I'd do a heap o' things different if I could."

Were those tears in his father's eyes? Surely not.

"I was hard on you, yeah. Because I knew you was strong. You were—you were my world."

No, the *ministry* had been his dad's world. He'd been an unwanted afterthought. Creed swung around. "I'm leaving."

"Hold on."

Even after all these years, that tone from his father could still stop him in his tracks.

Dad closed the space between them in three quick strides, boots crunching on the gravel. He crossed his arms and stared Creed down with a gaze like a gun barrel. "I wanted to make sure you didn't make the same dumb mistakes I did. You think my pa cared enough to make sure I wasn't out foolin' around? Only thing he cared about was findin' another woman to run off with. I ain't never been easy on you. Yer right about that. So if somebody needs to tell you this, 'pears like it's on me."

"Dad, I don't have time for more—"

"Creed, yer gonna listen to me for one dang second 'fore you leave me eatin' dust again. You wanna never talk to me again? You can do it, I s'pose. But I'm here to tell you that to be any good to anybody a'tall in this dang world, yer gonna hafta to learn to live with yerself. An' that's somethin' you still haven't figgered out. You still think it's all about you."

"What are you saying?"

"You say I shouldn't blame yer filmin' for you gettin' in scrapes. An' you know what? Yer dang right." Dad's voice was rising, his tone more closely resembling the bellowing father Creed remembered.

"Ain't nobody but yerself starts chasin' stories and forgets everythin' else. Ain't nobody but you that won't own up to nothin'. Yer still not thinkin' of nobody but yerself. An' yer still runnin' hard." He jerked his head toward Creed's arm. "Runnin' Wolf. One of these days, yer gonna figger out you cain't run from yerself. No matter how bad you want to. But until then, every word I say gonna go right through them ears of yers. An' yer gonna keep hurtin' yourself and everybody close to you till then."

"Well, great news, Dad. I don't have to listen to you anymore." He was shaking, Avery's words and his dad's words choking him. Anger and regret throbbed like poison in his bloodstream. "So you don't have to worry about me, okay? I'll leave just like I did before." He turned away, leaving behind every ghost his father had just raised. "And this time, I won't be back!"

CREED STILL HADN'T CALMED down by the time he arrived back at his camper. He kicked the door shut behind him, then slapped his hand against the *kapemni* on the wall. Blasted sign. It meant nothing. It never had.

The memories were burning through his mind like a runaway blaze. He closed his eyes and let the fire come, let himself relive that summer of sparks and wind.

All his energies had belonged to the Rez project. The one that had fully captured his heart and soul. His soul had never been the right shape to fit nicely at the ministry—he'd never spoken the language, never accepted the unstated rules, never felt at home in the board meetings where the leaders showed more excitement over the size of the bank account than the glory of God. So his work at the ministry had been awkward at best, soul-sucking at worst.

But when he'd found the film workshop that summer, he'd thought he'd found a way to blur the lines between the halves of his life—combine his roles as the dutiful son and the creative videographer.

Attending that workshop was like hearing a joyous song to which he'd almost forgotten the words. He put himself through his paces in the fake-hype *"prayer gatherings"* and the finance-focused board meetings, but his real life began each day when he drove off with his camera in hand. And the six-week workshop culminated in a final project: a short documentary-style video on *"a place that mattered."*

The choice had been easy, because he'd always and only belonged to the Rez. As a misfit kid and a turbulent teen and a restless young adult, he'd been at home there, in the forgotten corners of the land. The tangled grass whispered to the wind that ceaselessly searched the prairie. The sun watched with the probing eye of God. And the people lived their lives flinging forward faith from the past, reaching for a better future.

And so it was the stories of the land he'd decided to collect. He'd visited twenty people throughout the Rez, recording their own beautiful ways of telling their ancestral legends. He'd focused on capturing the emotions that lingered in the details: the cadence in their voices when they spoke of Coyote the trickster or Buffalo Woman the soon-to-come...the way their hands moved as if shaping the myth from the air...the way the lines around their eyes squinted as they peered into the brightness of the past.

All summer, his heart found its home in the work. Behind the camera, he was safe from his dad's endless pressure to fit the missionary mold, from his increasing disenchantment with the ministry, from his angst-torn questions about the God it claimed to stand for. He'd poured his whole self into the project, and by the time he finished, he knew without a doubt it was his best one yet.

Which was why he'd been excited to present it to the ministry leaders at the next board meeting. He'd hoped that it would prove the worthiness of his aims. Provide a video that could be used for donations. Even inspire them to soften some of the square edges of their consistent misunderstandings of Native culture.

He could still remember the pride he'd felt, watching the video play out on the big screen, reliving the interviews with his Native friends. He'd been so thrilled.

Until he looked at the other faces in the room.

Pastor Young cleared his throat as soon as the video ended. *"Creed, I'm sorry, but we can't use that for marketing."*

"Uh—" What had gone wrong? *"Why not? I thought you could send it to potential donors or show it at—"*

"It doesn't accurately reflect the goal of the ministry." There was no mistaking the disapproval in the man's tone.

In the back of the room, Dad started to say something, then stopped. Never defending him. Like always.

Creed fisted his hands. He was on his own. *"I'm sorry, Pastor Young, but I don't understand why not."*

"You're encouraging people to remember the old myths."

"That's my concern too." Mr. Bradford, the treasurer, nodded grimly. *"We shouldn't be celebrating stories like that. People will think the ministry isn't Biblical."*

Creed blinked. *"They're the people's culture. I'm trying to—"*

"A culture that's not in line with Scripture." Pastor Young gestured out the window. *"Why do you think we're here? To rescue these people from these kinds of superstitions and teach them the truth."*

Rescue these people. The words had a bad taste. *"Why can't it be both?"* Creed spread his hands. *"What if the myths point toward truth? What if you could use the myths to talk about spiritual things, things that—"*

"There is no agreement between light and darkness. The Bible teaches that." Mr. Bradford crossed his arms, a brick wall with no doorway. *"If we introduce these pagan elements, we only end up compromising, and confusing everyone."*

"I fully agree. This jeopardizes our mission." Pastor Young's mouth had turned down. *"To be honest, Creed, I'm highly disappointed that you pursued this project. Frankly, it's not the kind of behavior we expect from a staff member here. We are to uphold the Word of God in word and deed, and you have instead—"*

Creed opened his eyes and sat up. He didn't need to replay the rest of the conversation. Didn't need to remind himself of the frustration he'd felt, trying to convince the leaders that God was bigger than the tiny box they'd fit Him into. Didn't need to feel the pain all over again of trying to explain that he found God far more profoundly in a sweat lodge than in the church. What little he understood of the Scriptures, he'd found in applying them to the land around him. And if the Holy Spirit was real, then He was most like the untamable, unpredictable, unmistakable prairie wind.

Yet the sacrifice he'd laid on his own altar was being treated as sacrilege. Misleading the people. Misrepresenting the ministry.

And all through it, his dad didn't say a word.

Creed had been utterly broken when he finally stormed out of the meeting that had disintegrated into a witch hunt. He'd been guided solely by instinct as he tossed a shovel and an armload of kindling in the backseat of his Jeep, as the big tires spun in the soft dirt roads and carried him to the prairie at the end of the Rez. He'd cleared an area, arranged the logs, and struck the fire-breath of a match. And when the flames began to lick the logs, he'd crumbled a handful of sage over them.

The *péta wakan*. The sacred fire. The one his Lakota friends built when they were opening their hands to the sky.

He'd closed his eyes, focusing on the darkness behind his eyelids, and let his cry rise with the smoke. *God, Who are you? You're more than who they say You are. I have to believe that. So show me. Reveal to me what You want me to know. I'm here. I'm listening. I'm ready—*

But as he'd poured his heart out, he'd heard not the voice of God, but a hungry, crackling roar. He'd opened his eyes to see that the fire had escaped its bounds and was racing across the dry prairie grass.

Not Heaven, but Hell, had come to him.

It had all fallen apart after that. He'd raced into the flames, wielding the shovel, ignoring the searing pain that ripped across his hands and forearms. But he was too late. The wind he'd trusted had turned on him, and the blaze was running hot. It spread faster than a malicious rumor before the fire trucks could come wailing in from the station in Piedmont.

The ambulance had rushed him to Rapid City, where doctors had used words like *second-degree burns* and *smoke inhalation*. But his worst injuries had come not from the fire—but from his father.

He'd lain in that hospital room tugged between burning pain

and freezing fear. He'd needed guidance. He'd needed prayer. He'd needed...his dad.

When he'd heard his father's footsteps in the hallway, he'd nearly cried with the relief. He'd barely croaked out the word as his father walked in. *"Dad..."*

"What in all of dad-blame heck did you think you were doing?"

Dad had roared at him until Creed was sure everyone on the hospital floor could hear. Accusing him of being irresponsible and immature. Ranting about how filmmaking had corrupted his character. Finishing up by telling him he was a disgrace. *"I'm not gonna have my son destroyin' this ministry. I swear, yer burnin' down faster'n we can build. On all fronts."* He'd crossed his arms and stared Creed down. *"Yer goin' back to yer mother as soon's yer healed up. An' yer not comin' back till you can prove I can trust you again."*

And with that, his father had turned and stormed out of the hospital. Leaving Creed the way he'd now learned to live his life. Alone.

The memories were bringing back the anger, sharper and hotter than any out-of-control flame. Creed slapped the wall of symbols, the heat within his chest finding no escape. He'd thought he was managing it better, but hearing Dad's accusations, letting Avery down—it brought it all back.

Yer still not thinkin' of nobody but yerself.

Really? So his dad didn't care that he'd found a successful job doing what he loved? Or that he netted a salary bigger than what he could ever need in a year? Or that he'd done such a good job for Skyla that she'd promised him a recommendation?

No, his dad would never think well of him. Never admit any fault. Yet somewhere in the back of Creed's mind, hadn't he sort of hoped that by pleasing Skyla, he might earn his dad's approval as well?

He had, and the realization doubled his frustration with himself. What was wrong with him? Why after all these years was he still trying to beg crumbs of the old man's favor?

Maybe because he was still right where he had been. Sitting by the fire with an unanswered prayer.

God, Who are You?

Why had he ever thought it would be different this time? No, just like before, he'd let them all down. He hadn't been enough. And everyone had gotten hurt.

Especially Avery.

The same feeling he'd had when he saw the blackened fields sagged around his neck like a millstone. And suddenly he realized how worthless it had all been. This quest for redemption, this relentless drive for success, this stockpiling good deeds to present to Dad.

None of it would ever work.

He stared at the *kapemni* on his wall. What a joke. Heaven didn't touch Earth. And there were certainly no open doors for him. Only a silent sky and an ash-strewn soul.

Which meant it was time to forget Heaven and Earth and whatever shimmering space he might have thought existed between them. It was time to go back to what he did best.

Running.

UNFLAPPABLE. That was how Lance's mentor during his psychiatric residency had defined him on his final report. *Mr. Potter has a professional demeanor and sincerity that appeals to clients. He is unflappable in the face of any circumstance.*

That word had sunk deeply enough into him to remain a part of his internal self-definition for thirty years. He and Beth had even laughed about it one night. He could still remember the teasing in her voice. *"Unflappable? Makes sense. You're the steady one."* Shadows had crept into her tone. *"I'm the flappable one, I'd say."*

Well, now she'd managed to make him *flappable*. If that was even a word.

His eyes burned from the strain of his computer screen. He rubbed them and glanced around his office. The practice had been closed for two hours, yet he found it more productive to stay late and finish client notes then. That way, he could tie up all loose ends at work and then let his mind wander during the drive home.

But his mind was already wandering. As it had been ever since he'd seen the obituary.

He stared back at the in-progress document on his laptop.

Patient demonstrates severe guilt in response to perceived mistakes. We discussed the universality of regret as an experience, normalizing its presence for humans. I also shared research regarding the prevalence of regret in those with inflexible moral standards and encouraged the client to take a more self-compassionate approach. Client has been advised to begin reading Making Peace with Ifs by Joseph Stoddard and to begin practicing a mindset that is more...

Ironic, that he was giving guidance to a client with his own struggles—and no mindset shift or trendy self-help book was going to help him.

He stood and paced to the window, staring into the darkness at the lonely glow of the Bank & South building across the street. What was the matter with him? He and Beth were ancient history. She was gone. It was done. As it had been for years, anyway. So why couldn't he just put it to rest?

His reflection stared back at him in the window. He narrowed his eyes at his ghostly shadow self, tried to psychoanalyze the way he would a client. Okay, so he felt regret, sure. He wished that he'd known Beth was dying. He wished that she were still alive.

And he wished that he hadn't been a part of her downfall. What he'd done was—wrong.

He frowned. That made no sense. He'd spent a career encouraging clients not to think in the archaic black-and-white dichotomy of right/wrong, good/bad. He helped his guilt-ridden clients reframe their actions not as moral decisions but as instead natural and expected curves along the path of learning. *Make choices in accordance with your personal values and well-being. Follow what brings you joy. Seek to achieve better insight into what constitutes a meaningful life.*

But, as frightening as it was to admit, all of those mantras felt like dead leaves blowing away in the wind of reality. He'd followed that kind of thinking, and look where it had gotten him.

Well-being? The situation with Beth had fretted him like a blister for decades.

Joy? He couldn't remember the last time he'd felt light enough to laugh.

Meaningful life?

Well—if he had that, he wouldn't be staring at a dark window, staying alone in his office so he wouldn't have to stay alone in his house.

He'd spent his life relegating morality to a support framework for society, a largely arbitrary set of rules that brought people stability in exchange for a boatload of guilt. But—he couldn't reconcile his own conduct with that. Because what he'd done with Beth had been wrong. Plain and simple. No rationalization, no justification, no explanation could wash that away.

He rubbed a hand over the back of his neck. He was breaking his own philosophy, betraying the core of what he'd taught and lectured and written and counseled for decades. Ulys especially would scoff at him. *"You want morality? Go to church and let some dummy behind a pulpit stack rules on you."*

It had been unappealing then. It was unappealing now. And yet —he'd been wrong. He knew it. And now—he needed to fix it. Somehow.

In the religious context he avoided, you might call it *atonement* or *penance*. To use his more clinical jargon, it was *seeking closure* or *finding symbolic release*. But whatever it was called, he needed to try it. And then, maybe his mind would finally let go of this. And everything could go back to normal.

He took a deep breath and nodded at his reflection. Then he crossed to the storage closet on the side of his office and opened the door.

No skeletons in this closet, but something even more terrifying. An innocent-looking cardboard box in the back corner. With one word Sharpied on the top.

LANCE.

He'd opened the box only once, the night he'd found it on his porch when he came home from work. Then, he'd sorted through the contents feverishly, hoping for some clue that Beth had changed her mind, that she wanted him to come back. But there was nothing in the box for him.

Only for the girls.

Now that he knew about her diagnosis, things made more sense. That was probably a big part of why she'd pushed him away. And in the tumult of her chaotic life, she'd apparently gathered up the most important things and given them to someone she thought could be trusted to deliver them.

Him.

And he wouldn't let her down again. Especially not now.

He went back to his computer and closed out the client file. He'd finish it later, after he thought of some regret-removing homework for the client. Or himself.

He opened a new tab, his hands hovering over the keyboard. The words came slowly as he typed.

Addisyn Miles.

He'd done this Google search more than a few times over the years. But not in the past eight years. Not since Beth had pushed him away for the last time.

He hit the search bar and watched the results load. So much information, yet no answers to any of the real questions.

He skimmed the screen. Most of the results had to do with Addisyn's skating career, which he already knew about. But it appeared she hadn't been in competition for a few years now, after a defeat at Regionals. So what had she done since then?

One thing was certain—after the spotlight, the river of information about her life ran nearly dry. There were one or two links to a court case involving somebody named Brian Felding, a former skating coach who'd been convicted of sexual harassment and a few other serious-sounding offenses. Addisyn had been a witness in the case.

But that was still back in New York. According to the obituary, she was in Colorado. Why?

A thought struck him. He changed his search terms. *Addisyn Miles Payne.*

The first result was the staff page for the Denver Ice Center. He scrolled through a list of coaches' photos until a face he knew only from years of Googling jumped out at him.

But the Addisyn in this picture looked more relaxed, more confident, more at peace than she'd ever seemed during her years of competition. She was flashing an effortless smile at the camera, her glossy brown hair swept over one shoulder. He studied her, looking for any resemblance to Beth—but Addisyn's features were softer, her eyes darker, and certainly her smile easier.

He blinked at the name on the photo next to hers. *Darius Payne.* So did Addisyn's husband work at the center too? It made too much sense to be coincidence.

Nice-looking young man, if that was the case. Black hair in a ponytail, thick beard, gentleness in the lines around his eyes.

There were links to email the coaches beneath their photos. Lance hovered his mouse over the button but hesitated. Addisyn had a good life now, obviously. Who was he to barge in? His presence would only cause more chaos.

He returned to the search bar and changed the terms.

Avery Miles.

If the results had been insufficient for Addisyn, they were almost nonexistent for Avery. Clearly she maintained a low profile online. But then, according to Beth, Avery had always been a closed door. Kept her soul behind a barred gate.

He frowned at the first article. *"Raptor Center Spreads Its Wings at Fort Collins Schools."* What under the canopy did that have to do with anything?

He clicked the link anyway. A photo loaded, and he sucked in a breath. It was Beth again, the age she'd been when they'd met.

His eyes raced across the caption. *Avery Miles and Tyler Trine, of the EVMC, answer questions at Southcreek School in Fort Collins.*

Not Beth. Avery.

In the photo, a young, serious-looking guy was speaking, but Lance's eyes were glued to Avery. She was smiling at a small group of students, a hawk balanced on her outstretched arm. And—oh, she was Beth all over again. Same eyes, same delicate face, same build, same hair—although hers was chopped at her shoulders.

He leaned back in his chair. So Avery was working for a conservation center? In Fort Collins? Where was that?

Not that it mattered. Lance rubbed his chin. Trying to contact her would be an even bigger mistake than emailing Addisyn.

"Avery knows about you." He still remembered Beth's words.

His heart had jerked with something that even then had felt too much like guilt. *"You told her?"*

"I had to." Beth's voice was as worn as her eyes. She rubbed a hand over her forehead and patted her pocket. *"It's time for my meds."*

He'd already seen her take three doses, and he frowned. *"What did Ulys prescribe you? Are you sure—"*

But Beth already had the bottle open. She rattled out two pills with trembling hands and reached for the bottle of water on the table. When she finished, she wiped the back of her hand across her mouth, her shoulders relaxing slightly. *"I had to tell her."* Fear flashed in her eyes, and she hunched almost involuntarily. *"Are you mad?"*

"Beth, no." Every time he saw how badly Ulys had broken her spirit, he wanted to put his fist through his former business partner's jaw. *"But what about—what about—"*

"Addisyn?" Beth let a breath out slowly. *"Avery says no. I—she wouldn't let me talk to her."*

He gripped the edge of the table until his fingers ached. *"Did you tell her—"*

"I told her everything. She's always been—protective of Addisyn. Too protective." Beth's face twisted into something harder. *"Doesn't trust her own momma, I guess."*

Lance bit his lip. *"It's me."*

"No." Already Beth's words were coming more slowly, her eyes glassing over. *"It's me. I screwed up with both of them a long time ago."* Abruptly she got up from the table. *"I need to lie down."*

He'd asked no more questions. Not about Addisyn. Not about

the medicine. Not about her waning energy levels. And by God, he should have.

He dropped his head onto his fists. He could claim there was no such thing as regret, but the ghosts of his every choice were chattering at him tonight. Only one thing might shut them up: getting that box in the closet back to the people it was always meant for.

Beth's girls.

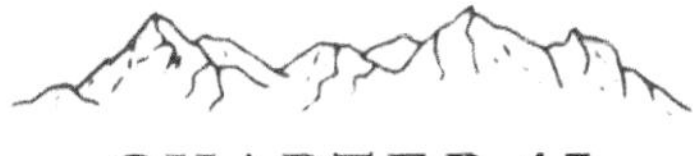

CHAPTER 17

When Avery opened her eyes the next morning, a single, fragile moment of blurry peace was instantly shattered by the events of the night before. She groaned and covered her face with her hands. Skyla. Creed. Addisyn. Laz. The weight of the judgment they surely felt for her pressed her into the mattress. And she could no longer hide behind excuses or explanations.

She rubbed her eyes and sat up, rotating her stiff neck. Well, she would do the next right thing. She would go to the center and teach her Saturday morning class. And try to hold her head up.

Her phone rang while she was finishing dressing. When she saw Skyla's name on the screen, her throat constricted. "Hello?"

"Hello, Avery."

The woman's voice was hard to read. Avery swallowed. "Skyla… about last night. I am so very sorry. I—I just—" How could she explain her conduct? "It was an isolated incident. It won't—"

"Avery, please do not apologize." Skyla's voice was gentle. "I can see that you are indeed fighting many shadows. But I have known that for a long time."

Fighting many shadows? Avery frowned. "That's not—"

"And the chairman of the board has spoken to me as well this morning. After our conversation, I must ask that you take some time off work."

The words were a dull blow. Avery sucked in a breath. "I—I'm being fired?"

"No." Skyla's answer was quick. "You are being given the time you need to gather yourself and begin to face what is before you."

Not her job. Not when she was losing everything else. "Skyla, please." The words were almost a cry. "I promise it won't happen again. I'll be more careful, I'll—"

"Avery, forgive me, but this has happened before. You have had difficulty with your classes, with your coworkers, in meetings—" Skyla's sigh was sorrowful. "I do not doubt your promise, Avery. I only doubt your ability to keep it."

Her denials dried up. She shoved her free hand in her pocket. Blinked back the burn in her eyes. "So—my class this morning—"

"Liv has agreed to stand in."

What must Liv think of her? "O-okay."

"She sees no shame in this. As I do not either."

Oh, but there was. The deep, dismal shame of having failed again, of having been once more not enough.

You're the strong one, Avery.

But her mom was wrong. She wasn't. Had she ever been?

Skyla was still talking. "It brings me no joy to say this, Avery, but I must. Before you can offer healing to those who come here, you must walk the path yourself."

"I have. That's my whole story." Didn't Skyla know? "I left everything and came to the mountains and found—"

"It is possible for the body to move to a new place and the soul to stay behind. You have heard Creed speak of the sky-mirroring, yes?"

That day at The Loch seemed far away now. "Yes. The *kapemni.*"

"Exactly." Skyla's words were still gentle but held an authority. "These words of power you know, Avery: 'What has been decided in the spirit-world above is what you will decide on earth.' And that is what I say to you. You must let loose your life to mirror that above."

What on earth was Skyla talking about? "I—I am following—the good road." Skyla's term for faith came most naturally. "I am trying to do the will of—"

"Yes, you are trying. Trying too hard. This is about—receiving.

Letting loose. And I think the person to be let loose is yourself." Skyla sighed. "Just take this next week, Avery. Please look behind you and before you. And after these days, we will talk."

When the call ended, Avery took a deep breath and snagged her jacket back on the hall tree. Mercy whined and looked in confusion at the door. Avery patted her head. "Sorry, girl. No work today." *My fault.*

She'd let the anxiety ruin everything. Wasn't that what Creed had said?

You act like it's all behind you, but it's not.

She shook her head. He was wrong. It was behind her. Far behind her. Well over the horizon.

Except that it wasn't.

She roamed the land behind her house all afternoon, turning Skyla's words over like smooth stones in her mind. *Look behind and before.* Even if she'd wanted to do that, how?

Addisyn called a couple of times, but Avery let both of the calls go to voicemail. There wasn't much to say anyway.

Soon after sunset, rain brooded over the mountains, pounding her roof with a lonesome rhythm. She took her time brewing a cup of coffee. As if caffeine would solve her problems.

Not much good coffee won't fix.

Creed's words, and for a moment, a sharp pang of longing clamped a vise around her ribs. If only—if only she could go to him now. Tell him what had happened. Talk about what she should do next.

Ridiculous. They had no common ground—last night had proven that. And he was back in Arizona by now, wasn't he? With his girlfriend, and his videos, and his climbing. Those things mattered to him.

And she did not.

She gulped the unexplained lump in her throat and forced herself to think, to peer into the clouds over her future and look ahead.

Or maybe Skyla would tell her to look back.

Look behind and before.

Behind. To Syracuse, maybe. Where Addisyn wanted her to go.

She cradled the coffee mug in her hands and watched her reasons for not going melt into the steam. Handling the legal aspects would be easier that way. Work certainly wouldn't be a problem now. Addisyn would finally settle down. And really, how bad could it be? She'd go, take care of the last lingering traces of their mom, and come home. To her real life.

And anyway, Mom had died in Aston, right? And Aston was a good twenty miles from their former neighborhood. So it wasn't really like going back to—that place. It was merely handling a business matter. Plain and simple. Cut and dried.

Unless—

Avery glanced at her desk, where that ragged envelope folded itself ominously around the secret inside. *Lance Potter.* She took another drink of her coffee. Surely Lance wasn't around anymore. If he hadn't appeared since the funeral, he wasn't going to now.

Dread settled in Avery's stomach despite her reasoning. But she drained the last of her mug, then swiped on Addisyn's number. Her sister answered almost before the phone could ring. "A? I've been trying to call you."

"I know. I've been busy today." Ha. She'd been the most un-busy she'd been in her life.

"Okay—" Addisyn's words sounded like uncertain footsteps, trespassing on sacred ground. "So, listen, about last night—"

"I'm fine. It's no big deal."

"But, A, I think we need to—"

"Addisyn, I said I'm fine." Avery took a deep breath and forced the words out before she could change her mind. "Let's book a flight. We're going to New York this week."

CREED DROVE late into the darkness on Saturday night. Drove until exhaustion overtook him, trying to put as many miles as possible between him and the mountains. When he caught himself drifting across the yellow line around Salt Lake City, he pulled over in a Smith's Food & Drug parking lot. The night was cool for early June. He reached into the backseat for his red anorak before the realization hit him.

Avery still had it.

The thought brought a pain that made him want to never stop driving south. He dug another jacket out of his backpack and slept in his car until the early sunlight reached through his window and tapped him on the shoulder. He waited fifteen minutes for the store to open, then went inside to the restroom and then to the in-store Starbucks counter, where he bought a bagel and a larger-than-life espresso.

The routine was familiar, part of the rhythm of life on the road. Already it felt as if he'd never really stopped living the nomad life. Everything about the last month was blurring into memory like hazy-filtered film.

Everything except Avery.

He shoved away the thought and looked instead at the wolf on his arm. The one that covered some of the scars from old burns. The one that had been born to run.

He steadily clocked away the southward miles, arriving at the Sedona campground by six o'clock. The sun was still hovering well above the horizon in these long summer days. He found the space reserved for him next to the other guys' campers and was just dragging the picnic table into place when his phone pinged with a text from Austin.

> Bro, you in town yet? We're all grabbing drinks
> down at the Blue Moon. If you're here, come join
> us and watch me dominate Rusty at pool!

He left the text on read and shoved the phone back into his pocket. He wasn't in the mood for spending the evening in a techno frat party. He needed to sleep. Recover from his travels. And from everything that had come before them.

By the next morning, some of the exhaustion overshadowing him had drifted away. He woke with the cactus wrens and ducked out of the camper to stand in the breaking light of a desert sunrise.

He'd forgotten what a magical place Sedona truly was. The scarlet streaks of sunrise on the red rocks were almost otherworldly. It was nothing like Estes, of course. But wasn't that the goal, after all? Something new?

Although who knew how many sunrises he'd have to chase to find that.

Already the desert was radiating heat like an oven. In Estes, the morning would have been cool and fresh and fragrant with possibility.

He headed back into the camper and had just pulled out his computer when a knock rapped on the door. And then a familiar voice. "Creed, my man! What's the scoop?"

For some reason, the greeting grated on him today. Creed sighed as he swung the door open. "Austin. Good to see you again." Was it?

"Same, man." Today Austin was wearing fraying cargo shorts and a T-shirt that read GO BIG OR GO HOME. "Glad to see you made it back." He narrowed his eyes slightly. "Erica said you got pretty attached to Colorado."

He searched for an answer. "It wasn't bad."

"Well, glad you didn't mind it too much. I spent some time in that place a few years back, you know. One-horse little town, man. Pretty boring."

Creed's gut twisted oddly at the reference to Estes Park. The little mountain town had more going for it than Austin thought.

"At any rate, I need you, bro." Austin lightly punched Creed's shoulder. "Wait till you see the setup I've got planned here. It's gonna be lit! Our biggest shoot yet. In the meantime—" Austin glanced around as if looking for a place to sit. "Small place you got. Sure you wouldn't rather get a hotel room? The channel would pay."

"I'm sure." Defensiveness rankled him. So maybe the camper was small, but it was his. A hard-earned home.

"Okay. Suit yourself." Austin shrugged, finally perching gingerly on the edge of one of the folding chairs. "All right. I'll get straight to the point. Creed, you've done a remarkable job. When I hired you all those years ago, I knew you were talented, but as I've watched you over the last several months, your abilities have just seemed to keep skyrocketing. And that video…I saw it this morning. Let me tell you, it was good stuff."

The video. Avery's face, Avery's voice. Creed swallowed. "Well. Thanks."

"So—" For once, Austin's expression was completely serious. "The international spot is yours."

He'd done it. The goal he'd pursued for years, delivered into his hands. Yet where was the elation he'd expected from this moment? "I —wow. Thank you. I'm really honored."

"You're a talented videographer. Super good at what you do. But you've also got drive. I know you'll put in the work. And you like life on the road." Austin shrugged. "This will require a lot of traveling, but I know you like that."

"Yeah, definitely." He did like that. All of it.

So why wasn't he more excited?

He had to say something. "Austin, that's so great. Thank you for trusting me." The words sounded stilted. He tried again. "I mean, I'm really honored—"

"Here." Austin tugged an envelope from his pocket and dropped it lightly on the table. "Job description is in there. And contract."

Contract. One signature, and he'd have the life he'd dreamed of for years. Best of all, he'd finally show his father that the man had been wrong about his filming. Finally leave his past behind for good.

So why did he feel as if he'd swallowed a rock?

"We can announce it on Wednesday at the team meeting." Austin nodded at him. "You should show your video then too."

"Okay. Sounds good. Thank you."

"Yeah, no problem. Glad to do it. Well, I gotta run." Austin stood and squinted at the symbols above the couch. "You took a crayon to your walls, man?"

Creed flinched. "They're Lakota signs."

But Austin was already halfway down the steps. "Oh. Cool. Well, see ya."

Avery had wanted to know what the symbols meant. Avery had touched the *kapemni* like a prayer.

Avery had asked him why he worked for Austin.

Creed stared at the envelope on the table. He'd worked for Austin for one simple reason: to finally reach this moment. All the months and years of editing unending footage, traveling across the country, and pandering to Austin's whims—it had all paid off.

And in seventy-two hours, his entire team would know.

AVERY'S HANDS didn't shake at first. Not as she drove to Denver in the predawn light, not as she left Mercy with Darius and picked up Addisyn, not as they navigated the labyrinth of security, not as the plane rose above the tarmac.

But when she looked out the plane window, the mountains were vanishing beneath her. *Her* mountains. She was beyond the protection of her sanctuary now, heading back into the eastern world that had nearly destroyed her.

And then the shaking started.

"A?" Addisyn's voice was timid.

Avery tucked her trembling fingers into her pockets. "Yeah?"

Addisyn picked at a fraying edge on the plane seatbelt. "Do you remember Lucy?"

Avery reached back through her memory to the hazy half-formed shapes of her early childhood. "A little. Maybe. Mom used to visit her. Sometimes she took me with her."

Addisyn nodded slowly. "Why don't I remember her?"

"Well—they must have only recently reconnected, because by the time you would have remembered, they'd lost touch."

"Because of Dad?"

"Well..." They weren't even back to New York yet, and already she was having to dance around the issues. "Mom didn't get out a lot after you were born."

"Oh."

The syllable was small, and for the moment, Addisyn looked like a lost little girl. Avery's heart squeezed. If only she could get them off this plane. Get them out of this story. Get them back to the beginning and start over with a mother who never left and a family that always protected.

El Shaddai, if I can only lead her through this without hurting her. Please. That's all I want.

She swallowed the ache in her throat and wrapped an arm around Addisyn's shoulders. "It'll be okay, Ads."

Addisyn nodded quickly, keeping her eyes down. "Uh-huh." She blinked and sniffed. "I wish—"

"You wish what?"

"I wish she had come back for us."

El Shaddai. Some mix of frustration and desperation tangled in her chest. Would Addisyn be forever longing to return to something they'd never really had?

She took a deep breath, releasing the hard edges of her emotions. Part of this process would have to include hearing Addisyn with no judgment.

"I know, Ads." There was nothing else to say. "I know."

Addisyn slid closer, pressing more securely into Avery's arm around her, and laid her head on Avery's shoulder. Within a couple of minutes, her breathing had slowed to the light, even rhythm of sleep. If only Avery could rest that easily. And if only she could protect Addisyn from everything that lay ahead.

She flexed the fingers of her free hand and forced her breathing to match Addisyn's even tempo. Okay. That was better. She just had to get to New York, do what had to be done, and escape back to Colorado.

And then everything would be okay.

Rain was pelting the runway when they landed in LaGuardia, the airport humming and crawling like the brimming dome of a giant beehive. Avery held Addisyn's hand as they made their way through security and into the crowded concourse. Whether she was doing it for Addisyn or for herself wasn't a question she examined.

"A, where did Lucy say she would be?"

"By the baggage claim." Avery shouldered her backpack more securely and peered through the clustering crowd. This place was more of a wilderness than the Rockies had ever been.

"Is that her?"

Sure enough, a woman with wide doe eyes and a gentle face was nudging her way through the thickness of passersby. "Oh, girls! It's so good to see you!" She reached Avery first and grabbed her in a warm hug, then stepped back and cocked her head. "My goodness, you look so much like Beth."

Avery flinched, but the woman had already turned her attention aside. "And you must be Addisyn."

Something in her tone rang a warning bell. Lucy didn't know the secret, did she? *No. Please don't say—*

"I'm just so happy to see both of Beth's girls." Lucy squeezed a hand on each of their shoulders. "My car's right outside. Any luggage?"

"No." Avery glanced to make sure Addisyn was still towing her carryon. She'd encouraged her sister to pack lightly. That made it harder to stay and easier to leave.

Once in Lucy's SUV, Avery watched the swishing windshield wipers and said as little as possible. Which proved easy, since Lucy kept up a stream of talk that meandered from the weather to local gossip to her family. Finally, right as they passed a sign that said WELCOME TO ASTON, she made her way to Mom.

"I'm sorry I wasn't able to do more for poor Beth." She pressed her lips together and glanced sideways at Avery.

Platitudes like *It's okay* or *I do too* or *You did all you could* died in her throat. Avery kept her eyes on the wagging wipers.

"How did you know our mom again?" Addisyn leaned forward from the backseat. The look of longing in her eyes made Avery want to leap out of the car.

"Oh, we met in high school." Lucy flipped on her blinker for a turn. "I had just moved to Aston from Chicago. And she was lonely, even then. We hit it right off. Even after I got married, we were still at each other's houses a good deal."

"What happened?"

"Well." Lucy rubbed at an invisible smudge on the steering wheel. "Ulys and I never got along that well."

"Oh."

Lucy cleared her throat. "So, we lost touch for a long while. It was only in the last few years that she reached out to me. By then, she knew about the cancer." Lucy blinked hard, watching some memory in the rain. "I think she was scared of—of being alone."

Scared of being alone. A sudden image burst into Avery's mind. Nine-year-old Addisyn curled up in the middle of her bed, swallowed by sobs. *"Avery, you won't go away too, will you? I don't want to be by myself."*

Yeah, it would take a lot more time before she could muster sympathy for her mother's plight.

She had just begun to hope the subject was dropped when Lucy spoke again. "I was her maid of honor, you know."

"Really?" Addisyn was clearly storing all these details.

"Yes. I wonder where those wedding photos got to." Lucy frowned and glanced at Avery. "Do you have them?"

"No." The syllable was all she could force out.

"Well, maybe that's another missing thing." Lucy sighed.

She shouldn't even ask, but—"Missing thing?"

"Yes." Concern pinched between Lucy's brows. "When I boxed up her things after she passed, there was a lot I couldn't locate. Her family album, for one. But perhaps she left that with Ulys."

Avery shook her head. "I don't think so." She remembered the bulky album, but it had disappeared when her mom did.

"See, I don't know where it got to. And then her journals." Lucy shook her head. "She was always writing in her journals."

"Avery journals too!" There was way too much enthusiasm in Addisyn's voice.

Avery gritted her teeth as Lucy offered her a hopeful smile. "Really? Well, maybe you got that from her."

Avery could only pray that she'd gotten *nothing* from her mom.

"Still, I wish I knew where the rest of her stuff went to." Lucy sighed and shook her head. "Oh, well. I've boxed up all I could salvage for you girls. Right here at—" She pulled into a gravel driveway and turned the car off—"her house."

A low red-brick structure slumped before them, a couple of shingles buckling like warts on the roof. The yard was soggy with rain, a coffee-colored puddle forming in the middle of the driveway. A vacant rocking chair swayed listlessly on the front porch.

So this was where Mom had lived. And died. Sudden chills tingled over Avery's arms. She was a trespasser in her mom's life.

"So, the house is part of the estate." Lucy sidestepped a cracked plastic pot of wilted geraniums as they made their way across the discolored concrete of the front porch. "We'll know more after we see the lawyer. I think he has some paperwork for you to fill out."

Avery nodded vacantly, her attention absorbed as she stepped into the main living room. She glanced around, both hoping and fearing to see her mom's fingerprints on the house. Although her mom had been gone so long. Too long for Avery to recognize her in paint colors or flooring choices.

The furniture was plain and mismatched, the cobbled collection of thrift-shop finds. A frayed blue rug underfoot clashed with the faded teal curtains.

"—moved in here about five years ago, is what I always understood. I tried to get her to find a place closer to town, but no, she wanted to be out here—"

Where were the personal touches? The details that would have put flesh on the skeleton of this house? The only decorative accent seemed to be a small framed art piece, nearly lost in the blank expanse of the wood-paneled wall. Avery moved closer, studying it. A line drawing of a wilting rose drooping in a bottleneck vase, dropping petals like tears.

"Your mom's art."

Avery jumped slightly. When had Lucy approached? "I'm sorry?"

Lucy stroked a finger reverently over the rose. "She took up drawing when she got sick. She was really quite good. At least, I think so. There's a folio of her other artwork. I'll make sure you get that."

"Wow." Addisyn's eyebrows rose. "That's pretty."

Her mom had been an *artist*? A heavy heat throbbed in Avery's chest. Her mom didn't deserve art. Didn't deserve whatever crumbs of beauty she'd tried to catch.

Lucy lifted the frame from the wall. "You'll probably want this."

Avery jerked back. "I—I'll get it later."

The rest of the house didn't take long to see—living room, bedroom, bathroom, laundry room. Finally Lucy pushed through a set of swinging doors into the kitchen and indicated cardboard cartons stacked into a semblance of order. "These are all of her things."

Sad, somehow. And oddly disquieting. How could a whole life be reduced to the remnants in a handful of cardboard boxes?

"Anyway—" Lucy opened a cupboard door to reveal a stack of soup cans next to a single box of Ritz crackers. "I've cleaned out the refrigerator, of course, but I haven't had time to go through the pantry yet. Although she didn't have much in here. She was bad about her meals. I always said—"

Avery's eyes were still on the cardboard boxes. The walls were tilting toward her, the whole house like a soulless body aching with the absence of life. Avery took a step back. "I need to go."

Lucy paused in the middle of a sentence and raised her eyebrows. "Are you all right?"

"I—I just—" She was being ridiculous. She stuffed her hands into her pockets. "We should probably start heading to our appointment with the lawyer. It's at four thirty."

"Oh, of course." Lucy nodded. "Let's go there now. You can always come back and go through these things tomorrow, or the next day if you need more time."

Addisyn nodded. "We'll be here a while."

No, they weren't spending more than three days in New York. That was for sure.

"Or—" Lucy paused as they headed back through the living room. "Do you want to go ahead and take those boxes with you?"

Boxes of secrets and lies and a story from which she'd been unwritten. "No, thank you." Avery stepped out of the door, into the cooling rain. Finally, air that didn't smell like the staleness of an unlived life. "I'll deal with that later."

"ALL RIGHT, let's break for lunch." Austin clapped his hands. "Great work today, guys."

Creed barely suppressed a yawn as he fitted his camera back into the spider holster. A day of dirt-wheeling through the desert and scrambling up the rock faces and catching the shots Austin wanted. A day in which he'd be formally named to the international team. A day spent waiting for the excitement to kick in.

And so far, it hadn't.

"Creed, can you get the rough cuts done in time for the team huddle this afternoon?"

Team huddle. When had Austin's trendy lingo started to feel as irritating as a prickly-pear thorn? "Sure. Yeah." The rough cuts on the film wouldn't be hard. Not when every video followed a predictable sequence.

What was wrong with him? His great Arizona adventure was just feeling—boring. The climbing was the same. The videos were the same. The traveling was the same.

The videos for Avery, though, had been different.

Then, he'd felt the sparks, the creativity kindling within him the way it once had. Because he believed in the project? Because he believed in her?

Either way, he couldn't find that connection here.

His shirt was soaked and salt-stiff with sweat. He shrugged it off as he climbed the steps to his camper. Maybe the problem was just that he was tired. They'd been going hard the last few days, with Austin seemingly determined to climb every cliff that raised its head above the Arizona desert. No wonder he didn't have much band-width left for excitement.

Inside his camper, the clattering fan made his papers dance on the little folding table. It was really too hot to be sitting in the aluminum shell in the middle of the day, but this was the one place he could find some privacy.

He slung his wet shirt over the back of a chair, then powered up his laptop, connecting his camera. He would put everything in a folder and then wipe the SIM card. Start over with—

The first still shot on the roll hit him like a slap. *Avery.*

The moment from Lake Haiyaha, the one he'd captured on a whim. There she was, perched on the big stone, gazing across the sun-splattered lake with a dream in her eyes.

Resting on the rock. Looking to the sky.

Two things he'd long ago quit doing.

The air in the camper was suddenly too small. He glanced at the clock on the wall. He had three hours still before the meeting. Plenty of time later to edit today's footage, to fit it into the predictable pattern of all the other videos. For now, he needed to get out of here. And tired or not, he needed to climb.

He pulled a new T-shirt from his bag and tossed his climbing shoes and chalk in the back of the Jeep. The climbing gym wasn't far away—he'd visited it yesterday, even. But then, he'd been with the guys. Now he needed to be alone.

In the middle of a workday, the gym was empty, just as he'd wanted. A rock version of "House of the Rising Sun" was blasting from the speakers. He took a deep breath of the familiar climbing-gym smell—sweat and rubber and adrenaline. Normally, this environment motivated him. Made his veins throb with power. But now it all just felt—small.

He pulled on his climbing shoes and scraped chalk on his hands, then studied the routes. V10 today. No, V11. He'd ratchet the difficulty to a level that would force him to focus only on the task at hand, give his mind a rest from the exhaustion of thinking.

He dragged the crash pad beneath the route and gripped the first jug, swinging himself up. His muscles burned in response. He found a crimp with his toe and stared up, mentally navigating the next steps. A sharp righthand turn...okay. Then across...and up...and he'd have to swing to manage that overhang...and finish up there. Where the double yellow tape taunted him from somewhere impossibly over his head.

Swing, pull, grab. The rhythm beat a tempo with the rock music, and he flung himself forward, the holds rough against his hands, his body fluid with the familiar break and burn. He kept his eyes on that finish far above him. That X in the yellow tape that looked like a vague *kapemni*. Hadn't he always been climbing toward something out of reach? Toward that intersection? The place between Heaven and Earth?

His breath was rough in his lungs, his muscles quivering under the strain. His sweaty fingers slipped off the overhang, and he just caught himself with his elbow. He pressed himself against the wall for a brief moment of rest, dipping his fingers into the fresh chalk on his belt. Was it really true that if he kept climbing—kept achieving, kept working harder, kept moving forward—he'd someday reach the intersection of the *kapemni*?

Avery claimed she had. She had known darkness greater than his. Yet she was working for the healing of the land, the people. What had broken her still hurt her—that was obvious to him, if not to her.

But she'd still reached out, and he'd only drawn in. Made himself the sorry center of a life that was all about climbing—in every way.

He counted ten more seconds of rest, then leaped off again, catching his toes against the overhang and swinging his body into the next hold. Sweat stung his eyes as he glanced up. He was over halfway there.

But what waited at the top?

He hooked his heel into a tiny hold and pulled himself to the next section. The wolf on his arm seemed to accuse him. *Running Wolf.* He was always moving, wasn't he? Running from the past. Chasing the future. Pursuing his goals so intently, so unwaveringly, that he'd hurt Avery in the process.

And suddenly, a new thought hit him with the force of a landslide. Wasn't that what his dad had done?

His foot slipped from the hold, his legs dangling in empty air. He tightened his grip, forcing his arms to engage, pawing at the wall. Why couldn't he find a foothold?

His heart was hammering from far more than the physical strain. All these years, he'd harbored such bitterness against the man. Hated him for putting his project over people.

But in a single snapshot of rock-wall reality, he could see it now: he'd over and over done the same thing. The way Dad had put the ministry before him was the same way he'd sacrificed Avery's trust for his own mission.

His chest was burning, his arms ripping from his shoulders. He couldn't hold this position. But he could find nothing solid beneath his feet.

He'd refused his dad forgiveness. But he needed it too. And was that what he'd really been chasing all this time?

His sweat-slick hands could hold no longer. The wall whooshed away in a single disorienting moment before he was on his back on the crash pad, the impact jerking through him despite the cushioning. It took a few throbbing heartbeats to get his air back.

His arms were still burning, his body drenched with sweat. He groaned and swiped a trembling hand over his face. He'd fallen. Again. And that elusive yellow X was sneering at him. *You can't climb high enough, Running Wolf. Heaven is out of reach. Earth has its grip.*

But for just a moment on that wall, he'd seen it: forgiveness. That was it, wasn't it? The place where Heaven met Earth.

And now—he'd never have the chance to find it.

The dry bitterness of regret tasted like climbing chalk in his mouth. All this time, he'd believed there were no open doors. No places where Heaven touched Earth. But really, he'd been surrounded by them. In the flight of the hawks and the strength of Skyla's convictions, the sunrises over the mountains and the pleading in his dad's voice.

And the light in Avery's eyes.

He'd had his chances to finally find that place he sought all his life, and he'd walked right by every single one of them. If only there could be—just one more. One more sign. One more word. One more something, *anything*, that would lead him to the redemption he'd always needed.

But gravity had pulled him down. Again. And as he lay panting on the crash pad, Heaven was silent.

As always.

CHAPTER 18

So far, the visit to New York was nothing like what Addisyn had expected.

It had started yesterday, when Lucy first showed them the house. Addisyn had hoped to linger, to try to soak up some essence of her mom's presence that might be hiding in the wallpaper she'd chosen or the furniture she'd arranged. But Avery had hustled them through the house as if impatient to check the task off some mental to-do list. They hadn't been there half an hour when Avery all but dragged her out the door. They hadn't even gone back to pick up those boxes.

And then there was the lawyer, a stuffy guy with face like a tombstone who talked about *estates* and *probate* and stuff like that. It had felt wrong, almost, reducing their mom's death to what felt like a business transaction. But again, Avery had moved methodically through the mountain of paperwork, her *"professional"* face never slipping. Whatever Avery's emotions about this whole thing were—if in fact she had any—they were hidden deeper than the mythical ore in Eugenia Mine.

Even now, Avery was making herself busy around the hotel room. Had she stopped moving since the plane landed?

"Okay, Addisyn, you ready?" Avery shouldered her bag, pocketed the hotel room key, straightened an evacuation route sign hanging by the door. "We're going to go by Mom's house and pick up those boxes. The real estate agent is meeting us there too."

"Real estate agent?" Avery hadn't mentioned that. "You're selling the house?"

"Well, yes." Avery paused with her rental car keys in her hand. "I mean, neither of us needs a house here."

"I guess not."

"What do you mean, you *guess not*?"

"Well—I mean—"

"Addisyn." Exasperation flicked at the edges of Avery's words. "What would we do with it otherwise? We can't possibly keep or maintain a house on the other side of the continent. Even if we rented it, someone would need to be on site to—"

"Avery, I get it. It's fine." If she didn't halt this conversation, they'd have the kind of fight they hadn't had in years.

Avery twirled the car keys for a moment. Then she sighed. "Okay, listen, if you don't want to sell it—"

"No. I understand." She couldn't argue with Avery's logic, anyway. And was it really Avery's fault this experience didn't match her expectations? "Isn't this just kind of—quick?"

"I need to get it listed before we go back home, and we only have one more night here."

Well, that was because Avery had only booked them three nights there. Irritation rubbed Addisyn backward again. Wasn't this whole trip supposed to be about emotional closure? Finding their way to healing by revisiting the past? So why hadn't Avery made space for that in her invisible timeline? "Hey, Avery?"

"Yeah?" Avery was hunting for something in her bag with a preoccupied expression.

"Are we—" She'd been clutching this request since before they left Colorado, so why was it so hard to ask? "Aren't we going to our neighborhood before we leave?"

Avery froze. "Our neighborhood? Why?"

"To see our house, and—and to see where Mom's buried."

Avery still didn't move. Like a mouse in the shadow of one of her hawks. "Ads—" She finally straightened and shoved her hands in her pockets, the way she often did when she was stressed. "I don't think that's a good idea. Okay?"

"Why not?"

"Because—" Avery shook her head. "There's no point. We don't live in that house anymore. And Mom—" Avery's hand tightened on the strap of her bag. "Mom's been gone a long time."

"Well—I thought maybe it would help give closure." Although Avery seemed to be allergic to the word.

Sure enough, her sister's expression tightened. "We'll talk about it later, okay?" She glanced at the clock. "We need to get going. The real estate guy should be there any minute."

Later. How many weeks had it been since Avery had started using that word to shuffle all her questions to a tomorrow that never came? Addisyn had a smart reply all ready but bit it back. Sniping at her sister wasn't going to help either one of them.

When they pulled up to the house, Avery was out of the car almost before she put it in park. "All right. We've got just a little bit of time before the guy gets here. Let's start by clearing out some of the things inside."

"Clearing out?" Addisyn ducked through the front door after Avery.

"Yes." Her sister was clearly in full-on executive mode. "I'm going to sort through her clothes. You can go ahead and start looking in the cabinets. See if there's anything we want to keep."

Every drawer and door looked at her like an untold story. Addisyn knelt cautiously and pulled open the bottom kitchen cabinet, wincing at the slight squeak of the hinges. A lopsided stack of plates stared back at her. "Do we want to keep these?"

"What are they?" Avery's voice was muffled from the closet.

"Dishes." Addisyn slipped the first one off the stack—creamy white with a leaf design around the edge. Pretty, but badly scratched. And somehow sad.

"Probably not dishes. I left some trash bags by the door. Go ahead and sack up anything we're not keeping in those."

Addisyn pulled out the stack of dishes and traced the leaf design with one finger. What had made Mom pick these dishes? Had she thought the pattern was nice? Or just found them on sale?

Somehow Addisyn couldn't just toss these in the trash bag. They were remnants of her mom's life. A trail of crumbs to a destination she'd never find now. Her throat pinched shut. "Avery?"

"Yes?"

"Can you come look at these? I don't know for sure what to do." With the dishes. With the emotions. With anything.

She blinked back the moisture in her eyes. Good grief, if she was going to cry over every item, they really would never get done.

But somewhere in these dishes and clothes and belongings was what she'd really wanted to find all along.

Her mom.

———⧗———

ANXIETY WAS one of the most common mental health ailments that Lance treated. Every year, thousands of fear-ridden folks streamed into his office, panicking over everything from passing the bar exam, to asking a girl out, to existential wrestling with the possibility of Heaven or Hell—or both or neither.

The DSM—the psychiatric "*bible*," it was called, despite his aversion to the religious terminology—listed anxiety as one of the most clear-cut mental health conditions to treat. And throughout his practice, he'd agreed with that assessment. When all the jargon was boiled down, anxiety could be treated with only two strategies. SSRIs, and the old *face-your-fears* cliche.

Yet he couldn't imagine a single medication or exposure hierarchy that would help him face the fear that gripped him now.

The road to Aston was sinisterly familiar. He gripped his steering wheel as he made his way to the town in which Beth had apparently lived and died. Fifteen minutes from him. If there was a God, was this His idea of a dark joke?

He glanced in the rearview mirror. The cardboard box was still sitting in his backseat. His name scratched across the top in her handwriting.

LANCE.

A plea, maybe. A command. A sacred trust. Or maybe an accusation. That was most likely. As if even from the afterlife—or whatever shadowy post-death state might exist—Beth was still reminding him of how much he'd disappointed her.

Sweat prickled on his forehead. He swiped at his face, scratching the roughness on his chin. He needed to shave. Needed to eat. Needed to sleep without the gorilla of insomnia sitting on his chest. Needed to do something, anything, to get this godforsaken box out of his life.

But—would that really bring him the closure he sought? Or would he forever be haunted by his guilt?

The thought made his hands tremble on the wheel. What was happening to him? He preached rationality to his clients, soothing their souls with skill. Now insanity felt precariously close. As if God Himself were hunting him down, chasing him off the precipice.

He shook his head. God, pursuing him? Next he'd be seeing Bigfoot in the passenger seat.

The cemetery loomed in front of him. He took a deep breath and pulled into the parking lot.

He knew what was causing his emotions, right? He could chart out the complex chemical reactions that swirled into the cocktail of guilt. He could point to which area of the brain activated when faced with painful memories. And until now, he'd believed that was the extent of the phenomenon.

But this—this was different. And it was driving him into a whirlpool of despair deep enough to drown in. Next, it'd be him in a sterile psychiatrist's office, hearing the same techniques he'd once believed in. He'd wander through the remainder of his life, hag-haunted by all of his mistakes. And then one day—he'd be dead.

A cold shudder turned his stomach inside out. Suddenly the grave markers looked like bared teeth. Why had he never thought of that before? His path could reach no other destination except the ultimate end. Nothingness. X.

But if his regret couldn't be reduced to a chemical reaction, then maybe there really was—something more. Not the whole cartoony cloud-and-harp rigmarole, but some kind of world beyond the edges of his awareness. Some place where Beth might be, even now.

He swallowed hard. That was worse. Because if there was an afterlife, there might also be a deity. Some cosmic judge who ran a court without appeals.

And he didn't need to meet God face to face to imagine what a higher power would think of his conduct.

He shoved the truck into reverse, backing out of the cemetery. Not today. He'd come back. Just—not today.

Coward.

The word was nearly hissed in his ear, so almost-real that he jerked in his seat and glanced around the truck interior. Great. He really was losing it. Too many nights without sleep.

Coward.

Okay, sure, he was a coward. He'd been a coward all those years ago, refusing to take responsibility for what had happened with Beth. He'd been a coward when Beth had sent him away, not brave enough to go after her and face her rejection again. He was a coward at the cemetery, too shaken to walk across a hundred yards of turf and find her grave. And he was a coward with that box—too scared to reach out to Addisyn or Avery, too unsure what to do, too—too broken. In every way.

But the invisible thumb in his back wouldn't subside, the pressure on him redoubling to do something, anything, to try to lift the two-ton elephant of regret just enough for him to take a single deep breath.

"Okay!" He yelled the word, hard enough his throat scratched. "I'm a coward! I get it!" He slapped the steering wheel, the frustration of days—maybe years—churning inside him. "So, fine. God—if You exist at all—it's Your turn. Don't You think it's time for You to do something here?"

Silence. Of course. Yet also—an eerily listening one. As if someone really was—hearing him.

A shiver chilled the back of his neck, yet something in him had unaccountably settled at the same time. "I—I'm trying." He paused. If ever he would be honest, this was the time. "Well, I mean, I—I *want* to try. But—I don't know what to do."

The prayer—if that's what it was—dwindled. He breathed in the stillness, waiting. For what?

Ulys would have laughed at him.

But Ulys was also dead.

A sudden thought struck him, a single arrow of clarity finally winging through his confusion. What if—what if he went to Beth's old house? Surely someone was there. The girls were in Colorado, of course—even if they had come for the funeral, they'd be gone by now. But maybe the neighbors knew how to contact them on his behalf. Or maybe one of Beth's friends would be there.

He pulled off the road and thumbed through a quick Google search. In thirty seconds, he'd found the address of the property registered to Elizabeth Miles. And amazingly, it was only five miles away.

A sudden new energy propelled him forward, his tires eating up the miles. This was it. He'd get rid of the box. Be able to sleep again. Find a way to rebuild the rest of his life without—

The house number loomed in front of him. 312. And there was a car already parked in the driveway. Perfect. He'd be able to hand this stuff to someone.

He pulled into the driveway. So, should he knock on the door? Or maybe—

But the door was opening, and someone was coming out. A girl. A girl who looked like—

His eyes widened. His breath stopped. And if he'd ever been tempted to believe in God, it was at that moment.

Because walking toward him, out of Beth's house, was Addisyn.

Just as Addisyn had finished sorting through the dishes, tires had crunched on the gravel outside.

"Ads, why don't you go out and say hi to the real estate guy?" Avery's voice had been muffled from the closet. "I'll be there in a second."

"Okay." Addisyn had all but fled from the house.

Now on the porch, she drew a deep breath and swiped at her eyes. This was impossible. Especially since Avery wouldn't acknowledge the emotions brimming under the task.

Sure enough, a truck was idling in the driveway. A protective instinct thrummed inside Addisyn. She'd see about this real estate guy before she'd give him permission to sell her mother's house. It was just as much hers as it was Avery's, anyway.

She squared her shoulders and marched up to the truck window. "Hello?"

"Oh. Hello there." An older guy stared back at her uncertainly. He rubbed a hand over the graying stubble on his face. "Uh—are you —Addisyn Miles?"

He seemed awfully nervous for a real estate guy. Addisyn narrowed her eyes. "I'm Addisyn Payne, yes."

"Addisyn." He said her name in an odd way. Half wonder, half fear. "So you're Addisyn."

This interaction was getting weirder. Suddenly sorting the dishes didn't seem so bad. Addisyn took a step back. "My sister's in the house. I'll get her."

"I didn't come to see your sister."

What? Addisyn tilted her head. "I'm sorry, aren't you the real estate guy?"

"Real estate?" Now it was his turn to look off-balance. "No. No, I—" He rubbed his face uncomfortably again. Then he locked his eyes on hers. "I came to see you, Addisyn."

A shiver of fear slithered up her spine. This was getting creepy. "Do I know you?"

"I'm Lance Potter." He was watching her as if that name meant something. "I'm sure your sister has mentioned me."

Addisyn stared at him, but he kept going before she could respond.

"I—" He cleared his throat. "I was a friend of your mom's."

A friend of Mom's? Why had Avery never mentioned him? Addisyn shook her head. "She's—she's passed away."

"I know." Pain twisted his face for a moment. "My God, I know."

He turned off the truck and stepped out, squinting even beneath the overcast sky. Standing, he was a lot shorter than she'd thought, and his expression was the cringing uncertainty of a timid animal. The pressure of her fear eased somewhat.

He nervously fingered his key. "I—I had some of her things. Some things she wanted you to have."

"Me?" A sudden surge of longing overrode all her sense of caution. The next moment common sense flashed back. "Wait, why would you have things for me?"

"Because—" He looked down, fiddled with the keys again. "Your mother knew that I—that I had wanted to meet you." He looked up, a raw pleading in his eyes. "For a long time."

All of this was too surreal for her to find her footing. "Why?"

"Well—" He gulped a deep breath. "Because—because—"

"Because what?"

"Addisyn." His voice was soft, each word a hesitant step forward. "I—I might be your dad."

His mouth was still moving, but a wind was roaring through Addisyn's mind. Drowning out his words. Blowing away all her conceptions of reality. Reshaping her past into something she didn't recognize.

"You're lying." She shook her head, stepped back, her breath hard and heavy. "Avery would have told me."

"You mean she never—" His eyes widened. "I wouldn't have said anything if—"

"You're lying." She clung to the words again, seeking shelter in the safety of the idea. Of course he was lying. He had to be. And any minute Avery would come out and tell him—

"I'm not lying." He swore softly under his breath. "I shouldn't have come here. Your mother always said—"

"Addisyn?" Thank God, Avery was hurrying down the path toward her. "Is everything okay? I thought—"

One glance at the man, and Avery stopped as if she'd slammed into an invisible wall.

"Hello, Avery." The guy's voice was quiet.

"Lance." Avery forced the word through gritted teeth. "What are you doing here?"

"Avery." Addisyn grabbed her sister's hand. She wasn't crying, not yet, but somehow tears were running down her face anyway. "He says he's my dad."

The words were pleading to be denied. Instead, Avery's face crushed under the pain of some great weight.

And she said nothing.

"Avery!" The first dry sob racked her ribs. "Avery, tell him! That's wrong, isn't it, Avery?" She was losing control, her words slipping and sliding on each other. "Avery, tell him, tell him he's wrong, tell him—"

"Ads. Stop." The deadly quiet in Avery's voice cut off Addisyn's words. Her fingers tightened around Addisyn's hand, but her eyes were still on the guy. Lance. "You need to go."

"I—I see that." The guy shuffled his feet, turned back to his truck. "I—I wanted to talk to you. To both of you, if—"

"Lance, leave." Avery's voice was strained, as if bursting against some internal barricade.

"Avery!" The word was a wail, because her world was scrambling and spinning and squeezing in on itself. None of this could be true. Avery would not have lied to her. Would not have hidden such a secret from her. "Avery, tell me! It's not true! Right?"

But when she looked at her sister's face, she had her answer. Because for the first time since they'd come to New York, Avery was crying. The kind of tears she never allowed were twisting her face, and a mix of guilt and fear swam in her eyes.

And then the thin ice beneath Addisyn's hope splintered into wounding shards, leaving her drowning in what she couldn't face. Because if Avery was crying, this horrible hard-edged thing was true. And if it was true, nothing else ever had been.

"Ads, please, listen to me—"

But Addisyn ripped her hand from Avery's. And then she turned and ran into the house. The house where her mom had lived and died with secrets her sister knew.

Or was Avery even her sister at all?

THE MOMENT WAS like running through another night terror. A thousand times Avery had jerked awake with this same sinking of horror, this same darkness roaring in, this same frantic pulse of hammering heart and slick sweat.

But this terror she couldn't wake up from.

"Lance, no!" The scream ripped at the inside of her throat, some wild and wounded cry. "What did you tell her?"

"I'm sorry. I'm so sorry." Guilt twisted his face, and he rubbed an unsteady hand over his chin. "I thought she knew—I thought you would have told her."

No, Avery hadn't told her. And this was exactly why.

"I—I've been trying to find you girls for a while. I had some things that your mom wanted you to have." Sweat glistened along his hairline. "So when I saw Addisyn today—"

"You had no right to show up here and tell her anything." What *had* he told her? And what must Addisyn be feeling right now?

"I know, I know." His groan came from somewhere deep inside him. "I—I just wanted to get these things back to you or her. Maybe—"

A few raindrops spattered her face. She blinked them back. "Just go. Please." She had no time to waste volleying useless words with Lance when Addisyn was suffering somewhere.

"I'm leaving." He scrambled into the truck, turned the ignition, paused with his hands clenched on the wheel. "Avery? I—I really am sorry."

Sorry. The word burned like salt in a gaping wound. As she watched the truck nose back onto the street, Avery clenched her jaw so tightly her teeth hurt. This man had ripped their family to shreds. And he was still at it.

She jogged to the door, rolling possible explanations like dice in her thoughts. None of them would begin to repair this damage. She was still choking on her heartbeat, her hands trembling. This was the worst part of the night terror, the part right before she'd jerk awake.

If only she would.

She opened the door, stumbled back into her mother's suffocating world. "Ads?"

No answer. The house was dark and silent as a soulless body.

Avery cautiously stepped into the shadowed living room. On this rainy afternoon, the sunlight was too weak to filter through the dingy curtains. "Addisyn?"

"I'm here."

Avery started and turned toward the voice. Addisyn was huddled on the floor against the opposite wall, hugging her knees to her chest as if holding herself together.

Avery reached toward her.

"Don't touch me."

Avery swallowed. Stopped. "Ads—"

Addisyn raised her head and shook back her hair. Her expression brimmed with anger and pain and a lostness that made Avery's chest ache. "You lied to me."

Avery bit her lip. "Okay, Ads, listen. You're right to be mad. I understand what you must—"

"You knew about Lance."

Avery took a breath. Let it out. "I did."

"You knew that he was my—my—" Addisyn choked.

Avery gulped the knot in her own throat. "Yes."

"Is that why Mom left?"

The walls were all down now, and there was no use hiding the rubble. "Yes."

The word settled between them, soaking up all the air in the room.

Addisyn blinked. Her eyes were vacant, dazed. Like the expression of Skyla's injured hawks. "Mom left because of me."

Avery had had this conversation in her worst nightmares. She'd hoped to never have it in real life. "Ads, *no*. Okay? I don't want you thinking that way." She struggled for her breath. "I'll tell you the story."

"Sixteen years too late."

Avery swallowed the sick taste of the truth. "This was before you were born, but Mom worked for a little while for Dad at his practice. Lance was in partnership with Dad at the time. She met him then, and they became—um—well, they had some sort of relationship."

Addisyn was watching her with wide, unblinking eyes. No hint of how she was absorbing this.

"I guess Dad found out while she was pregnant with you. He and Lance had a confrontation and ended up parting ways. And then when you were born, Dad thought that you were—you know." She couldn't look at Addisyn anymore. "He and Mom fought about it a lot for years. And finally—"

"She left."

Avery twisted her hands together. "Yes."

Addisyn nodded vaguely, still with that dazed expression. As if the shock of the story was too big to be absorbed. "How did you find all this out?"

Round two of secrets. "She came to our house one night."

"She came back after she left?" Addisyn's monotone broke slightly.

"Years later." Avery curled her cold fingers into fists. "She wanted to take you to see Lance. He was asking about you."

"But she wasn't—she didn't want to stay?"

Every question was wrenching Avery's heart a little more. "Ads, I don't think she knew what she wanted."

"Why didn't you tell me any of this before?" The last word cracked, and at last, tears spilled over.

"I was trying to protect you."

"Protect me?" Addisyn's voice soared an octave. She scrambled to her feet, sparks kindling in her eyes. "By hiding everything?"

"By not forcing you to carry a burden that's not your fault." Avery spread her hands, willing her sister to understand. "Addisyn, don't you see? Whether Lance—it doesn't matter. You're my sister. It changes nothing in any way that—"

"Avery, are you crazy? It changes everything! To know that—that everything I believed was wrong? That Mom didn't even want me?" Fresh tears pricked Addisyn's eyes. "That it's my fault she left?"

"No, it's not your fault!" *El Shaddai, help me!* She'd expected this reaction. How would she make Addisyn see reason? "Mom didn't care anything about either of us. Okay? If she had, she would have taken us with her. No mother leaves her children with her abuser. You've got to see that—"

"So, if you think it doesn't change anything, then why didn't you tell me?" Addisyn jerked her chin up, the way she did when she was trying to be tough. "This is going to destroy us, Avery! Why would you do this?"

"Addisyn—" She was begging now, pleading for the fallout to not flatten them both. "I mean, I know it's a lot to reckon with, but we'll talk about it and—"

"Not *that*!" Addisyn made an impatient gesture as if shooing away all the bombshells she'd just learned. "The fact that you didn't tell me!"

Avery blinked. "What do you mean?"

"I'm strong, Avery." Addisyn crossed her arms. "I've been through hell. We both have. This hurts really bad—" tears misted her eyes—"but—but I could have handled it. What I can't handle is you lying to me."

"You mean—"

"I can't trust you anymore, Avery." Addisyn's voice was the unforgiving cold of the mountain granite. "All this time of telling me to be honest? To tell the truth?" A sarcastic laugh jerked loose. "You got on my case when I'd fib about my homework as a teenager. And meanwhile you were hiding this big secret." Addisyn's voice broke. "I trusted you. Don't you understand that? I trusted that even if nobody else would level with me, you would." She swiped angrily at her face with her sleeve. "But instead, I had to find out something life-altering from a guy I don't even know."

Even in her darkest nightmares, Avery had never imagined this twist. She'd been ready to deal with Addisyn's devastation.

But she'd never expected to be the cause of it.

Guilt stabbed a burning needle into her. "Addisyn, please. I—I wasn't lying to you. I mean—I was trying to protect you."

"Then you should have protected me from believing a lie. From wasting my time hoping my mom would come back. From finding out one day that everything I believed was wrong. If you wanted to protect me, that's how you should have done it!" Anguish turned Addisyn's words inside out. She jabbed a finger at Avery. "But you know what? You weren't trying to protect me. You were trying to protect yourself!"

"What on earth are you—"

"You know what I'm talking about!" Addisyn's voice was soaring again. "You've spent sixteen years running from our past, Avery."

If she heard another person—"Addisyn, will you stop saying that!" Her own voice was rising now. "Quit making this about me, because I'm fine!"

"Oh, yeah?" Addisyn widened her stance. "You didn't look *fine* at the fundraiser. Skyla obviously doesn't think you're *fine*."

Anger pounded a drumbeat through her. "Stop it, Addisyn."

"Why do you think you have panic attacks? Because you've got so much pain bottled up inside you that your body doesn't know what to do with it!"

"That's not—"

"And why do you think you're afraid of everybody in the world?" Addisyn flung out her hands. "You're too scared to let anyone close to you, Avery! Look at Creed! You finally met this cool guy, and you ran him off."

"Oh, Addisyn, you've got to be kidding me." When she calmed down, she'd probably regret her tone. But right now—"Look, regardless of whatever fantasy world you dreamed up, Creed and I were not—"

"Sure. Right. I saw how he looked at you. I guess you can bury your feelings so deep you suffocate them, but he certainly felt differently."

The heat that rushed to her face was annoyingly out of place for the middle of a nuclear argument.

"You're losing everything, Avery, because you won't face the past." Addisyn's voice quivered, but her gaze was strong. "You decided that ignoring everything was the way for both of us to deal with it. And you had no right to make that decision for me."

The words sank into her like bruising blows. And like an avalanche in the High Country, the fallout of her decisions was coming, roaring toward her in a wave of chaos that would reshape their world and bury them both.

Because Addisyn was right.

"Addisyn—" She reached toward her sister, but Addisyn sidestepped her and pushed toward the front door.

"We're done talking, Avery."

"Addisyn, wait!" She couldn't let her sister leave like this.

"No." Addisyn's voice was shaking, the pain in her eyes a forcefield. "Don't talk to me. Not one more word." She yanked the door open, a cool blast of rain-soaked air whooshing into the room, and glanced over her shoulder. "I guess you're not my *real* sister anyway."

And then she was gone.

CHAPTER 19

Three summers ago, Creed had been rappelling into Erebus Canyon in California when his line had snagged on a rock outcropping and nearly broken. He could still remember the way his head had whirled as he'd stared down into the canyon below him, wondering how far he'd fall.

He felt that way again now as he waited in the corner of the little room Austin had arranged for this meeting, nerves tangled, watching the space fill with his teammates.

"Hey, Creed."

He turned. "Erica. Hey."

"Austin told me the news." Her voice was quiet beneath the friendly hum of the room. "I just wanted to say congratulations."

"Thanks." He shifted his weight. "And, uh, thanks for your help."

"Of course." Her smile was smaller than normal. More cautious, maybe. "So—you're not going back to Estes Park, then, obviously."

The rappel-line feeling strengthened. "Yeah."

She tilted her head, her eyes measuring him. "It's not my place, but—what about Avery?"

His heart stuttered. "What do you mean?"

She shrugged. "You like her."

"What?" Heat prickled over his face. His laugh was mostly the strained pitch of his nerves. "No. Not like that. We are—were—just friends."

"No, Creed." Erica's smile was suddenly sad. "You and I are the ones who are just friends."

He opened his mouth. Closed it. Opened it again. "Erica—"

"Creed, it's okay. Really." She gave him her penetrating filmmaker's look. The one that had always been able to read the story. "I—I had hopes, sure. But—I've realized we're best when we're working on different stories. Not writing our own."

Guilt and relief played tug-of-war with him. "I don't want you to be hurt. You—you really are a great person, Erica." Another way he'd been a lousy guy. He should have been honest with her sooner. Shouldn't have strung her along to take advantage of her help. Was there anything he'd ever done right?

"I always kind of knew we weren't meant to be." She shrugged one shoulder, a real smile twitching at the corner of her mouth. "I mean, you think jalapeños improve every food. That's a dealbreaker if I ever heard one."

"Well, true." He joined her soft laugh. "But just because—just because we aren't the best pair—there's nothing between me and Avery." The words stung with unexpected pain. "We had a disagreement anyway. And really, it's better this way." *Better that I don't hurt her again. Better that I stay away. Better that I keep moving.*

Erica's brows knit in something almost like—disappointment? "Hmm. Okay." She hesitated a moment. "But—you can always go back to the storyboard and start over. Remember that, okay, Creed?"

Before Creed could respond, Austin stood and clapped his hands. "All right, gang. We've got a few things to talk about today. Starting off, this shoot in Arizona has been awesome. Let's go over some of the—"

You can always go back to the storyboard and start over. Erica's words rolled through Creed's head as Austin continued to talk about the filming highlights of the last few days. He frowned. Erica meant well, but it wasn't that easy. He couldn't scrub all his mistakes like a deleted video. Couldn't edit out his bad choices, the chances he hadn't taken.

"And now we have special news about one of our own. Creed."

He jolted from his thoughts to see Austin grinning at him. "This is an exciting time for our buddy Creed. Starting next week, he'll be joining the international team. It's an honor he easily earned with his work for the Estes Valley Mountain Center."

Polite applause pattered around the table. Creed forced a smile. "It was a—an interesting project." One that could have been life-changing. If he'd allowed it to be.

Austin was still talking. "In fact, Creed received an outstanding endorsement from someone on the board at the Rocky Mountain Video Project."

Really? Creed sucked in a breath. Austin hadn't mentioned that. Was this the same person Skyla had known? How had they seen his work?

"This man has also been a good supporter of this channel, and a loyal donor. Anyway, I got an email from him a couple days back." Austin slipped a single printed sheet from his folder and dropped it in front of Creed. "This is what he had to say about your work, my man. Great job." He glanced at the room. "Now, in a few moments we'll see Creed's video, and—"

Creed wasn't listening now. Instead, he was skimming over the words.

Hello Austin,

As I'm sure you know, Creed did an awesome job while he was in Estes Park. I know Skyla Wingo personally, and she was highly impressed. In fact, if he ever wants to come back to Estes, I will be glad to put in a good word for him with the rest of the board at the RMVP.

Creed is a driven young man with a passionate heart and a great deal of talent. And he is a fantastic storyteller. I don't think he realizes yet what great things he can do, but I have always believed in him. I would be only too proud to help him succeed in any way I could.

Who had written him such a glowing endorsement? He looked at the signature.

Sincerely,

Laz Jobe

Disbelief spun the room around him. Laz Jobe? His *dad* had written these words about him?

The paper was trembling in his hands, the lines of type blurring. Tears stung his eyes. His dad believed in him? Was proud of him? Even after everything, was offering to stand behind him?

He glanced up. Across the table, Erica was watching him. And the same message she'd whispered earlier was screaming in her eyes.

You can always go back to the storyboard and start over.

He took his first deep breath. This was grace. This was hope. This, right here, was Heaven touching Earth.

And this time, he wouldn't miss the moment.

"—so anyway, now we'll see this video. Come on up, Creed."

Austin was waving to him. Creed blinked and stood, the revelation still working its way through his soul, and moved to the front of the room.

Erica was right. Avery was right. Even his dad was right.

The wolf had run far and hard, but he could always turn around.

"Thank you, Austin." He squared his shoulders, his heart racing away. Was this how Avery had felt at the banquet? "Thank you all so much." He looked across the faces he'd come to know. His tribe, he'd called them. Yet not one of them had ever known the reason for the wolf on his arm.

"But as grateful as I am for Austin's confidence in me, I can't accept the position."

A ripple of confusion went through the room. He focused on the clock on the back wall and forged ahead.

"I am a storyteller. All my life, I've been comfortable doing that through film. But I haven't done it very well with my life." He rubbed his chin. Fought for a deep breath. "I need to take care of some things before I can move forward in this capacity. But thank you all again so much."

He finally looked back at the faces. Most held confusion or just plain shock. But Erica was smiling with a glad knowing.

"Whoa, whoa." Austin hurried to his side. "What's up, dude?" He lowered his voice confidentially. "Hey, listen. If it's the money, I'll see what I can—"

"No, it's not the money." Creed studied his boss. The man might never understand, but he could try to explain. "I just—I need to work things out with my family."

"Your family?" Austin's eyebrows peaked. "Dude, I didn't remember you had family."

Understandable. Creed shrugged one shoulder. "Neither did I." He couldn't help but smile at the confusion on Austin's face. "I'm sorry, Austin. Really, I am. And I'm very thankful." Austin had taken chances on him when no one else would. "But I need to stay in Estes Park."

Austin shook his head, as if he were still unable to stretch his mind around the turn of events. "For how long?"

"I—I'm not sure." He suddenly wanted to laugh at the craziness of the whole thing. But wasn't this his story? Doing things that seemed crazy?

Well, giving and seeking forgiveness might be his wildest escapade yet.

Austin still looked disoriented by the whole situation, but he nodded. "Well, hey, man, family first."

"Thanks." Creed dipped his head, the sudden gravity of the moment weighing on him. "I'll hate to leave the channel after all—"

"Who said you're leaving the channel?" Austin snorted. "Just—take some time, bro. We're not heading to Washington until August, so you'd be on your own till then anyway. See what happens and let me know."

Even Austin? All along, he'd been surrounded by so much more grace than he knew. "I—thank you." He nodded at his boss. "I'll be in touch. Thank you for giving me this time."

And with that, he unplugged his camera and walked out of the room. He had to get back to Colorado.

Because if Heaven was finally breaking in, there wasn't a moment to lose.

THE INSTANT the door slammed behind Addisyn, Avery collapsed to the floor. The reality of the situation crashed through her like an avalanche, flattening the flimsy barricades that had held the panic at bay.

The pain in Creed's words echoed in her mind. *Your sister is right. Until you're brave enough to face everything with her, neither one of you will end up anywhere.*

He'd been right. But she hadn't listened.

You should have protected me by telling the truth.

Addisyn couldn't understand that it wasn't that easy. She didn't know how deeply the urge to protect her was carved on Avery's soul. Avery had always been the wall between Addisyn and Mom. Between Addisyn and the world. Between Addisyn and the truth.

I'm stronger than you think.

She'd known her sister was strong. Had she truly believed Addisyn couldn't handle the truth?

Or...was it really that she didn't want to return to that place of pain?

Her mother's rose drawing was still propped on the sideboard where Lucy had left it. What had Mom thought as she sketched out those wilting petals? Had she been crying out for the lack of her own life?

"I'm with Lance now."

Simple words from her mom, that night on the sidewalk that had changed everything. And Avery hadn't been surprised. By then, she knew enough of her mom's affair to make her even more angry. *"What does that have to do with Addisyn?"*

"Lance wants to see her."

The protectiveness her mom should have had welled in Avery's chest. *"He doesn't have any right—"*

"Avery, there's something you should know."

Avery's scalp had crinkled with dread.

"Your father doesn't like Addisyn."

"I know that."

Her mom's voice had been low, maybe ashamed. *"That's because he thinks she's Lance's."*

There had been no air in her lungs. She'd stumbled right where she stood, her knees warping beneath her. *"Momma."* Weird, how in that moment she'd reverted to the childhood term she hadn't used in years. *"Is that true?"*

Her mom had looked down, shuffled. *"Wouldn't that be better? If she were?"*

"No." The word wrenched from some place that still needed to believe in her parents. *"Mom, tell me the truth."*

"I don't know." Her mom had evaded her eyes. *"There's a chance."*

Avery held herself still, letting the pieces of the new reality whirl into place around her, but her hands were already shaking. *"Mom— does she know?"*

"No." Her mom's answer was quick. *"But I need her, Avery."* Her eyes had squinted in half-hope. *"She drove your father and me apart. But she'll bring Lance and me together."*

Nausea twisted inside Avery at the thought of Addisyn being forced into yet another dysfunctional situation. *"No, Mom. I'm not letting you—"*

The curse her mom snapped out sliced like a whip. *"Fine. But you're only hurting her. She needs her mom."*

Avery had sucked in a breath. *"And I don't?"*

"You're a big girl, Avery."

The same thing her mother had been telling her since she was in kindergarten. She'd always been a big girl. A big girl who didn't cry or complain or feel.

Mom's eyes turned wistful for a moment. *"You're tough. Tougher than me. That's a good thing, you hear? You're the strong one."*

Oh, she'd tried to be.

A girl needs her mom.

Yes. But she hadn't had one.

A sudden rage and pain fractured through the memories. Before Avery could stop herself, she swept the rose drawing off the sideboard. The cheap wooden frame splintered across the floor, and the broken pieces of herself cracked right along with it. All those years, she'd built up strong on the outside, fractured on the inside. She'd never let either Addisyn or herself reckon with the past. And now that past was coming to collect a debt she couldn't pay.

Tears pressed at her throat, begging for release. Tears for Addisyn and herself and the wasted life that had ended in this house. Tears for the breaking that had never been mended, the hurting that had never been soothed. But she couldn't cry. She hadn't let herself truly cry in years.

Because she was the strong one.

It took only a moment to dig through her purse, to find that old envelope she'd stuffed inside, to pull out the crumpled business card. She stuffed it into her pocket and headed for the door. Right now, she had to do what she'd always done.

Fix this before it was too late.

———✕———

LANCE COULD BARELY REMEMBER how to get home.

He made the turns blindly, rain pelting his windshield like retribution. He didn't want to go home. Didn't want to go anywhere. Most of all, didn't want to think.

He pulled into his driveway and staggered into his house. Fifteen miles from Addisyn.

The pain on her face struck him again with a force that snatched his breath away. The pain wrung a groan from him, and he dropped into a chair. He'd really done it now. Ruined everything even worse than before.

He'd had grand ideas that he was fixing things, hadn't he? Instead, he'd only hurt Addisyn. And Avery too. And that stupid box was still in the back of his truck.

The elephant on his chest settled heavier, the list of his wrongs squeezing the air from his lungs. Getting involved with Beth. Taking advantage of her unhappy marriage. Carrying things to the next step and next step and next step even when he knew those steps were leading right to disaster. Refusing to avow his actions when she found out she was pregnant.

That was the worst one. He'd been stupidly scared that when Ulys found out, he'd cancel their partnership. As if that mattered.

But besides, Beth herself hadn't been sure. She'd constantly told him that. Even in one of their last conversations, when he'd pressed her yet again, she'd shaken her head. *"I don't really think she's yours, Lance. Not anymore. But I don't know."*

Well, he should have stepped up anyway. He'd known what Ulys was putting the whole family through. He should have pulled himself together, tried to bring good from what he and Beth had done, tried to shelter her and her girls. Never mind who had fathered Addisyn—he could still have been her dad. Or at least, he could have tried.

Although who could say? He'd probably have been just as bad as Ulys. He was still hurting her, even now. He could never forgive himself for the way he'd just burned down Addisyn's whole world. And Avery...

Beth's words floated back. *She's always been protective.*

Well, Avery had been right to try to protect Addisyn from him.

Tears were running down his face, dripping onto his hands. Tears? How long had it been since he'd cried?

He crumpled from the chair onto the floor, his knees hitting the wood as defeat pressed him to the ground. The sobs heaved in his chest until a single word ripped out.

"God!"

Never mind his guilt. Never mind his regret. Never mind the consequences. If there was a Being out there—anywhere—who could see him on this floor, at the rock-bottom end of himself—then he had one request.

"Help Addisyn." The words were a cry, a plea to the empty air in the room. "Help her—and Avery—to be okay after—after what I've done." Tears shattered behind his words. He hung his head. "Help my daughter."

He waited, his breath hanging heavy in the stillness. He'd live somehow, he'd die, and then he'd accept whatever punishment God had in store for him. But if Addisyn could be okay—that would be enough for him.

That strange, watchful silence he'd felt in the truck gathered around him again. His skin prickled.

"God?" His voice cracked. There was a new fear in this. Yet there was an odd calm inside him too. As though even the turbulent waters of his soul were still, waiting to hear—

A knock on the door broke the moment, and he blinked. Probably a delivery person. They would go away.

Another knock. Louder this time. He groaned and forced himself up, swiping the sorrow from his face as he headed to the door. The package must require a signature. Well, he'd take care of that and then—

He swung the door open. The daylight striking his tear-swollen eyes made him wait a moment to recognize the person on his porch.

Avery.

"A-Avery." His heart rate tripled. "How did you—"

"Mom gave me your address. A long time ago." Her voice was guarded, her arms folded tightly around herself. But there was a quiet resolve in her face. "I wasn't sure you were still here, though."

He'd stayed put, hoping against foolish hope Beth would find him again. He just nodded.

Avery's shoulders lifted with a deep breath. "Lance—I—"

"I'm sorry." The words burst out, tumbling over his fragile barricades. "I'm so sorry, Avery. I—I thought you had told her. Or Beth. Honestly. I would have never—"

"Lance. Wait." Avery unfolded her arms and shoved her hands into her pockets. Her mouth twitched for a moment before she spoke. "I forgive you."

He stared. Waited. Surely there was more coming. Surely she'd come to condemn him, to tell him again how he'd—

"We've all handled the whole situation around Mom in broken ways. You know that as well as I do." Avery's voice was still quiet, but strong. "I'm not here to pass judgment on you."

He tried twice to swallow before he found his voice. "W-why?"

Avery cocked her head. "Why what?"

"Why are you—" He couldn't even fit the question into words.

"We forgive as we are forgiven. This is what I believe."

"But—Addisyn—"

"Addisyn will be okay." Avery sighed, ran a hand over her hair. "Lance—I—I'm sorry too. Addisyn has had questions before now. I didn't want her to be hurt, so—I didn't tell her the truth. That's something she and I will have to work through. But—" Tears swam suddenly in her eyes. "If you want—if you want to see her—or—" She sniffed, swiped a sleeve over her eyes. "I won't stand in her way any more."

He didn't deserve the trust any more than the forgiveness. But something strangely like hope buoyed in his chest again. "I don't want to come between you two." He meant it. Avery had clearly devoted herself to Addisyn in ways both he and Beth had been too cowardly to do. "But—just—will you give her my number? And my email? In case she ever wants to—"

"I will." Avery nodded. She looked down, tracing the toe of her boot in a pattern on his porch. "You're her father. It's only right."

"Well—" He'd match her honesty with his. "Your mom was never sure about that. She told me at the end that she thought—she thought I wasn't. But—well, I wish I were."

Avery glanced up. A slight softness crept into her eyes. "She's a wonderful girl."

"I—I'm sure. And thank you, for—" His thanks were too large to package in words. "For everything you've done for her."

"I'd do it all again." Avery raised her chin, a resolve in her eyes that couldn't be broken. "She's my sister."

The fitful rain was lessening to a drizzle, the sky lightening even behind the clouds. Lance shifted his position in the doorway. "How long are you in town?"

"Just through tonight. We're going back to Colorado tomorrow. We only came to get all Mom's stuff taken care of."

He blinked. "About that. Please, come here." He hurried to his truck, Avery following. There was the cardboard box. Finally ready for its rightful owner. "Here. This is some special stuff your mom gave me. I think she wanted me to give it to you girls."

Avery stared at the box. "Really? Mom—meant this for us?"

"She left it on my porch, but when I opened it—there's an envelope on top. It's for you."

Avery bit her lip. "Did she—did she ever talk about us?"

The question was a hard-edged one. "Yes." He blew out a breath. "Not much. To be honest, I think she detached herself from everyone. Even me. But—well, you need to see the first thing in here."

He set the box on his truck seat and opened the flaps. And there on top, just where it had been when he'd first cut the tape on the box, was the framed photo.

Two little girls on a swingset.

Avery sucked in a breath. "I have that same picture at home." She looked at him, enough brokenness in her eyes to bring tears to his own. "She—she didn't forget us."

"No." He cleared his throat. "I'm sorry, Avery." Each time he said the words, a little more of the weight on his heart seemed to chip away. "I mean, really. For—everything."

The ghost of a smile passed over her face. "I told you. I forgive you."

She'd never looked more like Beth. Never sounded more like her, saying those words he'd always longed to hear from the love of his life. *I forgive you.*

He swiped at his eyes, but the tears coming now felt—different. Like a new start.

"My friend at home tells me that Heaven and Earth mirror each other. And what is let loose in one is also set free in the other." Avery glanced to the clouds, then back to him. "Be released, Lance. There's always a second chance. And there is always forgiveness from Heaven for you."

His throat pinched. "Thank you, Avery."

He carried the box to her rental car. Helped her fit it into the backseat. Watched her drive away, heading back to Addisyn.

And then he stood on the porch, where a gentle rain shower sifted down once more, carrying with it the scent of first-time prayers and long-kept promises and a God Who might—just might—still love his broken soul.

THE TRUTH HAD SHATTERED the ice beneath Addisyn's feet. And now she would drown in the freezing waters.

Addisyn ran blindly away from her mom's house, her thin shoes slapping the pavement, her breath snagging on tears and anger and fear. The rain was heavier now, dripping into her eyes, but she blinked it away and kept going.

No wonder Avery had been so guarded every time Addisyn had approached this topic. No wonder her sister had locked their past behind barred gates. After all this time Addisyn had wondered and worried and imagined, the answers were uglier than she could have ever dreamed. And hidden by the one person who'd always been honest with her: her sister.

Well, half-sister, maybe.

The thought pierced so deeply that she stumbled. She caught her balance and glanced up to see their hotel. Thank God. She forced herself to walk crossing the lobby, to slow her breathing on the elevator.

Back at the room, she slammed the door behind her and locked it. If Avery tried to follow her, she had her own key. And anyway, what Avery did wasn't Addisyn's problem anymore.

No. She was all alone.

Unless—she could call Darius. But no, not in such a state. She'd only scare him. Anyway, how could she tell him the truth she now knew? What would he think?

She ran a hand over her dripping hair. Her clothes were wet through, clinging cold to her skin. The shaking that had begun deep in her core had spread to her whole body. The high-strung angst that had powered her frantic run to the hotel was draining away, leaving something in its place that felt like morning sickness. But a whole lot worse.

She staggered to the bathroom just in time. After splashing cool water on her face, she leaned against the narrow counter, studying her reflection. The girl in the mirror looked tired. And sad. But mainly—lost.

She leaned closer, searching desperately for a resemblance that hadn't been important before today. She tried to summon a mental image of her father—well, Avery's father. Tried to hold the fleeting impression she'd absorbed of the stranger today. Tried to compare each of them to her until the shapes of noses and placement of eyes made her dizzy again.

She sagged against the wall and dropped her head in her hands. Who *was* she? She'd always triangulated her position off the immovables in her life—her parents, Avery, her home. She'd calibrated her identity off who she was to them.

Yet in a single moment, all her stars had scrambled, and she had no compass to follow. She couldn't even define the meaning of her own name.

All because of her mom.

She closed her eyes, and a sudden riot of rage and pain clawed the inside of her soul. All this time, she'd been chasing a ghost, hadn't she? The mother she longed for had never really existed. And now she could see those taillights again, feel her world fracturing. But this time, there was no one to anchor to.

She sank onto the indifferent cold tile of the bathroom floor and let the tears come. Tears for the mother she'd wanted to have, the caring woman from the tea party. Tears for the mother she'd actually had, the one who hadn't cared enough to stay.

But what if she did the same thing?

She caught her breath. Was that the fear, then? The gnawing anxiety that had driven her through her quest for answers? Had she all along been searching for evidence that she would never do this to her child?

A moment of pure panic seized her. She couldn't put her and Darius's child through what she'd gone through. But with such a heritage behind her, how could she possibly do any better? She had no one to follow, no course already blazed. She'd be a terrible mother. Just like hers. She'd fail all over again, and this time—

A sharp pain suddenly sliced through her abdomen, quick and

wrenching enough that she cried out. Like a knife. She let out a breath. Okay. That was better. It must have been from being sick earlier. Surely it wasn't—

The pain came again, sharper and harder and more insistent. She held her breath until it passed, the sweat prickling against her forehead. Her already racing mind accelerated into overdrive.

She stood and tried to stretch, then crumpled forward again. The cramps were insistent, concentrated in the pit of her stomach.

Something was wrong with the baby.

A wild terror she'd never imagined rose like a tsunami inside her soul, submerging all other concerns. Something was wrong. She had to do something. Had to protect her baby. Had to get help...

Darius. Her heart was screaming for him before she could even grab her phone. Three agonizing rings, and then his voice. "Hey, Addisyn. What's—"

"Darius!" Her emotions broke on the rock that was his name. She pressed the phone to her ear and snatched the words past the tears. "Something's wrong—the baby—"

"Wait, what do you mean?"

The urgency in his voice doubled her own fear. "It—" There was the pain again. Addisyn sucked in another breath, held it until her insides relaxed. "I'm hurting. Darius—"

"Okay, you need to go to the doctor. Is there a hospital near there? Or an urgent care—"

"I don't know." The thought of finding a hospital in a strange place and then dealing with unfamiliar doctors was overwhelming.

"What does Avery say?"

The question stabbed worse than the pain. "Avery's not here."

"What? Where is she?"

"We had a fight, Darius." She gripped her forehead. The time when she most needed her sister, and she'd pushed her away. "Our mom—it's a long story. But she's not here."

Darius paused for half a heartbeat. "Okay." He was back to equilibrium, his voice calm and controlled, although Addisyn could still hear the fear underneath his words. "Okay, sit down, all right? Sit down and take some deep breaths. Let me Google it, see what I can find."

"Okay." Sinking onto the side of the bed, she closed her eyes and pictured him, the way his forehead would be furrowed in concentration right now as he scrolled through Google results, his head tilted in that endearingly studious way he had.

Gosh, she missed him.

"All right." His gentle West Coast voice had never been more like an embrace. "I found it. Looks as if that's not uncommon."

She blinked. "It's not?"

"No. You can have pain at any point when you're pregnant."

Who knew how many things could happen when you were pregnant? "Really?"

"Yeah. It is something to take seriously, but it doesn't necessarily mean something's wrong. Any other symptoms?"

"No."

"Then let's see if this stops soon."

She couldn't relax. Not yet. "How soon is soon?"

"Well, have you had any more pain in the last few minutes?"

"Uh—no." She glanced at the clock. Sure enough, since she'd settled down and started taking deep breaths, the pain had eased.

"Then you're probably in the clear. Let's just wait."

Fifteen minutes later, the pain was still gone, and Addisyn's shoulders had finally relaxed. "So—nothing's wrong with the baby?"

"No." Darius hesitated. "Stress can cause this, apparently. Emotional upheaval."

Stress. A stress she'd been holding for months. And an upheaval that had ripped her apart today.

The tears welled again, and Addisyn hung her head. So, she could have harmed her baby just by getting upset? Who knew how much more damage she would create when the baby was actually here? A sob broke loose before she could stop it.

"Hey, hey." Darius's voice was still calm, soothing. Utterly safe. "What's wrong, pretty girl?"

Pretty girl. How long had it been since he'd called her that? "Darius?"

"Yeah?"

If she didn't say it now, she might never be able to. "I've been really—really hard to live with. I know that, and I'm going to make it up to you, I just—"

"Aw, hey." There was a smile behind his words. "Don't worry about that. Just talk to me. Tell me what's going on with you."

"I—" She didn't have the energy to hide from him anymore. She took a deep breath. "My mom had an affair. And Avery knew about it."

There was a long pause. Addisyn squeezed her eyes shut. She'd done it now, bared the messiest part of her pain to Darius. Would he be disgusted? Shocked? Embarrassed?

"Addisyn, I'm so sorry."

Well, he didn't sound mad yet. Even so, Addisyn shifted uncomfortably. "It's okay."

"No, it's not okay." His voice was still pure compassion, rich and gentle and warm. "Do you want to tell me about it?"

Before she could pull her defenses back into place, before she could make herself strong again, the whole story came flooding out. The strange guy who might be her father and the secrets Avery had kept and the whole disorienting discovery that it had been she who'd split the family apart. By the time she stopped, her face was burning with the vulnerability of it. What must he be thinking of her?

"Addisyn." There was pain in his voice for her. "I'm so sorry. That's a lot that you shouldn't have to carry." He sighed. "But I'm here, okay? I'm here, and you're going to be okay. Keep talking to me."

His words were like a cleansing exhale. Every broken part of her was spilling out, and he still hadn't turned away. "I—I—" The next words that slipped out surprised her. "I'm going to be a bad mom."

"What?" There was genuine shock in his words. "Addisyn, that's not true."

"It is." With the pent-up fear broken loose, the words tumbled out. "I don't know anything about this, Darius. Nothing. My mom was so broken, and that's all I knew, so how can I not turn out the same way?" Tears choked her words. "I'm so scared, Darius. I—I panic over this. I just know I'm going to mess up. I'm going to fail. I'm going to ruin everything for our baby."

Darius was quiet for a moment. Maybe he was silently agreeing with her. Maybe he'd say that she needed to—

But then he laughed. Softly, gently. "Would you believe me if I told you I'd been feeling the same way?"

Darius? The confident, calm one? Addisyn blinked. "What?"

"Yeah. I've been mainly worried about you." Sudden emotion trembled under his words. "I worried I wouldn't be able to protect you. To take care of you and the baby the way I needed to." He sighed. "I've been a nervous wreck, honestly. I've had to do a lot of praying."

Was that why he'd hovered over her? Because he'd been just as scared as she had? "So—I'm not the only one?"

"Definitely not."

"But—but you know so much more than I do." The weight dropped onto her shoulders again. "You had great parents. And a wonderful family. I don't know the first thing about taking care of a baby."

"Yes, you do. You're already doing it."

Addisyn frowned. "What do you mean?"

"Why do you think you're so nervous about this? Why are you working so hard to do the right thing? And why are you so scared of messing up?"

Because she knew how badly things could go wrong. Because she was tired and frazzled and upset. Because—

"Because you love our baby."

And just like that, his statement flipped her entire view upside down. He was—*right*. All this time she'd fretted and worried and researched...it was all coming from a place of care.

"You're already doing more for this baby than your mother did for you. Because you're loving this baby, and you're trying to do what's best for him or her."

All this time she'd worried about not being a good mom. But maybe she was already more than halfway there. She caught her breath with a half-sob, half-laugh. "You mean it?"

"Of course I do. And you're not alone. Okay?" His words were a caress. "We're a team. We'll do this together. And hey, we're both going to make mistakes. That's just how it goes. But we'll stay and fix them."

We'll stay and fix them.

Finally, her lungs could fully expand. Maybe that was the secret she'd been looking for. Maybe this wasn't about avoiding all mistakes, but about staying to keep fixing them. And covering the whole process in love.

And that she could do.

"You're not your mom. This is a different story." Darius's voice was light, reaching into what had been dark for so many months. "When things go wrong, we will stay." He paused for a second. "*I will stay.*"

A fresh wave of tears misted her eyes. Somehow, he'd read her deepest fears.

"And Addisyn? You said you don't have a good example to follow. But you do."

She frowned. "Not my parents."

"No." He hesitated. "Avery."

Walls shot up in her heart. "Avery lied to me."

"Avery made a mistake herself. And yeah, it was a big one." He was choosing his words carefully, fitting them gently into the cracks of her heart. "But—she was a kid herself then, Addisyn. And everything she did—even that—" He sighed. "She did it all because she loved you."

And suddenly she could see the tears on Avery's face again. Tears for her.

I didn't want you to be hurt...

She sighed. Her emotions were still a complicated knot, and it would take time to unravel them. This wasn't enough. Not yet. But it was a start. The tiniest speck of hope that she could work things out with Avery again.

"I love you, Darius." With the words came a release, a rightness she hadn't felt in far too long.

"I love you too." His voice was low, intimate, an embrace from a thousand miles away.

She'd missed this. She'd missed *him*.

After they said their goodbyes, she sat on the bed for a moment, hand over her stomach. *I love you too, little one.* She rolled Darius's words around in her heart. *Your dad is right. When things go wrong, we will stay.*

And then she stood and headed to the door. Nothing that came next would be easy. But she would not be like her mom. She would not run. She would not discard. She would not abandon.

No, when things went wrong—she would stay.

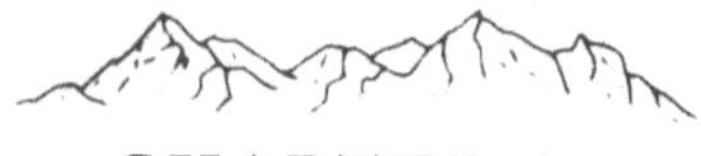

CHAPTER 20

The drive back to the hotel seemed to take hours, days, maybe weeks. And Avery's hands shook all the way there. *El Shaddai, help me.* What would she do when she saw Addisyn? What could she even say?

Or what if Addisyn was gone? She could have taken an Uber to the airport and be on her way back to Denver right now.

Avery was gripping the wheel so hard her hands ached. She forced out a deep breath. She could fix this, right? She always did...

Well, but she'd spent her entire life in fix-it mode. Yet here she and Addisyn both were. On the opposite edge of the map from okay.

She parked at the hotel and dashed inside and up the stairs. Just as she slowed to a panting walk in the hallway outside their room, their door opened.

Addisyn leaned out warily. Her brows lowered when she saw Avery, but she didn't go back inside. That had to be a start.

"I—I'm so sorry, Ads." The nickname slipped out from years of habit. Was it her imagination, or did Addisyn's eyes soften slightly? "Please just hear me out."

Addisyn ran a hand over her tangled hair. Her eyes were red, the tracks of tears still salty on her face. "I'm listening."

"I did all of this wrong." The admission clenched Avery's insides, but she pulled in a deep breath and kept going. "I messed up, Addisyn. I was only trying to protect you. I promise. I didn't want you to get hurt again, and—" She caught her breath. "And you—

you're right. I've been running and hiding, and that's not what I should have done. I didn't know how to handle this. Any of it."

Addisyn leaned against the doorframe. "If you had told me, we could have figured it out together." Her voice held more sorrow than anger.

"I know. I should have." Oh, if only she had. "I didn't want to hurt you, and—well, I didn't want to be hurt again either. I thought we were past all of that, and I didn't want to go back to that place and deal with it."

Addisyn looked down. "That doesn't make it okay, Avery."

"You're right. I realize that." She bit her lip, the regret aching in her throat. "I wish I could change it all, Addisyn. All I can tell you is I made a big mistake, but I did it thinking I was doing the right thing. And if you'll give me another chance—we'll face this together."

Addisyn studied her. She was guarded, but the door was still open. "What do you mean?"

Avery held out the car keys. "Do you want to go to our neighborhood?"

Addisyn looked from the keys to Avery. For an extended heartbeat, the question suspended in the air between them.

Then Addisyn nodded.

Driving the road into Syracuse was like traveling back through time. The bends and curves were still familiar, the shape of a word Avery had once known well. Addisyn didn't say anything, but her eyes were reading the story out the window. At the red light at Flint and Strauss, she pointed toward the street corner. "The movie theater is still there."

Avery blinked. "Oh, yeah. It sure is." The building was crying out for a new coat of paint, and the electro-neon marquis no longer looked as cool as she'd remembered. But that was the theater where—

"You would bring me here to see the lights. The projector that made all the little spinning lights on the lobby floor."

Addisyn's voice was softer, and the tug of the memory caught Avery too. "Yeah. You loved those lights."

Addisyn looked away, picked at her chipping fingernail polish. "You'd walk me down here every day in the summer. Just to see those lights."

"Yeah." *Because I love you, Ads.*

The traffic light changed. The movie theater shrank away in the rearview mirror.

Déjà vu haunted Avery as she drove through the maze of their old neighborhood, until her sweaty hands were nearly slipping on the wheel. Somewhere here, she might see the shadow of herself. Walking home from school, or learning to drive on the quiet cul-de-sac, or following the sidewalk to the library. All the old ghosts were waiting here, in the stronghold of her deepest nightmares.

And she was willingly going right back into it.

The sign loomed in front of her. CEDAR STREET. The road where she and Addisyn had lived a lifetime ago.

She made the turn and glanced at Addisyn. Her sister looked as disoriented as Avery felt. She wasn't saying anything, but she was back to picking at the fingernail polish.

Their house. Avery slowed, pulled off the road in front of the place that had once been as familiar as her last name.

The mailbox was new, and so were the numbers on the post. The fence was the same sharp pickets, but it had been repainted a jaunty white that softened its outline. Did the gate still creak?

And the house—oh, the house was as it always had been. The cream-colored siding, the smoke-gray roof, the many windows like watching eyes. It had looked just the same when it had been a cage, a trap, a Pandora's box the rest of the neighborhood didn't dare peer into too deeply.

Addisyn pointed. "The tree is still there."

Avery let out a breath. "Yeah."

Her tree. The parental oak right outside her old bedroom window. The one whose branches she and Addisyn had climbed down, on the night that they'd last seen this house. Eleven years ago. How had it been eleven years?

For a moment Avery had the sudden crazy desire to climb that tree back into their past, be once again the teenager in the bedroom, try to write the story differently.

The front door threw wide, and a dog exploded out with a joyous bound and an ecstatic flap to his lolling tongue. Two little girls with bouncing beaded braids rushed after him, their giggles floating across the lawn.

A woman appeared in the doorway behind them, peering out just in time to see the girls and dog collide in the grass. She stepped onto the porch and laughed in the soft hues of afternoon light.

A lump of bittersweetness swelled in Avery's throat. This was redemption, because someone was writing a new story for the old house. A better story.

She pulled away from the curb, the house watching her in the rearview mirror. The old place might recognize her. But it was getting its own second chance. She was no longer a character in its story.

And she knew where her path led next. To the cemetery.

The wrought-iron fence around the green was still like a phalanx of spears. Avery's hands were trembling by the time she parked the car and slipped through the creaking gate, Addisyn at her heels. The lukewarm sun had vanished again, the clouds spitting a sullen drizzle of rain once more.

She slipped through the tombstones and monuments, scanning the names. In the back section of the cemetery was a simple granite cross. The ground beneath it was still raw, unhealed.

Some power that wasn't her own helped her legs move forward. And there it was, written on the cross in the cold starkness of all that could not be changed.

ELIZABETH GRACE MILES.

No other words besides the dates of her birth and death. Because there was nothing else to say.

Addisyn's face warped first. She sniffed, tears dripping into the pain-plowed ground at their feet.

Death. Mom. Death. Avery didn't fall as much as melt, sinking on legs that wouldn't hold her any longer. The trembling in her hands was moving up her arms, and her heart was thudding like a stone in her chest. The panic was coming. Coming to eat her alive. She'd known this would happen if she came back here. She closed her eyes.

"A?"

She barely heard Addisyn's question before the jolt was upon her, the vortex whirling around her. Her pulse hammered wildly in her ears, and her chest exploded with bursting pain. She clenched her fists until her fingernails dug into her palms and curled forward.

"No!" She screamed the plea into the shadows of the cemetery, the word ripping against her throat. "No!"

This time, she wouldn't be able to make the panic stop. And it would kill her. She would die here, at the escapeless end of her mother's own story. She had faced the truth too late to change anything.

She gasped for air, but her lungs were cinched by an iron band. She hunched over herself, dug her fingers into the wet dirt. She would die, she would die, she would—

An arm curved around her, and hands gripped her shoulders. She pulled away, but the hands held firm. And then came Addisyn's voice, from somewhere beyond the roaring in her ears.

"Hold on, A. You'll make it through."

You'll make it through.

And with the words came the barest sliver of hope.

She blinked, tried to focus her racing mind enough to catch the tail of the thought. That was right, wasn't it? She'd hated the panic, she'd fought against it—yet she'd never died. She'd always made it through.

So maybe it was time to finally face it.

The memories were blurring together in her mind, as she'd known they would, but this time, she didn't try to shove them into the shadows. Instead, she pulled them into the light. The whole painful package of her mother's empty hands and weary eyes and drifting gaze. The weight the woman had heaped upon her shoulders, and the way she'd warped under the strain long ago.

You're the strong one. She'd hated that and hoped for it, all at the same time.

But—

The roaring in her ears faded. She blinked her eyes open. She'd been kneeling in the mud, and her jeans were soaked. But the pain in her chest was draining away, and like the first break in the clouds after a bad thunderstorm, the blurry world was coming back to reality.

Gingerly she sat up, studied her muddy hands. Her fingers were still cold, but they had stopped shaking.

"Hey." Addisyn was still crouched by her. Holding her together. She pulled back enough to look into Avery's face. "You okay now?"

"Uh—" She was sweating and shivery at the same time. And she felt as if she'd just run a marathon up the Rocky Mountains.

But as the panic flowed out, something else was flowing in. Strength. Because for once, she hadn't run from the panic. She'd let herself feel every ounce of it.

And she'd survived.

"Yes." Her laugh was shaky, the overflow of the new strength. No matter the fear—she would make it through.

Just as Addisyn said.

She rotated her stiff shoulders, then looked at Addisyn. "Thank you."

Addisyn just shrugged one shoulder, but there was a compassion behind her eyes that hadn't been there before. "You didn't tell me." Hurt crept into the edges of her voice. "That you were dealing with this, I mean. I—I didn't know till the fundraiser."

For just a moment, Avery wanted to dismiss. Hide. Pretend.

But instead, she sighed. "I—I'm sorry. It—it started several weeks ago. I should have told you then."

Addisyn nodded slowly. "Can we—talk about it?"

Talk. Hope flickered again. "Yes. I want to. I want us to talk through a lot of things."

Addisyn's expression softened. "I want that too."

Now was the time to tell her. Avery shifted. "I have some things from Mom for both of us. I got them from—from Lance."

Addisyn blinked. "You saw Lance again?"

"I did. I went to his house." Avery hesitated. "For what it's worth, he doesn't really know if he's your dad. But he said he wished he were."

"He said that?"

"Yeah."

Addisyn stared at their mom's cross and seemed to consider that for a moment. Then she looked back at Avery. "It doesn't matter, you know. Lance—or whatever—" She shrugged. "I didn't mean what I said. You're my sister."

The relief and hope of a second chance swelled in Avery's chest. She reached for Addisyn's hand, squeezed it tightly, and this time her sister didn't tug away. "I love you, Ads."

"I love you too." Addisyn dipped her head. "Will you—go through Mom's stuff with me? Not now. But sometime."

"Yes. Whenever you're ready."

The clouds were clearing, the westward sun beginning to slant underneath them. Light getting in, the way it always did. Washing over the place where Mom was dead...but Avery was alive.

Avery held onto the thought, turned it over in her mind. She was alive, right now. Right here. In this intersection of time and space, between the painful past and the forgiven future, she could still choose and think and act and change. The past would be forever buried in itself. But with every new sunrise, she could still change the future.

And maybe it all could start right here.

"You know what I need right now?"

"What?" Whatever Addisyn needed, Avery would get her.

"One of those pudding cups." Addisyn ducked her head sheepishly. "Weird. I know."

And suddenly all the complicated emotions overflowed in a soft laugh. Avery rocked back on her heels. "Really? That's what you need right now?"

"Well, not me." Addisyn grinned and touched her stomach. "The baby."

The baby. And there was hope, again, because Addisyn's child would grow up in the warmth of love. In the home Avery wished they had experienced. Which meant the next chapter of the story would be full of light.

"Well, then." Avery drew a deep breath, finally feeling the freedom in her lungs. "Let's find a grocery store."

Mom had been right. She was the strong one. But not in the granite grip she'd always thought. Instead, she was strong like the aspens that grew in the High Country. Looking to the light. Unafraid of the clouds. And rooted in something—Someone— much deeper and bigger.

She grabbed Addisyn's hand. She stood on legs that were shaky but sure. And then she led her sister away from the place of death, and back into the life breaking like eternal waves on the western horizon.

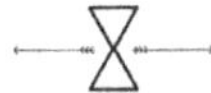

ESTES PARK, 20 miles.

Creed's heart rate kicked up to the tempo of the classic rock on his radio station. He was twenty miles from starting the long process of repairing his mistakes. Twenty miles from the place where his story had started. Twenty miles from his dad.

And from Avery.

He'd talk to his dad first, but then he had to find her. Try to see if there was any way she might let him apologize for all his stupid decisions.

Assuming Dad didn't kill him first.

The mountain road was sharp, steep, with curves that pitched his stomach. He rubbed his fingers uneasily on the steering wheel, remembering the frustration in his father's eyes. Maybe the man had said his last words to him. Maybe he simply didn't want to bother with Creed anymore. Maybe he never had wanted to repair their relationship anyway.

But the letter in his camera bag said differently.

He kept his eyes on the road ahead. Who knew what this day

held. But whether things were better or worse at the end of it, he was finally doing what was right. The way Charlie had always said.

He drove on through the town of Estes Park, past the filling station and Marys Lake until he reached Live Bigger. And there was the big pickup. His dad was at the store.

He parked under the creaking wooden sign, studying the hand-carved letters, the decorative trees at the edges of the words. His dad had made it, no doubt. He'd never noticed it before. But then, he hadn't noticed a lot of things.

The gravel scrunched under his feet as he crossed the parking lot. Odd, that when everything had fallen apart, his father had come back here to live. Back where they'd been before the divorce, before the ministry, before the Rez. Did his dad remember when their family had been whole? Did he still long for that?

His shoes echoed on the hollow boards of the wooden porch. This felt like trespassing. He stepped inside cautiously, and a bell over the door jingled. Taxidermied ducks spun lazily from the ceiling. Display racks crammed with outdoors gadgets faced him. Some old country music crooned from the speakers. John Denver, maybe.

And his dad was standing behind the counter, head bent over some papers. "Howdy, welcome to—" He glanced up, and his booming auto-greeting snapped off. "Creed."

"Dad." The awkwardness locked him in a chokehold. Some sudden emotion surged upward in his chest. All that he'd come to say was lodged in his throat.

His father came from behind the counter and moved tentatively toward him, floorboards creaking under his boots. "You came back." His tone was unreadable.

"Yes." Creed's hands were sweating. He was a teenager again, his dad's approval a climbing route he could never summit. "Um—the email. The endorsement you—you sent Austin." Heck, he was all but stammering now. "Uh, thank you."

Dad's mustache twitched. He studied the toes of his dusty boots. "Your work is good. Made that easy to write."

"But—" He couldn't find his way to the questions. "How did you even know—"

Dad cleared his throat. "Few years back, Miz Skyla showed me how to set up the MeTube."

He didn't correct the man this time.

"Anyhow, she fixed it up on my laptop back at the house so's I can get on there and just click the little picture thing and see what you been doin'."

Surely he didn't mean—"You've been watching my videos?"

"Ever' since you started with that channel. I kep' up." Dad dragged his boot along the floorboards. "Looks like you've done well for yerself. You've got a good thing goin'."

You've done well. The gift he'd always longed for, and now he could no longer accept it. "Actually, Dad—" He fingered the insides of his pockets nervously. "I'm sort of—on hold with the channel. As of Wednesday."

His dad's eyebrows rose, but otherwise his expression didn't change. "That so?"

"Yes." What would his dad think of that decision? "I—my boss offered me a promotion, but—but I didn't want it anymore."

His dad nodded slowly. "I see."

Silence settled between them. The silence of two stubborn guys who were neither of them good with matters of the heart. Creed took a deep breath. Time to say the words he'd come eight hundred miles to say.

"And—" He braced himself. Squared his shoulders. Locked eyes with the man he'd spent years blaming. "You were—you were right. I've handled some things wrong. Well, maybe everything. But I want to learn differently." Avery's face, Avery's voice in his mind. The rock underneath her feet. "And I thought maybe, if I were back here for a while, then—then you and I could maybe try—to talk some more. If you were willing." He licked his lips and kept going, to the hardest thing he'd ever had to say. "Because—I—I'm sorry."

The words all but choked him coming out, but behind them was the greatest sense of release. He was no longer clinging to the cliff, trying to hold on. Instead, he was back on solid ground.

"I'm sorry." His throat was pinching, but he had to say the words again, bask in the broken peace of them. "I'm really sorry."

Dad cleared his throat. Swiped a hand over his eyes. "Seems like I got heaps to be sorry for too." He squinted at Creed. "I tried to be a good dad. But tryin' wasn't enough. I let you walk out, and iffen you'd be wantin' to come back—" He sniffed. "I'd be right glad."

His father all along had been more gracious than he was. Creed shrugged a shoulder. "Well. Thanks."

"Eh—" The ghost of a smile touched his dad's expression. "Miz Skyla'll be glad to see you back. She always thought you'd show up here someday."

"Really?"

"Yeah. She'll be happy." His dad's expression turned more knowing. "An' so will Miz Avery."

The tips of his ears heated. "Yeah."

With steps that were slow, tentative, as though he were trying not to spook a wounded animal, Dad closed the distance between them. And then, for the first time in over half a decade, he pulled Creed into his arms.

Creed squeezed his eyes shut, but the tears came anyway, falling on Dad's flannel-clad shoulder. He wrapped his arms around the man and held on. Oh, he'd needed this. So much more than he'd known.

"I'm right proud of you, son." His father's words held a tremble.

The words he'd waited all his life to hear, and the rightness of them sank down into his deepest wounds. "Thanks, Dad."

And in the softening air between them, he'd found that first toehold in the rock. It would take time and talk and probably many more tears. But finally, he believed he and his father could find their way back to each other.

Because for the first time since the fire, his dad had called him *son*.

THE MORNING after she arrived back in Estes, Avery called Skyla, who answered with her usual calm grace. "Greetings to you, Avery."

"Hi, Skyla." Suddenly she had no path into the conversation. She fiddled with a seam on her hiking pants. "I—I just got back in town. I've been gone for a few days."

"Indeed? I did not know. Did you go to Canada with your sister?"

"Not this time." Avery swallowed the dryness in her mouth. "Addisyn and I went to New York. To handle the situation with our mom, and—everything else."

"Oh." Skyla's soft syllable held volumes. "And—how was this?"

The question was too big to hold in one hand. A million images jumbled together in Avery's mind. The fresh dirt at the gravestone and Addisyn's raw grief and Lance's guilt-ridden face.

But also, the happy family in her old home...the patience of the big tree still outside the window...the peace in Addisyn's face when she'd fallen asleep next to Avery for the flight home...the light slanting in behind the clouds...the way the panic had washed her pure as the rain.

She took a breath. Let it out. "It was—good."

Because *good*, she was learning, was a word big enough to hold all manner of broken things—and to trust that something beautiful would rise from them in the end.

"This is welcome news. I am glad you made the trip."

Avery nodded, her eyes on the stack of boxes inside her door. The stack that would be ready whenever she was. "So am I."

"But you wished to speak with me?"

Here came the hard part. "You said to—to call you when I was ready. To talk about—about my job."

"Ah. Yes." Skyla's voice held a knowing. "Would you come to the center, if you would do this kindness? We can speak heart to heart there."

Dread hovered over Avery as she drove to Allenspark, but she kept her eyes ahead. She already knew what she'd say.

In the parking lot, the *kapemni* on the sign caught her eye, and a wave of longing crested over her. *Creed.* Even now she halfway expected to see him capturing the center with his camera, watching everything with his storyteller's eyes. But instead, he was out in the desert somewhere, running like the wolf on his arm. Running as she had once been, without knowing it. If only she could tell him he'd been right.

No sooner had she stepped through the door than Liv attacked her in an exuberant hug. "Avery! Galloping geese, we've missed you around here!"

No hint of judgment in her eyes, and part of Avery's fear lifted. "I've missed you guys too." Avery squeezed Liv in return, then looked around. "Um—Skyla. Is she here?"

Liv nodded. "She said you were coming and to send you out to the flight cages when you got here."

Her face held a curiosity barely kept under wraps. Skyla must have instructed her to ask no questions. Avery suppressed a smile. "Thanks, Liv. I better head on out there. I'll see you later."

Sure enough, Skyla was standing inside one of the flight cages, watching a Barred Owl strengthen her wings. As Avery let herself in, Skyla turned at the creak of the hinges. "Ah, Avery. There you are."

"Yes." Avery breathed in the familiar ambiance of the flight cage —lattice light and the smell of sawdust and the flutter of wings over-head. "I'm back."

Skyla folded her arms and leaned against the wall of the cage, her attention fully on Avery. "And now you feel you are ready to talk."

"Yes." Avery gulped. This would be the worst part. She started to shove her hands in her pockets but stopped. *No. Not anymore.* "Skyla, I'm so, so sorry. You were right. There were things that I truly —I did not have a handle on." She stopped. Skyla deserved her honesty. "Well, really, there still are. There's a lot I have to work through, about my mom, and with Addisyn. It's a long story, but I was burying too many things. And it was—it was affecting my work here."

Skyla was still watching. Nothing in her face except total concen-tration on Avery's words.

Avery took a deep bracing breath. "And so, I—I realized you were totally right. What I was going through—it wasn't letting me show up here the way I wanted to. The way you and Tyler and Liv and— and all the students deserve." She swallowed the growing lump in her throat. "I think—I think you're right. I'm not qualified to try to bring healing here when I haven't found it myself. It would probably be best for me to step away."

There. The job she'd longed for and loved, bare and broken on the altar.

But Skyla was—smiling. One of her rarest smiles, brimming with the miracle of the alpenglow. And there was a rejoicing behind her eyes.

"Avery." She shook her head. "This is indeed the place for you."

Avery blinked. Did Skyla not understand? "No—what I'm saying is—"

"I prayed much for you. At all times, but especially while you have not been here. That the Spirit would blow fresh wind across your heart." Skyla glanced around the enclosure. "Many times we have stood here together, have we not?"

"Yes." Skyla had delivered truth to her in the flight cage when she'd been caring for her first injured bird, Isaiah, while rebuilding her relationship with Addisyn. And again when she'd struggled to find her purpose after Addisyn moved to Canada.

"And have I ever delivered you unto crooked paths?"

"No." That answer came easily. Skyla had always seen her soul with the patience of a prophetess and directed her toward ways of peace.

"Then I speak again words of power to you now." Skyla gripped Avery's hands with a sudden strength, her voice somehow drawing the resonant ring of the mountains into her words. "What is released is also redeemed. And when the good ground is broken, the seeds of strength come forth in restoration."

Avery sucked in a breath. *Redeemed. Restoration.* These were precious words. The words she'd been seeking all this time, without knowing.

"I told you then, and I tell you now, that there is healing in your hands and your heart." There was no mistaking the sincerity in Skyla's voice. "And there is no better work for a healer than to seek healing themselves. This is not the place for the perfect, Avery. This is the place for those in progress."

"Do you mean—"

"I mean that I have long desired to see you reach a moment of breaking down and building up. And now you are here."

Forgiveness. Grace. The hope glowed in her heart, but she was too afraid to look directly at it yet. "Are—are you saying that I can—"

Skyla squeezed her hands. "Please, Avery, join us again in the work. Your job is waiting. And there are many souls to see." Her gaze moved over Avery's shoulder, and her eyebrows lifted. "Starting with that one, perhaps."

And Avery turned to see her second miracle in that many minutes.

Because pulling into the center was a very familiar dusty orange Jeep.

CHAPTER 21

Creed was sweating under his T-shirt as he pulled into the parking lot of the center. This might be even harder than talking to his dad.

The beat-up green truck was parked near the sign, and his stomach flipped. Avery was here.

By the time he stepped onto the porch of the center, his courage had already drained away. Maybe this was a bad idea. Maybe he should find a campground, get the camper set up, try to regroup and come back when—

"Creed?"

The voice he'd been longing and fearing to hear. He swung around to see Avery standing beside the porch, watching him with the deep green knowing of the forest in her eyes.

"Uh—hey, Avery." His thoughts scattered from his mind like birds in flight. He ran a hand over his hair. No doubt he looked terrible after twelve hours of travel.

"You came back." She sounded slightly breathless, as if she'd hurried from somewhere. The wind tugged at her hair, and she shoved it behind her ears.

"I—I did." He couldn't think beyond those words, because the truth was coming into focus—full-color and high-resolution

You have feelings for her.

Erica had read the story, even when he hadn't. He'd lost his heart to this woman with the evergreen eyes and the mountain wind in her hair. *When? How? What to do now?*

"Creed?"

He snapped back to reality. "I—I'm sorry?"

Avery's gaze slanted with concern. Great. "I asked why you came back."

He forced himself to concentrate on the conversation. "I, uh—it's a long story. I talked to Dad."

She blinked. "You did?"

"Yeah." He rubbed the back of his neck. There was so much he wanted to tell her, about the mountains and the mystery and the way she'd shown him to live. "Um, a—a lot has happened. But first, I'm sorry. I'm really sorry." He was getting better at saying this. "I shouldn't have used your videos without asking you. It was a last-minute idea because you—you did great on them. And I tried to ask you, but—I should have tried harder. It's my fault."

Her face eased slightly. "Well—thank you."

"And—you were right. About—about needing to stop running."

He braced for *I-told-you-so*, but instead heaviness clouded her eyes. She looked down. "Creed, what you said when—"

"I know." He winced. Here it came, and how could he ever make it up to her? "I'm sorry. I shouldn't have ever—"

"I—no." She rubbed her hands together as though they were cold. "What you said was the truth." Her eyes, her face, held a vulnerability that tugged at his heart. "You were right. I've been running and scared, and I hadn't dealt with what should have been faced."

He opened his mouth. Closed it again. Still didn't know what to say.

"But—" Her hands were trembling, and she fisted them at her sides. A new strength glowed within her expression. "Addisyn and I —we just got back from New York. To take care of things with our mom."

Avery had gone back to the place she hated? Then her story of the last few days must be as radical as his. "Oh. Wow. How—how was that?"

"Tough. But—good." Her laugh was soft, a little sad. "It will be hard to rebuild everything. But I'm finally ready to try."

"You'll do it, you know."

She quirked an eyebrow at him. "Why do you say that?"

"Because—you're brave." His face heated, but he kept going. "While I was in Arizona, I kept thinking—you showed me another way to live."

Her own cheeks turned pink. "And—that's why you came back?"

"I came back to be different. To make things right with Dad and —and with you." He was watching her reaction. Silently crying out for her to be proud of his choice. "I'm on hold with Guys in the Wild. I don't want to be who I've always been."

Her eyebrows lifted. A cautious expression—was it hope?—filled her face. "So—you'll—you'll be staying around?"

"I'll be staying around. However long I need to." He stepped closer, willing his sincerity to sink into her heart. "This—this is where Heaven touches Earth. And—I hope you'll give me a second chance too."

A smile crept onto her face. "Yes." She shrugged. "We'll learn together."

"Exactly." He looked down again, to her still-trembling hands. Then he reached out slowly, watching her face, and covered her hands in his.

Her breath caught and her eyebrows lifted, but she didn't pull away. Her fingers were delicate, but strong. Hands that could reach and touch and heal.

He rubbed her hands, feeling the tightness in her fingers ease. "There." So much more he wanted to say, but maybe this would speak more than words could. "Does that help?"

"Yes." She whispered the word, a heartbeat away from him. "That helps a lot."

"Avery?"

Skyla's voice from around the corner of the center. Avery jerked back, yanking her hands from his. "Yes?"

Creed bit back a smile. It was okay if she pulled away for now.

He'd give her the time and healing space she needed. But in the coming weeks and months—well, maybe then he'd be able to tell her how she fit within his heart.

"Avery, did you find—" Skyla stepped around the corner and smiled. "Well. Creed Running Wolf. Running no longer?"

"Running no longer." There was solid satisfaction in the words. "Thank you, Skyla."

"Of course." Skyla smiled at them both, then squinted at the bluebird sky. "Heaven is near, yes? And there is joy in the beating of wings."

"WHAT'S THIS? A COW?"

Addisyn smoothed down the corner of the last piece of wallpaper before peering at what Darius held. "A cow?" She tossed him a mock glare. "Excuse me, that is a bear, thank you very much."

"Hmm." He wrinkled his nose as he gazed at the little wall hanging he held. "Still looks like a cow to me."

"Would a cow say 'Beary Cute' under it?" Addisyn unrolled the next section of wallpaper and smiled again at the design. After the two of them had done a lot of haggling—she'd been picturing something white and chic, and Darius had wanted a full-on hockey theme—Avery had finally found this decor online and bought the whole set as a surprise. *"A gift for my future niece or nephew,"* she'd said. The room was gently mountain-themed, with woodland designs and friendly forest animals and—Addisyn's favorite—a hanging arrow print that said FOLLOW TRUE NORTH.

Following true north was what she'd been trying to do every day since Syracuse. One step at a time, one decision at a time, one prayer at a time. Her problems certainly hadn't magically vanished in New York. But she'd come back west a little lighter than before, with a hope she hadn't had.

And she'd come back to Darius.

She sneaked another look at him as she pasted the next piece of wallpaper. He was still wrangling the crib components, studying the screws on the ground with a bemused expression. His hair was slipping loose from his ponytail, and his brow was furrowed in the adorable expression he gave when he was concentrating.

Her breath caught all over again. How grateful she was for him, for his quiet ways and his abiding faith, for his love that reached patiently through her every attempt to push him away, for his strength that absorbed all of her whispered fears.

And now they were getting the nursery ready. The nursery where their baby would be in less than six months. A twinge of the old uncertainty pricked at her.

"Hey." He glanced up and gave her a quizzical look. "What are you thinking?"

Before Syracuse, she would have pretended it away, told him *nothing*, put up her wall. But now, she was practicing being more honest. "Well—" She took a deep breath. "We don't have long to get this ready."

"It'll be done in time." He gave a crooked grin and gestured to the mismatched fragments of crib on the floor. "Don't you see how much progress I'm making?"

She bit back a giggle. "It looks almost like destruction instead of construction."

"Hey!" He pulled a mock hurt expression. Then he laughed. "Okay, so maybe I'm not the world's best builder."

"You have other skills." Addisyn took a deep breath. "But that's not what I was thinking. I was just thinking—well—" *Get it all out there.* "Things will change. Soon."

Understanding softened his face. "That's true." He crossed the room and sat next to her on the floor, pulling her into the safe circle of his arms. "But it will be a good change."

"Yes." For the first time, a spark of excitement kindled to meet this baby. This combination of her and her husband. "Darius?"

"Yeah?"

She leaned more fully into his arms. What a comfort it was to know that both she and the baby could find refuge in his strength. "Thank you."

His chuckle vibrated in his chest. "For my crib building contributions?"

"No." She ran her finger along the tattoo on his forearm. "For being you. For being here."

His arms tightened around her. "I'm always here, Addisyn. For you and our son."

"Our son?" She leaned back just enough to swat him on the arm. "That's enough. We're having a girl."

"Oh, yeah?" He cocked his head at her. "How do you know?"

"A mom knows these things." *A mom.* The rightness of the statement settled into her.

"Hmm. With all due respect to the intuition of mothers, I think you're just guessing. And I hope you're wrong." Mischief glinted in his eyes. "One woman is all I can handle."

She laughed softly. "Well, I don't want to be outnumbered by men."

"We'll see."

We'll see. Yes, they would see—all the firsts and lasts and nexts that lay ahead. And somehow there in the bright nursery, where she was wrapped snugly in Darius's arms, the future seemed as welcoming as a sun-soaked path extending into the cloudless day. Especially since through all the twists and turns of that path, Darius would be there with her.

"Thank you, Darius." She looked up, savoring the sight of him. His thick dark beard, longer than when they'd been dating. The depth in his blue-green Pacific eyes. The warmth in the arms holding her close. "For being here."

"I love you, Addisyn." He kissed her, the kind of kiss that still took her breath, then gently stroked her stomach. "And I love our baby."

The tears that started to her eyes were ones of hope and healing. She wrapped her arms around his neck and pressed her forehead to his, safely back within the circle of his love. "And we both love you."

⟡

THE FIRE SNAPPED, a celebration of sparks spinning into the summer air. On the bench next to Avery, Liv laid her guitar aside and stretched her hands toward the blaze. "Beautiful, isn't it?"

"For sure." The fire was breathing light into the darkness, the flames in the melting heart of the wood quivering with an intense electric blue. Bluer even than the heavens over the Rockies, or than their reflection in Lake Haiyaha.

Avery gazed at the faces around the fire, each illuminated by the finger of the fire's flicker. Liv and Tyler, Skyla and Chayton, Laz and Creed. Breathless thanks rose to her heart. For these people, who lived their lives to bring healing. For this place, that waited to welcome those who came.

And for the God Who had brought Heaven to Earth.

"I told you this would be a good idea." Liv sounded proud of herself. "You have to have a bonfire on the first night of summer. It's, like, a rule."

"This is indeed a sacred time." Across the circle, Skyla leaned forward, the reflection of the flames dancing in her thoughtful eyes. "A fire at the turning of the year often holds meaning. And—" her eyes found where Creed stood at the edge of the ring of light. "This was well kindled by one who has long waited."

The firelight glanced off Creed's hair and sparked in his eyes as he reverently moved to the fire, sitting on the bench next to Avery. "A sacred fire." His voice was soft. "My prayer, finally."

The fire caught the light of Skyla's copper bracelets as she stood. *"'Let your prayers rise like smoke to the Great Spirit, for He will see and answer you. Every step is a prayer, and as you dance upon the earth for the things you seek, the way will open before you. In the same way, as you search for the true ancient pathways, you will find them. Answers will come to the ones who ask, good things will be found by the ones who search for them, and the way will open before the ones who keep dancing their prayers.'"* Her eyes found Creed's across the circle. "It is good, He Who Believes. Keep dancing."

He bowed his head. "I will."

Liv reached for her guitar again, and the moment relaxed into her gentle strumming and easy conversation. Avery slid closer to Creed, keeping her voice low. "I'm glad for you, Creed."

"Thank you." His smile tipped upward. "This—it's a special place."

"It is." God's country, and for every day he spent in it, Creed seemed more at peace. He was fighting hard, climbing higher, seeking a rock on which to stand. And he'd find it. Because he was that kind of guy.

For a moment, the knowing tugged at her memory again, the picture she'd seen. The flames wrapped around Creed. She still didn't see the fullness of what the vision meant. But watching his sacred fire rise tonight, she was starting to have an idea.

Beside her, Creed's camera came to life with a whir, and he peered through the viewfinder. "I can get some great shots of the fire here."

She grinned. "That's cool." It was endearing, really, the way he studied everything with an artist's eye.

Without warning, he suddenly swung the lens to her.

"Hey!" She clapped her hands over her face, her mock protest spilling through her laughter. "Don't take my picture. I've been with the birds all day. I probably look terrible."

He smiled and lowered the camera. "Trust me." His eyes held hers, and his expression shifted. "You could never look terrible."

An unfamiliar—but far from unpleasant—discomfort under his gaze burned heat into her cheeks. She quickly looked away. Did he mean—

Nonsense. No doubt she was reading too much into his comment. Creed was a good friend, nothing more. But lately, she'd begun to wonder if—

"Heard from your sister?"

She shook off the odd emotions. "Um—she called this week-end." She and Addisyn were finding their stride together, blazing a trail through hard honesty back to hope. "We talked about what we'll do with the box."

"The box?"

"It's a box full of my mom's stuff that Lance gave me in New

York." She shifted position on the hard bench. "Addisyn asked if we could look through it sometime soon."

"Are you ready for that?" His voice was gentle.

Something between a laugh and a sigh escaped. "No. And yes."

"Hey." He gently nudged her arm. "You'll be okay."

For a moment, the shadows of all that lay ahead fell around her, thick as the night. "We'll see."

"No, you will be." There was a fervor, a strength in his voice. "You're grounded here, you know. You're standing on a hundred feet of bedrock granite. Just like your faith." For a moment his smile turned wistful. "And even if everything has crashed down, with that kind of foundation—you can build again."

He was right, and the hope that had been rising in her heart for the last few weeks swelled again. She still had El Shaddai. Still had His Presence wrapped around her. Still stood on the mountains to which He'd led her.

Still had a trail to follow.

Thank You, El Shaddai. Thank You for Your country that mirrors Heaven. Her God would be with her, as faithful as the sunrise. And she had Skyla, and Liv, and everyone here.

As long as...

She twisted her fingers together. "Creed?"

"Yeah?"

"Will you—are you planning—" The words she wanted to ask caught in her throat. "I mean, you'll be here, right?"

His smile came softly, like the alpenglow after night. "Yes, Avery." There was a resolve beneath his words. "I'll be here."

I'll be here. Words that had never been spoken by her mother, but had been offered by so many others in her life, people who loved her, valued her. And each time she heard them, her soul healed a little more.

On the horizon, the dark shoulders of the mountains rolled against the navy-blue sky. So much lay ahead. So much terrain to climb.

But the rocks would be firm, and the sun would be steady, and the wings would still fly. She'd released what was bound, and she'd faced what she'd found. The trail ahead was long. But by the strength of El Shaddai, and the fire of those around her, she would reach the peaks.

Liv strummed her final chord, then grinned in the patter of applause and stroked her instrument lovingly, the firelight shimmering on the strings. "My fingers need a break. Let's tell ghost stories."

"Holy Ghost stories." Laz smiled at Creed. "I'm thinkin' we all got some o' those."

"This is a good idea." Skyla clapped her hands softly, bracelets jingling, and glanced at Avery with a question in her eyes. "Avery? Would you like to go first?"

Avery took a deep breath and gazed around the fire. Now, she didn't see judgment, or fear, or a strained strength that had nearly snapped her in two.

She saw grace. Grace in the story—both for the telling and the listening.

"I'd love to." Her voice was steady. Her hands no longer shaking. The power of her mighty mountain God was with her, and she no longer needed to run. "If Creed will help me, I'm going to tell the story of the *kapemni*."

Creed smiled and leaned forward on the bench. Beside her, Liv flashed a thumbs-up. Across the circle, Laz shot her a wink and nod of approval.

She looked up. Past the night below, to the night above, and the place where the sparks and the stars danced together in the space between.

"Where Heaven mirrors Earth."

KEEP READING!

Thank you for joining me on this journey, dear reader! I hope you were blessed by this story. If you enjoyed this book, would you please consider taking a few moments to leave a rating or review? Reviews are one of the best ways you can support my writing as well as help other readers find books they might enjoy. Thank you in advance!

Now, I have more exclusive content for you—the Climbing Higher Library on my website! This virtual library contains exclusive content—including a prequel scene from Addisyn and Avery's escape to New York, a scene of Skyla's backstory, and even a collection of gorgeous mountain-themed phone wallpapers. Just scan the QR code below or visit www.ashlynmckaylaohm.com/climbing-higher-library to download all the special content today!

THANK YOU!

Dear Reader,

Ask any author—the most common question we hear is, "What's your book about?"

I love this question, because I so appreciate the heart behind it, the desire of the asker to understand more about my writing. But I also dread this question, because it's terribly hard to answer. As if I've used up all my words in the writing of the book, I usually end up stammering out something that sounds like a description of a fever dream—*um, this girl works with hawks, and she has this younger sister who's trying to uncover a secret—and oh yeah, then this good-looking guy with a wolf tattoo shows up—*

Apologies and gratitude to any politely curious person who's patiently waited while I trip over my own book description like that!

The reason this question is so hard, of course, is that this is a question that goes deeper than the characters, than the setting, than the story itself—right down to the bedrock about what I believe, and why. And in that sense, this is not a story about a girl who works with hawks, or an overly curious younger sister, or even a good-looking guy with a wolf tattoo. This is instead a story about—me. And you. And all of us.

Like everyone, I've been hurt wounded on the sharp edges of others' apathy, or hostility, or yes, abandonment. Spiritually, I've been left behind, and left out, and left for dead. And if you're nodding your head along with me, then you understand that even worse than the event are the questions that follow, the same unknowns with which Avery and Addisyn grapple—*why did they... why wasn't I...where is God...what do I do now...*

And like my characters, I too have sought different ways to handle the pain—succumbing to the grip of fear and frustration, searching obsessively for explanations, running from the situation until it can't be ignored and the scars finally bring me to my knees. And it's there—on my knees—that I come back to the center, that I lay hold of the truth, that I finally look up and remember that the God of Heaven is still reaching toward Earth—toward me. And I face down one of the most intensely spiritual yet utterly practical teachings of Jesus—forgiveness.

Now, contrary to what some would say, forgiveness is not a free pass for the offender or a panacea for emotional wounds or a gimmick of conjuring charitable feelings. It doesn't mandate reconciliation, it doesn't negate consequences, and it doesn't require us to ignore or forget the past. Instead, it's a resolve—a firm and steady decision that your light will not be dimmed, your anger will not become your default, and your past will not put a period on your story. It is slipping the heavy yoke of bitterness off your shoulders and exchanging it for something much freer and lighter. In fact, while I'm not a theologian or a therapist, I'd say that forgiveness is basically trust in action. When we trust that God will vindicate us, defend us, and transform even the most horrible circumstances to good, then we don't have to cling to our stubborn right to resentment or yield to the urge to self-protect. Instead, we free ourselves to live, as Skyla would say, in the reflection of Heaven. The Scripture she quotes to Creed (Matthew 6:12, 14-15) equates forgiveness with release. And as anyone who has forgiven or been forgiven knows, that release is real.

And in the final analysis, that is the truth that has helped me through the rawness of hurt, the glory that has overshadowed my dark moments—I myself have been released. Two thousand years ago, the Son of God canceled my debt and took on His shoulders every way I had spit in His face. And out of the eternal fountain of

His love for me, I can, with grace, pour a glass of water for one who has wronged me.

So, my dear reader friend, this is my prayer for you. May you rise to the sky on newly healed wings and soar even in the curl of the clouds. May you stop your restless striving and find peace in the Love that is offered to you. And may you live in the grace that breaks new like each sunrise—the grace that walks alongside us here, between Heaven and Earth.

— Ashlyn McKayla Ohm
June 2025

MORE BY THE AUTHOR

Enjoy more writing by Ashlyn McKayla Ohm! Find more information about her fiction and nonfiction on her website, or follow her writing on Substack at words fromthewilderness.substack.com.

Climbing Higher

Sisters Addisyn and Avery Miles have chosen different paths in life to cope with the fallout of their tumultuous past. But now, their stories have intertwined, and in the majesty of the Rocky Mountains, the two sisters must navigate threats from the past, new opportunities for the future, and the same fears that have always threatened to tear them apart, all while climbing higher...not only into the mountains but also toward the God Who still moves them.

A Year in the Woods

What if encountering God in a fresh new way is as easy as stepping outside? Step away from a stressful world and enjoy a full year of inspiration with this peaceful book— fifty-two nature-themed devotionals are complemented by full-color original photography and space for journaling. Experience God's world through the lens of His Word with this popular devotional!

High Country Hymnal: Poems for the Mountains, the Valleys, and the In-Between

This collection of lyrical poems, prayers, and contemplations not only celebrates mountains in a geographic sense but also provides an honest yet hopeful perspective on the spiritual terrain through which we all journey. Through stunning original photography and deeply heartfelt writing, you'll come face to face with the breathtaking glory of not only the mountains but also the High Country to which faith will lead.

*Find out more about any of these books by scanning the code below or visiting **ashlynmckaylaohm.com/my-writing/** today!*

A worshiper of the Creator and a wanderer of creation, Ashlyn McKayla Ohm is most at home where the streetlights die and the pavement ends. She is passionate about shaping stories that weave together unfailing truths, vivid characters, and dramatic natural settings —bringing readers face to face with not only the mountains but also the God Who still moves them. Her work has been featured by publications such as Clayjar Review, Truly Co., Proverbs 31, Calla Press, Vessels of Light, and Heart of Flesh. If she's not daydreaming about her next book, you'll find her hiking, birdwatching, or otherwise getting lost in the woods.

Follow Ashlyn's writing at her website, ashlynmckaylaohm.com, or on her Substack, wordsfromthewilderness.substack.com!

ACKNOWLEDGMENTS

A story may start as an idea tucked away within the author, but it takes so many hearts and hands to bring it to the light. It is with humility and immense gratitude that I acknowledge all who have helped me along the way.

For my friends who prayed for me, believed in me, and never laughed when I told them I was going to be a writer. If I began to list names, I could fill this entire book, but please know you are all so dear to me.

For my fabulous cover designer, Hannah Linder. Thank you for taking my sketchy vision and translating it to a cover that captures the spirit of the story.

For Mercy, who is just as good a dog in real life as she is in the books.

For my amazing creative community at The Rabbit Room, The Habit, and Redbud Writers Guild. Thank you all for the ways you strengthen and encourage me, not only as a writer, but also as a believer.

For Lena, my dear friend and sister from the Spirit. Thank you for always looking for the light.

For my amazing parents, Ralph and Derri Ohm, who gave their all to write a good story for me. You have been the steadiness in my sunrises, the patience in my seasons, and the wind to bolster my wings. Your constant love walks with me on my every path, and if I could count the stars, I might be able to tell you how much I love you too.

For my Savior, my Shepherd, my mighty God of the mountains —Jesus Christ. What could I possibly say to capture the glory of Your gift? Thank You for not only stirring this story in me but also for writing my own life so lovingly. In the darkest nights and the brightest days, You are still the sacred song around me. May You continue to lead me by the paths of peace, and may Your fire fall on the altar of my pages and my life.

www.ingramcontent.com/pod-product-compliance
Lightning Source LLC
Chambersburg PA
CBHW061917130726
47908CB00017B/1665